PRAISE FOR PRINCE OF GLASS

"When I tell you Matey writes like a god, I mean she writes like a GOD... This is an epic fantasy you just can't miss. The character work in this book is on a level I haven't seen from anyone other than Brandon Sanderson and Stephen King."

— BAILEE CONDIE

"Prince of Glass is a hauntingly poignant, epic tale that you won't be able to get out of your head... Moving, gripping, and unforgettable.

— A. M. LIBBY

"Captivating, compelling, stylish."

— T. R. RINGNALDA

"Packed with raw emotion, Prince of Glass is a deeply moving journey... This story will captivate audiences looking for an edge of your seat, give you the chills, jaw-dropping, heartwarming rollercoaster of an adventure."

— M. R. OSWALT

"A harrowing, hauntingly beautiful, and poignant epic journey... this is a book you can't miss if you love gritty, grimdark fantasy or masterfully written morally grey antiheroes. This gripping tale will stay with you in the corners of your mind long after you turn the last page."

— MARTA TORIĆ

PRINCE OF GLASS
THORN & ASH SERIES
BOOK I

S. A. MATEY

Independent Publisher

COPYRIGHT

For James

THE OUTERLANDS
MAP OF
IERIS
THE WHITE SALT SEA
HOUSE LIGHT
KOR TOFEL
GREYFELL
AURVOIR FOREST
GOSTERAL
FOLOGIA
NOWN-JIN
HOUSE RING
PEARL GREEVILLE
THE CUTLANDS
CASTEN
NORTH WINDLIN FOREST
WORTHWOOD
PEARL FASTALL
RIVER OF COINS
GODSWOOD
GREATWATCH HOLD
VALVIGNUS
PEARL KORSON
KENDALL RIVER WEST
TENSUIR VONN
CASTLE VANGITT
EFRIIN-HAL
IRI MOUNTAINS
THE GREAT PLAINS
THORIAN
PEARL GLASAVILLE
KENDALL RIVER EAST
KOR VENSURITE
PEARL GLASTIN
THE HILLTOPS
PEARL JIN
EFRIEL'SHU
HOUSE GLASS
RIVER OF KOFEE
CREEVILLE OUTPOST
PITNEY
FIELDS OF 10,000 FLOWERS
PORTSBANE ISLAND
THE KNIFETOPS
TORMAIN AL NEMILLE
AL DUIR
EFRIEL
THE HIGH PENNISULA
SHORT RAIN
NUI VERSUSCIA
VELLE ESBE
CRE LEDAA
FORT GRAINS
SOUTH WINDLIN FOREST
NYLADIIR
THE BLACK BLADES
OLDSWOOD
NARROW'S WATCH
THE GORGE
HEFE
NER ESBE
BLACK SEA
TARROT
VALLEY-LANDS
THE GREAT PENNISULA
CASTLE UNADA
NOVITOPP
FAERIEL
KELS-JA
THE GREYLIGHT MOUNTAINS
THE FINGERLINKS
OZMAHL
THE WHITELIGHT MOUTNAINS
TYL ETAN
THE FALLING RAINS
VAR TRELN
SHEFFAL
THE NUUJIN VALLEY
THE TAIL RIVER
VAR TALOB
SOUTH GREYLIGHT RANGE
AREF-USA
THE GREAT MARSH
AREF-MAL
HOUSE SLATE
AREF-NOKKA
VANDEL PROVINCE
AREF-JOULA
YURDRAIN
GTIS DAL
THE SOUTHERN WASTE
AREF-MARA
AREF-UBAL
THE MIST
THE ASH PEAKS
BLACKMOUND ERUPTIONS
THE UKNOWN

PRINCE OF GLASS

A SONG OF THORN & ASH

Herein lies a story all creatures know

The root of the root, the seed left to sow

A history of yearning, of great sorrow and pain

Told to me as a warning, told to you just the same.

In the beginning, the Father-Graven had two sons

Who tore the boundless heavens apart

In salted stardust, Geiin birthed a world

And Mithre corrupted its heart.

The world fell to a night deep and starless

The spirits of men filled fully with darkness

Geiin ascended and in his wake

Left four brothers, each an Anathema remade:

A Father to rule dumb creatures
A Father to keep Ieris living and green
A Father to be mankind's healer
& a Father to balance, sort, and cleave.

What was faultless turned to rust

A world once beautiful turned to dust

At the end of all things but this stands true

All spirits return to one of two

Geiin or Mithre, holy or shrewd

Until the end we will slay what has strayed

Hear this song and be afraid

Never again let Anathema see light of day.

— **Harring Rickson,** *"Songs of Warning for Youths: The Four Fathers"* 768
A.A. — written in the 34th year of Our Lord Cicero, High King and
First of His Name.

PART I: OBSESSION

❧ I ❧

THE HUNTER
{THIRTY-SIX DAYS BEFORE}

Vasily Miinriel stood watching a cloudless sky, his formidable build casting a small dark shadow. A waxing moon hung heavy over House Slate, cold and untouchable as the frost pressed outside the window. Vasily could almost feel his father with him on nights like this. Perhaps Babas was up there now, resting among the stars he once looked upon so fondly.

Just say something. Anything.

Vasily placed a scarred palm on the glass window-wall, the moon so close from where it hung it the velvet sky. The room was settled in the coldest, most isolated spire, and that was just the way Vasily liked it. He never felt the chill that stalked the room like a starving dog, not with a rage inside such as his.

It's all over now, came that lonesome voice. *You have to let it go.*

Vasily searched the heavens. *But how can I let it go, and still hold onto you?*

As always, the winking stars stayed silent.

Vasily rested his forehead against the glass and sighed. His eyes followed the long fall down to the base of the House, and just for a moment, he let himself imagine how the plunge might feel. The kiss of air. The weightlessness.

I

A long fall indeed. House Slate jutted out from atop the spines of the Whitelights, a black-stone castle so old and extensive it'd even harrowed down into the heart of the mountains when it grew too tall to build up any further. The House had long ruled over Faeriel, a realm that somehow felt incredibly friendless despite its healthy population of mountain-dwellers and valley-men. Those of the mountains kept their clans among the cold and stone, and the valley dwellers shadowed by the curving Whitelights did just the same. This reclusiveness made House Slate the singular bastion of warm civilization for thousands of mountainous miles.

There was much to do, as king of such a House—councils that needed tending, armies that needed leading, banquets that needed hosting, the whole of a country that needed to be held together, and held together *tightly*—but Vasily spent most of his days alone in Babas' old study.

He simply didn't know what else to do with himself.

Vasily pried his eyes from the plunge and rested them once again on the heavens. *Father, if you would only tell me—*

A voice shattered the silence. "A fine night, isn't it?"

Vasily whirled around. A familiar ache clutched his chest as soon he spied the dark-haired shadow by the door—his youngest sister, Yena, had so much of their Babas in her, from the black of her eyes to the proud tilt of her chin.

Yena also reminded Vasily of himself, back when he'd not yet seen more than ten winters. Back when life was only the future, when the world could be anything he imagined.

Now, Vasily had seen near thirty winters. Now, he saw the world just as it was.

"Seems rather lonely up here," Yena said, shuffling her feet as she waited for proper admittance.

Vasily frowned. "How did you get in?"

"You left the door unlocked." Yena shrugged. "Besides, Finya and I thought you might want some company."

"Ah," Vasily sighed, drifting back to the window. "Where is our sister, then?"

"Distracted talking to that *boy*."

"Don't tell me—the kitchen boy again?"

"The very one! With the green eyes." Yena's grin turned wicked as she followed Vasily to the window-wall. "*'Oh, Telgin, your eyes are like emeralds. However do you carry those bags of flour so eaaaasily?'* She talks about him all the time, but he's literally dumber than Mortle's hen. The one that pecks at her own feet!"

Vasily couldn't help but laugh a little. "Girls are silly, aren't they?"

"I'm not!"

"Of course you aren't. You've not yet reached ten winters."

Yena reached up to take Vasily's hand and peered out the window. "When do girls get silly, then?"

Vasily squeezed her palm, so small in his own. "When they start noticing a boy's *dashing emerald eyes* before they notice his wit."

Yena went cherry red. "I didn't say his eyes were dashing! You added that part!"

"Did I? I could've sworn I heard you say such a thing."

"Va-a-a-sily—"

He reached down to ruffle her hair. "Go fetch your sister before she gets into trouble and visit Mari. I'll be down shortly. "

"But I just walked up so many stairs! All the way to see my favorite brother!"

"I'm your *only* brother." Vasily nodded to the door with a smile. "Now off you go."

Yena was almost gone when she turned back and said just the wrong thing.

"I miss Babas, too, you know."

Vasily froze halfway between the window-wall and Babas' desk. The weight of her eyes on his back was a terrible thing.

"You were just a babe when he died." It was all he dared say when he faced her.

"I remember him looking at me," Yena said, her little face curiously still.

Vasily could hardly breathe—it was as if she spoke of the woodsman who'd stocked House Slate's firewood before he died two summers ago in the Hilklepts riot. Or Finya's little dog who ran off. Or that blonde kitchen-maid who disappeared into the snow one night. Not their father, their Babas. He was too precious to be spoken about like this, like he was never really there in the first place—

"His eyes were just the same as yours," Yena said with a tight shrug. "It isn't hard. I see him when I look at you."

Vasily couldn't think of a thing to say. Yena waited, staring at him by the door.

"Move along, Yena," he managed at long last.

She disappeared without another word. Vasily got to the desk, pulled out a half-empty flask, and returned to the window-wall as if pulled there by chains.

The bottom drawer of his father's desk was locked, and the key hung from a cold chain around Vasily's neck. Within that drawer laid five amulets, each of which once belonged to Babas' murderers. The amulets were his only assurance that their former owners' souls would never find relief in the Long Wait. That Vasily had claimed his vengeance. That it was *finished*.

Vasily nearly lost himself back in the open face of the moon and the surrounding abyss of stars when the door slammed open again.

He startled, his drink nearly sloshing from his flask. "Yena, I told you to—"

"My lord?"

Vasily turned and found Babas' seneschal stooping in the doorway.

"Nuest?" Vasily said, "You're back so soon! I trust the journey went well—"

"I've come straight from Nown Jin, my lord, from the Pearl herself. I finally established a contact," Nuest answered, swallowing reflexively as he shuddered beneath a heavy cloak. The old man was built like a scarecrow, his wire-thin arms and spindly legs poking out from a frame long-since collapsed in on itself. He could not stop wringing his age-spotted hands as he hovered in the doorway, the corners of his beard still edged in frost.

"Yes, very good," Vasily said. "What news?"

The old man held out a hand to keep Vasily from coming any closer. "Terrible news, I'm afraid."

Vasily stopped short. "Is it Auryn?"

"No, no..." Nuest broke off as a rogue tear stole down his bearded cheek. "My lord, a Prince of Glass *survived*."

THE THIEF

The Prince of Glass himself, rumored to be the most dangerous man in all of Pearl Jin, was getting beat to a bloody pulp in the dilapidated alley behind *Kaljen's Tavern & Fine Dining*.

The early spring sun was just dimming above the Pearl, casting the languishing mists of the city in a lazy blue light. But the afternoon's sleepiness was not shared by Taein, who was having the absolute shanking *time of his life*.

Two thugs were busy beating the living daylights out of him—one comically thin and capped with yellow hair like a straw-man and the other a brute-faced boulder that some half-wit god seemed to have mistakenly animated into a man.

In the span of a half-breath, the pair plucked Taein off his path, knocked away both his cigarette and his shiv, and pinned him. Then, without so much as the courtesy of introduction, affiliation of gang, or declaration of intent, they commenced thrashing Taein with an overzealous efficiency he rarely saw anymore. The big one alternated pounding him between the moss-eaten brick wall of the tavern and the slime-slick cobblestone street below, while the skinny one yanked away Taein's satchel and pawed through his stuff.

Taein winced as the twin Mendolniese knives he'd pilfered but days ago rattled about in one of the many well-hidden compartments of his satchel.

All that work, for nothing. But these habitual muggings were one of the few consistencies in Taein's chaotic excuse of a life—one he'd arguably let go on far too long, sure. Still nothing else made him feel so alive as this.

"Hell-shanking-dammit!" Skinny growled as he rampaged through Taein's satchel. "Stoppit for a minute, Steeve!"

"What for?" The big thug said after delivering one final gut punch.

Taein doubled over, slid to the ground, and vomited as Skinny kept cursing.

"Come rip this thing apart for me!" he said, shooting Big a glare.

Big furrowed his brow. "Whaddya mean?"

Taein watched blearily as Skinny twisted in angry circles, boots squelching on the cobblestone, one arm still thrashing inside the bag as curses poured forth from his mouth like water boiling over some furious pot.

"I *mean*, there's rich stuff hidden in here, halfwit! I just—I *swear*—you hear it too, don't you?"

Taein spat out a mouthful of blood, eased back against the wall, and enjoyed the show. A worn travel map, a change of socks, and a half-rotten apple each dropped onto the street as the muggers dumped out the contents of the main compartment. It'd been six years, and still no thug had ever figured Taein's satchel out.

He grinned again. *It never gets old.*

"There ain't no pockets. There ain't even no loose seams!"

Big snatched the satchel from Skinny and tried to rip it apart, muscles straining and veins bulging on his forehead, to no avail.

"What's *wrong* with this thing?" he growled, giving the bag a violent shake. The sweet, metallic clang of Rightfellow metalwork sang out just above the muffled pound of untuned instruments and bawdy laughter on the other side of the tavern wall.

"Had enough yet?" Taein chirped.

A tense moment passed. The thugs glared at each other, each with one hand still on the secretive satchel, before their twin glares slid onto Taein himself.

"*You*," Skinny hissed, just as his burly friend clamped a hand around Taein's neck and forced him upright. Big pinned him against the wall again, then Skinny hauled back and let fly with a mighty slap.

"Empty out that cursin' bag for us and we'll leave you living," Skinny snarled.

"No thanks," Taein said as he tested Big's pin. It wasn't just his bag that had secrets—his coat also had a myriad of hidden pockets, one of which housed a one-of-a-kind steel creation imported directly from the Outerlands. "You blokes can steal your own stuff—"

That was when Skinny slapped Taein again, so hard he busted open Taein's bottom lip. Taein's head smacked back and he bit his tongue. Also hard.

One would think I might learn. The thought circled dimly as he drew in a gasping breath and spat blood, but silly notions like 'learning from mistakes' and 'breaking bad habits' had never really been his specialty.

"Dammit," Taein managed. "You've just got to take all the joy out of this for me, don't you?"

"Hush up," Skinny growled, foraging through Taein's accessible coat pockets. "That bag got some sort of magic key?"

"You already emptied it." Taein said.

Skinny's eyes narrowed. "That bag still got a money-sound innit."

"Have you always had such a rampant imagination—"

Skinny smacked Taein's head back against the wall. "Hush now," he growled, frisking beneath Taein's shirt. "What's this? You ain't even got an amulet?"

Taein didn't say anything. Just held the thug's eyes and tried to look scary. He always loved this part.

Skinny swallowed hard. "How'd you like it if my associate 'n me turned you to a Shallow, then?"

"It would be my greatest pleasure," Taein said. "Now get your hand out of my shirt, skiv."

"You in one of them weird cults? Folk warned us about you freaks even 'for we got here," Skinny asked.

"Bold of you to assume I've even a soul left to save."

"Dramatic one, ain't you?" Skinny said, stepping back and wiping his hand on his shirt as if he'd discovered Taein carried some sort of transmittable insanity.

"Don't even get me started." Taein pitched forward as soon as the mugger released him and caught himself from face planting at the last minute, one palm placed oh-so-conveniently over the shiv the thugs had knocked away from him and forgotten.

"Well... what now, Steeve?" Skinny asked.

"Dunno," Big said, having resumed his fixation on trying to rip the satchel apart. Sweat was rolling down his forehead, the satchel still not even slightly torn. "Suppose now is when we kill him?"

Taein bit back a scoff. *Good luck.*

Skinny gave Taein another glance, then looked back at Big. "Are we really that sort of muggers, though?"

"Ain't that just how things are done here? The Pearl's pretty cutthroat, Murph. Best we keep up with the competition."

"Suppose so. I just didn't think we'd catch one so soon."

Big shrugged and shook the satchel violently again. "Must be lots of easy marks in this neighborhood."

"You insult me, gentlemen," Taein interjected, slipping the little blade up his sleeve. "I like to think of myself as quite a challenge."

Skinny shook his head. "Sorry, mate, but you didn't put up no fight."

"Not *yet* I didn't."

"Not *ever*, you didn't." Skinny poked Taein. "Maybe the bossman will know how to get the rich stuff out that bag, Steeve."

Big nodded. "Let's split."

"Lets. But before we go, you got rit on you?" Skinny asked, looking Taein over.

His stupid, smarmy gaze came to a sharp stop at Taein's right arm. His sleeve had gotten pushed up and the rough tattoo of a crow's silhouette—the tattoo no one alive was *ever* supposed to have in these parts—showed bright and black on his bruised skin.

The tattoo that made Taein a *legend* in the Pearl.

Skinny raised his eyes back up to Taein's, face blanched of all color, fresh sweat breaking out on his forehead.

"Sweet Geiin. You're him."

Taein grinned. *"Say my name,* skiv."

Instead, Skinny did the sensible thing, and punched Taein as hard as he could. That's when Taein realized that he had a fat, three-pronged gemstone ring, right as it tore the skin off his cheekbone.

That's also when Taein decided this was not even a *bit* fun anymore.

He braced his aching back against the wall and kicked hard at Skinny. His boots, toed with silver, hit the mugger square in the chest and sent him stumbling.

Taein hit the ground. There was only a second's gap between one thug losing a grip on him and the other sweeping in, but a half-second was all he needed. Taein slid the cool engraved metal of his flintlock from a pocket hidden deep inside his coat, got one thug in his line of fire, and squeezed the trigger. Flint hit frizzen with a sharp smell unlike anything else in Ieris, and sparks flew gold in the dark of the alley. Within the same breath, Taein dropped the shiv from his sleeve and slashed. Big took the bullet and Skinny a slice across the throat. The same expression of disbelief splashed over one thin face and one broad, and both thugs collapsed as one.

For a long while, the alley was quiet. Taein looked around, his heart settling beat by beat, and fully saw the alley. Sweet Geiin, he usually never let things get *this* far. So much blood was in the air that it clung to the mist with an oozy, metallic waft, mixing with the stench of sweat, mold, and tavern-filth.

A wave of revulsion stabbed at Taein's gut, but he just sighed and wiped one gloved hand clean on his pants. The pain wreaking havoc on his body was just a far-away throb, held at bay by adrenaline and spite.

Taein staggered over to Skinny and slid the three-pronged ring from the mugger's rapidly-stiffening finger.

Then a hoarse cough split the quiet. Taein's eyes darted back to Big as the mugger's grip on his satchel finally gave out. The bag rolled onto the blood-slick cobblestones with a wet *thump*.

Big was still alive. *The sucker.*

Taein strode over, slipping the ring into his pocket as he bent to retrieve his satchel. Then he crouched down next to Big, sliced open the mugger's bloody shirt, and tugged on the rosewood piece around his neck.

"Now, now," Taein said. "You have a choice. Sleeper or Shallow? It's not too late for me to relieve you of that pretty rosewood amulet, you know."

"Bastard." Big wheezed as real fear went spreading over his features like spilled ink leaching across new parchment.

"I am, actually," Taein said, smacking away Big's flailing hand with the jagged flat of his shiv. "Been a while since I got a good look at one of these."

Big started shaking like a leaf as Taein turned the rosewood piece over in his hand. "*Please.*"

"You idiots were getting workplace experience, I was getting enough adrenaline to kill a horse..." Taein shook his head. "We were having such a time, and then you went and mucked it all up."

"You ain't gotta take my amulet from me, man. We didn't know who you was!" Big pleaded. Were those actual *tears* welling up in his eyes?

Taein lifted a brow. "Such *theatre*. There's nothing scary about getting lost out there in the Between, you know, once your body's gone and given up on you. *All spirits return to one of two: Geiin or Mithre, holy or shrewd*, as they say. All men like you and I ever have to fear is one day getting found."

"Shank off, you faithless skiv!"

"Then say my name," Taein said as he rose and adjusted his coat. "You know *exactly* who I am."

"You're the Unkillable Kid—" The mugger said through a froth of blood, his squirming growing weaker.

Taein picked him up by the lapels and drew the mugger's face so close he could see the broken blood vessels in his eyes. "Say. My. *Name.*"

"*Taein*," Big said, and he burst into tears.

AND TAEIN HE WAS, AFTER ALL.

He was the prince of purloining, scourge of the streets, survivor against all natural odds, reckless to the point of delusion. He was *Taein*, survivor of the BlackBlades, the Unkillable Kid himself, (or unkillable as far as he *knew*, at least), and if a good thrashing was all that could beat back the numbness anymore, even just for a few adrenaline-soaked moments, so be it. It was better to feel *anything* other than his usual state of abysmal emptiness—even pain—because that emptiness haunted him like a starving child, dogging his heels every waking minute, leaching through his very bloodstream as a hard frost crawls along a windowpane.

He was *Taein*—terror of thieves, conductor of chaos, sweetheart of spite—and if brushing hands with death was all that could shake him halfway to life anymore, *so be it.*

After the thug's wheezing got too pitiful to bear, Taein silenced any further complaints with another lead ball and staggered off to Regor's.

This led him limping along the endless side streets that went curling under bridges and along canals toward the heart of the city. The Pearl was composed of three main districts—District Shardain, where the politicians, college fellows, and general wealthy populace lived; District Keenwin, home of the Nomen—the poor, desperate, and dangerous; and District Willville, the city's sector of grandiose lawlessness and melting pot of all things illicit, which was splattered in Pearl Jin's heart like an inkblot. Inside this last hub were numerous smaller divisions where merchants, industrialists, gang-bosses, and scrapping operations of all manner of ill-repute held occupation.

Taein found the Willville in its signature chaos. The mist tinted the air purple as it languished over the square like a wet blanket. He pushed his way through swarms of people, ignoring hockers of all sorts as they cajoled at the crowds. People from every realm in Ieris were buying and selling, gambling and fighting, all squeezed in among an ocean of tents and trading booths. Taein pocketed a few packs of good Venrian cigarettes from a vendor who was quick to look the other way and finished pushing through. He entered one of the many alleys snaking through the ramshackle boarding houses and moss-eaten taverns on the precarious verge of collapse that ringed the main square, opened a pack, and let the smoke take the edge off his stinging cheek.

Rain started plinking down again, so he hurried up with his smoke. It was spring in Pearl Jin, a season that was supposed to herald hope, and spring in the countryside did have its green, lush appeal. Such charms were lost in the Six Sister Cities, however—here there were only cobblestone streets to pock full with gray puddles and dirty alleys turned to mud and peaked mossy roofs to grow new leaks.

Taein flicked the cigarette away and finally headed straight for Regor's tent, stealing a glance at the sky. Regor never worked through the afternoon, and evening was coming on fast. If there was one thing the old boss hated more than a tardy scrapper, it was missing the evening races.

"Hello, Dorthy, long time no see! Did you miss me?" Taein chirped as he reached Regor's tent—a hulking, brightly colored sanctuary set as far from the muggy square as possible.

"Name's Dory," The guard, just a tower made of corded muscle capped with a shining bald head, growled in response. "You *know* my name's Dory. And you're late. Bossman ain't happy—"

Taein didn't look up as he dug through each of the six different compartments in his satchel, searching to unearth the Mendolniese blades. "Take it easy, Darla, it's only the 21st."

"It's *Dory*—"

Taein looked up at the bruiser. "That can't be right. Dory is a *girl's* name."

The giant let out another growl as he stooped down and gripped Taein by the shoulder. "No, it *ain't*. And today's the 22nd, you idiot."

Taein struggled under the weight of Dory's paw and cursed. "Son of a bitch, I could've *sworn* I had my days straight this time."

"Can't imagine you keep anything straight with boots like that."

"Now, Demi," Taein said, plucking a cigarette out of the bruisers' shirt pocket, "play fair—"

Dory dragged Taein forward and shoved him through the tent entrance before he could finish his retort. He blinked in the sudden change of light, shrugged off the ache from the bruiser's grip, and headed straight for one of Regor's many mirrors.

No one seemed to be inside. The pleasant scent of something woodsy and clean permeated the whole tent, so different from the ever-changing and mostly-rank smells of the city outside. Chandeliers hung from the tent's ceiling every few paces. Their candles, each partially encased with multicolored glass to prevent fire, sent shards of soft pastel light glancing about the room.

Beneath this gentle glow was a menagerie of exotic indulgences from around Ieris—plush woven rugs and deep purple hangings from the art museums of Kor Vensurite in Ersii, blackwood furnishings from the best craftsmen of the Eastwin District, paintings from the Isle of Winsor, and even a hand-carved wiinwood desk from the realm of Faeriel.

Taein stopped by the desk, pausing to drop off his satchel and pick up a gold-crusted lighter. Only after puffing on the cigarette he'd stolen from Dory did he feel up to facing the mirror hung above an overstuffed couch.

The image that greeted him was not a pleasant one. Both eyes were blackened and swollen, and the cut on his lower lip throbbed worse than a bee sting. The gash on his right cheekbone was deeper than he'd thought, too. Beneath the layer of grime and gelling blood, he could catch a glimpse of raw bone.

His stomach turned hard. *This is nothing new,* he reminded himself, squeezing his eyes shut. *It'll heal, it always heals.*

"That's gonna scar."

Taein didn't startle, nor did he turn to greet the old man.

"How's about gettin' off my couch with those filthy boots?" Regor said.

He was referring to Taein's perfect, pristine, *dearly* cherished leather boots. With the gold scrolling and leaf-and-rose inlays and silver toes. The boots Taein's brother gave him, all of those years ago, and he never went without since. And boots like his looked too good to ever be called *filthy*.

Taein hopped down. "Boss," he said sweetly, "you're as vain as the day is long. If anyone has some magic liquid for scarring, it's you. And mud or no mud, my boots are shanking *beautiful*."

Regor just swore under his breath as he lumbered to his desk and unlocked a drawer, pausing only to chuck someone's hand aside on the end table.

Taein stared at the severed hand for a beat, then to the man who had presumably removed it.

Regor looked just the same as the day Taein had met him, some seven or eight years prior. He was a stout barrel of a man with squat legs and thick arms, dressed in the most pompous velvet tunic and striped silk breeches to be found. A slouching, oversized hat shaded his round, sun-darkened face, which was half-covered by a short beard. He had the calloused hands of a working man and long articulate fingers, both of which were curious to Taein as he never saw the old man do much beside lavish over his many, many knives... which he was presumably still deft with, judging by the graying fist still oozing blood on the end table.

Regor shuffled back over with a bottle, rag, and bone-needle box before he parked his bulk back in front of Taein.

"Sit down and let me look at you, kid."

"Just hand over the bottle," Taein said on a smoke-tinged exhale. "I can take care of myself."

"Sit."

Taein hesitated before lowering himself onto Regor's plush carpet. "Somebody got caught keeping too many marks aside again?"

A grim smile slid onto Regor's face. "Learn from Ken's example." The old man blew out a low whistle. "Who did this to you?"

"Dunno, really. They were new, got me in an alley."

Regor scoffed as he opened the vial and dropped the crystal stopper into Taein's palm. "I don't understand what the hell you're thinking, letting all these bastards rough you up like this."

"Ah, but I love the attention so very much and none of the resident brutes will give it to me anymore."

Regor shook his head. "Don't change the fact that you're ruining your face."

"Maybe I like the scars," Taein said, trying not to flinch as Regor dabbed the cloth onto his gash. "Just think, with every new brawl, my reputation as unkillable grows. It's all politics, Regor."

"It's all insanity, is what it is. Don't you want to meet a nice girl one day?"

"Ha! The more thrashings I survive now, the less I'll have to dodge when I finally get old and brittle like you. It's *reputation*—hey!" Taein said as Regor plucked the cigarette out his mouth and chucked it onto his turquoise ashtray.

"They take your wares?" The old man asked.

"Not a chance," he managed, pulling the blood crusted ring from his pocket. "And this was my consolation prize."

"*Our* consolation prize."

Taein slipped off the ring and dropped it into Regor's waiting palm. "Of course."

Regor patted Taein's good cheek. If he noticed Taein's flinch, he had the good graces not to say anything. "That's why you's my favorite. But you're still way past return time, boy, don't think I didn't notice."

"Well that's *never* happened before." Taein steadied his stomach as Regor threaded the needle and commenced stitching the gash. "Now what do you want? There's no chance you're doctoring me out of the goodness of your rotten old heart."

"I've got no heart, only a chest for coins." Regor tied off the stitches before he stood and wiped his hands on his pants. "Come over to my desk and we'll have us a little chat."

Taein frowned and followed, where Regor eased into a plush chair and curled his hands together atop his stomach. He leaned back and looked Taein in the eye for a long while.

"What is it?" Taein asked, a wisp of unease curling down his spine.

Regor gave a sly smile. "Now, I think, is a good time to *remind* you of where you came from, and what you *owe* me."

Taein's grin slipped.

"Oh... scrawny, stupid little teenaged you..." Regor shook his head as he reminisced. "Found ya slumped over half-dead in some rit house with your brains oozing out your ears, skinnier than a rat trapped down a dry well. Remember?"

Taein nodded, of course he did. He felt the old aches whenever he passed some knocked-out ritter in an alley, felt the aches in each and every scar littering the insides of his arms, felt the aches when he woke up and went to sleep and every moment in between.

It was *forgetting* that had always been the trouble, that drove him to the drug in the first place.

Regor held Taein's gaze. "There was a reason I did the world the great disservice of keeping you alive, Taein. Not because I *liked* you, but because of what you told me when I had Vincent drop your ass and we turned to leave."

Taein swallowed hard, beginning to sweat.

"You told me you would thieve from anywhere in the world, even from the ruins of House Glass, even from the *Blackblades,* and when I laughed in your face and called you crazy, you laughed too. And then you told me you were the last Prince of Glass."

Sweet Geiin. Taein's heart began to careen around his chest, but he popped his boots up on Regor's desk, leaned back in his chair, and concocted a lazy smile. "Malarky, old man. You're lying to me."

Regor knocked Taein's boots off his desk and smiled right back. "No, I ain't."

"Well, I sure as shit didn't say that—"

"Ain't my word law 'round these parts?"

Taein felt his face drain white. "Look, I would've told you anything—"

"You told me everything, is what you did. Now the time has come for me to use such an audacious and unwise claim to my advantage."

"Regor, boss, I was lying to you. I couldn't possibly be—"

"For once, you were telling the truth. You think I can't tell the difference?" Regor chuckled. "Drugs make most men into liars, but drugs made *you* an honest man. Now relax. This job should be a cinch for the likes of you."

Taein stood. "You can't be serious. You have no proof—"

"Look, it ain't about who you are right now, boy," Regor snapped. "It's about your uses."

"Isn't it always about who I am?" Taein snapped back. "What you're accusing me of is a death sentence—"

"It is, isn't it?"

Taein fell silent, glaring all the while. "What the hell could you possibly be after?"

Regor's blackbird eyes lit with a hungry gleam. "Oh, it's a tricky one this time. The Outlander himself has put out a... demand."

The Outlander. Taein barely heard what Regor said. His palms were as slick as if he'd plunged them in a barrel of fish oil.

"But what is it?" he asked.

Regor leaned forward and looked Taein deeply in the eyes, something akin to a grin curving his features.

"Not a *what* this time, boy. A *who*."

❦ 3 ❧

THE HANDS THAT ARE EMPTY
{THIRTY-SIX DAYS BEFORE}

"**M**y lord, a Prince of Glass *survived*."

Vasily's grip gave out and the flask crashed down, splattering wine like blood across the marble floor. For a long while he could do nothing but stand there and feel the shuddering of his destroyed heart as the world pinched in on itself.

"It cannot be," he breathed.

Nuest shook his head. "I came as soon as I could."

Vasily drew back, no longer able to see Nuest or even the study. The glass chilled his back, his pulse just a slow shiver in his veins. Just when he thought he'd finally made amends, when he could finally set aside this black fire in his heart and search for something quieter... a *survivor.* How could he have failed his father *again*?

Vasily wavered, one boot sliding on the wine-slick stone. It was not possible. It *wasn't*. He caught all the sons of Glass, burned their bodies to ash with fire just as they turned his father to ash with a mere *touch*. He denied them their amulets, broke every ritual. He took everything, even their half-deaths. They paid and they would *suffer*.

"Are you certain?" he managed.

"Beyond all doubt, my lord." Nuest said.

"But..." Vasily's eyes darted around the room. There had to be an

19

explanation. "Nuest, I watched the life leave their eyes. I took their amulets."

Nuest shook his head. "I saw him with my own eyes."

Vasily turned and slammed his fist into the window-wall. Blood smeared onto the glass as it absorbed the impact without so much of a tremor. The wash of pain did nothing to settle the creature turning over in its sleep inside him, that monstrous *thing* Vasily had spent every day since the war trying to rid himself of.

"Which is it, then?" he bit out.

"The half-prince."

The bastard, then. Vasily closed his eyes as the creeping chill about the study grew fierce. The urge to go down to the crypt in the bottom of the House where his ancestors lay sleeping, to surround himself in the cold deep where no one would hear his frustration or his grief, swept over him like a wave.

But that was just the problem—there was no tomb for his father. Lord Taegart of Slate had been denied his place among the silent stone hold of their fore-fathers. Vasily hadn't even the chance to lay his body to rest, to embalm him so that his stranded spirit might be soothed to sleep by the touch of a rosewood amulet. No tomb for bodies that no longer existed.

And now here stood Nuest, standing there with fat tears rolling down his face, telling Vasily that a Prince of Glass yet lived.

The silence lingered for a long while before Nuest spoke, broken only by the blood dripping from Vasily's knuckles onto the floor.

"I am sorry, my lord."

Vasily opened his eyes. "What for?"

"That you must hunt the boy again. If one could even call such a creature a mere *boy*."

Vasily looked away from Nuest's tears. He couldn't stand the old man's grief any more than he could stand his own.

"I can't even remember him," he said, clenching his fists to hide the way they shook.

"I only remember him from before your father's passing, when he was still a lad. Just looking at him *startled* me, my lord. Something about him seemed so... starved."

Vasily risked another look at Nuest, expecting to find the old man still lost in his reminiscence. But Nuest was looking straight at him, his eyes terribly grave.

"He frightened me even when he was a boy, Vasily, in a way none of his brothers could rival. And they were warriors even then, grown men they were. I can't imagine what the bastard has turned into as a man himself."

"Geiin in heaven," Vasily marveled, "are you insinuating he may cut me?"

Nuest didn't look away. "I think he would kill you, if you gave him the chance. He's built up a fearsome reputation in the city. They call him the 'Unkillable Kid'. Apparently he is in possession of some new device from the Outerlands called a flintlock. It is a mighty defense—"

"Ridiculous," Vasily snarled. "He'll die at my hand, easily as any other."

"But he *isn't* any other man, my lord. Is he not of the line of Glass? Is he not kin to the one who turned our late Lord to ash with the mere touch of his bare hand?"

Vasily gritted his teeth. "He will be no challenge to me."

"Then... it will be as you say, *Alaskiae*."

Vasily flinched at the use of Babas' pet name for him. *Alaskiae.* Little Wolf.

Nuest shook his head. "Perhaps it's only a bad feeling... but there is nothing more dangerous than a man whose hands are empty."

Vasily couldn't stand looking at the old man's weepy face any longer. He turned back to the window and sifted through the stars, searching for his father's stolen warmth.

Help me, Babas.

"*Mie durksil menwi tu son gaethoa*," Vasily said softly.

Nuest replied without hesitation. "*Mie durksil menwi tu son gaethoa.*"

I was born a shield. The honor-pledge of his father, and his father's fathers before them. The way of the sons of Slate.

"I will destroy the last Prince of Glass once and for all," he vowed. "No matter the cost."

"Of course, my lord," Nuest said. "You are your father's son, after all."

Something gripped Vasily's heart and squeezed hard. Five stolen amulets lay untouched in the locked desk behind, a key wrought of false security resting cold around his neck.

"I am," he murmured, more to the moon than the old man hovering behind, "and I will not fail him again."

THE BOUNTY

Taein had thieved for the Outlander before, of course.

The Outlander was a strange creature who *looked* like a man, but most certainly was not. He was the only creature from the distant Outerlands to ever return to Ieris after two-thirds of the First Men (and a host of other strange creatures) first fled across the White Salt Sea from Lithriin's corruption two thousand years ago, just before the waters turned savage and forever separated the two continents like brothers torn apart.

This particular Outlander arrived back on the Jinian coast some five or six hundred years ago, an imposing, willowy figure with eyes of pure obsidian and ears that slanted back into points, and had been outliving Ierisians ever since. Being the only creature ever to survive crossing the monster-swamped, storm-socked, ice-shredded White Salt Sea entailed certain privileges. It meant that if the Outlander wanted someone hunted down, it happened. And it happened *fast*.

Or at least it used to, 'till the Jinian authorities got sick of him medaling in their politics and business and worst of all *embezzling their precious money,* and banished him from the realm. That had been five years ago, and they hadn't heard a peep from the Outlander since.

But despite all this, it truly *wasn't* a job from the long-lost Outlander that was sending Taein's heart into this ridiculously frenzy as he stood staring like a downright podge at Regor.

Only one thing was capable of frying every barricade Taein ever bothered to construct around his nerves to such a blackened crisp: *the truth.*

He sat there, too stunned to function, and stared at Regor. "You want me to go after *what* now?"

"You're not going after anything. I need you to simply move... cargo. From point A to point B."

"Easy enough—"

Regor cut Taein off with only a look, then turned behind him.

"You can come out now," he said, and out it came.

Well, not quite an *it*. Rather, the *it* was a *she*.

A little girl crept out from behind the life-sized porcelain statue of a tiger near the back of Regor's tent. She wore a dirty, torn blue dress dotted by once-white flowers, mousey brown hair falling scraggly into her face as she crept forward and glared at Taein. Her eyes, the palest, coldest green he'd ever seen looking out of a tan human face, locked in on him and filled with seething, black-tar hate.

Taein's breath caught. He looked back at Regor, desperate to get those strange pale eyes off of him. "What does the Outlander want with a *kid?*"

Regor set his jaw. "Apparently he's been hiding out in the Lost Realm—"

Taein groaned. "Not *Efriel-shanking-Shu.*"

"Efriel Shu indeed. He's put out a contract, asking Chevaliers for..." Regor drew off, gazed at the kid for a long while before continuing. "People of interest to him, I suppose. This one here fits his criteria."

"What's he doing in Efriel-Shu, of all places?"

Regor shrugged. "None of my business, none of yours. But I can tell you this much, son," he said, jamming his thumb at the girl, "He's willing to bleed coin out the ass to get the kid. Now sit."

Taein sat.

Regor motioned for the kid to come, then leaned back in his chair.

She paused at the edge of his desk, eyes snapping to the severed hand before landing accusingly back onto Taein. Her glare deepened and Taein wanted to snap at her that *he* hadn't done it, but Regor was talking again.

"Listen, Taein. I know your little secret, which means your days of refusing jobs are long over," Regor said, watching with bemusement as the kid took up one of his emerald-crusted pens and a leather-bound ledger before settling on his carpet to draw.

Taein glared. "You can't prove anything."

"You really think *I* need proof?" Regor looked hard at Taein, then began pulling all the many knives from his coat and piling them up on his desk. That caught the kid's interest—she looked up from her drawing and zeroed right in one a wickedly-curved cleaver. Regor kept the blades coming, and Taein counted some thirty before the old man spoke again.

"I know who you are, Taein. *What* you are. Princes of Glasses aren't just any old princes, are they?" he stared Taein down, unflinching, and then he said it.

"*Anathema.*"

Anathema. The forsaken descendants of the long-dead Four Fathers, who lived with curses in their veins and targets on their backs, who had all long ago been hunted to extinction—most recently including the sons of Glass.

Or, so they thought.

"Well, shit." Taein sat back and ran a hand through his hair. "What are you going to do? Turn me in to be flayed alive over something I said when I was so high off my socks I could've taken flight?"

"Relax, kid," Regor said with little patience, depositing what Taein fervently hoped was the last of his knives on the table and beginning to polish them one by one. "You're safe, but only so long as you are bound to me."

Of *course*. Taein fought back the seething frustration brewing in his chest and gripped the arms of his chair.

"Now I can't just reveal what you are and hand you over to the highest bidder, since you got that very-specific crow's tattoo even I can't just stamp on your replacement. That damn crow enables you to truly thieve from anywhere, Geiin knows how you got it. If you could get in and out of the Blades, surely you can get in and out of the Fallen Realm."

"So you're blackmailing me. For the rest of my shankin' life." Taein said.

"Think of it as a small... tax for your continued protection within my sacred fold," Regor said, setting down a cleaver and picking up a curved, emerald-crusted Venrian dagger. The kid, remaining eerily silent, tracked the old man's every movement.

"What you're gonna do for me is use those twisted survival skills of yours. Use such fine and unscrupulous talents to get our friend here to the Outlander."

"You can't make me be your little nursemaid," Taein sputtered.

"Don't care," Regor scoffed, losing interest in Taein's protest before Taein could even really get it underway.

"Give her to Hank, he's done way more jobs for the Outlander—" Taein scrambled.

"No dice."

Taein gave Regor his best smile and perched on the edge of his seat. "Regor. Boss. You know I hate people more than anything. Kids especially."

"I couldn't care less about your pretty little feelings. I got my reputation, and more importantly, good cold marks tied up in this deal. So swallow your silly 'Half-Siou' pride and *get it done*. He'll be waiting for you at a drop point," Regor said, handing Taein a piece of paper with some scrawled coordinates.

Taein slumped back and stared at the kid, who was still fascinated with the blades and totally ignoring the conversation around her. His heart sank slowly to his toes.

Not this. *Anything* but this.

"I'll even sweeten the deal with some marks, if that'll help the pill go down easier," Regor added. "But what's better is a successful return buys you the precious jewel of not only continued protection, but my silence."

"It won't buy me anything," Taein snapped, "because I'm not *him*—"

"Oh, right, because you're only *half-Siou*." Regor smirked and handed the emerald dagger to the kid. She took it up, admiring her reflection in the steel, before glaring again at Taein with a creepy half-grin on her face.

"Taein, the Half-Siou, who calls himself the Unkillable Kid," Regor mused. "My, my... what a mighty small world we live in."

Taein's mouth went dry. Between the freak of a kid smirking at him with a knife and Regor's prying for the *terrible truth,* he was getting a little lightheaded.

"Well, *Taein*... you're walking on dangerously thin ice, as per shankin' usual, But my word is law 'round these parts, and any other part of Ieris you think might be safe. Botch this job, and there will be nowhere to hide," Regor said, keeping Taein's gaze hostage as he set about tucking each newly cleaned knife (excluding the kid's dagger, which she was somehow allowed to hang on to) back into his clothes. Each blade disappeared into the old man's person as if they were as much a part of him as flesh and bone.

"What's the Outlander want with her?" Taein asked. It was all he could do to keep himself from bolting as far as his legs could carry him and then some.

"Who cares?"

"Someone should," Taein said, trying not to look back at the kid as she crept a little closer. "She some relation of his?"

The kid shook her head violently before Regor could speak. The old man gazed at her for a while, then shrugged. "Just get it done, Taein. It doesn't matter who she is."

Taein folded his arms. "Find someone else. I'm not doing this."

Regor opened a drawer and withdrew a corroded chain, from which hung a tiny bounty disc of dull silver. He looked at Taein and smiled his executioner's smile.

"No, I think you will."

Taein's stomach twisted hard. He'd seen similar chains hung around the necks of Regor's bounty hunters many times before. They were made of eldrwrought silver from the southern mines, a metal Regor exclusively controlled in the Pearl. When a bounty was created, such discs were engraved with the name of the mark, and whichever bounty hunter ended up returning the mark with the tag got the reward. Taein himself never dreamed he might wear one—much less one etched with his *own damn name*.

Regor stayed silent as he took out a razor-tipped mechanical torch-burner and flicked the heating-flame on to life. "I'm making two of these, Taein. One for you, to remember what's at stake. One more for me to give to our associates, if you forget. The deal has been cut—if you don't get the kid to the Outlander safe and sound, your life is forfeit."

Taein just nodded. There was nothing to say. Once the old man's mind was set on something, he was immovable.

"How much are we talking?" he thought to ask.

"500,000 marks."

The panic in Taein's chest took a back seat. That was an *unheard* of sum. Taein wasn't sure if Regor himself even possessed that much money.

Regor harrumphed. "Now here comes my final bribe: get there and back again in a month, and I'll part with seven percent of the cut. Minus expenses, of course. That's all you're gonna get out of me, considering I could just hand you over and keep it all. Think of it as a... present, and your life the real payment. But *only* if you get her to the Outlander, and fast."

Taein's mouth went dry. *35,000 marks*. That was enough to buy a man damn near anything—even a life spent alone. No more scrapping, no more cities, no more people. A life where Taein, in all his selfish, spiteful glory, could buy some farm on a far-off hillside and live out the rest of his days alone. A life where he could *win*.

"You leave tomorrow," Regor said, the glow from the burner's flame illuminating his face.

"I'd be a fool not to," Taein said, glancing at the kid. She'd settled herself back on the carpet, balancing the knife Regor had yet to retrieve from her on one knee while scribbling doodles in his ledger.

"What's your name?" he asked.

She didn't look up, nor respond. Her hair—dirty and matted, once a soft brown—shielded her gaze from him, and Taein was thankful for that. Without those ungodly eyes burning holes right through him, she looked like any other grubby brat from the street.

Regor took the white-hot burner and put the razor tip delicately to the bounty disc. "She's mute, by the way."

"But she can hear, can't she?" Taein asked.

"Oh, her hearin' is good as a cat's. Getting her to listen is the real problem, according to Ka-el. Which brings me to the part of this conversation I like least." Regor set the torch burner aside and waved the freshly-engraved disc to cool it. "You remember Vince, don't you?" Regor asked as he tossed the bounty disc over, the still-hot words carven into the metal flashing *Prince of Glass*.

Taein caught the chain, slipped it over his neck, and tucked it beneath his shirt. The disc, no bigger than his thumbnail, lay warm against his skin. "Sure do."

As much as he loved working on his own, Taein had developed an unfortunate soft spot for Ka-el and his crew over the years. Ka-el himself was a lanky, dark-haired tracker, twice Taein's age and a hundred times more honorable. His crew consisted of Venny, a slender blonde with a bad leg and a knack for cracking locks, and Vince, a bearded mountain made into a man who possessed the personality of a field mouse, and served as the crew's bodyguard.

"What about them?" Taein asked.

Regor picked at a spot of blood on the desk, then glanced back at the severed hand on his end table as if he'd forgotten its existence. "They're the ones who brought this kid to me in the first place. Encountered her and some funny business out in the wilds."

"What kind of funny business?"

"The kind Vince can fill you in on, when you pick him up."

"You can't be serious," Taein said, dropping his face into his hands. "Not the kid *and* Vince. Are you trying to kill me? Just hand me over to the law for Geiin's sake!"

Regor rolled his eyes. "I'm not sending you with Kory or Arvin—"

"I *hate* Arvin," Taein groaned from behind his hands. Arvin always made fun of his boots and it was against Regor's rules to thrash fellow scrappers while in his square, so Taein always had to just sit there and take it like a podge.

"But you like Vince," Regor said. "He's got nothin' to do anyway."

"I don't *like* Vince," Taein said, dropping his hands from his face. "And I thought you weren't assigning him jobs for a while after that incident with the Vandel diplomat."

Regor scratched his nose. "Don't remind me. I ain't paying him 'till he brings you back *alive*. Now listen—back at the rithouse, I told Vincent you were lyin' through your teeth to get us to save you. He don't know any better than that. I haven't told him where this job is heading, either."

Taein's stomach churned. What the hell was *happening*?

"You meet him tomorrow morning and don't be sneaking off before." Regor paused to glare at Taein. "If you bring any of my horses back lame, I'll turn your hide into curtains and string your guts along the city walls, no shit! And get a new amulet! And—"

"Regor, what *is* her name?"

Regor faltered, then looked at the kid. She was still ignoring them, sketching some hooded figure and a horse with a frenzy.

"I don't know." The old man quieted, his gaze drifting away from Taein and to the pale fractures of pastel light glancing atop the ceiling.

The gentle glow softened his features, eased away the years hard living had carved into his face. He eased up from his chair and bent down, then said a few hushed words to the kid. Taein listened half-heartedly as the old man explained the situation, absorbing the kid's hateful look as she realized she was being made to go with him. Taein had nothing to say to her to try and make the situation better—she was cargo. She was a job, nothing more.

That's how it had to be. That was the only way he could survive this.

Still, his heart couldn't help but prick with a tinge of sympathy as he saw the honest-to-goodness tears on her face. Regor got her to her feet, helped her tie on a muddy rain cloak, and set a fine-woven silk bag in front of her, into which he not only deposited his leather-bound ledger book and gaudy pen, but also that glittery dagger she'd taken such a shine to. Then he nudged her in Taein's direction.

Regor returned his gaze to Taein. His eyes took on a steely sheen.

"The Celestial will decide what happens to her once this is all over. All I'm asking is to keep her safe, Taein."

Taein turned, heart tight and bruises aching, and disappeared into the night.

The kid, silent as a ghost, followed.

❧ *5* ❧

THE FAREWELL
{THIRTY-FIVE DAYS BEFORE}

Before he left, Vasily paid a visit to his mother.

He said goodbye to his sisters, held Finya as she sobbed into his chest while Yena turned her back with a silence that went lancing right through Vasily's heart as a harsh winter wind bites through an old coat.

Now he was standing in front of mother's door, his shirt still damp from Finya's tears, his heart already so tired.

Vasily braced himself and knocked.

"Come in," came his Mari's voice through the white-washed wood, and Vasily turned the knob and stepped inside.

The room was quiet, save for a scattering of trickling fountains. The air was perfumed by sweet incense burners trailing faint blue smoke and pots upon pots of blossoming plants, which lined the walls on straining shelves. Legions of unruly vines slithered down along the baseboards like thin green serpents from some warm foreign jungle. The room was rather like a garden, bright with sun and full of silent growing things, but the peace held a sort of finality that never failed to set Vasily on edge. It seemed as if the room was almost *too* easy to rest in. A room where one might drift asleep and never fully awake.

32

Vasily found his mother gazing through the window by her desk, standing between two large pots of tall orange lilies.

"Mari?" he called.

Lady Terigyn Miinriel looked back, her features laid bare by the truthful light of the window. She was pale as the gray morning sky, closed up in a light blue dress sewn with hundreds of silver beads. Her hair was done up in a polished swoop, and Vasily could tell that she had rubbed her cheeks with rosy pigment that morning. There was a healthy flush to her cheeks that he knew was not really there.

Vasily crossed the room to kiss her cheek. "Good morning, Mari."

She gave a slight smile. "Ah, there he is. How does my favorite son fare?"

"Wonderfully, what of you?"

Her eyes drifted away and back toward the window. "Quite well, Vasily, don't fret. I hate to see you worry."

"I know," Vasily said, evaluating. Mother and Auryn—his eldest sister, only a few years younger than him who'd been long away in the warmth of an Ersiin court— were the only ones to differ from the dark eyes of their family line. Theirs were light and pensive, the color of a winter dawn. But Mari had changed since Babas' death. Those eyes, once peaceful and assured, now held a sort of fragility, a searching. And it bothered Vasily. He knew she was looking for something he could not replace.

Vasily closed his eyes for a moment, willing away the hot rage that was always so quick to spring up at the mere thought of Babas' death. Mother's headaches had come but days after Babas died, and since then she spent her time drifting from bout to bout of wasting fatigues.

"Nuest told me you're leaving again," Mari said. "To where?"

"Just on some business." He hesitated. "I'm worried for you, Mari. Even if you don't like to hear it, I am."

She set her jaw. "Why won't you tell me where you are going?"

Vasily shrugged. "It isn't important. What I wish to talk about now is your health."

"All I wish to talk about now is my son." Her eyes took on a hard glint. "And I am worried about *you*."

Impatience welled up inside. Vasily strained to keep his voice level. "What in Geiin's name for?"

She laid a thin hand on his chest, her eyes searching his seriously. "Your heart. In you I sense—"

He tried to move away, rolling his eyes. "Mother, please—"

"Vasily."

He stopped, reaching up to fidget with the rosewood amulet lying beneath his shirt before remembering himself. Mari searched his face for another too-long moment before reaching up to cup his cheek with her hand.

"You remind me so much of your father. Never at rest."

"And are you at rest, lady mother?" he asked.

"No." She said, "I will not rest again, not in this lifetime."

Vasily closed his eyes. Her hand was cold against his cheek, and the fire in his heart was raging.

"But I am old, Vasily, and you are young. You deserve to find peace."

"I am trying."

"You should take a wife." She withdrew her hand from his cheek. "Find a lady to serve your house."

"If I wanted to find peace, the last thing I'd do is get a wife." At her blank expression, he looked down and continued. "Besides, you aren't old. If you'd just listen—"

She scoffed. "You may be the lord of this house, Vasily but I still see you as you are." She tapped his chest. "I see your heart."

He brushed her hand away. "And what of it?"

"Vasily... he would want you to move forward. Away from your grief."

Vasily's heart sank. "Don't do this—"

Her voice broke as she spoke again. "Your father would want you to be *happy*."

"Don't speak of him like this," he whispered.

"Why not?"

It hurts. He couldn't force the words.

All the previous warmth seemed to have drained from the room. Vasily let himself sink into the silence until mother finally spoke again.

"Tell me where you are going."

He looked up and found her watching.

"Tell me, *Alaskiae*."

He sighed. "Why does it trouble you so?"

Her eyes drifted back to the window as if pulled by some imaginary thread. The valley far below the Whitelights stretched out long and dark and green, threaded by silver rivers. A land with no end. A land to fight and die for.

"I foresee great suffering on the northern winds," Mari said. "I see this... *pain* reflected in you."

Vasily fought another sigh, reminded of her silly habit of wind-reading. "It is no great matter. A simple loose end that needs cutting."

"I sense Nuest's agitation."

Vasily smiled. "Nuest is always agitated."

"Not like this. I know you'll think it's silly, but I feel something strange stirring deep within the fabric of the land. When I close my eyes, I see things that should not exist. Plants that shine with a cold light even in the high sun, wild animals twisted from their natural states and turned savage... things that were, Vasily. Remnants of a past age." She frowned. "I feel a coming darkness, in my very bones. And I'm afraid for you."

Vasily stepped forward, captured her hand with his own. "I promise you," he said, "that everything will be fine. *Mie durksil menwi tu son gaaethoa,* mother."

Tears glimmered in her eyes, but she somehow kept her voice level. "Wherever you go, I will be with you."

He squeezed her hand. "You are always with me, Mari."

"And so is he, Vasily." She smiled as if the action could hide the single tear slipping down her cheek, quiet as longing, cold as want. "He lives in you."

I am not worthy, he thought.

But he squeezed her hand once more, and left.

The gray morning had eased away into a clear afternoon by the time Vasily finally trudged to the Aerie, that unshakable weight still marinating in his very bones. He hadn't slept since Nuest told him about Glass.

Vasily walked down the long, high-ceilinged hallway that attached the Aerie to House Slate until it ushered him into the great vaulted spire itself. He stilled, taking in the tower before him.

The spire reached some five hundred feet in the air, almost half House Slate's height, and never once failed to take his breath away. The tower was topped by a great stained-glass dome that poured in multi-colored light on the forest of cobalt firs below. Among these ancient trees lived some fifty or sixty bloodhawks, each one bred, fledged, and taught to fly within the spire's dizzying height.

The bloodhawks were small, sociable animals, their feathers colored in shades of red, gold, black, and white; no bigger than a common hawk but possessing of a steely intelligence that rivaled the dragons and basalt deer of the long-lost Unfallen Age.

The Aerie was quiet save for the small, high whistles of the hawks talking among one another and the *swoosh* of silken feathers shifting cold air. Vasily took out his horn and called for her. Bellan appeared a minute later, her feathers a mottled gray and white, soundlessly displacing the air as she sailed down to alight on his arm.

It was Babas himself who helped Vasily tame her some twenty years ago, and together they taught her to come at Vasily's call, to track any quarry without breaking focus, to understand human words as well as any man. Bellan remained a constant companion through all his life, there even when it seemed everything else had been torn apart. She had even helped him hunt down the sons of Glass.

Vasily frowned. How was it possible they *both* missed one?

"I see Bellan has already found you, my lord," a voice said from behind.

Vasily turned to spot Nuest. "Good morning. Is—"

"I've seen to everything, sire. You have but to be on your way."

Vasily nodded, the bloodhawk heavy on his arm. He and Nuest made their way to the stables in silence. Vasily focused on the bird perched on his arm and ignored the way his heart seemed to sink lower with every step.

House Slate's stables made up a modest wing opposite the Aerie, built with thick boards to keep away the cold and a heavy thatched roof to shelter its inhabitants—twenty resident stablemen and some four hundred horses—from the year-round mountain top snow.

Vasily himself owned but one—a strange shadow of a horse, so unlike the muscled destriers to which he was once well accustomed. She was tall, a plain dark bay color without a spot of white, and rarely made a sound. Nuest had already saddled her up and she stood waiting in the aisle.

"Hello, old girl," Vasily said. The grooms called her *Falaksi*, ghost-horse. Vasily himself had no name for her.

He set his bloodhawk on a saddle rack and was reaching for a pack on the floor when the silver cuff on his wrist slipped forward. Vasily held back a sigh as he shoved the cuff further up his forearm where it belonged. He was only a boy when Babas placed the cuff on him, naming Vasily heir to House Slate in front of thousands. The cuff was too big then, designed never to be removed and only grown into, and Vasily had always been so worried it might slip from his wrist, and to this day it still didn't fit quite right.

Back then, he was so excited to one day be *Lord Vasily Miinriel of Slate*, to grow into the looming shadow his father cast. But what was he now? Standing here in killer's garb, ready to hunt down a man whose only crime was existence.

The silver glinted in the dim light, and Vasily shook his head. This wasn't his father's shadow he'd grown into, and he knew that. He'd slipped into a shadow of something Babas had never been, no matter the battles he fought and men he felled. Something Babas always fought *against*.

Murderer.

Still, Vasily straightened his shoulders and pulled himself into the saddle.

It didn't matter. He would find this Prince of Glass and plant his sword in his heart before the bastard could even comprehend what killed him. He would make things right. He would *finish it*.

Vasily shook himself from his thoughts and looked to Nuest. The old man was sitting on a bale of hay, smiling to hide his worry.

"I very much look forward to your return, my lord," he said.

Vasily smiled back. "Until we meet again?"

Nuest nodded, his eyes growing watery. "Geiin be with you."

"And you," Vasily said. He clicked to Bellan and she swooped into the air and headed for the open stable door.

Vasily nudged the bay after the bloodhawk, her hooves striking loud against the stone floor. A single stolen amulet lay deep in his pocket, its former owner the prey ahead.

6

A WHISPER OF SNOW

There were many things that made Taein stand out like a sore thumb in Pearl Jin—he looked *Siou*, of course, all sun-starved skin and dark eyes and unruly hair, and at the end of the day that would always put a target on his back. He also looked weak, at first glance, too scrawny to be a bruiser, too meek to compete as a thief or a mugger, too fine-featured to be a shake-down or a slash. Nothing about his appearance made him look particularly deserving of respect, save for his weird little smile, which he could make sharper than a blade at a second's need, and his tattoos.

Ages ago, House Ring created the Council of Coins and accorded the board power over each of the Six Sister Cities. In a bid to separate the educated and decent from the criminal class, the Council created a caste of six distinctions, most all with a corresponding tattoo: Royalty of Ring, Councilors, Rightfellows, Countrymen, Chiselers, and Nomen.

This made Taein a sort of anomaly, because he was a criminal by trade and therefore considered a Noman, the only class to not have any instituted tattoos, and yet he sported *two*. The first was a fern, the mark of Regor's crew, which covered most of his left forearm and part

39

of his wrist. This one alone was enough to stop most thugs in their tracks, because Regor was Regor, and he was shanking *scary*.

But it was the second tattoo that single-handedly earned Taein the moniker of the *Unkillable Kid.*

He had the silhouette of a *Blackblade crow* tattooed on his right forearm, and that was a tattoo no one ever saw, except for on the dead.

The Blackblades were a string of outposts sat on the west coast of Nown Jin, sequestered from the rest of civilization by a cropping of mountains called the Septets. As the criminal underbelly of Nown Jin grew, so did the need for a place of concentrated violence. A razing was beginning to happen, stirred up by a sea of kingpins, gang bosses, and criminal henchmen who all had scores to settle and needed a place to settle them *freely*.

Born of a need to spare the Six Sisters from a violence that could not be quelled came the Blackblades. Newcomers to the Blades got tattooed with a crow, and no one got out alive without having that crow tattooed over by a black rose.

But Taein didn't have the rose. He still had the crow. And that meant not only did he survive the Blackblades itself, but that he *broke out.*

And that tattoo was what made Taein the Unkillable Kid to most. The tattoo put every city's RAC and the entirety of the Blade's Garrison on his tail for years before they finally gave up and resorted to permanently denying not only the tattoo's *authenticity*, but Taein's very *existence*. The tattoo is what made muggers cross the street, what made rivals leave him alone, what kept his apartment permanently un-burgled—but it wasn't to him. What made Taein the Unkillable Kid was more than surviving the war that tore his realm apart and the hunt for his life that followed. It was more than almost starving to death in the wilds, it was more than the addictions that still hungered for his life. More than his time in the Blackblades, more than evading the Garrison, more than all the thrashings and scraps and botched brawls he'd ever gotten himself into. What made Taein the Unkillable Kid was the *truth*—that he literally *could not die.*

And Taein knew that for a fact, because he had tried to die more times than he could count.

. . .

TAEIN DRIFTED FROM REGOR'S TENT, THE BOUNTY FOR HIS OWN LIFE slapping against his chest all the way, and headed straight home to his tiny apartment building.

This humble hovel was set in the massive sprawl of the Keenwin District, his apartment one in thousands of near-identical slum houses stacked atop one another to staggering, precariously tilted heights. It was almost impossible to distinguish one house from another, with their ramshackle peaked roofs that always leaked and dark sagging doorways and claustrophobic rooms.

The kid's eyes grew wide and frightened as they cut through dark alleys and foggy side streets. Taein understood why. The Keenween was a place where even the most optimistic felt despair, every inch of it covered in squalor.

The district was populated by perhaps a hundred thousand people, all of them unidentifiable, unimportant Nomen to the realm—hunched men smoking rit and loitering on tavern stoops as if cemented to their rotting steps; women with ratty hair and silenced voices sulking down alleys on the prowl for something—*anything*—to throw in their pots; young people with drumweed joints hanging from their lips and hard slants to their lancing bodies; legions of obligatory children with dirt-smeared cheeks and blood-filled mouths, running in tightly knit gangs and bullying one another with the same ferocity as the adults did screw and shank and sabotage each other. Taein didn't believe a single one of them was literate. There were so many stabbings a day that the RAC long ago stopped keeping track.

Yes, the Keenwin District was an excellent place in which to get lost—disappear, even, in a sea of sameness and ruination. That was why, to Taein, Keenwin District was paradise. It was as close to safe as he'd ever really come in the last decade. But it certainly was no place for a child, no matter how many were unfortunate enough to live there.

Taein shouldered open the door to his apartment, set on the fifth story of a complex called *Fanshin Manor*. His eyes fell to his gloves as soon as he shut the door. They were so old now, held together by scuffed patches and fraying stitches. The fingertips had been worn away to nothing and patched too many times to count, but he didn't care. He couldn't breathe without them. The damned gloves were the one thing that kept him—and everyone around him—the slightest bit safe.

Until now. But Taein had always known that even without gloves this day was coming. There was only so long he could hide in plain sight before someone looked too close and saw him for who he really was.

But Geiin... he'd told *Regor* of all people. Sure, he'd been so strung out that the old man could've burned him alive and he wouldn't have even noticed. But he never thought, even with all the drugs, the truth could ever leave him like that. He'd always been such a good liar.

You idiot.

Taein stood in the doorway, the kid facing him in her too-big cloak with her too-pale eyes in her too-quiet face. He opted to ignore her, allowing himself a moment to let the tension of the day dissipate like black smog into the silence. The kid moved to a corner and hunkered down, pulling her knees up to her chest. She pulled out Regor's ledger after a moment and wrote, then held up the page for Taein to see.

Taein read from across the room. *It stinks here.*

He scoffed. "It stinks everywhere in Pearl Jin."

But she *did* have a point—his apartment once smelled of the drumweed habit he'd brought with him, before turning to the bitter scent of his short-lived affair with shank. But the infamous amber powder was far too stimulating for his nerves, and he hated the way it burned his nose and stained his gums. So shank was traded for an even shorter waltz with crystelin, the warm, lavish, and *extraordinarily* expensive opiate of high society, before that fell apart too and his long drift with rit came, forever staining the room with the soft, arid scent that accompanied it.

But he beat even rit eventually, though evidently not before making a *great mistake,* and went back to smoking through several packs of cigarettes a day until the pining for rit dulled enough to be consistently tolerated.

The kid was still scribbling. *It smelled nice in Regor's tent,* she wrote.

"Well, pray the Outlander shares Regor's taste for fine scents," Taein snipped.

More scribbling. Taein just shook his head before crossing the room and dropping his cloak at her feet.

"Here. If you get cold. And whatever you do, don't even *think* about leaving. This city will eat you alive and spit out your bones for the dogs."

She stared at him, her shock quickly turning into a glare, and snatched up his cloak.

He could feel her eyes searing him alive, even as he shut the door and locked it.

THERE WAS NO WAY TAEIN WAS SPENDING EVEN A MOMENT ALONE with the kid. He couldn't bear the weight of her eyes, much less the sheer shankin' responsibility of it all.

This commitment to avoiding the kid and her bog-child glare led Taein to the nearest tavern, where he spent the rest of the night cajoling as much cherry wine from the bartender as was possible to hold. At half-past two he was finally booted out and began the hazy navigation back home, meandering about until he finally ended up back at his front stoop.

He thought about going inside and that only made him immediately nauseous, so he waited for dawn leaned up against his door and picking at the stitching on his gloves.

The hours crept by one after another. Each of his wounds protested every movement; his head still spinning, his ribs bruised, the stitched gash throbbing.

His mind kept returning to the job ahead and each time it did the bounty disc only grew heavier.

Oh, that shanking *bounty on himself*. How could he ever get out of this job? There was no way he was taking a *kid* anywhere.

Taein stared at the wall opposite for a long time, the leather encasing his traitorous hands as comfortable as a blanket brought in soft and sun-warmed from the line.

The scents of mildew and pipe smoke were still heavy in his nose, the lingering taste of sour mulberry ale seared onto his tongue. Taein leaned his head against the door, and allowed darkness to sweep him away.

He jolted awake not long after to the too-familiar whisper of falling snow, sweat cooling on his heaving chest.

He clenched his fists tight, trying to fight back the usual sudden bombardment of memories. Each time he blinked he saw snow behind his eyes, heard the muffled sound of a body falling.

When the *incident* happened, the first thing Ruein did was drop his goblet. Taein could still hear it, no matter how hard he tried to forget—the way the crystal met the marble floor, the way the world broke apart. It was the sound of their entire house collapsing.

It was autumn solstice. A good, warm day. A holiday for all four realms to mingle and mix and work on furthering a peace that had been held for the past two decades.

Then Taein's brother turned the late-king of Faeriel to ash, and their whole world broke like *it* was what had been dropped, and not that damned goblet, as if Taein's brother had been holding their world itself in his careless hands and never knew it.

But the sound of shattering glass wasn't what stayed with Taein, and neither were the screams that followed. It was what came some months after, all those years ago, in the snow.

Taein closed his eyes against the blue bars of light shining through the broken shutter slats of the window opposite, wishing the sound of rain drumming on the tin roof above might drown out the snowfall caught in his mind.

His heart picked up again, so he riffled through his pockets until he found half a pack. Golden light flared at the touch of a match and he took a long drag. There was no use fighting for sleep any longer. His long-job pack lay waiting on the other side of the door, prepped and ready for a quick exit as always. All he had to do was go inside his apartment, wake up the kid, and leave.

He got up, bones creaking, and immediately hesitated, one gloved hand resting on the doorknob.

It wasn't too late to refuse. Regor *literally* couldn't kill him, not even if he ditched the kid with Vince and took a vacation far, far away instead. Sure, he'd accidentally let Regor in on the truth, but what did it really matter? He was nothing but a sick ritter back then.

But Taein saw the hungry glint in Regor's eyes again, saw all those beautiful marks piled gleaming before him. Felt that hunger mirrored in his own heart.

This job wasn't just about survival. It was about *release*. Money couldn't erase who he was, but it could do a great deal in keeping him comfortable. Even a fraction of the fortune this stupid job promised was more than enough to keep his fireplace hot and his roof dry and himself perfectly bereft of company for the rest of his spiteful little life. A lifetime of peace and quiet and *aloneness* was worth a couple hellish weeks of work.

Right?

Taein squared his shoulders, and turned the knob.

ROADS PAST & ROADS FUTURE

❦   7   ❦

Taein sloshed through a waterlogged pothole as he made his way toward Vince and Ka-el's apartment, the kid tailing him like a shadow. She hadn't made any effort to communicate with her little book since they left his apartment—just as well. She kept her wide eyes on the streets, absorbing the filth of the city like a sponge, and Taein left her to it. The less they interacted, the better.

He found Vince's place soon enough. Taein perched on the stoop to escape the growing precipitation as a suffocating humidity broiled the misty air, and knocked.

A moment passed before the door was almost jerked off its rust-eaten hinges by the brown-eyed, shaggy-haired, bushy-bearded mountain of ink and muscle himself. This creature was called Vincent, but Taein mostly just called him Vince.

He was some seven and a half feet of pure, corded brawn, covered neck-to-toes with intricate tattoos—likenesses of foxes, hawks, and a stag decorated his left arm, his right encased in roping chains and abstract spikes that harkened to mountains, along with a large fern just like the one Taein sported himself. He had roses inked on his neck and warnings on his hands, with one set of knuckles spelling *start* and the other *riots*.

Taein didn't know a single person in all the Pearl who had that many tattoos—only Right Fellows had access to decorative ink like that, but then here was Vince, sporting a whole art gallery on his massive frame as he went about his job of punching the fear of Regor's name into politicians and gutter rats alike. Taein had been asking why Vince had them and where they came from for years, to which Vince would always smile in his easy-going way and shrug and change the subject.

"Surely we're not leaving *this* early," Vince said, stooping down to peer at Taein.

"We surely are, old man," Taein chirped.

Vince frowned and rubbed a hand over his face, his many rings glinting in the faint light, then pointed at the kid. "Who's this little bugger?"

"Our cargo."

Vince pinched his brow. "That don't seem right."

"Ask the big man yourself, if you got doubts," Taein said, trying to step inside. Vince stretched an arm across the door frame and leaned in.

"You heard yet?"

"Heard wh—"

"Wait, what happened to your face?" Vince cut Taein off, reaching out a paw to probe Taein's battered cheek.

Taein swiped Vince's hand away. "Just remnants from a little scrap the other day, it's nothing."

"Who—"

"Some newbies, it's fine. They're dead, anyway. Can I come in? Regor's making you come with me and our new little ward on account of some 'funny business' on the outside, and I wanted to ask Ka-el if he's seen..." Taein trailed off, catching sight of what Vince's frame had been blocking as the giant stepped aside.

A body lay on the floor, covered in a black sheet.

Was that... Taein hid his falter and stepped inside, trying not to stare at the shrouded figure. The sweet, stale smell of basalt embalming solution hung heavy over the room. Ka-el was sitting on the edge of his bunk facing the body, his eyes clouded, face swollen and blotchy.

"You can say hello if you want," Vince said, lowering his voice. "But he's no good for conversation right now."

"Why... what happened?"

Vince shifted. "Ka-el turned back up way past his deadline about a week ago, dragging Venny with him."

Taein stilled. Ka-el was *Faeish*. The fact that he'd been kicked out of his country had done nothing to curb his silly honor-bound ways— the man was never late to anything.

"How'd she die?" Taein asked, a shiver of uncertainty trailing up his spine. The kid stood at his side, staring at the body. Taein spared her a glance, expecting her little freckled face to be all teary and afraid, and instead found her perfectly still, not a trace of emotion, good or bad, to be found.

"You ever seen a body?" Taein asked.

She gave no answer, seemingly frozen in place.

"Ka-el won't say nothing certain," Vince said. "He just keeps going on about glowing foliage and dogs made of shadow and forests covered n' flames that ain't burning. You didn't see nothing like that when you were out, did you?"

Bile rose in Taein's throat, but he shoved it down and just shook his head. Silence hovered between them for a long while and the dread in the pit of Taein's stomach began to spread.

"Well, interesting," Taein said at last. "She's gone Sleeper, then?"

"Yeah. Dogs didn't get her amulet away, at least."

Taein moved over to the dark-haired tracker. The man staring at the sleeping corpse didn't look anything like who Taein remembered Ka-el to be. His proud shoulders were stooped, his eyes unfocused, his body so much thinner. Ka-el didn't even seem to notice when Taein sat down next to him.

"Hey, man. Heard you got knocked around out there."

Ka-el turned his baleful gaze onto Taein, who immediately wished he hadn't. The grief in the tracker's eyes was a tangible thing, and it hit Taein right in the face.

"There were dogs," Ka-el said, his voice strangely matter-of-fact and devoid of the emotion so conspicuous in his eyes.

"Oh, I don't need to know—"

Ka-el pressed on. "The dogs are what got her, but they weren't dogs at all. I swear on Geiin..." he drew off, eyes darting around the room as if the creatures were there among them. "They were made of shadows, Taein, living shadows, I swear on Geiin, on Venny's own soul. They weren't real and yet they were *tearing* at her. She was screaming and trying to protect this *kid* and nothing I could do would help... and now no one believes me."

Ka-el's composure slipped word by word as he carried on, clutching his hands in his lap. Taein looked to Vince, begging for help.

Vince shrugged. "Don't look at me, boss. Like I say, I can't even move the body."

"She has to be in state for a week," Ka-el snapped, "or her spirit will belong to those *beasts* and—" he cut himself off the moment his wild-eyed gaze landed on the kid, who stood hovering close by the door.

"*You*," Ka-el said, sliding off the bunk and onto the floor. He stabbed a finger at the kid. "It was *your* fault. If you hadn't been with us—"

Vince stepped in, quick to haul Ka-el off the floor and back to his bunk. But he'd said enough—the kid's marbled features finally cracked, and Taein caught the hint of tears in her eyes. He looked away quickly. Regor had said that Ka-el and Venny were the ones to bring her, but not at this cost. Where did she come from, for such danger to be following?

Because sure as shit *dogs* weren't what had done this. It had to be another Chevalier's crew, fighting to take the kid. Or road bandits, or.... Anything else.

"...but she ain't a Shallow," Vince said as he tried to calm Ka-el down. "You got her taken care of, now she's sleeping. So why not at a church? Or we could call the RAC and have her taken down to the Citadel of Silence."

Ka-el looked back at Vince as if the notion they put Venny in the massive labyrinths buried below the city with the thousands of other

Sleepers was akin to him growing two heads. "Because this is where she lived, you *imbecile*. You know nothing of Vandel tradition. If she..."

Ka-el broke off. He was silent for a full minute before bursting into fresh tears, and that was when Taein decided it was very much time to go.

"Let's head out, Vince," Taein said, giving Ka-el an awkward pat on the shoulder with one gloved and very uncertain hand.

Vince nodded and turned about the little room, gathering spare shirts and various knick-knacks to stuff in his already-overfilled pack. Taein found himself looking back toward Ka-el, who continued to sob like a little kid.

How come I never cried like that? Taein found himself wondering. He never collapsed in on himself like that when Ruein... went.

Taein dropped his eyes to the grimy floorboards, blinking fast. Now was not the time for that nonsense. Not now, not ever.

"Ready," Vince said softly, a scuffed guitar in one hand and his overfilled pack in the other.

Taein followed him to the door, which opened to the dull roar of rain slapping off metal roofs and down onto cobblestone. He glanced back to make sure the kid was following. She hovered in the doorway for a moment longer, staring hard at Ka-el. The tracker took no notice, lost again to his grief. She turned slowly away and trailed after them, putting up the hood of her too-big raincloak as she went. But before the shadow of the cloak fell to hide her face, Taein caught her look.

She'd gone emotionless again, her face still as a statue, eyes glued to the ground. Taein almost began to wonder what was wrong with her, before reminding himself that he didn't care.

"You should've told Regor that he's keeping her body in there. It's doing nothing but making him sadder," Taein said, flipping his own hood up and following Vince into the deluge. He couldn't help but keep looking over his shoulder to make sure the kid was still with them.

"I know," Vince sniffed, slinging the guitar over one impossibly broad shoulder and the pack over the other. "I slept at a boarding house across town yesterday, but I ain't got the marks for another night. Regor hasn't given me a single assignment since the incident with that diplomat bastard. And he *still* ain't paying me for this, not till we get back."

"Well, don't squash the next target so much and maybe he'll forgive you," Taein said as he turned back and shoved the kid between them, tired of feeling her eyes burning holes in his back.

"It was an *accident*," Vince sighed. "And it was the door that squashed that man, I just bumped into it. How was I to know he was hiding there?"

"Nice sob story, I'm still not going to give you any of my marks."

"Well, color me shocked. How big a price are you getting, anyway?"

Taein looked up to Vince, unease still tight in his gut, and changed the subject. "Do you think he's telling the truth? Ka-el, I mean."

Vince rubbed the back of his neck. "Ah... dogs made of shadow." He shook his head. "Who's to say? I've seen odder things. I once saw a man with eight fingers on his left hand."

"How is that in *any way* odder than dogs made of shadow?"

"You'd have to see it, boss. Made my gut turn, just lookin' at the kid."

"Ridiculous," Taein said as he stepped out of the alley and onto the narrow, rain-darkened street that led to Regor's stable. "I—"

But before he could finish his sentence, the kid tugged on his arm. He looked down, hiding the way he flinched at her touch, and squinted to read as she stuck her book in his face.

The rain-dotted paper read, *There were dogs. Scary black evil dogs. The nice lady died helping me.*

"What's it say?" Vince asked.

"Nothing." Taein pushed her book away and just kept walking.

The kid's glare did the impossible thing, and darkened even further. Taein left her outside with Vince as soon as they reached the stable and went their separate ways—Vince to the draft-horse wing, Taein to where Regor kept his racehorses.

He soon found Lorrin, the apple of Regor's eye, in the largest stall in the stable.

"Wake up, nag," Taein whispered, sliding the door open. *Nobody* was allowed to take Lorrin on a job. He was Regor's most treasured racehorse, jet black and lanky, as ugly as Nown Jin itself and in just as perpetually foul a mood. But Lorrin was fast, and had an unbeaten track record to prove it. The way he ran was like *flying*—those long legs barely touching the ground, hard hooves striking thunder, mane waving like grass in the wind.

Sure, *'nobody'* was allowed to take Lorrin on a job. But Taein wasn't any old nobody being sent on any other mission, was he?

"I love that horse," Regor had said with all the puffing and pride of a new father the first time he showed Lorrin off to Taein. *"I love him more than all my stuff I got. And I do love my stuff."*

Here's hoping you love the marks I'll be bringing back more, Taein thought, and with that he took Lorrin, found the kid a little white pony, and rejoined his sorry excuse of a crew.

Taein found Vince and the kid standing next to Vince's impossibly huge chestnut draft, who the giant affectionately called Maple. The steed was a dopey, quiet creature, his great floppy blonde hair falling in front of dark, gentle eyes, but he was strong enough to tote even Vince across the county, and that's all that really mattered. Vince was eyeing the kid in silence, looking thoroughly confused, as she petted Maple's shaggy leg (which was the only part of Maple she could reach.)

It didn't take Vince a second after laying eyes on Lorrin to start up his protest.

"Oh, hell no! There's no way Regor said you could take him!" Vince bellowed. The kid turned to see Lorrin and the white pony and *almost* grinned.

Almost. But it was the first expression of joy Taein had seen on her little freckled face since Regor pulled out his knife collection. At least this smile wasn't prompted by the possibility of violence.

"Well he didn't say I *couldn't*," Taein said, unable to hide a grin of his own.

Vince looked from Lorrin, to Taein, and back again to Lorrin. "Taein, he's going to lop off your head. And then *I won't get paid.*"

Taein waved a hand. "He'll never even notice Lorrin's gone."

"Never notice! He's got a race tomorrow, for Geiin's sake! Put him back!"

"This one here's for you," Taein said, ignoring Vince as he handed the pony's lead rope over to the kid. "Ever been on a horse before?"

She stroked the pony's gray mane and shook her head.

Great. Taein bit back a curse and heaved her up onto the pony's saddle before she could protest.

"Look, just hold onto the saddle horn and grip with your legs. All you need to worry about is not falling off. She'll follow along behind."

He turned to leave, but the kid snagged his sleeve again. He held back another curse as she took out her book again and scribbled.

What's her name?

"Dunno, anything you want it to be," Taein said. He paused, flexing his gloved fingers. "What's *your* name?"

All she did in response was snap her book close and busy herself with putting it back into her little pack.

Taein took the hint and swung himself up on Lorrin. If the kid didn't want to tell him her name, fine. All that mattered was getting her to the Outlander alive.

"Off we go," Taein said, starting down the street.

Vince sputtered and swore some more before clambering onto Maple and following. The kid's little pony trotted right after them, and Taein couldn't help but smile at the brief giddiness that flashed on her face.

VINCE WAS STILL GRUMBLING ABOUT LORRIN BY THE TIME THEY made it to the eastern edge of the city, where a smuggler called Miin ran a sector dedicated to the horse trade just before the East Gate.

That once-familiar scent of sweet hay and sour manure soon arrived, hanging around Miin's square as heavy as the morning smog. There were horses absolutely *everywhere*, standing jammed together in paddocks made up of rusted roofing panels pieced-together with strands of corroded barbed wire and frayed rope.

The kid, her pony sticking close and well-behaved to Lorrin, was looking around with those huge, overwhelmed eyes again. Her shock made sense—Miin's square was more than a zoo of horses. It was the first sector every trader had to pass through when entering the Pearl, and as such was always chocked *full* of people.

Foreigners from all over made up the crowds—men from the

Vandel Providence clustered together in their traditional red trading *kesjlas,* laughing and shouting with no real regard for the chaos all around, while native Jinians, less obvious in their varied appearances, both bought and sold. A few Faeish travelers stood in a tight circle, looking around with the same sort of bewildered expression as the kid.

Taein had been just as mystified as the kid when he first stepped into the city years ago. Miin's square was the first bit of civilization he'd entered after that long, lonesome year spent wandering the wind-swept wilds of Efriel Shu. By some strange play of fate, he was picked up by a less-than-scrupulous Ersiin farmer on the westward border, heading to the Sister Cities with a wagon full of hay.

"Hullo," He had said in his thin, flowing accent, peering down at Taein from beneath the narrow brim of a grass-weave hat. "You look like a lad in need of a job. I shall give you two half-marks if you help me haul my load to Pearl Jin."

Taein looked at the farmer, the sweet summer hay piled in his cart, and the long-eared donkey hitched to it before the gnawing in his stomach reminded him that two half-marks could buy something edible other than the wild rabbit and hedge greens he'd been existing on for far too long. He knew that two and a half marks were a piss-poor wage, but he also knew that he was half-Siou—and a very hungry half-Siou at that.

So stupid little fourteen-year-old Taein found himself in a hay cart riding from Ersii right to Pearl Jin, the crown jewel of the Six Sister Cities, where he managed the dust-choked, sweat-sticky work of unloading hay into one of the rangier shack-stables in Miin's Square.

Afterward, two corroded half-marks dropped into the dirt at his feet, along with a new amulet. Taein looked from the amulet, to the farmer, and back to the amulet.

The farmer shrugged. "Ain't nobody deserving to go without."

Taein just stared. The rosewood was so terribly white against the dirt. It'd been over a year since he last touched an amulet. How had the farmer even noticed he didn't have one?

"One thing," The farmer said as he clambered back onto his cart.

He nodded to Taein's gloved hands. "You'll need to be losing those if you'd like to stay alive, boy."

Taein looked down to his grimy gloves, ground down to nothing by the wear of a year spent living in the wilderness like an animal. The tips of his first two fingers on one hand had completely worn away. Something twisted hard in his gut as he looked at his gnarled fingertips, at the wasting leather. He was still staring at them when the farmer clicked to his donkey and the cart rolled squelching down the muddy street. And just like that, Taein was left alone in the largest city in all of Ieris.

Time passed. Too much time. He took his half-marks and left the amulet where it lay in the dirt.

Ain't nobody deserving to go without, the farmer had said.

But then again, he didn't know Taein, not really. He didn't know what Taein was, and he sure as hell didn't know what he'd done.

Ain't nobody deserving to go without.

Nobody, Taein amended as he set off down an alley, those grimy half-marks clutched in his fist, *except me.*

The first thing he did was try to buy a new pair of gloves, tossing the farmer's warning right over his shoulder without another thought. But the city was quick to swallow him like an eternally hungry snake from some rain-choked jungle in the Outerlands, a continuously-combusting eruption of people and animals and things; of crumbling stone buildings stitched together by rope and mortar but also grand wooden villas shaded by potted trees and rich purple awnings; of the mingled scents of perfume and manure and sweat and sizzling food and the tang of distant White Salt Sea and the faint scent of the copper marks that were *everywhere* all the time, changing hands like water rushing down a river.

Suffice to say, Taein never found a vendor.

Instead, he found himself holed up beneath a bridge as the gray sky let down a steady drizzle, bereft of both half-marks and with two black eyes to replace them, the sharp ridges of his jutting spine pressing painfully through his thin shirt against slime-slick stone.

He stayed there for a whole day, his heart hammering, flinching at every strange noise (there were a lot of them) and picking at his peeling gloves as the crowds moved all around him like great waves on a ceaseless tide. He remembered being scared out of his mind that someone would notice him. But nobody ever did.

As evening came to soften the drizzle and allow a hint of warmth from the setting sun, Taein came to a blissful realization more precious than all the marks in all of Ieris.

There, beneath that dilapidated bridge in that great foreign sea of a city, amid the crowds and fog and rain and buildings, he was *lost*. He was truly, completely, irrevocably lost, more so than he'd ever been before, hidden by a veil of hundreds of thousands of human souls.

If anyone was still hunting, they would never find him here.

Taein felt a sudden wash of relief that hadn't come in what seemed like whole ages. Beneath that bridge top as the rain danced down from above, he took his first real breath in ages.

Soon enough, they passed through the city gaits and were well into the countryside surrounding the Pearl. Taein assessed the growing storm clouds above as the first inklings of thunder rumbled in the distance. The rain was starting to truly pick up.

"We're behind already, Vince."

"Sticking with the status quo, I see," Vince said. He glanced back at the kid before kicking his draft closer. "You know, something just don't feel right about this job. What're we doing with a damn *kid*, of all things?"

Taein squinted at the sky as a jagged bolt of lightning cut through the purple clouds, then flashed his lair's smile at Vince as thunder rippled over the city.

"Trust me, Vince. This is about to be the adventure of your life."

8

SHANKING TAROT'S BOYS

The day was melting into a hazy evening, and Taein was *bored*. Vince was off in his own little world and the kid was stone-faced as usual, so Taein busied himself by tracing the eagle soaring lazy loops overhead for a while. But the eagle flew off and Taein was left unamused as ever in the grassy expanse he'd dubbed The Field That Went On Forever. They'd been cutting south through the open, rolling Hillsteps for a day now, just to avoid the Godswood and the overly-armed sap harvesting crews that came with the forest.

Here, beneath the westward shade of the mountain range that separated the Blackblades from the rest of Nown Jin, the lush expanse of the Hillsteps seemed to go on forever, an infinite land of high rolling hills, dotted with the occasional patch of woods or under-hill house.

Springs in Nown Jin were so different from the springs Taein had grown up within Efriel Shu. In Efriel Shu, spring was a slow awakening —snow easing off wind-carved hillsides, sleepy grass unfurling, washes of wildflowers painting the endless plains, rain falling in hazy sheets for days on end.

Nown Jin held none of the same quiet rhythms. Here, spring burst through at the earliest opportunity, beating off the snow in bouts of torrential rain to spread an explosive green across the countryside. Ivy-ridden trees seemed to erupt with buds in mere hours while flowers struggled up and pushed out blooms in every color imaginable. The weather was always changing, turning from thunder to hail to cold gleaming sunshine in the span of a half-hour. It was beautiful in its own way. But it wasn't home.

Taein sighed as his thoughts strayed to the destination ahead. Talk of Efriel Shu drifted through Pearl Jin now and then. Such gossip was perpetuated by traders trying to boost the value of trinkets they'd pilfered from near the fallen realm's border and amplified by overly-honored veterans of the war Faeriel had spearheaded all those years ago. Efriel Shu itself was said to be cursed these days—people spoke of a land plagued by wraiths and ghouls, buzzing about hordes of Shallows walking unchecked and kelpies swimming in the rivers and krakens terrorizing the northern shore. Taein told himself it shouldn't matter, that it didn't. All they had to do was get near the border, not infiltrate the shankin' realm.

Still, he couldn't help but wonder.

At last, The Field That Went On Forever gained some elevation. Taein drew Lorrin to a stop as they crested a particularly tall hill and looked down on Farthing, a little village of ten or so shacks and maybe seventy residents. People, most of them Countrymen, were still milling about on paths that all converged upon a single tavern.

A coil of unease snaked around Taein's core. Sure, these blokes were so lulled by their field-slaving, beer-slobbering lifestyles that no one blinked twice when a half-Siou such as himself rode into town. But Farthing had no sea of bodies to hide in like Pearl Jin, no chaos, no density. The village felt too exposed.

But Vince would insist, of course, and there would be an argument that Taein would lose, and despite a warm mug and too-hammered-to-care company, he would spend another night awake in a cold sweat, just waiting for someone to beat down his door and stab him where he lay in the sheets. And he would live through it, no matter how well and thoroughly they shanked him, and that would cause a whole *new* barrel of issues.

"Well, what are we waiting for?" Vince asked, finally breaking his long silence.

Taein glanced back. "I was just thinking we should keep a low profile. Considering the stakes of this particular job and all."

Vince scoffed. "I always keep a low profile."

"Vince, you're over seven feet tall. You couldn't keep a low profile if you tried."

Vince raised a brow and leaned forward to rest an arm on his saddle horn. "Oh, I see where this is heading. You won't win, kid. Best to just save your breath and get a move on."

"But I think it would behoove us to—"

"*Behoove*, that's a mighty big word. Do you even know what that means?"

Taein glared. "Yes, and it would *behoove* you to know I have more of an education than anyone in the entirety of Pearl Jin, college districts and all. Think on that the next time you try to get the upper hand on me in an argument, tough guy."

"Sure you do, rit-head. Spell *condescending*," Vince said, nudging his draft down the hill. The kid was quick to prod her white pony after him.

Taein let out a frustrated growl. "Vince, I'm serious this time! This is *my* job—"

"—And this is *my* favorite tavern in the world," Vince interrupted. "Ain't nobody going to keep me from a mug of Teffold Valley beer right at the break of spring, kid. I've been thinking about it ever since we left the city and I'm pretty sure that havin' to deal with you for the next few weeks makes me *more* than entitled to my choice of lodging, considering how your signature peachy attitude is known only to sour the further along we get..."

The giant drew off as a quartet of riders cantered into the other side of Farthing. The villagers wasted no time in scattering, darting out of sight like field mice under the shadow of great wings.

Taein squinted, trying to sort out what all the fuss was until it dawned on him that the riders weren't wearing sleeves—the entirety of their arms were all blacked out with ink. Those were the *shanking Tarot's Boys*.

In theory, Tarot Murphin himself was just another of the many Chevaliers in Pearl Jin. He was a middling-boss with a mid-sized crew who worked 12th through 31st street, the well sought-after streets that connected the good side of the Pearl to the bad. What made him scary was that Tarot Murphin was the only Chevalier to start his criminal career scrapping for old man Regor Snevets, *betray* him, and survive the consequences.

Or, well, most of him did. Tarot lost both of his arms to Regor's punishments, which was why he made every member of his gang black theirs out in ink.

It was also probably why he *hated* Regor, and by extension Regor's crew, with such a flaming hot passion, and did everything in his power to shank up, steal, and otherwise sabotage their jobs.

Including this one, so it seemed.

"We really aren't stopping for a brew this time, Vince," Taein gritted as he booted Lorrin around.

"Yeah, no shit," Vince said, quick to follow.

They had no more but turned the horses and started cantering back up the hill when a holler sounded out, and Taein looked back to catch sight of the gang hauling ass after them.

And there was the kid, doing absolutely nothing as her little pony plodded lazily up the hill after them. Taein swore and wheeled Lorrin around again, forcing the racehorse back in time to snatch the pony's lead and haul her with him.

But they barely had time to crest the hilltop and start off toward a distant cropping of woods when two riders galloped in front of them, the other two coming up swiftly from behind.

"Well, shit!" Vince said, reining in his flustered draft.

"Hello, boys," drawled out one of the scrappers, flashing a smile missing a few teeth. Taein recognized that crooked grin as Sig, one of Tarot's smarmy lieutenants. "Almost fancied that you rats got too far out the city for us fellers to find."

"Didn't *fancy* rushing out," Taein said as he fished for his flintlock. He flashed the weapon in the dying light of day, then leaned on his saddle horn. "What can I do for you, Sig?"

"Just hand over the kid, that's all," Sig replied, glancing at Taein's pistol from atop his piebald gelding. "Didn't think the Outlander offered you's boss a closed deal, did ya? That just ain't his style, not at all. Efficiency, however, is. And as you know—"

"*Efficiency is the name of the Tarot gang,*" Taein mocked as he slipped his other hand into his coat and dug for a bag of greyscale. "Shank off back to the Pearl and get your own deal."

Sig leaned uneasily on his own saddle horn and laughed. "Well, I know better than to go messin' with the Unkillable Kid, now don't I?"

"You sure as hell should—"

But before Taein could finish his sentence, one of the riders lurking behind spurred their horse forward and leaned down to snatch the kid from where she sat sullenly on her pony.

Time for action. While shooting Sig straight in the face was Taein's first instinct, every shot taken had to be individually loaded and there were four of them, each one mounted and ready to take off with their all-important cargo.

So Taein did what felt incredibly smart in the moment. He shot the rider reaching for the kid, and in the next breath pulled out that bag of greyscale dust and chucked it hard at Sig.

Here's what should've happened, considering just what greyscale was: the powder, made from the pricey, toxic scales of gorrin-fish and imported from the Vandel Province, was quite useful in implementing a glittery, blinding fuss.

Such a glittery mess is exactly what Taein had in mind as he went chucking the bag at Sig. The greyscale was supposed to hit Sig square in the chest, burst on impact, and send out clouds of irritants for him and his friend to choke on. Then Vince could take care of the rider on his right, and they would be free to gallop off before the toxins drifted their way.

And Taein *did* manage to shoot the scrapper on his left and launch the bag of greyscale—only to watch Vince smack it out of the air as he swung his guitar at the rider on his right. The giant knocked the bag out of its precious trajectory toward Sig and sent it right into the ground between them and the enemy.

And then it didn't even go off. Which was shankin' *ridiculous,* because Taein had mixed that bag himself.

A long, ludicrously tense moment crawled by. The scrapper Taein shot fell off his horse, foot still caught in his stirrup as his horse backpedaled away. The kid, freshly misted with blood, whirled around to gape at Taein with her raging eyes. The scrapper Vince hit with his guitar was on the ground, rubbing his bruised forehead and peering at the bag laying so innocently on the grass between them all.

Sig was the first to start laughing. Then his crony next to him, and then the one with his ass in the grass.

They were all laughing, and Taein had just started to panic, and then the greyscales finally detonated.

A *pop*. Blue-grey glitter everywhere. It got very hard to breathe in the span of a half-second.

It should've been their cue to enact a swift getaway. But instead, the bag went off with far too mighty of a bang and the whole of their group, Taein, Vince, and the kid included, were instantly enveloped in that shimmering cloud of toxins.

Too much gunpowder, Taein thought, and then Lorrin reared up and dumped him.

He hit the dirt hard—nope, that was a rock. He was suddenly coughing so violently he couldn't make sense of his own thoughts.

Then he wasn't thinking at all, and all around lay the dark.

9

THE TROUBLE WITH HAVING
A HEART

Taein woke up still coughing. He opened bleary eyes to a dim world and rolled onto his side. His flintlock lay by his hand, those silver fern inlays smudged with dirt.

Sig. The kid. The *money*.

He grabbed his flintlock and forced himself onto his feet, head spinning. Vince was propped up on his elbows a few feet away, hacking his lungs out and looking thoroughly pissed.

Taein swiveled, trying to stifle his coughs as his eyes and throat burned. This was no longer a darkening twilight they were standing in. It was getting lighter. It was *morning*.

The horses were gone. Sig and his boys were gone. *But the kid was gone, too.*

"Oh... shank me," Taein breathed, fisting his hands in his hair. He whirled around. "Vince. Vince for the love of Geiin get up. They took the kid!"

That got the giant up on his feet and straight into a tirade. Taein tuned Vince out and set his mind to figuring out where the kid could've possibly gone. There was a mess of hoof prints all around them, the horses having panicked when the greyscale got to them as well, but when the tracks settled they all led in one direction—Vince's draft's ginormous hooves included.

The idiots hadn't just taken the kid—they'd also taken the horses.

Taein set off following the tracks, Vince close behind and still swearing up a storm. They weren't halfway down the rain-slick slope when something caught his eye—in the distance, spiraling high above twin hilltops, was a plume of smoke. Taein stopped and squinted.

"What's with all this stopping?" Vince asked, glaring. "C'mon, boss, she could be dead, or dying, or—"

"Does that look like chimney smoke to you?" Taein asked, pointing.

Vince squinted. "Not by my eyes."

"That's woodsmoke right there."

"So what?"

"So nobody's burning slash this time of year."

"You think it might..."

Taein set his jaw. "Where there's trouble, there's Tarot's boys."

Tracing the plumes of smoke led them deep into a grove of woods. They skirted the base of one of the twin hills standing watch over a little valley, following the hoof prints.

Vince looked around. "I have a bad feeling about this."

Me too. Taein kept the notion to himself and instead threw another jab at the giant.

"You *are* a bad feeling, Vince."

Minutes passed as they ran deeper into the valley and the smell of smoke became more pungent. Almost sweeter, like the sickly tang of scorched meat. The trees cast odd shadows and Taein tried to ignore both them and the pit in his stomach.

They came upon the valley floor at last. It didn't take long to spot the source of the smoke.

No village. No smoke house or slash piles. Just a sight so sad it made Taein's heart frost over with that too-familiar numbness.

Before them lay the remains of a small farm, what Taein guessed was once two or three buildings. The area was still smoldering, thick dark smoke puffing up from the blackened remains of houses as if the earth was an old man smoking pipe, and the little shacks had been the match he used to light up. Several horses milled around the scene, tossing their heads and snorting at the fire... including one tall, pissy black stallion harassing a giant chestnut. The only one missing was the little white pony.

Taein stared, fingers itching for a cigarette. There was no way Sig would've left all the horses behind like this. Not without something terrible happening.

"We should go," he said. "This has to be a trap."

"What if she's still alive 'round here?" Vince said. Taein looked over with a glare and found the giant fixated on the wreckage, his brow knit tight.

"Nobody's alive in that."

"I just... we should make sure," Vince said, and with that he slowly closed in on the ruins.

"Vince..." Taein tried to plead, but the giant didn't even look back.

He stayed still for a long moment before desperation got the better of him and he hurried after Vince.

Just ditch him. Taein shook the thought away and looked around.

"Anyone here?" he shouted.

Why was his voice pinched? If anyone was still alive, surely they would've run for help already. Taein bit back a barrage of curses and redoubled his efforts.

Ash drifted through the air, sticking in his hair and tickling his lungs with every breath. Last time he saw a settlement razed like this, two of his five brothers had been in it.

"Hello? Anyone?" he said again. "*Hello?*"

No response. A burning beam collapsed into cooling rubble, shooting clouds of ash and sparks into the air. Taein stumbled upon one of Sig's riders, left aloft from a pool of his own blood by a large, sharp tree branch that had seemingly shot straight up from the ground to spear his heart.

It was an odd sight, to say the least.

He hurried faster, darting to each house, glancing around. Ash, charred wood, burned meat smell. More of Sig's companions, each one skewered by a tree or strangled by roping vines. All of them very dead.

He's here, came that snaking voice from deep inside. *Someone* had to kill them all.

No. It wasn't possible. If *he* were here, Taein knew he'd already be dead.

His brain was not working. All he could think was *oh Geiin oh Geiin oh Geiin* on an endless loop. He stopped short at the third mangled corpse, drumming his fingers as fast as he could on his leg, trying to figure out a coherent thought.

Sweet Geiin, he was such an idiot. Why did he ever step foot in this valley? Accept this job in the first place? Try to do anything other than to bury himself in the deepest, darkest hole he could dig?

You're good at digging holes for yourself, came that familiar voice, *and tumbling headfirst into them. One of these days you're going to dig yourself another hole and realize you've finally dug your own grave.*

Taein scoffed. *If only.* He took three steps well on the way to his desired and instinctual pace (run), and then someone coughed, and he whirled around so fast he fell on his face.

He staggered back up, blood pumping so hard in his ears he could scarcely make out the sound of the second cough.

Bump-bump-bump-you're-an-idiot-bump-bump-bump went his heart.

Cough, went someone else, and Taein didn't think he'd ever been more terrified in his twenty-three years of existence.

"Who's there?" he said at length.

No response, no more coughs. Taein set his jaw, then put a hand on the flintlock tucked into the waist of his trousers. He took a deep breath, steeled himself, and started to walk away. And that was when he spotted it.

There, in the ruins of the second building, the one with the beam jutting out. The slightest sound. A hint of breathing.

There—another cough. Taein padded over the thick blanket of ash surrounding the wreckage, ignoring Vince's distant hollers. He finally found Sig, the smarmy lieutenant staring with dead eyes at the morning sky, his head all bashed in.

He sure as hell wasn't the one coughing. Taein hurried forward until—there. Just beneath the beam. A glimmer of blue.

He crouched down, heart plummeting. And there she was.

Taein squinted, trying to see if the kid was hurt badly, when what was protecting her from being crushed by the house debris caught his attention.

The beam was held aloft by the thickest blackberry stalk he'd ever seen. It was thicker than Vince's own forearm, even thicker than the giant's entire body. And the kid... Taein could barely see her from beneath the beam and blackberry stalk. A thick tangle of branches, weedy grass, and newborn saplings continuously jutted up from the charred earth, from beneath that terrible layer of still-hot ash, *growing* in the face of all this death.

Taein watched, unable to trust his own eyes, feet growing hot in his boots, as the infant shoots withered away from the simmering heat only to be replaced seconds later by new shoots flushed with a pulsing, unnatural light.

The kid. She was being... protected by these plants. From the beam and the heat and the ash. Nestled in a safe green bundle of her own creation.

Taein's memory flooded with the story he hated more than anything in the entire world.

Geiin ascended and in his wake left four brothers, each one remade...

He rubbed his smarting eyes, and the plants were still there. That little hint of blue was *still there.*

A Father to rule the wills of dumb creatures, he thought, the scorn he usually felt at the boyhood verses now distant, *a Father to keep the world living and green...*

A Father to be mankind's healer...

And one to balance and cleave.

Taein sank down. Before him was not just their kid, but a small, wounded, *Anathema* kid.

Anathema. Four strains of blood, cast in ruination. The blood in his own veins, cursed forever.

And hers, apparently.

So this was why the Outlander wanted her. This *surely* had to be the reason. This was why his life was forfeit if he failed.

It was all Taein could do to stare as a terrible thought entered his mind. *How good it would be for her, if she just... stopped coughing.*

He gritted his teeth. That was a rit-headed, rotten little thing to think. But... to live a life like his was not a happy one. It was a life of survival and spite with precious little room for anything else.

Taein glanced back at Lorrin. The stallion was several paces off, calmly eating grass and fixing to step on and snap his reins, while Vince's draft ran around spooking with the rest of the horses.

Taein scanned for Vince and spied him on the other side of the wreckage, examining something in the dirt. He raised an arm to wave the giant over before thinking better of it. Regor said that Vince didn't believe he was a Prince of Glass, and therefore didn't think he was Anathema. It was a bad idea to bank on the giant defying the status quo and allowing this *distinctly*-cursed kid to live. Maybe he could get Vince to Farthing, leave the giant to his pints, and then come back for her.

But what then?

Taein glanced back. She *was* unconscious, after all. Clutching that emerald-crusted Venrian blade Regor had given her with white knuckles even in her sleep.

She'll be fine on her own.

There it was, the second terrible thought. He wanted to smack himself.

"Have a heart, Taein," he told himself.

But most of the time, it felt like he'd left his heart somewhere back in those snow-choked mountains. Back where he left someone he loved for the very last time, and just kept running. And never really stopped.

Just go.

Taein barely managed to turn around before smacking into Vince's chest.

"Sorry, boss," Vince said, reaching out to steady him.

Taein shoved him away. "Geiin's thumbs, Vince! You can't startle me like that!"

"Sorry, sorry. Did you find something?"

"No—*don't*—"

But before Taein could do a thing about it, Vince crouched down and peered into the growing bramble.

Silence. Taein took three steps back, adrenaline spiking hot in his veins, and waited for Vince to make a move. If Vince went to kill the kid, what would he do? There was no chance he could beat Vince in an outright fight, and he couldn't just *shoot* him. Well, he *could*, but he would probably feel bad about it, and the last thing he needed was more guilt to carry around.

Tense seconds went by that seemed like whole days, and Vince just stared. Taein shifted. If Vince attacked, did he even care enough to *try* stopping him? If he did, Vince would know the truth. There was no coming back from this now, Vince had already heard him shankin' *say* he who he was once before. There was no Regor here to tell the giant to believe differently. And then Vince would try to kill *him*. And then—

"Well... you found her," Vince said at last.

"Looks like it."

Vince dragged both hands though his shaggy hair, blinking hard. "Them little plants are growing, Taein. Why... how are they growing?"

Taein kept quiet.

"She's... oh. Oh, sweet Geiin," Vince said slowly. He rose and looked at Taein, brow bunched. "She ain't looking too good, boss."

Taein stared at Vince, every muscle tensed. *What the hell are you thinking?*

"We probably should get her out, huh?" Vince said.

Taein blinked. "You want to help her?"

Vince shrugged. "Look... she's cargo, ain't she? And she's just a little... erm, *magic* girl. Don't mean we can leave her."

Taein looked at Vince, and Vince looked at Taein until he couldn't stand it anymore. "*Magic* is just another word for Anathema."

"I know... little growing things and such."

Taein looked at Vince, then to the girl inside the bramble, then back to Vince.

And then he snapped.

"Look, Vince," he said, "you better tell me what you're going to do right now or I'm gonna drop dead. And you don't want that on your conscience, right? *Right?*"

Vince folded his huge arms and seized Taein's gaze. "Everybody talks about you in the city, Taein, but no one makes a move to find out for certain if it's all true. You know why?"

"No," Taein whispered. Vince had never seemed taller than he did right now.

"They're afraid of you, *Mr. Too-Big-For-His-Britches-Unkillable-Kid.*"

"They should be," Taein managed even as his throat got tight. How much did Vince weigh, some three hundred pounds? A cold sweat broke out on Taein's forehead.

"Well, I ain't."

"Everyone else is." Taein's eyes were drawn to the multitude of thick rings Vince wore on every finger. He thought about how bad his cheekbone still hurt from being punched by that sod wearing just *one* ring and got a little lightheaded.

"But I ain't 'everyone else.' I'm your friend. What reason do I got to be afraid?"

Because I shouldn't exist.

Vince seemed to wait a while for Taein to say something, but there wasn't a thought in Taein's brain besides *run, you dumb podger,* so the giant continued.

"Look, boss. You can kill a man with a rock, or a tree branch, or a pencil. You can kill a man by breathin' on him, for shank's sake. If you wanted to kill me, Anathema or not, I'm right sure you would've by now. But you ain't done that."

Taein forced himself to nod. "I do appreciate your discretion. How are you feeling about the kid, then?"

Vince glanced at the bramble and rubbed the back of his neck. "Reckon she could use some doctoring. You get her out, and I'll go to Farthing for some medicine."

"We have a deadline."

"Ain't more important than gettin' her fixed up."

"Regor would beg to differ."

"Regor ain't here."

Time crawled by as rain began to pitter-patter down again. Taein drew a deep breath.

We should leave her.

It would be the smart thing to do. The consistent thing.

Are you really that shanked-up a man?

The answer was a resounding *yes*, and it'd been that way for a long time. Taein Glass was not the kind of scrapper who coddled lost kids or fed stray dogs or helped grandmothers cross the street. He was a thoughtless smart-ass, an unrepentant thief, and a grand dodger of consequences, sustained solely by spite and the strange burning desire to *stay alive,* no matter what it cost or who it hurt, because if nothing in Ieris could kill him, he was going to make it *everybody else's problem.*

Taein Glass was an asshole. He knew he was.

But somehow, standing there staring at that stupid scrap of blue that was their cargo—the *kid*—somehow still breathing, he couldn't walk away.

Not again.

"Should've gone the East Route," he muttered as he kneeled down at the bramble.

❧ 10 ❧

THE KID

{THIRTEEN DAYS BEFORE}

The air smelled of storms. A wild static scent coursed through the thick silver sky, driving June deep into the forest.

She sat alone with her knees pressed to her chest, perched atop a flat boulder and surrounded by young trees through which she could easily spy on Gram's dingy old house. The cottage sat off-center in a large, sloping meadow ringed by a wall of brooding dark firs and bushy green maples, with whom June was now holding silent vigil.

Mama had told her to wait in their own cottage, which stood in marginally better repair adjacent to Gram's, but June couldn't watch Gram's door from her room. She couldn't see just what Mama was doing that she'd been so expressly forbidden to watch.

For something *finally* happened with Gram, who'd been rasping, wheezing sick for as long as June could possibly remember, and June was desperate to know just what.

She leaned forward on the rock and squinted at the house as little raindrops plinked down through the tree-top covering and the sky kept on grumbling.

Minutes went by. The air grew wilder and the gray sky rattled with white lights. June stayed still as the air played with the ends of her hair and rose bumps on her skin, and waited.

At last, the door swung slowly open and Mama stepped out onto the worn stoop.

Mama was a steady figure, seemingly carven from the very trees they lived among. Mama was tall where June was small, her hair a river of midnight waves where June's was the color of acorns. Mama was proud and kept her shoulders back and her chin level at all times, moving with the quick silent gait of someone who never seems all the way at ease. She was always watching—but for *what*, June was never quite sure. Nothing seemed to ever happen in their valley if she didn't count the time they watched a wildcat pass through.

"June?" Mama hollered against the wind, shading her eyes with a hand as the sky lit again with a pale, fiery crackle.

June wanted to reply for a moment as the sky let out a deep, rolling grumble—she reached for words and came upon the wall in her throat that had been in place since she was four years old.

June bit her lip as she slipped off the rock and hurried toward Mama, weaving around trees and watching the forest floor to make sure she didn't step on anything pokey. It'd been a while since she even thought about wanting to speak, or had words rise only to die like that. Speech had left her long ago, but sometimes she still couldn't help but wish she'd never had it in the first place. She hated the reflex of words. Their natural rise and their unnatural end, as they inevitably hit the rock wall of scar tissue that had replaced her vocal cords.

Mama was looking in the wrong direction when June reached the cottages and poked her side. Mama jumped and whipped around, her braid flying over her shoulder, eyes wide until she spotted June.

Her face clouded over in an instant. "June, you *know* you're not supposed to go into the woods when it storms like this."

June grinned. *Lightning never hits the little maples,* she signed, hands fluttering like leaves in the wind.

Gram taught June signs when she was little, since Gram used to teach school back in a city called Pearl Jin and remembered pieces of how the deaf there would communicate. Mama and Gram learned to read it, and June learned how to sign as fast as they could talk.

Mama shook her head. "It's not safe, little."

June squinted her eyes at Mama. Did she always have to be so serious?

I don't want to go to my room, she signed.

"When do you ever?" Mama paused. "Would you like to help me, then?"

June nodded furiously. *Yes. What's wrong with Gram? Why won't you let me come in?*

Mama sighed. She crouched down to June's level and looked at her very seriously.

"Gram was very old, June, and very sick. And you know how much she missed Grandpapa."

June furrowed her brow. Grandpapa had been gone so long June couldn't even remember him. And Gram was always sick, and always old. It's just how things were.

Mama sighed again. "Oh, Geiin help me," she murmured. "Alright, June, just come in, and then I can explain better."

June hurried in ahead of Mama, darting along the narrow hall as she'd done countless times before, usually to find Gram in her sun-warmed kitchen with oven-fresh pastries.

But Gram's cramped, cluttered kitchen was dark when June passed by, and Gram's room ahead even darker. The bedroom was lit only by a small, lonesome candle that lent the room a scant orange glow. The light was not even remotely strong enough to overcome the shadows cast by the closed, moth-nibbled curtains Gram and Mama had spent months embroidering.

There, on her lumpy old bed, lay who June *assumed* was Gram, bereft of her favorite blanket and instead wrapped head-to-toe in starch-white cloth. Only her wrinkled face was exposed, her eyes half-open and sleepy, her forehead sprinkled with red powder. Her amulet laid above the wrappings, the white wood turned amber by candlelight.

June stood in the doorway, trying to understand. She heard the sound of Mama approaching and jammed a thumb toward Gram.

Why's she all wrapped up? Why—

Mama bent down and took June's hands in her own to stop her signing.

"Slow down, little. Let me explain."

June waited.

Mama brushed a stray hair back from her face and led June closer. Something strange and cold seemed to cling to the corners of the room, bending the shadows closer, and that flickering orange light grew smaller as the sky continued to rumble outside. The walls had never seemed more eggshell-fragile, the room never more unfriendly. A strange, icy scent hung stale over the bed.

June and Mama stood hand-in-hand at the foot of Gram's bed, and for a long, long time, only the sky above was bold enough to break that heavy, sacred silence.

"She's gone asleep, June," Mama said at length, her voice strangely hoarse. June looked up just in time to catch a tear sliding down Mama's cheek before she brushed it away and squeezed June's hand tighter.

June pulled away and signed. *So... she is taking a nap?*

Mama offered a tight smile and drew in an even tighter breath. "No, it's more... it's a forever kind of sleep. Most people call it the Long Wait."

Waiting for what?

Mama almost laughed, voice still choked. "I'm going to have to tell you everything now, aren't I?"

June nodded, looking between Gram and Mama. *I'm confused.*

"I know. You've never seen half-death before."

But Bessie died last year, June signed.

"Cows aren't people. Our deaths are not the same." Mama squared her shoulders, retracting back into the usual strong shape she always held herself in. "Help me get Gram outside, little. Then I'll do my best to help you understand."

THE STORM WAS ALL BUT MOVED ON BY THE TIME JUNE AND MAMA managed to get Gram out of the cottage and to the base of her beloved old apple tree, which had been blackened to the roots and robbed of every leaf by lightning two springs ago.

At the base of the tree was a deep, rectangular hole. Mama had dug it four months ago in the dead of winter, out there amid the snow and frozen earth with a shovel and a pickaxe, furiously hacking away at the earth as Gram hacked her lungs out inside her cottage. Whenever June asked what the hole was for, Mama refused to answer. June's best guess was a watering hole for a new cow, but that didn't explain why Mama had felt the need to dig it in the freezing winter cold with such a violence.

Now Mama stood in front of the dead apple tree, evaluating, still stubbornly silent. Her sun-browned arms were folded across her chest, eyes red-rimmed. June waited, looking between the tree, Mama, and Gram behind.

At last, Mama came back to life and shook her head.

"This is unacceptable."

June sat down among the grass. Sure it was, but what could they do about it?

As if Mama had heard June's question, she lowered herself down to the base of the tree and laid her palm atop the blackened bark.

June watched. Mama was always worrying over plants. Sometimes, it seemed like she never left her garden behind their little house at all and just lived among her strawberries and sweet peas entirely.

But something happened.

Really, it was a *something* that had happened many times before. June had seen little flashes of this pale green light while playing in Mama's garden, caught glimpses of plants in full bloom that'd only sprouted the day before.

June always assumed the plants loved Mama just as much as she loved them, and grew a little extra for her. But now, watching as the charred roots beneath the earth lit with a vibrant pulse, watching as Mama's eyes closed and her brow went tight with concentration, watching as that fried tree *came alive again*, June wasn't sure which was sillier—that she once thought the plants could love someone, or that Mama was actually *making* them grow.

There was a soft, earthy sigh from the tree, like it was releasing a long-held breath. The tree struggled and contorted and was suddenly standing upright again, all new spring leaves and unfurling buds just as if lightning had never struck it in the first place. The cracking and creaking faded, the breath dissipated, and the leaves began to settle.

June looked up at Mama, who sat still touching the ground. But she didn't say anything. The grass around waved a deep green in the calming breeze, grown perhaps a good three inches taller.

June clapped to get her attention, then signed, *Mama?*

"Yes?"

How did you <u>do</u> that?

Mama shrugged. "Well, I reached for the roots, I... Gram needs her favorite apple tree. Grandpapa gave it to her, you know. All those years ago."

June nodded as if that made any sense at all and waited for a real explanation. But as the moment grew longer and Mama stayed still at the base of the new tree, gazing up at it with that far-away, critical look she usually got while reading the annual Jinian paper, June just wanted to ask *how* again. And *why*. But mostly just *how*.

Still, Mama stayed quiet, even as she turned and tugged, pushed, and pulled Gram into the hole at the base of the apple tree.

June flinched as Gram went in with a heavy, ungraceful *thump*. Mama stood at the base of the hole, sweat on her brow and her eyes glassy, before her whole body wracked with one long, singular tremble.

Then Mama sank down, pulled her knees to her chest, and sobbed.

June came close, her own chest growing tight and confusion coating every single thought, and leaned her head on Mama's arm as she continued to cry.

Mama never cried. Not when their cow died or when she and Gram talked about Grandpapa late at night. June had never seen her cry before, not once, not even when she got stung by a bee.

As such, she hadn't the slightest idea what to do. So June just sat there, the last remnants of the storm still drifting quickly away, and waited.

Twenty or thirty minutes passed. Mama stopped crying and sat still, leaning her head atop June's and staring up at the newly-reborn apple tree standing tall above their heads.

At last, June finally gave in and tugged on her sleeve. When Mama looked, she signed *How?*

Mama's features clouded back over in an instant. "What, June?"

June narrowed her eyes. *I asked <u>how</u>. How did you make the tree come back? And why is Gram in the hole? And—*

June cut herself off as Mama sat there, frowning and blinking as if June had just said a bad word.

"It's time, then," Mama said, "for the truth I hoped I'd never have to tell you."

June swallowed. She didn't like it when Mama looked at her like this. Like she was going to put something heavy in June's arms and expect her not to stumble. June's arms weren't anything like Mama's strong brown arms. Her arms could carry anything. June was not so sure about herself.

"You know how I love my garden." Mama smiled. "I feel as though I've spent half my life there."

Because you like your garden more than me?

Mama laughed a little and wiped her nose. "Well, I certainly *like* my garden more sometimes, but I love you most. Now... this is a truth that all creatures here in Ieris know, and even those in the Outerlands beyond, from the time they are very young. It's an explanation, and a warning."

June frowned. She didn't *like* warnings, and they were all Mama ever seemed to talk about.

Mama plucked a blade of grass, held it aloft until it pulsed with her strange light before reciting some strange poem.

Herein lies a story all creatures know
The root of the root, the seed left to sow
A history of yearning, of great sorrow and pain
Told to me as a warning, told to you just the same.
In the beginning, the Father-Graven had two sons
Who tore the boundless heavens apart
In salted stardust, Geiin birthed a world
And Mithre corrupted its heart.
The world fell to a night deep and starless
The spirits of men filled fully with darkness
Geiin ascended and in his wake
Left four brothers, each an Anathema remade:

A Father to rule dumb creatures
A Father to keep Ieris living and green
A Father to be mankind's healer
& a Father to balance, sort, and cleave.

What was faultless turned to rust
A world once beautiful turned to dust
At the end of all things but this stands true
All spirits return to one of two
Geiin or Mithre, holy or shrewd
Until the end we will slay what has strayed
Hear this song and be afraid
Never again let Anathema see light of day.

The world seemed to still and slow down as Mama spoke, the thunder ceasing its now-distant grumbling, the wind settling. Even the birds seemed to pipe down and listen. June stayed still, watching the sun creep from behind the fading storm clouds.

"Does that make any sense?" Mama asked. "That poem is called a Song of Thorn and Ash. It is how your Gram taught me what we are."

What we are? June signed. *What does <u>that</u> mean?*

"It means we are of the Four Fathers." Mama chewed on her lip before continuing. "As the poem tells, the Father-Graven, the great Celestial, once had two sons. These are called Geiin and Mithre. Geiin created our world, and stayed there for thousands of years until his brother-god Mithre turned his creation away from him. Because of Mithre's jealousy and deception, Geiin was rejected by the men he had created and pushed out. But before his ascension, he named four human brothers to rule in his stead. At his touch, the very fabric of the brothers' humanity was rewritten, and that of their descendants, for all time. How's that for clearing things up?"

Not any better, but June just nodded and signed *good.*

"Very well," Mama said. "Now... the first of the four brothers, Ithlil, was given power over the living land. At the touch of his hand, even the mightiest tree would bend its branches, the wind stir, the waters part. All that withered was his to renew. From him we are descendants, June, and that power in turn lives in us."

June blinked. *Me?*

"Yes, even you."

June signed as fast as she could. <u>*Now*</u> *I have questions. How do I use my power? Is it exactly like yours? Will I—*

Mama held up her palm. "Let me finish the story, then we can talk about our gifts."

June slumped back. Who cared about the history of a bunch of dead guys, when Mama had just told her of a magic *she* could use?

"The second brother, Dormaan, was also given a gift of life," Mama said. "He was given power over all animals, called to be a good steward of the dumb roaming creatures of earth. He was the first man to tame the horse, befriend the wolf, walk with the silent mountain cat."

Wow, June signed, her mind racing. That one seemed way cooler. If she had such a power, she could use an army of sparrows to pick the summer blackberries for her instead of pricking her fingers a million times over, or have fish jump out of the creek for dinner without having to sit for hours with a net, or—

"Are you still listening?"

June looked up. *Yes.*

Mama gave her a look that meant *I know you weren't*, but kept on with the story anyway.

"The third brother, Saer, was given the gift of healing—with a touch he could knit flesh back together, cure all ailments, soothe all sickness." Mama faltered, picking at her cuticles. "And the fourth brother was called Lithriin. Geiin gave him a gift unlike any other, a gift that mankind had never known before. Geiin called it balance, but to men it is known as death."

The hair rose on June's arms. Suddenly the thought of Gram down in the hole sent something other than intense confusion through her mind.

Mama continued. "With a touch of his hand, Lithriin possessed the power to turn anything to ash. This brought many firsts into the world—the first patch of sterilized earth, the first withered leaf, the first creature sent to sleep. The first true death. It was after the Four

Father's creation... that many things came to be which Ieris had never seen before. Men, beasts, and the land alike began to grow old and die. Magical creatures were hunted to near extinction. Eventually, the strength of men grew weak. And men the Four Fathers were, despite their gifts. Men who easily succumbed to their own desires.

"Lithriin grew weary of being feared, as the story is told. So tired was he of mankind's scorn that he refused to continue governing death, and chaos ensued. His three brothers turned against him out of desperation and a war erupted that gripped the mortal world for a decade, and it tore the fabric of Ieris asunder. The bloodshed ended only when Lithriin had killed all three of his brothers. Then, driven mad with grief, Lithriin lost control of death, and death became him entirely. Without anyone strong enough to fight the spread, Lithriin ravaged the land and he walked alone for ages through fields of ash. But at long last, Geiin took pity on mankind and intervened, helping the armies of Ieris arise and drive Lithriin to extinction. The race of men set a High King on the Isle of Winsor, a mortal with a kind heart, and for many generations Ieris knew peace, and healed. Geiin gave one last gift to mankind by creating the Windaerwood, from which our amulets are made to protect our spirits from half-death until we come home."

Home?

Mama tugged at the grass all around. "It is said that at the end of all things, the Father-Graven will bring those whose spirits burn clean across the last stretch of the unknown world. Through a sea of stars and into a place of white shores, where the sun never sets and men forget the taste of death."

What about the other spirits? The bad ones?

"They will cease to exist."

June nodded, soothed only a little. What kind of world *was* this? She had lived the last eleven years one sunrise and sunset after the other, never giving a spare thought to what might happen when the sun finally set and *didn't* rise again.

"More questions?" Mama asked. "I know that look."

But for once, June couldn't think of a single thing to say. She stared at Mama and tried to comprehend it all, mind spinning. The story was so vast. So unbelievable.

"After Lithriin was overthrown, the memory of Geiin's touch meant nothing to most folk. They hated all magical things, especially anything descendant of the Four Fathers."

Like us, June interrupted.

"Yes, like us." Mama sighed. "So Geiin withdrew his hand completely, for the world now scorned him more than ever, and those he once touched either lost their way and were killed, or were killed trying to find it again."

I don't like this story.

"True stories are often uncomfortable, my June. We do not learn in the arms of comfort."

June held one finger up, and then signed. *How did the race of men fail so badly, Mama? If Geiin made them and loved them, why would they reject him?*

Mama sank into deep thought as she looked across their green valley.

"It is a sad thing," she said, "how the hearts of men grow to see only themselves. We forget how big and fragile the world is. Forget how easily we can crack it." She smiled a little. "It must sound strange to you, to speak of people this way. Our valley has always been good to us. A safe place. The outside world is so different."

I cannot even imagine evilness in people, Mama.

Mama reached out and ruffled June's hair. "I hope you never can."

The sun was warm and distant on June's skin. *So all this is why we never leave the valley,* she signed. *People hate us.*

"Yes. And this is why we never will."

We're... Cursed.

"We are called Anathema, not Cursed. That's a sort of slur against us."

A rock sunk in June's chest. *But isn't there more to see than this little patch of trees and grass?*

Mama shrugged. "Of course. But even I haven't experienced the world we live in, I've only ever learned its history. The farthest I have ever gone from home is to Farthing for trade. I'll take you there, one day. We have to be careful, but—"

What an adventure that will be, June signed as she flopped down with a huff.

Mama shook her head. "There is nothing beyond the valley for us. Nothing but death."

Death is here, too.

"Death is everywhere. But Gram is *sleeping,* June. She's not really gone. No one ever is."

June stared at the sky. *Why did you wait so long to tell me the truth?*

"I didn't want to scare you."

I'm not scared.

"I didn't want you to be scared of *me.*"

June wanted to laugh. *Who could ever be scared of you? You're just my Mama.*

A shadow crossed Mama's face. "Everyone, if they knew the truth."

June got to her feet and folded her arms over her chest, absorbing the strong look Mama gave her.

"Knowledge is power, June. You must swear to me that you will be careful. One day, your gift will come—"

Curse, June signed.

"Whatever you will call it, you must keep it hidden. You *must* stay in our valley."

June set her teeth. This wasn't *fair,* not at all. It was as if her world had been turned over and spun around a few times and she was expected to carry on without noticing.

She looked back to the hole that held Gram, and tears sprung back up behind her eyes. When June looked back at Mama, her eyes had gone glassy again, too.

So this is goodbye, June signed.

Mama managed a smile. "Only for now."

II

STRANGE COMING DARKNESS
{THIRTEEN DAYS BEFORE}

A storm was rolling in.

Vasily toyed with his amulet as he cantered through another of the many lonesome fields occupying the hollowed abyss that was central Nown Jin's countryside. Nuest had told Vasily that Glass constantly traveled to and from one city—Pearl Jin. Vasily hoped to run into the creature somewhere in the countryside nearby, but if he wasn't so fortunate, he'd simply wait for Glass in Pearl Jin herself. But for now, all he had to worry about was the rain-choked sky and the expanse of tall grass rolling away beneath his mare's hooves.

He let his mind wander and as always it wandered straight home, where all his love and all his pain seemed to rest together. But he was ripped from his thoughts before he could even begin reminiscing when his mare slid to a stop and shied violently to the left. Vasily swore and scrambled for the reins, scanning for the source of her spook. Was there a wildcat near? There seemed to be nothing worthy of such a start. It was just them and the field—

Vasily's heart skipped a beat as his eyes came to rest on the small, brightly glowing toadstool in front of them. It couldn't have been more than three or four inches tall, its white stalk and wide dotted cap alight with a strange turquoise luminesce, bright as a star against a patch of thin, withered gray grass.

Blazingly bright, even in this full sunlight.

Vasily struggled to keep the mare from bolting, and looked up. Beyond that toadstool was another, this one mottled between that same bright blue and a rare, glittering violet. Beyond it was another, and another, and countless more. They were choking out the whole field, the surrounding grass hoary and gray. If he looked hard enough he could catch glimpses of a dimmer light beneath the soil. Even the root system tangling beneath the earth was alive with pulsating light.

His mind flashed unbidden back to what mother had said, before he left. Her warnings of strange happenings... glowing plants.

It cannot be.

He squeezed his eyes shut and tried to clear his mind, but when he looked again, the toadstools were still there.

I feel a coming darkness. And I'm afraid for you.

The bright lights seemed to mock Vasily as he slid from the saddle, still fighting to keep control of his horse, and took a few cautious steps toward the nearest toadstool. The color seemed to be lit from within the stalk, which glowed a glacial white.

There has to be a logical explanation for this, Vasily thought as he crouched down to pluck the fungi. The cap snapped off and released a puff of glittering ash, sending Vasily into a coughing fit and his horse into another panic. She backpedaled and Vasily found himself dragged in the wake of her spook, his boots skimming over the grass. She finally stopped a good fifty paces from the mushrooms, shying away from the cap Vasily still held crushed in his free hand.

He rightened himself, still coughing as if he'd inhaled straight dust, and peered at the cap. Bit by bit, the luminescence blinked out. As soon as it vanished, the cap dissolved fully into ash.

Vasily let the ash tumble through his fingers, disgust and sordid fear roiling in his gut.

Glass. This had to be his doing somehow.

A deep rumble shook the earth then, something beyond the incoming storm—a sort of grumbling, the sound of a giant turning over in his sleep. Vasily felt fear twist like a knife in his gut as the earth seemed, just for the slightest moment, to quake beneath his feet.

He looked around, his heart picking up speed. What in Geiin's name was that?

Moments passed, and the earth stilled again. Vasily shook his head, finally looked away from the toadstools, and mounted.

He would stop at the nearest farmhouse or settlement and ask questions. Maybe Glass had recently been through this place.

The wind was cold on his face and loud in his ears as he spurred his mare into a canter, almost enough to drown out the off-kilter beat of his heart that seemed to only worsen with each new day. Glass' old amulet felt impossibly heavy in his pocket, an anchor drawing him inescapably deeper into this strange coming darkness.

12

THE STRANGER

{THIRTEEN DAYS BEFORE}

The afternoon was slipping by. Mama had sent June away again so that she could finish burying Gram, so June spent the remainder of the day deep in the forest. Dinner time was near and her stomach was grumbling as she lay on a patch of sun-warmed grass, still trying to sort out the puzzle pieces of all this 'truth'.

Why hadn't Mama told her all of this sooner? Why wait until Gram was... sleeping? She could've been prepared. She could've understood that the time they had with Gram was as limited as the time they shared with their Bessie the cow or a plucked flower or the very seasons themselves. That there was an *end*, and it was near.

June chewed on the inside of her cheek. She didn't think she'd ever understand the ways of her mother.

She plucked a dandelion wisher growing next to her and waved it around. The little white fuzzies took flight and whirled away. June stared at the now-bald stalk, then fidgeted with her amulet. Cursed... if that was true and she was just like Mama, then she should be able to make the stalk grow a whole new head of wishers, right?

But... how? Reach deep inside herself? Concentrate on plants? Chant some fairy spell in her head?

She snorted. *Absurd.* Maybe Mama was making it all up. How did she know all that, anyway? If it all happened ages ago, how could the facts possibly have stayed true? If Lithriin really was dead, who could verify Mama's tale?

June shook her head and got to her feet quick. Time to go home. The truth could wait for another day.

June set her feet to the deer path that led home. Mama should be making dinner by now. If June was lucky, maybe it would be *potato soup.* Mama had gone to the market a few days ago, maybe she had picked a block of cheddar. Maybe they could bake crumpets—June stopped short.

She'd reached the edge of the forest and was looking down the slope toward their cottages. A man in a rain-stained cloak astride a plain bay horse was talking to Mama, who stood at the base of Gram's half-filled grave.

Mama. Who always hid them whenever a traveler came too close to their valley. Mama, who was so careful and quick, who never let her guard down, who was always ready for everything all the time.

June crouched down. Maybe this man was an old friend?

The man's voice raised. His voice was rough and clouded with a strange accent that June couldn't understand. Why was he mad?

June watched as Mama put a hand low by her side and signed. Somehow she knew June was watching. How did she know?

Wait, pay attention. What was she saying?

Once again, Mama signed.

Run.

June felt the hair rise on the back of her neck.

13

THE PRICE
{TWELVE DAYS BEFORE}

A mist-choked dusk lay heavy all around, and the sky continued to weep. Vasily huddled beneath the viridian bows of a fir tree, unsure of his location, his cloak pulled tight around his frame. The bloodhawk was perched on his knee, her eerie amber eyes closed as she swayed along with Vasily's trembling. The shakes wracking his body had nothing to do with the spring chill or the heavy rainfall.

He rode for twelve hours straight after the *incident*, until his mare couldn't go on any longer.

Now he was here, hunkered down beneath this tree.

The woman in the settlement. She'd been so engrossed in the simple task of burying a body that she never heard his approach. He watched her pause shoveling, watched as she laid a palm on the apple tree just beyond the grave, watched as the entire tree pulsed with a flare of golden *life*.

He squeezed his eyes shut. Just how many Anathema were there? Surely there must be hundreds, for him to have stumbled upon one by *chance*. Hundreds and hundreds in hiding. Thousands, even, living amongst them in plain sight. Inhuman monstrosities, threatening his kingdom, his house, his family.

I would do it all over again.

He leaned his head against the tree and tilted his face to let the rain pour down on him as if it could wash away all these coldblooded sins. He murdered her, the Anathema woman. Burned her and her home to the ground.

I would do it all over again.

The woman had a child. A girl not much older than Yena, who came running out of the forest the second she saw his sword first fall, who fought him like some tiny, frail demon, intent not so much on living but vengeance.

Vasily's eyes grew hot. She was just so little. But he did it anyway.

He wanted to get up and run, or scream, or hack this stupid tree to the ground, to kill a whole army of men. He wanted to ride straight home and hug his sisters. He wanted to take the Prince of Glass' head in his hands and crush every last drop of life from it. Anything to relieve this awful panic buzzing inside. The grate of each breath wore hard on his nerves, each slam of his heart nailed the guilt in further. Vasily closed his eyes. It didn't stop the memories—the fear and shock on the woman's face, that apocalyptic hatred burning through the little girl as she rammed into him.

The little girl wasn't afraid, not at all. She *screamed* in Vasily's face as his sword fell upon her, but not with the scream of the dying, but of the robbed.

I will do it all over again.

Vasily dug his fingers into the rain-soaked dirt, Bellan's amber gaze his only tether to reality. He made himself focus on home, on Mari and the girls. If this was the price he must pay, this resurrection of the monster he'd long strived to rid himself of, *so be it.*

There was no other way.

14

REBIRTH

June was drifting. Lost in the dark and the quiet. Sometimes she would wake up, peek open her eyes. Fractals of light. Faces roving. She couldn't feel much other than her hands. Feel the dirt under her nails, the blood stained on her palms. Her hands felt dry and cracking, they shook even when she was falling asleep.

But June was not alone in this dark and quiet place. There were glimpses. Fire. Mama's screaming. Mama telling her to go back, to run away. The sound his blade made. *Him*, the Raincloak Man, and fire all around. This stranger who walked through the flames and cut her world away.

Well, *almost* all of it. June was dead, so certain she was dead—and then she wasn't. She hadn't felt a thing since she woke up after the fire, hadn't felt a thing when the nice lady and grumpy man found her and brought her to the Rich Man. Hadn't when the Rich Man gave her over to the Giant and the Idiot, hadn't felt a thing since then, not now, not ever again. She had seen more faces in the last month than she imagined were in the whole world, but only one showed clear in the darkness of her mind, as she slept and fevered and dreamed. June drifted, half-aware of her aching body, and realized that *it was not going to end.*

It couldn't.

Not, at least, till she found the Raincloak Man again. Not until fire was repaid by fire. Not until his skin was the one split by a blade. Not until he endured what he did to Mama with fire and blood and steel, just the same.

Everything was different now. And this *burning* inside... it would not be gone until June could rest in the dark, and not see his face.

❧ 15 ❧

A PLAN CALLED PRETENDING

The night was choked with mist and rain by the time Taein confiscated the kid's knife and carried her to the tree line where Vince had set up a quick camp. Taein tucked her in with his bedroll and let her be while Vince made a fire and ate more for dinner than Taein thought himself capable of eating in an entire month. All was quiet for a long while, save for Vince strumming softly on his guitar. Night set in, and the rain turned to a downpour. Vince fell asleep and Taein into deep thought, his back pressed against the base of a tree, water pitter-pattering down on his head. He lit a cigarette, smoked, and thought.

Damp. Miserable. Behind schedule. He needed a plan.

One soon presented itself, which Taein affectionately dubbed *The Plan of Pretending*, and it went like this:

When morning came, they would wake the kid up, make sure she wasn't too hurt, and carry right along as if nothing had happened.

No matter how *mighty convenient* it seemed that Regor would have his only known Anathema take his Anathema cargo to the shankin' Outlander, who Taein could only presume had the worst in mind. The marks at stake were worth the risk. The marks were worth it all, because they would fix everything.

They would finish the job, because nothing really *had* changed. Then Taein could wash his hands of the whole incident and buy his happily ever after and have written on his tombstone *'Here Lies Taein of House Glass, the sole surviving son of the bloodline of House Glass, who all you podges never managed to find and kill, who died a natural death so rich he used marks to start his fireplace every morning. He truly was a great fellow.'*

Easy-peasy. Taein smiled a little, twirling June's knife through his fingers. He'd always been good at pretending, especially with himself, so therefore this was just a little hitch in the road.

Early morning finally came around. The rain retreated, and the sky was brewing a soft predawn gray when she woke up.

The kid startled half-way to consciousness, her eyes half-open but resting on nothing, lips parted and moving without a sound. It was a strange sight. Taein didn't know what to do so he stayed a few feet off, leaning against his saddle with the emerald blade balanced on one knee, and just watched. The morning light revealed the dark stain of blood gathered above a deep wound between her shoulder and neck, and a larger cut on her lower leg.

Dammit. Those weren't wounds he could bandage in a hurry. Taein looked over at Vince to ask for help, but the giant was still asleep.

He frowned and looked back at the kid. Her eyes were closed again.

"She needs help, you idiot," he said softly to himself.

"I agree on both accounts," Vince mumbled.

"Oh, so you *are* awake."

Vince cracked open an eye. "The kid got an amulet, at least? You actually check for one?"

Taein glared. "Yes, Vincent, the minute I pulled her from the bramble."

Vince grunted. "Well, at least she got that. If she goes, you know. But the goal here is that she *don't* go, Taein." Vince looked up at him sharply. "Hey, wait a minute. You ain't still on that no-amulet-wearin' kick of yours anymore, right?"

"Relax, Vincent," Taein snapped. "I'm the Unkillable Kid, remember?"

"But what if something *happens* and you turn into a Shallow and—"

"You just know I'd haunt the shit out of you," Taein said, folding his arms.

"No, but I do want my money. I'll even loan you mine. Just wear one *please*, even if only for the trip—"

Taein shook his head. "Nope."

Vince drew in a breath, then released it with excruciating restraint. "Why *not?*"

"Amulets are bad luck."

Just like that, Vince lost all his hard-fought patience. "For shank's sake, Taein!"

"My, Vince, it's almost as if you care."

"You're the stupidest little shit I ever met, Taein!"

Taein ignored Vince's whining, unable to bring himself closer to the kid. He kept his hands tightly folded in his lap as light rain plinked down on his hood and picked at the stitches where he'd mended his gloves. He remembered watching their lady mother fuss over Ruein's various scrapes and gashes loads of times growing up. Ruein could find trouble better than any other Siou in the Ieris. It was his greatest talent.

Taein gazed at the tree line on the other side of the valley as the gray light grew stronger. He could still see mother—well, *Ruein's* mother—stitching up a particularly bad gash on Ruein's knee. How Ruein caught Taein's eyes and winked.

Taein's hold on the past was slipping like a drunk on black ice, but *hell below*, he would never forget his brother. Sometimes, looking at Ruein felt like looking into the mirror reflection of what Taein himself could've become in some better, alternate universe; but Ruein embodied luck and freedom and good fun, always smiling, always warm, and Taein was everything he was not. Taein was slight and shadowy growing up, the half-hearted whisper of someone else. He had three features of distinction; chief of which was a sharp little smile, a grin that looked like it belonged to a liar—which it did. This singular feature promised a strong penchant for malevolence that was promptly betrayed by Taein's skin, which looked eggshell-fragile, and his eyes, which were dark as strong coffee but devoid of Ruein's warmth; fearful, mistrustful, cowardly holes in him that Taein could not reforge into something better no matter how he twisted and contorted the rest of his persona. He could batter and bruise his skin in meaningless brawls, he could sharpen his smile with words that cut, he could walk as a silent menace and steal from orphans and needle rit and poke a hole into his earlobe and always shoot and stab and swing first. He could burn down and remake every weakness lurking in his sliver of a being, reforge Mikhael Glass into Taein, the Unkillable Kid who took no guff from no one, who weighed 160 pounds but made most bruisers cross the street.

But he couldn't change a thing about his eyes.

Taein sucked in a fast breath as the thoughts grew more and more unruly. *Focus. The kid.*

He snuck another glance at her and nearly jumped out of his skin. The girl was looking back at him, fully conscious, and in her eyes of the palest green was pure, flaming murder.

"Take it easy, kid," he said, sitting upright.

Those unnaturally pale eyes darted around his face, clouded with confusion. Mouse-brown hair hung in stringy clumps to her shoulders, her blue dress covered in mud and ash, her face caked with the same debris but for twin trails cutting white paths down her cheeks.

"What happened here?" Taein asked.

The kid froze. In the mist, with the pale rising daylight beating down to further illuminate those alien eyes, Taein could've sworn she was some sort of bog-child, a wild and unnatural blight he wanted to get as far away from as possible. For just a second, he understood why everyone was so afraid of the Anathema.

Of something so strange as this.

The kid's eyes roamed from pile to pile of still-smoking rubble. Then she looked back at Taein, and the desire to get as far away as possible hit him like a shovel to the face.

The hair rose on the back of Taein's neck. "Did you kill all those men?"

The kid ignored him and instead lurched to her feet before sinking right back down, confusion and hurt and that terrifying hatred still twisting her entire frame. She looked back toward the ruins again, let out a low, keening noise, and began to soundlessly sob. Little shoots of new grass came popping up from the damp earth all around her. That rust-colored splotch was seeping through the side of her dress again, as was the gash on her neck. Sig and his boys had definitely done a number on her.

Taein looked back at the smoldering remains of the settlement as a weight settled hard inside. This whole scene was too familiar.

We have to get out of here.

His attention snapped back to the kid as she tried to stand again, giving one last effort to get to her feet. She almost made it this time before the wounded leg gave out and she crashed back to the muddied ground, choking on tears and clotted blood, her eyes gone wild. But she didn't scream or even cry; the only sound she made was a sharp gasp as curled in on herself, her eyes shut tight and mouth twisted in pain.

"Look, kid, I promise we won't hurt you," Taein said.

Silence. Her breaths came in short, fluttery pants. More and more slender shoots of new grass came curling out from the dirt around her, punctuated by tiny yellow flowers.

They could still leave. She obviously didn't want anything to do with them. She never had, not since the beginning.

The thought sent something dark jittering through him. *Just how many people are you going to leave behind?*

No. He curled his fingers into his palms and gave it one last effort.

Taein scooted a bit closer. "I'm only going to ask one more time. What happened?"

Her eyes opened, darting to Vince and then away with alarm. She struggled to sit back up in one explosive movement, eyes on fire again, and stabbed a finger toward the ruins.

Taein furrowed his brow. "I don't understand."

She blew out something like a hiss, entire body quaking, and set about moving her hands in strange shapes with such an intensity that blood began dripping from the wound on her side again. Taein watched her go off, dirt-caked hands fluttering like strange startled animals, before shaking his head.

"What's she doing?" Vince asked.

"I think she's trying to... communicate. Hell, who knows." Taein shook his head. "Where'd your book go?"

She shook her head, then burst into tears. Taein glanced at Vin, who just shrugged.

"Alright..." Taein dared to move forward a little. "Can you at least tell me your name?"

She scratched in the dirt with a finger, hands shaking so badly that Taein could barely make out the scrawled letters.

J-u-n-e. So that was it.

Taein ran a hand through his hair. "Not to be blunt, but I can't foresee you living much longer if you don't let me patch you up."

She wiped her nose, smearing blood across her face. Taein's stomach flipped. He dared to move even closer before sitting down just a few inches from her. Beneath the dirt and ash and congealed blood, he could tell that each wound was a clean, sharp line.

"No one's going to hurt you again," Taein said, trying to catch her eyes. "I won't, Vince won't. He's nice. Aren't you, Vince?"

Vince nodded. "I'm very nice."

The kid just sniffled.

Taein softened his voice. "Was this all an accident, or—"

She met his eyes for the first time, and slashed her hand through the air as if to say *no*.

Taein's eyes strayed to the wound on her neck. "Why did they attack you? Because of your powers?"

She nodded. That hateful look in her eyes was back.

A chill lanced through Taein as blurry memories of fire flashed in his mind.

Oh, sweet Geiin.

His first instinct was to get them on their feet and hightail it away, but one look at her crumpled frame stopped the idea before it could take form. Her face had faded into an ashen shade of gray, and looking around it was easy to see why. Blood was sprinkled everywhere— congealing on her dress, clotting in her hair, speckling all the newborn grass around her.

Taein asked one more time as Vince's stare became too heavy to ignore. "Please let me help you."

Finally, she nodded.

Taein moved forward. He peeled blood-soaked fabric away from the wound on her side and held his breath.

"Hand me my pack, will you?" he asked.

Vince handed him the satchel and Taein rooted through its contents until he found his canteen. He then tore several strips of fabric from the hem of her skirt.

"I'm going to have to clean your gashes and bind them really tight, alright? It's going to shank—" he caught his profanity when Vince coughed with a furious glare. "...hurt."

June's eyes flickered up for just a second. It was the only response he could coax out of her.

Taein soaked a strip of fabric with water from his canteen and set about cleaning the wounds. When they were as clean he could manage, he met her eyes and offered what he hoped was a reassuring smile.

Please don't cry.

His breath caught in his chest, Taein began wrapping the gashes as tightly as he could. If he didn't stop the bleeding, especially from the wound on her side, he knew she wouldn't last much longer. He worked slowly, expecting her at any minute to flinch away or snap at him or do *something*, but she stayed frozen.

"Still alive there?" he asked, fumbling with the fabric.

No response. He looked up at her and froze—she was unnaturally still, hardly breathing, eyes shut tight. Taein dared shake her shoulder before realizing that she had slipped back into unconsciousness. For a long while he stared at the pallor of her skin, the sickly hollows beneath her eyes and in her cheeks, the tiny flutters of her breath.

She was so still he thought, just for a moment, she had died.

He hated the relief that flooded his body.

"What's the plan now, boss?" Vince asked.

Taein hesitated. The Plan of Pretending suddenly seemed awfully far-fetched with the condition the kid was in.

"Dunno," he said.

"Well, I do know for certain we ain't taking her to the Outlander. Do you... you think he knew? And that's why he wanted her?"

Taein narrowed his eyes at Vince. "What do you mean, we're not taking her to the Outlander?"

"Well... we ain't taking her *there*. Beyond that it ain't really my call."

Taein glared. "No, it's *not your call*. She's going to the Outlander."

"We ain't taking her there, that's for sure," Vince said, rooting through his pack for food. "I won't let you."

"You're shankin' with me."

"No, I ain't. Once, my only real opinion rested in where I wanted a beer, which I might remind you I was most tragically denied. Now, my opinion is that we are not taking her to the Outlander. He'll hurt her for sure. "

"You don't know that!" Taein sputtered. "He could have no idea what she is! She could be a relative, or—"

"You should eat something, boss," Vince said, "you get angry when you're hungry."

"Trust me, I'll stay pissed either way." Taein snapped. "If we're not taking her to the Outlander, we're leaving her here. Let the Celestials decide what happens to her next."

"Geiin already did," Vince said through a mouthful of food. He pointed a sausage-skewered knife at Taein. "We got her back. That's gotta count for somethin'."

"Accounting for what? Providence? The will of the Divine?" Taein scoffed. "Doesn't matter if it was the intervening hand of Geiin himself, we've got no business taking on a kid."

"We already did, though."

"That was when she was cargo."

"And now?"

"Now it's different. Now we know what she is."

"Then where in the world is it safe for an Anathema?"

"Nowhere." Taein tugged at the grass. "That's the shankin' trouble of it all. That's why we're taking her to the Outlander. She isn't safe anywhere, so we might as well be rich."

"We'll find somewhere better," Vince said resolutely.

Taein rolled his eyes. *What the hell am I getting into?* The mere idea of him attempting to function as some kind of parental figure made a peal of bitter, biting laughter well up in his chest.

He already was the world's worst brother. He would most certainly be the world's worst parent.

He tracked the kid's shallow breaths. He could leave, and she'd never know. She probably wouldn't even wake up again.

He closed his eyes, sickness welling up in his chest. He shouldn't think like that.

But he was still Taein Glass, the bastard baby who was never supposed to exist in the first place. His business was keeping himself alive, plain and simple. He'd proved it to himself, time and time again. Life and death would converge and he didn't get a choice—he lived, no matter what it cost, no matter how badly it hurt. No matter *who* it hurt.

And yet, here he was. Wasting time looking after this strange, hateful little kid who was only going to cause him trouble. The Plan of Pretending wasn't going to be nearly as easy as he thought.

You owe Ruein this, he thought, and he tore off another bandage.

———

PART II: THE LONG ROAD

THE SHADOW GROWS

Dusk. Slivers of a bright crimson sunset stabbed out from behind Nown Jin's usual dense clouds as Vasily searched the horizon for a sense of serenity. Bellan flew overhead, steadily guiding him north. Vasily took in a deep draught of the cool evening air, heavy with the scent of rain and spring growth, and breathed out slowly.

Everything will be well.

He'd been clinging to the thought ever since the incident at the little settlement. He wasn't sure if he believed it just yet, but every stride further away eased off the guilt.

Little by little, it will leave you.

He wasn't sure if he believed that, either. Because even if he didn't remember every Siou face that had fallen on his blade in the war that followed Babas' tragedy, he never quite shook the weight. No matter how justified. The last thing he wanted was to make such a burden heavier. He just wanted to go home. He just wanted to forget. He just wanted himself back.

And yet. Here he was.

Vasily adjusted the reins and sent the mare into a trot. They cut across the highpoint of a hill, the only sound in the coming night that of the long grass brushing the mare's legs. It was still. Almost too still.

The night deepened, the red sunset all but gone, and Vasily looked up. He could see the faintest hint of his father's stars, still dim in the receding light, through a minuscule hole in the cloud covering.

I will honor you, Babas.

Silence.

Vasily's throat tightened and he looked down to the mare's dark mane, his amulet bouncing against his chest beneath his shirt, a constant dogging reminder of the death right his father had been denied. Babas' amulet had turned to ash along with the rest of his body.

Vasily just barely soothed away the ache in his heart when his mare stopped short and nearly tossed him from the saddle as a deep, rolling groan shook the earth. He righted himself with a muffled curse just in time, looking around wildly for whatever startled her. *Again?* Ancestors above, could it be more of those glowing mushrooms? And what was that *sound* again, that shifting of the earth? Could it—

No. He caught a glimpse of something dark and shadow-like moving in the grass. A passing coyote, perhaps? But when had his mare ever startled at a lone coyote?

Vasily drew up on the reins and gave the bay a reassuring pat. He traced the shadow as it cut across the field, hardly visible in the grass, toward what looked like... was that another? He squinted as the animal stopped short, becoming aware of his presence, and looked over. Sharp ears pricked up above the grass and unearthly eyes, glowing an eerie, reflective green in the dying light, stared him down.

Seconds crawled by like a held breath. Bellan, sensing something was wrong, glided down and perched on Vasily's arm. He watched, unable to get a clear view of that *thing* through the grass. It was as if the creature was moving underwater, as if its dark figure was curling at the edges like smoke.

It was in that moment of stilted uncertainty that the creature tilted a pointed nose to the sky and loosed a horrendous *shriek* of a howl, shattering the previous tranquility of the night like the wail of a starving baby. Vasily struggled to keep his mare under control as she spooked again and spun in a tight circle. The animal's companion took notice and lifted its own head, the mangled leg of some unfortunate prey still clenched in its jaw, before dropping the limb and joining in on the hellish cry.

Then another canine voice joined the two, and another. And another.

Vasily watched with growing horror, his blood gone cold in his veins, as more and more dark shapes darted out from the surrounding clumps of forest and cut across the field to join the two, yipping and snarling with horrible, humanlike shrieks as if their victims were somehow still screaming from within them.

"Oh, stars." Vasily whispered, as seven—no, *eight*—dogs clustered together some hundred feet before him and stared.

The dogs stalked closer, ashen bodies shifting in the gaping dark, those unearthly eyes glinting green fire, and Vasily sent Bellan into the air and booted his mare around into the fastest gallop she could manage.

He heard the pack shriek from behind and knew that he could not outrun them, that he had not gotten a far enough start. And sure enough, not ten seconds passed before two of those dark shapes darted in front of his mare and cut her off. She shied again and this time, his balance failing and heart rising in his throat, Vasily went toppling from the saddle.

He landed hard, the breath knocked from his lungs, and jumped to his feet just in time to rip his sword from his sheath and slash out at the first dog to leap at him. He toppled to the ground, a scream he didn't recognize as his own tearing from his throat as the thing snapped with blade-like teeth but a hair away from his face, rent by his sword and still scrabbling and snarling after him with rabid intensity. Vasily rolled over and ripped his sword clean through the thing, slicing the dog's emaciated body in half just to watch it dissolve away into a smear of ash.

Just like how Babas died.

Vasily hadn't time to shake himself from the memory, his heart a frantic drum in his ears, before the rest of the dogs arrived. He struggled to his feet and hacked at the dark shapes, half-aware of

Bellan as she swept down and raked at the dogs with her talons. He barely managed to slice another into ash before he was back down again and fighting to keep his throat in one piece. There were so many. There were too many.

Help.

Vasily gritted out a harsh breath and braced his sword against the dog snapping at his face. He would not be sent to his Long Wait at the hands of these *animals*, while Glass was still alive and roaming free. *No.* It would not happen.

Vasily threw off the dog with a roar and slashed his sword in a wild arc, catching two dogs with the blade as he kicked off another trying to snap his leg. He could see his mare tearing around the field in the distance, her reins flapping loose and two dogs at her heels, and a flash of white just beyond.

White?

Vasily whirled and brought his sword down just before a dog tackled him, watching as a man astride a muddy white workhorse tore through the field toward him, screaming at the top of his lungs. Behind him ran a group of farmers, all bellowing as if they were charging into battle.

The creatures paused their assault to stare down these new prospective victims. Vasily seized the opportunity and kept hacking at them. The remaining dogs took off after the newcomers, leaving Vasily bloodied, panting, and somehow alive. Bellan swooped after them, still snatching at their backs with her talons.

Vasily stood dumbfounded, his heart still racing in his chest as the group clashed against the dogs, until his legs could hold him no longer. He sank to the ground as his adrenaline gave out and the pain surfaced beneath his mangled skin like a drowning man fighting for air.

Vasily eased his right pant leg up and grimaced at the mess of shredded skin beneath the blood-splattered fabric, the hollering of the farmers against the shrieking of the dogs a terrible cacophony in his ears. His other leg didn't look much better, and both arms were dotted with deep punctures. He struggled to his feet and spat out a mouthful of blood before limping toward the group of men as they struggled to dispatch the last dog, catching his mare as he went.

Vasily stopped the bay and rooted through his pack for his canteen of *varjla* just as Bellan returned to perch atop the saddle horn. He sank back down and set about pouring the alcohol on each of the punctures, biting his cheek to keep the curses at bay.

A sharp cry came from the last dog as the villagers finally managed to pin and kill it. Then the blessed quiet came again.

Vasily looked up as the group approached him, led by the man atop the white workhorse. He raised his hand in greeting, his heartbeat picking up pace. They were just peasants—surely he'd never seen them before, nor had they ever seen him.

"Are you hurt badly, lad?" The man hollered, stopping his horse a few yards away.

"I've survived much worse." Vasily replied.

If any of the party recognized him, they didn't show it. They were a group of dirt-faced villagers, men worn by life at the governing whims of the land. Definitely farmers, Vasily supposed, by the collection of shovels, hoes, and pitchforks they wielded as make-shift weapons.

"What business have you in this part of Nown Jin?" The man atop the horse inquired.

Vasily gritted his teeth as he wound a rag around the worst bite. "I'm only passing through. Thank you for coming to my aid."

The man nodded, unimpressed. "Aye, though we didn't intend any such thing. We've been huntin' that pack for a week now, lad. It ain't nothin' but a fine coincidence we caught up with the bastards when we did, or you'd be just another carcass for burnin'."

Vasily shoved back his unease and rose, ignoring the sharp bolts of pain shooting through his body. "I imagine you gentlemen would know what those Geiin-forsaken creatures are, then?"

"Oh, for certain," said the apparent leader, leaning on his saddle horn, "though I can't fathom how you'd be traveling through these parts without already knowin' yourself. We call them bastard's shadow-dogs. For right obvious reasons, you know. The bastard's been killin' our flocks for weeks now, and our folk, too, when they can get them."

Vasily moved slowly around his mare, checking her legs for bites. She was somehow uninjured, thank Geiin.

"Any idea where they herald from?" Vasily asked.

The leader scoffed. "Sure I do, lad, everyone does."

Vasily struggled up into the saddle, biting his cheek so hard it bled to keep from crying out. When he had settled himself, he looked back to the leader. "Well?"

The man squinted. "The *mists*. Are you dense?"

Vasily blinked back his surprise. "The mists. As in the *Southern Mists*, in the Vandel Province?"

Laughter rippled through the group as the leader scoffed again. "Are there any others?"

Something cold crawled through Vasily's gut. "How did they come here?"

The man shrugged. "Rumor has it that the mists are fallin', that the creatures inside are gettin' loose. I don't know what to make of it 'cept for that we've lost three men and a wee little girl to those things," he paused, stabbing a finger at a smear of ash in the grass, "and more sheep than I've fingers to count five times over."

Vasily winced as the mare took a step. His mother's warning echoed in his head.

I sense a coming darkness, Vasily.

Was this it?

The man looked back to his group. "Well, we best be off. There's more out there we've got to get before they turn and get us like the shankin' bastards they are. Keep moving or they'll get at you again for certain, you hear?"

Vasily nodded and moved his mare aside to let them pass. "I will, thank you."

The group passed, their farming implements poking up over the overgrown grass like strange thorny branches. Vasily watched them walk off before his eyes were drawn to another smear of ash amid the grass.

Ash.

Something clicked in Vasily's mind with a bolt of terrible certainty. Perhaps *that* was what Glass was doing—the bastard was lowering the mists. Surely, he had *something* to do with it. First those mushrooms, now the dogs, and *him*. All connected by ash, by that terrible curse.

With an oath, Vasily pulled Glass' old amulet from his pocket and held it out to Bellan. She contemplated the thin rosewood disc, then launched into the air.

"Find Glass." He called out to her.

The bloodhawk circled above once before gliding away. Vasily watched until she melted entirely into the night. Then, his heart grown heavy and body afire with pain, he turned the bay southwest toward the Vandal province.

And the Southern Mists.

✵ 17 ✵

THE SAINT

Quite disappointingly, the kid kept on living.

Vince left for Farthing to get real medicine, which left Taein alone with the kid and solely responsible if she bled out. Somehow over the hours Taein managed to hold steady his frayed nerves *and* get her wounds to stop oozing—this was a mighty accomplishment that deserved attention, so he made sure to point it out as soon as she woke up.

"Hey, I actually managed to patch you up!" he said, "You wouldn't believe me how long it took me to figure out how to bandage the cut on your neck. What an inconsiderate angle..."

June just glared, pale eyes like hot coals.

"No appreciation? I'm hurt." Taein offered another jagged smile. "Hungry? We got food."

She shook her head and looked down the hillside at the settlement ruins.

Taein kept trying. "How about dried beef? It's alright, honestly. I've had better but beggars can't be choosers. Not that you're a beggar. Or that *I* am for that matter..."

June didn't seem to hear him, her eyes still searching those distant

III

blackened heaps. With tiny, pain-shocked movements, she pulled herself upright and away from him.

"Want an apple?" Taein said, attempting to draw her attention away from what once was her home. "We've got some potatoes I could fry up. But the fire's mostly out, anyway... blueberries?"

The kid didn't bother with so much as a shake of her head.

"Booze?"

The kid finally looked back. And burst into tears. Taein didn't know what to do, so he sat and stared at her like a podge. Why was she crying?

He struggled for words. "Look... I'm sorry. For whatever you're on about."

He sat and waited, deep discomfort tramping around his chest. June shook her head slowly, flinching as she strained the wound on her neck.

"No?"

She pointed to the ruins, frustration crumpling her features.

"I looked through every pile after we found you," Taein lied. "There's nothing but ash. What could you even want here?"

She collapsed right back into silent despair. The sight of her, this bloodied, vicious little thing, crying her eyes out without a sound, was so disturbing that Taein couldn't help but look away. He dropped his eyes to his muddied boots and just let her cry.

I wish someone else would've found her, he thought, *I wish we never would've recovered her at all.*

"Well, have it out now I guess. We're leaving just as soon as my friend gets back."

June shook her head, reaching for a small, half charred stick Taein had been using to prod the fire. In the dirt, she wrote, *Mama said go to House Light.*

Taein laughed as he fetched a water-stained pad of paper and a pen from his pack. "You can't possibly mean the *Ersiin* House Light."

She looked at him with no small disgust and snatched the writing instruments, slapping the pad down in the mud and stabbing the pen at the parchment. The letters were cramped and crooked, but he could make out her sentences with some trouble.

Never been to Farthing, she wrote. *Only the big city and the Rich Man's house. And your house that smelled bad. I never left home before it happened.*

"What's happened?" he asked.

This is my <u>home</u>. She wrote and underlined the word three times. *The Raincloak Man came two weeks ago and burned our home and my Mama. He killed everything.*

Taein stilled. "You lived here?"

Yes.

"Sig and his boys weren't the ones who trashed this joint? It was already burned?"

June wrote, slowly and deliberately, underlining the important parts.

The Raincloak Man burned everything except me. Then the other man and the nice lady found me and took me to the big city with the Rich Man, Regor. And he gave me to you, and then the men with horses tried to take me but I ran away back home. They followed and saw me.

"And then what happened?"

She clammed up, stopped writing.

"Did you do it on purpose?"

She looked down, hugging her legs to her chest.

"Or were you just... scared?"

She nodded once.

"And then things got out of hand, didn't they?"

Another nod.

Taein could tell she needed a moment, so he stopped prodding. Something far worse than the thought of her crazy plant powers was making Taein squirm in the dirt where he sat.

From the moment they'd entered this little burned-out settlement, Taein had felt *his* presence in his very bones, as if the hunter marked the earth he walked upon with every step. The scene was too familiar, it had been from the start.

"You're absolutely, positively sure that your mama knew someone at House Light? *The* House Light?" Taein asked.

Mama said find Lady Marguerite, she wrote, swiping away her tears.

"Well, I sure as sweet hell won't be taking you there."

June stared, eyes blank. *Why not? Mama said the people in House Light are friends. She told me if I ever got lost, go there. She <u>said so</u>.*

"You have no idea how far away that is, do you?"

She concentrated on writing. *Where are you going that's so important? You were supposed to take me somewhere anyway.*

"None of your business, that's where."

She looked up from the dirt at him, glaring, and then wrote, *Idiot.*

"You're a fresh one, aren't you?"

Her jaw clenched and she scribbled for a long while.

Don't want help. You + the Giant are in a hurry. You just go, then I'll find Raincloak Man and go to Lady Marguerite on my own. Where is my knife?

He bit back a laugh. "I don't think you quite understand the nature of the man who 'did this'. Did he have a strange white bird?"

The hatred that flashed across her face chilled Taein to the bone. June nodded once.

There it was. Confirmation.

What's he doing, roaming around again? Is he... he couldn't be. The hunter thought Taein was dead. There was no way Taein would've lived this long if the hunter had any notion of his existence.

But somehow the Outlander had gotten a notion of more Anathema roaming around. With a shanking bounty for his own life hanging from his neck, it wasn't too hard to assume the hunter had the same intel.

And if that really was the case, they were totally, irrefutably *shanked.*

Taein bit back a barrage of curses and explained. "Then that's the same man who killed my family and wrecked everything I ever had. So you can forget about that little pipe dream, kid. He hates people like you and me and makes it his business to burn us dead or alive."

She blew out an angry breath. *I don't care.*

"You will when he starts hacking at you. You think Sig and his boys tore you a new one? Wait until you get a taste of the hunter's handiwork."

She ignored his question, scrawled a quick sentence, and then stared him down.

You lived, she'd written.

Something clenched tight in his chest, but Taein managed to give her a small smile. "I was lucky."

For the first time, the kid was looking at him with something other than contempt. *But you lived. How?*

Inside, that cold constant *something* that was always twisting around Taein's ribcage pulled a little tighter.

"I ran away."

The contempt was back. June didn't write a response, instead opting to ignore him and trying to get to her feet with slow, careful movements.

"Look, I'm not going to let you go and track him down. If you ever found him he'd kill you in an instant, and I sure as hell don't need that on whatever's left of my conscience."

She tossed a contemptuous glower toward him, making it unsteadily to her feet. The injured leg trembled from her slight weight.

"No chance we can take you to House Light," he said, "We're going where there's marks to be had."

She stared at him for far too long, eyes burning like the white-blue flame of a candle, before shaking her head.

Taein scoffed. "What, you think you've got a choice? Besides, it'll be an adventure. Your first one ever, what fun!"

She shook her head again, face pinched into a tight grimace, and began hobbling down the hillside toward the piles.

Taein stood and caught her wrist and barely managed to hang on against the wave of anxiety that shot straight through his gut. Not that it took much—the kid stopped, shoulders sinking, eyes still glued to the wreckage. After a moment she hung her head and gave a little sigh.

Taein sensed an opportunity and softened his voice. "Your mother wanted you to go somewhere safe, did she not?"

The kid's shoulders sunk even lower.

"Then the Outlander is your best bet."

June turned and faced him before scrabbling for the pen. She lowered herself gingerly to the ground and then wrote with fury.

I don't care. I'll find the Raincloak Man. You are a coward and an idiot and I don't even want your help. I just want my knife back.

He brushed away the insults. "Cowards survive. And how do you even know I have your knife? Maybe you lost it."

Her glare only deepened. The pen flew as she further punished the pad.

The rich man said your job is to steal things from people. So of course you have my knife.

"Maybe I do. What's a kid need with a knife, anyway?"

More scribbling. *You only want to help me to make <u>yourself</u> feel better, don't you?*

Taein stilled. "Trust me, the only thing that would make *me* feel better is ditching you on the spot and finding a new job that ends with me *distinctly* richer." He paused, patience running thin. "Besides, you're too little to know anything about the world, much less about me."

June started signing and stopped just as fast, hands quaking, rage glinting in those bog-child eyes. She went still, sat upright on her knees, her jaw clenching and unclenching as if she was chewing on the words she could not voice. Her entire body shook before she exploded back into motion, snatching the pen back up and scrawling *<u>I know I want my Mama back.</u>*

She underlined each word three times, so hard the pen almost snapped.

Taein faltered. The only person he ever truly loved was Ruein and perhaps sometimes his father, in the same silent, begrudging way Taein assumed his father loved him. But a mother... he didn't know what to say.

June choked in breath after breath, trying not to cry, and sat in the dirt.

"For what it's worth, I really am sorry."

More scribbling. *I don't want your <u>sorry</u>. It's not fair."*

"What is?" Taein looked away as she started sobbing again. He watched the sun glide through the sky as the day ebbed away, his heart tightening and tightening.

He never let himself cry for anyone like this, not even Ruein. He kept his grief stuffed in the back of his mind alongside all the guilt and the shame and the hurt. He'd kept it all down so deep for so long he didn't think he could feel anything at all anymore, not even if he tried.

But really, what did it matter? There was no room in the world for the immensity of grief. It plain took up too much space.

But even so, Taein just picked at the grass and let her weep.

THE KID WAS ASLEEP AGAIN—CRUMPLED UP AND SNORING underneath Taein's coat—by the time Vince finally came back.

"You sure took your sweet time." Taein said as Vince swung down from his draft.

Vince flung a burlap sack over his shoulder and grinned. "I finally got my Teffold Valley brew! There ain't more than an hundred grown men in that whole village and still the line was out the tavern door and back the alley—"

Taein narrowed his eyes. "Of *course* you did. We don't have any time to spare and you've gone and spent the whole day chasing booze—"

Vince chuckled. "Settle down now, it ain't like that. I had to wait hours for the village leech to get the medicines ready." He opened up the sack and pulled out a few bottles. "One for staving off infection and the other for sealing wounds."

Taein grabbed one and peered through the violet-tinted glass at the murky liquid inside. "How much?"

"Ten and a half-mark each."

Taein scoffed. "Roadside robbery."

"That's a good idea, boss. If we run out of marks on the road," Vince said as he finished picketing his draft. "Speaking of, we need to talk about the job."

Taein glanced at where the kid was sleeping before sitting down himself. "What about it?"

Vince arched a brow. "Where we're taking her that's not the Outlander, obviously."

Taein set his jaw. "Look, I found out some things about the kid while you were gone. None of which are good."

Vince folded his arms behind his head and leaned back against his saddle. "Shoot."

"This was her old village, Vince. She ran off before Sig got ahold of her, and when he caught up she accidentally revealed her powers, I'm guessing. Then they attacked, and she killed them all. But they lived here, in hiding. Some man came and burned the whole joint down a month ago and killed her mother, so she's got nobody."

"Figured as much," Vince said. "No one in Farthing knew a thing about her."

Taein grimaced. "The only person her mother wanted her taken to just so happens to be *the* Lady Marguerite of House Light. All the way in shanking Ersii."

"Not exactly on the way to... wait a minute. Where were we headed, Taein? Regor didn't tell me, just said east of the Pearl."

"Well, we *were* heading to Efriel Shu."

Vince chuckled. "Ha. Funny."

"Deadass, Vince. That's why he sent you with me, in case I ran into whatever Ka-el and Venny did. I'm the only scrapper he's got who will do the job."

Vince sat up. "You're kidding. Tell me you're kidding."

Taein shrugged. "Not like it matters now."

Vince opened his mouth, searched for words, and swore. "This is because Regor's mad at me about the door incident, isn't it? It was a shanking *accident*!"

"Count the marks if you're lucky enough to get them and quit complaining." Taein leaned back on his elbows and shoved away a wash of dread. "Based on what the kid told me and my prior... *run-ins* with similar situations, I'm pretty sure the man who killed my whole family is the same man who attacked June and killed whoever else was here."

Vince went still, his eyes boring into Taein's with an unexpected intensity. "The king of shankin' Faeriel? You can't be serious. What... what's he doing *here*?"

Taein struggled under the weight of Vince's gaze. "I'm trusting you because I don't have a choice here, Vincent," he said, toying with a fraying fingertip on his left glove. "I'm pretty sure the hunter doesn't know that I'm still alive. If he's lurking around we gotta get a move on before he gets wind of my name. The kid said all this went down a month ago, but I got a bad feeling."

Vince furrowed his brow as Taein caught the slightest hint of sweat glinting on his forehead. "You're saying he could be hunting you? Why?"

Taein stared at Vince, and Vince stared right back as his fog of confusion slowly drained away.

"Oh," he said. "So you weren't lying, back then in the rithouse."

Taein didn't say anything, just stared Vince down for a long while.

"I'm saying the hunter is after *Anathema,*" Taein said after the pause became too excruciating. "I think he stumbled on her home by chance... but if he gets a hint of... my existence, he'll burn the whole world down just to put a sword through my back."

Vince swallowed hard. "What's the plan, then?"

"We take the kid to the Outlander. Make the trip fast and quiet."

Vince shook his head. "No, we take the kid to Ersii."

Taein laughed. "We're sure as shank not abandoning the job."

It was Vince's turn to get tough. "We're not taking the kid to the Outlander, either."

A long, tense moment passed. Taein glared at Vince, Vince glared right back.

Taein gritted his teeth. "Well... what if we dump her off at Myrtle's?"

"Who the hell is Myrtle?" Vince asked.

"This old crone who runs an orphanage nearby."

"How do *you* know about some orphanage way out in the sticks?"

Taein shrugged. "Regor sent me there a good while back."

Vince narrowed his eyes. "What for, Taein?"

"It was just a little pick—"

Vince cut Taein off with a burst of disbelieving sputters. "For shank's sake!"

Taein rolled his eyes. "Oh, please, you've worked for Regor twice as long as me, don't go feigning morality now."

"What the hell did you even steal?"

"Unimportant. What *is* important is our plan. Getting her to Myrtle's shouldn't set us back more than three days, four at most. Then we'll find a substitute, I'll still be rich, and you'll regain the old man's favor. Then both of us get what we want."

"That's a bad plan." Vince said, shaking his head. "That still means we're handing *a* kid over to the Outlander."

"He'll soon find out our substitute is a fake and toss her back to the streets, I'm sure. What's it even matter? I don't see you offering up any brilliant suggestions."

Vince frowned. "What if our kid has a family in Ersii? She might not ever get to them if we don't—"

Taein shook his head. "That's my final offer, Vince. It's the orphanage or Outlander."

"Are you really this terrible?"

"Yes!" Taein threw his hands up. "Look, Vince. We dump her off and conjure up a new fake Anathema. *That's* how you and me get what we want, and you don't bruise your little conscience."

Vince went quiet. At last he shrugged and finally spoke. "Well, I reckon so."

Taein narrowed his eyes. "You don't agree."

"I didn't say that."

"Yes, but you obviously don't."

"Well, I'm not obligated to like it, Taein. Just to go along with it."

Silence swept in as the sky continued to gray toward darkness. Taein turned the bottle of medicine over in his hands, mindlessly tracing the engravings running down the sides of the glass. His hands were cold even beneath his battered gloves.

I hate this, he thought. But in truth, he'd always known this day would come.

You can't hide forever.

Taein frowned and trained his eyes back onto Vince, trying to puzzle out his character, to sift through what made Vince *Vince,* besides the beard and tattoos and bulk. He'd always trusted Vince more than the other bruisers, trackers, scrappers, and bounty-hunters in Regor's service, but never stopped long enough to really ask himself *why.* Was it because he'd run with Ka-el for so long, and there was no one more moral than Ka-el in the whole city? Was it because he knew that when Vince was off the job he slept more than a cat? That laziness was a virtue in Taein's eyes. It was the ambitious, hungry scrappers that made him nervous back in the city. He understood that hunger all too well. What he *didn't* understand was Vince's quiet, subdued ways.

Maybe that was a good thing.

Taein uncapped the disinfectant and soaked the rag before walking over to the kid.

"You're doing the right thing, you know. At least sort-of," Vince added as Taein began to dab at the wound on the kid's neck.

"Yeah?"

"Yeah." Vince withdrew an apple from his pack. "It's just, usually you don't go miles near the right thing."

"Figured I'd give everything a go at least once," Taein said.

Vince nodded. "Well, I think this will be a nice change of pace. Especially if we take her where she really belongs."

"Which is an orphanage, considering the marked absence of both parental units. I truly am a saint."

"If saints cut corners for the sake of marks," Vince grumbled.

"Hey, it's your ass as well as mine, pal. Returning to the Pearl without marks won't be putting us on Regor's good graces, and that's leaving the Outlander's wrath out to begin with."

Vince went quiet, and Taein left him to it. He looked down at the kid in the fading light. Her skin was still so very gray, her breathing so shallow.

What if she dies, and this is all for naught?

Taein scoffed and dismissed the thought. All the more reason to not waste the time it'd take to haul her to House Light.

Still, he found himself looking at the amulet around her neck. A little sunflower was painted on this disc, the yellow petals distorted by blotches of dark blood. Taein brushed at the splatters with his thumb, but they'd already stained deep.

Taein sighed. She was just a kid, after all. No matter how filthy and feral.

"I certainly hope you appreciate all this effort," he grumbled, and went back to treating her wounds.

THE WASTES

Vasily rode harder than ever before, each day just a blur, the sky above cycling through periods of light and dark, the earth hard and unforgiving as it rolled away beneath his mare's drumming hooves. The pain radiating from his mauled legs was a far-away thing, dulled by the force of his fixation on the destination ahead.

The mists are falling.

What would that mean for his family? For Faeriel, no less? He was only one man. Who was to say there wasn't a whole army of mist-altered men and half-decomposed Shallows behind those lowering gray walls, just waiting for their chance to re-enter a world long since lost to them?

Vasily shook his head and leaned forward to twine his fingers in his mare's sooty mane, his back aching from days of cantering across the countryside. Cold air whipped his cheeks, drew tears from his eyes. It'd been long since he'd last slept. Too long to even remember anymore.

He didn't care. He was too *close* to care—the rolling, wooded hills and torrential rains of Nown Jin were long behind, as was the lush Nujin Valley and its scattering of rice farms that marked the beginning of the Vandal Province. It wouldn't be long at all before the mists would rear up on the horizon, a distant, towering wall of gray smog some thirteen stories high and three times as thick.

But first came the Wastes.

Vasily bit back an oath as the mare stumbled, jarring his legs. Pain splintered through him as the scabs cracked and pricks of new blood dotted his past-ruined trousers.

Almost there. He gritted his teeth and rode on.

Vasily felt the mists before he saw them.

Twelve hours had passed. The mare's neck was black with sweat, the scent mingling strangely with the dust and sage. The cracked sand floor sparkled white as snow in the dying sun, which cast a fiery crimson glow over the flat landscape as it sank low and bathed the world red.

This was the Southern Wastes, an arid desert of pale glittering sands and abysmal oceanic skies; a place where sandstorms swirled with erratic fury and the sun blazed with either cold indifference or practiced orange fury and never any manner in-between; a place where nothing much grew but craggy green sage and carpeting amber crili flowers; where the poisonous crimson arrinvale would explode into bloom at the first touch of fall and turn the salt flats of into a fragrant garden of death; a place of unparalleled and savage beauty, sacred to the Vandals and religiously avoided by most everyone else.

Vasily wasn't in the Wastes long before he felt the chill in his bones. He remembered the feeling from the only prior trip he had made to see the mists, back when he was some fifteen or sixteen years of age, and Auryn much younger. The feeling was carnal, an instinctive sense that there was *something* ahead, and that *something* bore the mark of the unnatural. The feeling was alive inside Vasily, cold, alien, and afraid, the reaction of any sane man drawing near to a site that still bore the touch Geiin's own phantasmal breath.

Vasily had been afraid when he was a boy, and he certainly was now.

He drew his mare to a halt and looked out beyond the white sand to the looming wall of gray on the horizon. The sinking sun infused the mists with an eerie, shifting crimson glow.

Vasily leaned forward, his breath catching.

"There it is."

He'd grown up on stories of the mists, like all Ierisian children. There were a thousand different legends that revolved around the wall, as many different accounts of how it got there and what it contained as there were years in Ieris' history, and yet they all still held tight to a pair of singular, unopposed truths.

The first truth taught that the mists were brought down by Geiin himself, a claim that was as good as irrefutable. Even some hundreds of miles off, Vasily could feel the mark of *his* presence. No natural thing held that sort of power.

The other truth regarded just *what* Geiin had decided to contain— or rather, *who.*

Vasily was also brought up on stories of the Four Fathers, long before he knew to fear their presence in the supposedly free world he lived in. He knew the tales of their miraculous origin, their immense and unthinkable power, their rise and world-ending fall. And even when he knew the Four Fathers with a child's blind perception, before he ever felt the cold power that was the mark of Geiin's touch on the land or seen that same unrivaled power in a living, breathing man, he was afraid. And really, there wasn't a single child who *wasn't* afraid of Lithriin, the ancient king of death, who was universally rumored to still live within the cage Geiin himself had made. The fallen Father who dwelled in the Southern Mists.

When Vasily had first seen that cage as a child, he had been struck by the vastness of the mists. His father had caught him gaping and leaned down from atop his destrier.

"Geiin looked down and found his own creation so fearsome that he built it a cage with walls some ten miles thick and three hundred feet tall. Can you believe that, Vasily?"

Vasily remembered having to swallow the boulder in his throat before he could answer. *"He must've been a terrible man, Babas. The Lord of Night."*

Babas laughed then, a deep, rolling sound, rich like the dark forest soil of their homeland, a sound which had always filled Vasily with incredible warmth.

"Lithriin wasn't a mere man, boy," father had said. *"Geiin doesn't throw common mortals like us in prisons of supernatural mist. Geiin caged Lithriin because he was more."*

Vasily looked to Auryn then, expecting to find her staring with the same wide eyes as him, her mouth agape, paralyzed with the shock he'd felt when Headmaster Mikaels first told him of the Four Fathers.

Instead, Auryn smiled when he looked at her, curiosity behind the paper-thin veil of apprehension in her eyes, nimble fingers toying with a fray in her braided reins.

But that was just Auryn—always brave, always sure in her storms, sure in her doldrums. The only time Vasily ever remembered seeing his sister afraid, *truly* afraid, was when he left her behind at House Light.

Now something different gripped Vasily's heart. How long had it been now, some eight years since? Nine? He was losing count.

Something else caught his attention. Vasily raised his eyes to the East and squinted. Far in the distance were two great plums of smoke —no, three. Were Vandel cities burning?

No, they couldn't be. Vandel would've called for help in the event of a crisis of that magnitude, to be sure. They would've used the Copper Fires, lit the aid-towers all the way to Faeriel. Vandel would never burn alone. Vandel would never burn in the first place.

Vasily looked back up to the distant gray wall and searched for Auryn's strength as he spurred the bay forward. Stars knew he needed it.

The mare trotted off, hooves kicking up sand, but something was amiss. Her steps jarred with uncertainty as she gazed ahead, ears pricked. Vasily drew her to a stop just as a shrill whinny priced the air.

He froze in the saddle. His mare was silent as ever and stayed frozen. Her nostrils flared as she sampled the breeze, and Vasily knew they were no longer alone on the Wastes.

He twisted in the saddle and saw a distant cloud rising toward the right. He instinctively booted the mare into a gallop before catching himself and spinning her back around. The land stretched endless every direction, a flat white expanse rapidly dimming in the absence of the sun. Where could he go? The bay was largely spent, he'd never run her this hard nor for this long. And even if they tried to escape, there was nowhere to hide and even less a chance of outrunning presumably fresh horses.

He wheeled her back around to face the growing cloud of dust with a curse.

Vandels. What in Geiin's name could they want? The Vandels were never fond of foreigners traipsing about their sacred Wastes, but it wasn't as if passing through was unheard of. Ambassadors and sentries from the other realms were often sent to check on the mists for their respective lords some several times a year.

Vasily watched as the Vandels, trilling and hollering, crossed the expanse in what seemed like only a few short breaths, turning from distant clouds of dust to discoverable shapes—some thirty or forty men, astride the slender, hot-blooded Venrian horses whose ancestors they stole from Siou stock hundreds of years prior.

Vasily held still, waiting as the distant murmur of hoofbeats became a rolling thunder he felt in his very chest, waiting as the cloud of dust blew toward him and coated his clothes, his hair, his face, *waiting*, uncertain and already unamused with the situation, until he realized that *they weren't going to stop*.

With a bolt of splitting panic, Vasily whirled his mare around and kicked her into a gallop. She sprung forward, straining to devour ground as the riders bore down behind them, shouting in Venrian, their clothes dim flashes of purple, orange, and red beneath the cloud of dust.

He didn't make it more than six strides away before the Vandels cut him off, encircling him in a second. He spun the bay in a tight circle and bit back a barrage of curses. Someone ripped him from his saddle before he could regain control of his mare and threw him down. He landed hard on sand, barely comprehending what the hell was happening, and struggled to his knees before a boot met his back and he found himself pressed face-down on the Waste flats, breathing snow-colored sand and tasting salt as a fit of white-hot anger flickered to life inside and melted away his former fear.

That anger was snuffed out like a half-used candle when a second boot connected with his temple. Vasily toppled headfirst into the black, out before his eyes even shut.

BACK WHEN HE WAS A BOY OF EIGHT, VASILY BECAME OBSESSED WITH the Vandel Province.

The Province was something of a conundrum, really—the land the Vandel's occupied as their own actually still belonged to Nown Jin, and therefore House Ring, and had ever since the Vandels first created Sheffal, the Shifting City on the Green Grass Sea, and stole a band of horses from Efriel Shu.

Both feats were a thing to behold, really. Back then, the southern portion of Nown Jin was an unoccupied wasteland made up of stinking marshlands home to a million and a half insects and a snow-colored desert only the hardiest, most poisonous plants could call their own; and Efriel Shu was the most powerful realm in Ieris, running with a calvary unchallenged.

But up came the Vandels, then led by the long-defeated Westerlys who had once called House Ring their own, and they *changed* things, making the marshlands of the untamed South a trading paradise and rooting their capital cities deep in the Waste. They acclimated to the poisons, fended off the harsh weather, grew tall gleaming castles and high sacred cities and spice gardens and a whole new way of life where there once had been nothing but sand and bloody arrinvale and a looming mist behind. They were *strength from nothing,* as their national motto became.

Vasily had always thought these accomplishments wonderfully bold and unique, especially when his own way of life had been the same ever since the Old Men first settled in the Faeish mountains and banded together under the common banner of Faerran the Pine Cleaver, a largely unchanging cycle of family, clan, house, and country, no matter who occupied the House Atop the Mountain or how harshly the long winters raged.

But shortly after, Vasily learned about the Enti and their Mist Exchange. Learned just what the Enti *did* with Mists.

He was eleven the day he decided that the Vandels were nothing but packs of hypocritical sand rats protected by a group of honorless body traders with spears, still a boy, still fueled with the black and white morality that made up the Faeish way of life.

He was near thirty now, and his morality had long since muddied and grown gray. He was older and he was *tired*, and he had just woken with the red-dusted tip of one of those accursed Enti spears stuck directly in his face.

Vasily struggled to focus his eyes, his head still spinning as he surfaced from the black. Waves of Venrian chatter went silent as another pair of boots hit the sand. Vasily struggled, sand between his teeth, and tried to free himself as the boots approached.

He wondered if he was about to be beheaded without so much as a word, when a voice cut through the newborn silence.

"*Bruhalsa onya.*"

Hands clamped down on his shoulders and hauled him onto his knees. Vasily threw his hair back and met the black-steel gaze of a Vandel no older than himself, his tanned face marred with a scar that stretched from temple to chin.

The man wore a rich, multicolor cowl beneath a white leather breastplate cut through with a singular crimson stripe. An arrinvale blossom was tattooed atop both hands—the mark of an Enti. Vasily stared at the swirling black arrinvale petals etched into the man's skin, and realized how utterly *damned* he was.

The man's hair, braided in a long, glossy rope down his back, swung forward as he crouched down to Vasily's level. He just looked for a long while, his dark eyes impassible.

Vasily spat sand and glared. "Are you in command of this unit?"

The corner of the man's lip quirked as he straightened and nodded to the men behind Vasily. Instantly, they knocked Vasily back into the sand and resumed the beating. Vasily tried to struggle up, only to get shoved back down as *another* boot caught him in the face. Stars exploded in his vision and he curled in on himself, choking on the blood that was pouring from his nose and his mouth. He wasn't sure if he'd bit his tongue or lost half his teeth—both, perhaps.

The beating stopped as abruptly as it began and the silence swept back in, broken only by the shifting of horses and Vasily's own gasping breaths. At length he regained control of himself enough to struggle onto his hands and knees and look up to the commander.

The commander was still watching, brow tight, jaw set.

"What the hell do you want with me?" Vasily bit out. "Do you know who I am?"

The commander looked to the closest soldier and spoke a few words in Venrian. Vasily fought hard to concentrate, but before he could decipher a thing the commander turned back to him and spoke in perfect, heavily accented Jinian, the foreign words oddly sharp on his lilting tongue.

"You are trespassing, *stajerno*."

"I have my reasons."

The commander smirked. "As do all." He assessed Vasily for a long moment before speaking again. "You are Faeish."

Vasily glared. "I'm the *king* of the Faeish."

The commander's dark eyebrows flew up as open amusement curved his tan features. "Sure, *you're* the Unseen King, standing before me in peasant's clothes."

"I'm on a most sacred mission—"

The man cut Vasily off with a burst of laughter. "Next to no one has seen Vasily Miinriel in some seven years, and you expect me to believe that he's meandering through the Waste, soaked in blood upon a half-dead horse? You would do well to listen to yourself before you speak."

Before he could answer, a pair of Enti descended and riffled through each and every pocket. Vasily shoved down the urge to plow his fist into the nearest one as the soldier withdrew Glass' stolen amulet and tossed it to his commander, who caught it and tucked the rosewood into his coat with little care.

Vasily set his jaw so hard he thought he might crack a tooth before speaking, taking time to summon every ounce of patience his father had ever instilled within him. "I swear to you, I *am* Vasily Miinriel."

The commander scoffed. "Right. We will take you to the Shade, *Vasily Miinriel,* check you for the disease, and let her decide whether you live or die. If you resist now, we will leave your body for the *raz-jyala.*" He smiled, an odd gleam in his dark gaze. "The shadow-dogs."

Vasily paled and started to struggle to his feet. "You will do no such thing. You—"

"Wait."

Vasily waited, halfway to his feet, his heart spasming in his chest. The commander withdrew Glass's amulet, turned it over in his palm.

He lifted his eyes to Vasily. "This is a Siou amulet."

Vasily's eyes snatched to the tiny horse painted in black in the amulet's center. He nodded, holding the commander's eyes.

"I took it from a Prince of Glass myself."

The commander's gaze flickered with a strange light. "You... took their amulets?"

"Every last one."

The commander looked back to the amulet, caressed the faded horse atop the rosewood with a gentleness out of place amid his fierce figure.

"Please, if you would *listen*—" Vasily's voice rose as the commander, moving slowly as if to exaggerate each motion, bent down and ripped Vasily's own amulet right from his chest.

"You cannot!" he bit out, throwing himself against the soldiers restraining him.

The Enti commander turned Vasily's snowy amulet over in his palm, the once-pristine disc now splattered with dirt and stained with old blood, before tucking it into the same pocket in which he put Glass'. He grinned at Vasily.

Vasily glared back, something inhuman broiling up, trying to claw out of his throat. "*Give. Them. Back.*"

"If you pass the Shade's examination, I shall."

Vasily lunged forward. "You gutless—"

He found himself immediately cut off by the touch of cool steel at his neck. He clamped his mouth shut, rage brewing in his gut, blood oozing from his temple, and let himself be hauled toward the bay. An Enti swapped the mare's bridle for a rope halter as another forced Vasily up into the saddle and set about binding his hands to the saddle horn and legs to the stirrups. Vasily waited, that pale fury broiling beneath his skin.

"Do we hood him?" A soldier asked as the commanding Enti swung up into the saddle.

He glanced back. Vasily felt the commander's challenge and did not look away.

"No," he said at length. "He is *Faeish*, Bahkal. His eyes already see nothing."

Coarse laughter rippled through the group and Vasily trembled with rage, the rough rope binding his hands to the saddle horn biting into his skin.

As suddenly as they had descended, the Vandels sprung into a canter and hurried back the way they came. Vasily, a prisoner atop his own horse, was towed after them, away from the mists, and *away from Glass*.

❧ 19 ❧

AN INNOCENT MAN

The night swept down and blanketed the white sands with heavy darkness, dusted through by a scattering of minuscule stars so small they seemed like white insects awash in an unending sea of ink. Vasily kept his eyes on the heavens as the Vandels rode on, his aching body jostled relentlessly by his worn-out mare's shambling gait, his face caked with blood and the taste of iron seared on his tongue. He searched for his father in those stars, but it wasn't long before a cloud cover blew in and stole away the small comfort.

Vasily lowered his eyes to watch the sand fall away beneath his mare's hooves, overcome by exhaustion and rage, and listened to the rolling hoofbeats and the soft creaking of leather instead of the murmuring talk of the Vandels in their lilting foreign tongue.

The complete darkness was eventually broken by a distant glow of orange torchlight that promised a coming civilization. Vasily opened his eyes and watched as the group entered a war encampment made up of hundreds of red-canvas tents, the settlement lit by orange torches and populated exclusively by Enti brothers. The group split up, half of the riders breaking off toward the center where Vasily caught a glimpse of a corral, while the second half rode straight on toward the northernmost edge.

As they neared, Vasily caught the sound of weeping, and that simmering rage inside faltered.

Before a trio of great black tents stood a long line of iron cages, some five feet tall and twenty feet wide. Inside those cages were a gaggle of men, women and children, all of them obviously Vandels and sorted in no discernible order. The smell of piss and unwashed bodies hung in the air like a thick cloud of fear.

Vasily didn't have time to more than glance at the cages before the Enti stopped and dismounted. A trio of soldiers descended upon him and hauled him off his mare, who another guard led away toward the corrals.

Vasily realized then that they intended to cage *him*, and the fire inside rose to a roar.

He dug his heels into the sand and threw his elbow into the Enti on his left, ripping his arm away the moment the man's grip loosened. He swung at the guard on his right and caught the man in the jaw, feeling his knuckles split open just as the third guard booted him in the gut and threw him on his back. Vasily reared up, gasping for air and searching for solid footing, only to catch the butt of a spear to the side of his temple. He crumpled down, bright lights flashing behind his eyes for the second time that day, and felt a scream tear from his mouth as the world turned to black again.

When Vasily jolted awake, the darkness was dimming toward morning and iron was pressing into his back.

He lifted his head from his chest with a groan and looked up.

He'd never been in a cage before. There was blood crusting in his hair and on his clothes. Around him, the gentle morning sounds of the camp awakening were just beginning to break the night's quiet—pots and pans clattered, food sizzled over fires, water sloshed in wooden buckets, voices murmured and laughed, steel grated against whetstones. Each noise felt like a blow to his aching head as a kind of exhaustion he hadn't felt in ages clung to him like a black fog. He leaned his head back against the bars and sighed, allowing his eyes to slip back shut. He could hear the other captives shifting in their cages and an occasional cough or sniffle, but no one dared to speak.

He groaned and reached for his amulet, only to grasp at nothing. A chill settled over him, and he dropped his hand back to his side.

Father, why am I here?

Really, why were *any* of them here?

He opened his eyes and looked at the other prisoners crammed in the neighboring cages. A motley mix of men, women, and children, all Vandels, their features all proud high cheekbones, smooth tan skin, haughty dark eyes. Other than that, there was no commonality among them—there were men in the rich, loose garb of black market tradesmen and men in the worn clothes of the Nujiin farmers, there were women in scanty, shifting silk *kelyas* the color of ripe summer fruits and women in pale lavender shawls that covered them head to toe. There were wide-eyed, well-dressed children, their bright clothes soiled, and dirtier children made of sharp edges who seemed to make the better-dressed ones cringe back into the worse corners. There was even an Enti brother sitting cramped in the very back of an overcrowded cage, his eyes closed and body trembling. A small boy was curled next to him, his head resting on the soldier's knee.

Vasily's ringing head couldn't decipher what the *ever-loving hell* was going on. Perhaps the caged Enti was a deserter? But that still did not justify the other Vandel citizens. Surely, these were not victims of the Mist Exchange—these looked like everyday, average people after a week without baths or proper toilets. Not the sort that deserved eternal banishment.

If learning about the Shaff Army was the beginning of Vasily's childhood obsession with the Vandel Province, learning about the Enti and their accursed *Mist Exchange* was its end.

It was old GrandMaestor Hordon who taught him all he knew about the Vandels. He taught Vasily of the Shaf Army, made up of thousands of mounted soldiers loyal to Vandel Crown, famous for their tradition of riding into battle without armor or shields of any kind, save for silver wrist-guards. An army where men became brothers and rode in the harshest conditions known to man under the bright savage sun and the grim shade cast by Southern Mists, all for the betterment of their people. The Shaf were great, fighting with their long spears and light, fast horses. They were brave, noble, good men. Vasily *idolized* them. He got his own long spear and learned how to use it atop his own horse, and for many more months the obsession continued unhindered.

Vasily then graduated to learning about the *Bavarti* and the *Jal*, and the divide that split the province into the clean and the common, the sacred and the sinful. The Bavarti was a caste made up of Venrian royalty, mages, and priests. They alone were allowed in the sacred Wastes, while the Jal, the working class, kept to their scams and scandals elsewhere. The separation made sense to Vasily and in no way affected his desire to pack up his mountain-dwelling life and leave the family he was born to protect to go join the Shaf. It was when Maestor Hordon turned to page. 768 of *Narnarth's History and Atlas of Ieris* and began to read in his slow gravel voice about the *Enti* that Vasily's dream finally went crashing out of the sky and died.

The Enti too fought with Venrian spears, he learned, and they rode horses just like the Shaf. Enti and Shaf often rode together, in times of war.

That was where any similarities ended.

The Enti were not an army of discipline and sacrifice, but instead a lot of honorless bastards who spent their sorry existences blood-bound to their savage-born brotherhood, dipping their long spears in ruddy arrinvale powder to poison their enemies, breath-sworn to the sorcery of Order Maage and *not* the royal family, serving as border guards to keep the unclean out of the Wastes—*except* for those brought in for the Mist Exchange, the management of which was the chief duty of this accursed group of murderers, marauders, and men without honor.

The Mist Exchange was what the Enti named their practice of taking in live criminals and Shallows alike from all over Ieris and disposing of them in the Southern Mists, along with the obligatory legions of unwanted, uncared for Sleepers they were also paid to get rid of. Dumping these criminals, lost spirits, and half-dead alike inside the mist to wither and rot and to turn into strange, altered creatures, instead of allowing them the simple mercy of a Long Wait. It wasn't as though any of these people were Anathema. They were simply unwanted. And even as a child, Vasily knew that disposing of them this way was wrong.

In Faeriel, any criminal guilty of a capital offense met his father's own sword, swung by Lord Slate himself. The body would be embalmed with its amulet and disposed of with honor and dignity, not left to contort into something *cursed*, to add to a looming problem that Vasily's father once eyed with great concern.

To Vasily, the Mist Exchange was worse than despicable, worse than cruel. It was *dishonorable*. And for the Enti—and all of Vandel, really—to profit from such an honorless practice, was far too much.

Thinking too long on the subject only intensified Vasily's nausea, so he closed his eyes again until the soft pad of boots approaching his cage piqued his interest.

The commanding Enti had exited one of the large black tents and was walking down the line of cages, pausing now and then to examine the silent occupants. Vasily wondered what had stilled them so, while he was unconscious.

At last, the commander stopped before Vasily's cage and looked in. Vasily sat up straight against the bars and met the man's eyes.

After a moment the Enti spoke in Jinian, his voice sharp and melodic.

"You asked me when we took you captive whether I knew you," he began, "and I called you by your race. I must know your true name now, *stajerno*. No games."

Vasily drew his knees up, rested his arms upon them, and leaned forward to stretch his aching back. He looked up to the commander. "I've already told you."

The commander's eyes flickered with suppressed amusement. "You choose to maintain the lie?"

Vasily slid up his sleeve and revealed his silver cuff. "I choose to speak the truth."

"Let it be so. I am Rafael Argen, Third Hand to Next-Aal Llewryn Selle, commander of the Sand Brotherhood, the Order Enti." He didn't bother to look at the cuff but once before lowering himself down on the sand and crossing his legs. When he had settled, he spoke again, quietly and conversational, as if they were discussing politics over a polite dinner.

"I am glad we have not yet killed you, *Lord Slate*. My Aal does not crave war with Faeriel, nor does my sacred Order Maage."

"Giving my amulets back would be a good start to ensure things stay civil. What do you want with me?"

Rafael brushed a few pale grains of sand from his pants. "That will be decided once you have seen the Shade."

"And who the hell might they be?"

Rafael looked up, one dark brow arching and pulling at the tight, pink skin of his scar. "You really do not know? She has not visited you?"

Vasily gritted his teeth. "I have been traveling on business of the highest importance for weeks now. Until this point, I have not *visited* with anyone."

Rafael smiled. "Well, I hope you will not have to wait long."

"As do I, for your sake."

That earned a chuckle from Rafael, which sent a wave of heat washing through Vasily as if he had just taken a draught of especially strong ale.

Rafael, still smiling, shook his head and looked up to meet Vasily's gaze. "Do you remember the fall of House Glass?"

Vasily felt his brows pull together as something sunk inside. "Of course. I was there."

"*Vasily Miinriel* was there," Rafael corrected. "Whether you are him remains to be seen. But regardless... I did not have the privilege of witnessing such a spectacle as he, a fact which I rued for many years. I was twenty years old then, perhaps a little older, and you were around the same age, yes?" A glimmer came about his dark eyes. "I heard about what you did there, if you are who you say you are. How you burnt the House, the people, the realm. They killed your father and you killed in return. The natural reaction of any man in such a sad position, maybe. But then again, some would rejoice at the chance to see their fathers dissolve like that," he said with a snap of his fingers.

Vasily flinched as his heart seized with a sudden crackle of pain, the feeling so strong he thought he might throw up. Instead, it was all he could do to keep himself sitting rod-straight and silent, and hold the Enti's gaze.

Rafael spoke again as he examined his knife, something like a smile still on his face. His eyes flickered up to meet Vasily's. "Here, they call you *Aal Salava*, or 'lord of the balance'. I must admit, I was envious of you for some time, back when word of the fall of the Siou was the most interesting thing to happen in Ieris since the Outlander first washed up on Jinian shores. I wished to be in your stead back then, because sands know I would've liked to see *my* father turn to ash. But more than that, I wished for a very long time that I could've seen *them*."

The hair rose on the back of Vasily's neck.

Rafael raised his eyes to Vasily's. "The Anathema, I mean." His gaze took on a wondrous sheen. "To see the remnants of a world more savage and spectral than this empty land of iron and dust in which we are condemned to toil... the Anathema, they are remnants of a world where dragons and faeries and *Celestials* walked, living proof that Geiin himself did once stoop down and raise life with his breath. We are the dust of a mortal earth but they are the breath of the Celestial. I thought they would be..." he drew off, something sobering his gaze. "I thought they would be *more*."

Vasily felt a terrible weight descend upon him, horribly conscious of the people crammed into the cages all around. "You don't mean to tell me... it cannot be."

Rafael stared, something flickering behind his gaze. "Yes. Near all of these. We bring them to Shade in the night and she reveals to us which are, and which are not."

"It cannot be," Vasily breathed, looking wildly around at the men, women, and children sitting silently in the cages surrounding him. "But they're *your own people*. It—the line of Glass was all that remained of the Anathema."

But even as the words tumbled from his mouth, his mind was flashing back to the woman at the farm, her terrible curse. Her child, that raging little girl who undoubtedly carried the same unnatural affliction.

How many more?

Rafael tucked his knife back into its sheath and shrugged. "That is what we thought too, for many years. But then things began to shift. A squad of brothers escorting a shipment of criminals to the mists found them..." he drew off, searching for words. "The squadron leader reported finding them *shrunk*. Not much, perhaps only ten or fifteen feet, but a noticeable difference. And the mist itself was thin, weak. I thought it was lunacy, of course. So I went down to see it with my own eyes and saw that it was true. Around the same time, we began seeing strange, altered plants... wild creatures with terrible deformities, a fast-spread withering of the land. We did not know what to do or how to cure it, until the Shade came and directed our efforts to the unseen disease."

"The Anathema," Vasily supplied. "They are the reason the mists are falling."

Rafael nodded. "Why, we cannot understand. But the land has finally caught up with their presence, and it is turning against us."

"When was this?" Vasily asked.

"Some eight or nine months ago."

Vasily couldn't stop staring at the other prisoners. "Why didn't you raise the word?"

Rafael rose to his feet, brushing sand from his pants. "You may think it strange, but we hold the Wastes and the Southern Mists as our own. They are sacred to us, Miinriel, as relics of Geiin's touch. They enable a business that no other province can compete with and we rely on them like no other country to keep this near darkness at bay. The mists are a way of life. To see them fall is to see Vandel fall. We could not allow the word of this weakness to ruin everything we have built up in the face of nothing." Rafael gave a bitter smile. "When has Vandel ever needed help? We are strength from nothing. Until now, that is."

Vasily didn't know what to say. His mouth went dry with want of words, the presence of the other prisoners around him suddenly an intense, radiating heat.

He gave Vasily one last look. "Take heart. The Shade will soon see you and determine whether you are clean. For now, I have work to do." A shadow came over his face as he turned away. "The Shade has made her decisions in the dark and now I must see them through in the light of day."

Rafael rose and approached a squadron of some ten men, each heavily armored in a strange, glinting metal. Rafael said a few words and they dispersed. Vasily watched as they rolled in a massive wood round, stained dark and pocked with chips on one side. As soon as it was settled before the cages, a muffled cry rose from the inhabitants. Vasily watched, unable to move, his guts roiling, as the Enti brought out the first of the Anathema.

It was the young Enti soldier. They stripped him of his breastplate, tossing the pieces into the sand, and forced him down onto his knees. Rafael stood on the other side of the blood-stained wood round, his hands clasped behind his back. A few words were exchanged between the young soldier and the commander before Rafael gave a nod and another Enti forced the young soldier's head down. Only when his cheek touched the round did he begin to struggle, throwing his weight against the brothers who stood straining to keep him pinned down. He was repeating a single word that Vasily couldn't understand over and over, his voice rising toward hysteria.

"Angatento!"

His voice reached a new fervor as the commander's sword scraped free of its scabbard hovered aloft and flashing in the rising light. From behind, a child screamed in the cages.

Vasily felt the first signs of Waste's daytime heat beginning to eat away at the night's chill and saw the sweat darkening the young man's back as they finally forced him still, his face ground against the blood-stained round.

The sword waited in the air, the child still screaming.

Rafael spoke above the noise, arm still suspended. Waiting.

"Brother, I release you from your watch."

With that, the Enti burst into tears.

The sword came cutting down, and Vasily flinched as the Enti's right hand detached from his wrist and toppled into the sand. Blood spurted, hiding the arrinvale tattoo from Vasily's eyes.

Vasily swallowed hard as the child's screams grew more desperate.

Rafael spoke again, the sword hovering once more.

"I release you from the brotherhood."

"*No*," wept the Enti.

A second later, another black arrinvale blossom drowned in crimson as it fell upon the reddening sand.

"*Angatento*," the Enti bawled out again through his agony, smacking his forehead on the block again and again as if somehow the action could wipe out the pain, as if it could mask the stench of his own blood in the air. Vasily watched, unable to look away.

"*Angatento!*" The Enti wailed again, and Vasily finally understood.

Innocent.

"Wait!" he cried, finally coming back to himself, his heart rising in his throat. He scrambled forward and hit the bars, frantically trying to get Rafael's attention even as the commander dropped his sword into the final descending arc.

"*Wait!*" Vasily bellowed.

He flinched as the sword glanced off the side of the round, the blade cracking off a chunk of wood and smacking into the sand. Rafael shouted an oath and slammed his sword back into its scabbard before looking at Vasily. Beside him, the young Enti on the block shuddered and sobbed. Vasily realized the poor lad had pissed himself.

A silence fell over the cages, and Vasily then realized that they were all waiting for him to speak.

He swallowed hard, a sudden dryness overtaking his mouth, and raised his voice. "I will do it. To prove to you that I am who I say I am."

Rafael stared, unblinking, before barking a word to the nearest Enti. Vasily felt his breath hitch as the soldier hurried forward and hastily unlocked his cage. The iron door scraped open, and Vasily clambered out and straightened for the first time in what felt like ages. The Enti shoved him roughly toward Rafael, toward the block, toward the shuddering, sobbing, handless man.

Rafael looked Vasily over before nodding to the Enti next to him and taking the soldier's sword.

"How do I know you won't use this against us?" he asked.

Vasily met his eyes, all that too-familiar rage bubbling up again. "I swear to you as a man of honor that I will not harm a single innocent soul this day. I swear to you on the lost spirit of my father."

Rafael held out the sword. Vasily took it in his sweat-slick hands, the weight familiar, the sun already turning warm on his face.

Rafael nodded, and Vasily turned to the prisoner, shifting the sword in his hand until the grip felt right. A quiet fell over the Enti ranks as each Vandel brother watched, hands on the pommel of their swords or leaning on their spears, waiting to see what he would do.

Vasily just began to swing his sword to the highest point in its lethal arc, his breath catching, when that same child's voice cried out to shatter the stillness of the late morning, and he made the mistake of looking up.

The little boy he had seen with the Anathema Enti before was pressed up against the bars and screaming, his face red and streaked with tears. The boy caught him looking and lit with desperate hope, chirping *angatento, angatento* over and over again.

Innocent.

But Vasily knew that the man on the block was not, no more than the boy himself. They were condemned by the breath inside their bodies, a crime over which they had no control that could not go unpunished. A blight left to fester and bring this foul consequence.

A horrible knot pulled tight in the pit of his stomach. He looked down from the tear-stained child to the Enti on the block, and realized just what he was about to do.

Vasily looked to the surrounding Enti, their dark gazes heavy on him, waiting, watching. He looked down to the Anathema shivering with his face pressed to the block, gone silent, his tears drying to salt upon his cheeks. Vasily just watched him. Watched his breaths flutter.

Have courage for your boy, he wanted to say. The words stayed trapped inside his mouth. He saw there was no amulet around the man's neck. No chance of sleep in the Long Wait ahead.

The man looked at him, sweat glistened on his tan forehead. "Please," he whispered in broken Jinian. "Please. I am an innocent man."

Are you really going to walk this road again?

Vasily ignored the voice inside and met the man's eyes. "There are no innocent men like you."

He raised the sword and let fall, sliver in the rising red light, and metal met flesh and bone.

Vasily only dimly heard the boy shriek. The scent of copper flooded his nose and he forced himself to step back and handed the stained sword back to its soldier.

"There," he said, keeping his voice somehow stable, "Surely that proves to you my innocence from whatever stain you think I may share with them."

Rafael nodded. "A good demonstration, yes. But you have not yet been checked."

Vasily stiffened. "But I—"

Hands clamped down his shoulders and hauled him toward his cage. Vasily threw them off and stepped back toward Rafael, only to be stopped by the sound of every Enti sword in the vicinity scraping out of its scabbard.

He froze, his hands clenched so tightly his nails bit into his skin, and fought not to combust when he was hauled to his cage and thrown back inside.

"Wait for the Shade," Rafael called, "unless you want to do more of my work for me."

Then he turned his back and took up the sword again. Vasily heaved in breath after breath, watching as the body was cleared away and another Anathema brought out. This time, Rafael was the one to do the cutting.

And the blood began to flow.

20

HEAVIER STILL IS THE HAND

Rafael went about his work with efficiency. The red sand grew redder. Still, he didn't make them suffer.

Vasily watched the whole time. He knew it was the kind of watching that would never really leave, but he couldn't look away if he tried. His breathing went ragged with every swing of the blade. He jammed his hands into his armpits, all the screams around him dimming further and further away, and turned to praying as his nausea grew unbearable. The scent of blood in the air was not a foreign thing, not to him. But the origin of Vasily's walk with death —the *truth*—was a thing he could barely explain. Not even to himself.

The scent of blood first made itself known to him when he was a child learning to fight under his father's relentless tutelage, spilled from the various nicks, cuts, and scrapes any boy acquires while learning the art of the blade. The scent became familiar as he grew into the middling years of his childhood, rising from the bodies of felled stags and the corpses of the traitors and murderers whose spirits Babas had the solemn responsibility of sending to the Long Wait. But Vasily could barely remember the first time *he* took a life. It was a blurry haze—the purple night sky, the orange glow of fire. The way a man had shivered and cried at his feet, two arrows protruding from his back like broken wings.

But his first kill hadn't been a man, had it? The first man he killed was a Prince of Glass—he wasn't even sure which one. Though he had been well trained in the arts of violence, Vasily had not grown up with war. His culture was not a culture of death, and Faeriel had been at peace long before Vasily was even born, thanks to his father. He had still seen life be taken, of course—Babas had taken Vasily to his first execution at ten and to every one after for the rest of his reign. He liked Vasily to know the consequence of death. To see it as justice. A thing only done when necessary.

And *necessary* it was, to fix things once Babas had been killed. Vasily took two princes of Glass, there in the dark with the night burning at his back. He remembered how crystallized the world was, how simple everything seemed. A Prince of Glass had taken father from him, dissolved his father into ash before Vasily's own eyes. Vasily had a debt to collect, simple as that.

It was strange, how his first kill came only after he had been so terribly *robbed*, how it came only after his life was upended in a way that could never be put back. Babas had taken many lives during his reign, especially before Vasily was born and he was a young king dealing with an insurrection in the mountain tribes. Wasn't that the way of most new kings? Wasn't it the responsibility of every ruler to deal death as a part of their power, their responsibility? Wasn't death the cost of peace?

But that wasn't how it seemed to Vasily when he went for his sword with a Prince of Glass there in the amid the darkness, the Anathema prone on the grass and crying at his feet.

As soon as Vasily's hand touched the pommel of his sword, all the resolve drained from his body. His anger became hollow. The simplicity of it all evaporated. This was no *man* sentenced to death for crimes of evil. This was no soldier who understood the rules of battle. This *thing* at his feet wasn't even a man at all, and yet he lay there, crying and clawing at the dirt.

And yet he was crying. A monster, crying. A monster who *owed* Vasily, and he was *crying.*

And it bothered Vasily.

He pushed past his weakness and killed the first Prince of Glass. And then he killed the second one they'd caught that night. But the swing of his sword didn't feel like *responsibility*. It felt like a vain attempt to balance a scale that had been broken. It felt like trying to put back a world in its ruination. It felt like trying to restring the stars in the sky.

It felt impossible. But mostly, it felt *pointless*.

Vasily killed those two princes of Glass, as if their spilled blood might set everything right, as if their deaths might reset it all, might bring back what was lost.

And all the while, he knew it wouldn't.

Vasily knew that night he would never be a good king, just as he would never be a good son. Hours later, he ended up vomiting behind a line of trees after sneaking away from his battalion, crying and shaking and sick to his guts that he was so *weak,* that avenging his father felt so wrong when he knew it was right. When he *owed* Babas his justice.

Babas had turned to ash in front of Vasily. His ashes had stuck to Vasily's hands. *Stuck* to him. And he should want more than anything to kill every last person responsible for making him have to *wash his own father off his hands.*

Days went by, and Vasily made himself learn to want it. Beat the weakness out of himself. For the duration of his war Vasily sealed away the sickness that rose in him at the sight of death—he punished himself with pain when he caught himself faltering, fasted when he felt anything other than his rage and his righteousness and his consuming, soul-eating *grief.* He made himself a man and he burned Efriel Shu to the ground and closed off their realm from the rest of the world. He forged treaties with all other realms to enforce that the Siou border be closed off forever, paid bribes to divert all trade and smuggling, and cut down whoever stood in his way. Vasily made himself a man, and he set things right, and he made the smell of blood become a comfort, because Babas was dead and Vasily was left behind to sacrifice himself upon the altar of vengeance. Because dealing death was the only way he knew to make it right.

And then Vasily came home, thinking it was *over.*

It almost made him laugh, now—that he thought he could kill the good in himself and resurrect it later, that the unending rage inside would burn out once it was no longer needed, that he could turn himself into a monster to kill something monstrous, and not stay that way forever.

In the end, what separates a man from a monster, when he is trying to do right? And when the wars have been fought and the guilty have been killed and everything has been set as right as it can ever be set, how can he ever find himself again?

The terrible truth Vasily had been learning was that he *couldn't*. That taking lives the way he did took something in return, bit by bit, with every swing of his sword and every spilt drop of blood. Because the truth was Vasily had been anything but angry when that Prince of Glass killed his father. In that moment, as he watched Babas turn to ash in that foreign court for some foreign holiday with the best of all four realms watching, all he felt was *helplessness*.

And helplessness would not win Vasily a war. Helplessness had to be turned to rage. The kind that could topple mountains, the kind that could dethrone kings, the kind that could burn a whole realm down to the ground.

The kind that never, ever went away.

Heavy is the head that wears the crown, many said about men of power. But Vasily knew a different kind of truth.

Heavier still, was the hand that wields the sword.

No, the scent of blood was not a foreign thing to Vasily. It hadn't been for many long years. He was Lord of House Slate, after all, and for some ten years now it was *he* who lifted the sword to the worst offenders against House Slate, those who sinned against his family, his house, and his country, just as his father before him.

But even so, Vasily found himself retching out the bars of his cage as the stained sand surrounding the block grew redder and redder.

These were men, women, and *children*. No different from him, not on the outside. And these people were not responsible for his father's death. They likely never so much as saw Lord Taegart once in their lives.

So why had he done it? Why swing a blade against a simple Enti soldier?

In his heart of hearts, Vasily knew. He knew what lay beneath their skin, the damage they could wreak. They were poison to the earth. But here, under the cloak of terror and desperation, they just looked like the first Prince of Glass had, all those years ago.

They looked just like people.

———

21

MUDDY ROADS

TAEIN

Rain again. It floated down in misting sheets as Taein trudged along the mud-clogged path that led toward the orphanage. Long velvet ferns had grown into the path and reached out to brush against his boots like a friendly cat as he walked, the little creek running along the roadside flowed by with a bright and merry tune. If they weren't laughably off-track and behind schedule, Taein would've thought it a perfectly amiable day.

Instead, he sighed and cued Lorrin to pick up the pace. "I'd say I've had about enough of Nown Jin for a while, how about you?"

Taein waited for a response, but the kid gave no indication of hearing him at all. The kid hadn't done much of anything besides drift in and out of bouts of sleep since Taein sat her atop Lorrin and insisted that they were heading to the orphanage. Her wounds were slowly scabbing over and she ate whatever was offered and stayed totally silent otherwise. And Taein didn't mind, not a bit. It was better this way. Less hurt feelings for her when she got dumped at the orphanage.

Taein tugged Lorrin a little farther ahead of Vince and closed his eyes, imagining for a moment that he was blissfully alone in the countryside, the dewdrop air sharp in his nose, a breeze moving cool against his cheek and playing with his hair, his body warm and lean, free and alive.

He hadn't always savored the feeling. In the weeks that followed his separation from Ruein, Taein lived in a state of continuous, cyclical terror. Every snapping twig and shifting branch sent him into a frenzy, he constantly mistook the groans and whispers of the swaying Siou forest for hunting human voices.

He spent some two full weeks lost in the Iri Mountains, wandering alone beneath the shifting gray clouds and the puzzled, judging stares of gryniff owls and wood rabbits in boundless snow. He spent long days and longer nights huddled beneath the bows of imperious pines, bark digging into his back and sap matting his hair and snow choking the air, hugging his knees to his chest as hunger and fear struggled in a relentless battle for control over his narrowing husk of a body.

In the end, hunger won. Taein crawled out the cold mountains a shuddering frozen wild thing with frostbitten fingers beneath his tattered gloves and limbs grown gaunt as barren branches in the dead of winter.

Naturally, he scared the living daylights out of the first person he encountered, a lone survivor from the recently-destroyed Salt Watch who looked just as battered as Taein himself and ran the other way the second they met eyes.

It wasn't until Taein caught a glimpse of his reflection in a half-frozen creek that he understood *why*. He looked like a Shallow dug up from the grave, his hair an overgrown mess of matted curls, his skin papery-white and smattered with bruises, his bones jutting beneath his clothes like stilted wings.

He then set to work filling his stomach with any marginally-edible thing that crossed his path and waged war with his hair. But a more presentable appearance didn't do anything to change the reaction of the next person he encountered as he crossed from Efriel Shu into Ersii. The second—a woman hanging laundry on the moss-eaten branches of a young alder in a tiny farm settlement just across the border—screamed when she saw Taein and incited the appearance of a riled husband who bore both a pitchfork and an axe with a certain threatening countenance Taein didn't find himself quite fond of.

The third encounter featured a patrol of Faeish soldiers, which went as well as could be expected considering the current war, and took every ounce of conniving Taein was capable of to live through.

It was then, after he wiggled himself free of the soldiers with his head somehow still on his shoulders, that Taein finally understood what exactly had happened. It wasn't his hungry eyes or ghastly appearance that sent the deserter running. It wasn't the silent scared way he walked or the fear dogging his steps like a black shadow that made the farm woman scream. It certainly wasn't anything in his *presentation* that caused the Faeish soldiers to run after him like dogs set upon a rabbit.

It was the ivory of his skin, the dark of his eyes, the sharp curves of his features. It was the *Siou* in him, a new and inherent sort of guilt-stain he could never scrub away or cover up. Suddenly, the very fabric of who Taein was on the outside was wrong.

Just as suddenly, Taein learned the essential importance of being just *half-Siou*. A fact he had resented for the majority of his life became the deciding reason he was only *hesitantly* allowed to 'keep his life' by the common folk of Ieris in the months following Ruein's great, catastrophic, world-ending mistake.

But even status as half-Siou wasn't enough. Neither was changing his name from the very-Siou sounding *Mikhael* to the plain old Jinian name of *Taein*. And as the years wore on and he found himself still in Pearl Jin, finally off of rit and under Regor's protection, he grew weary of the nasty glances and the gobs of spit, the hushed whispers and the slammed doors. Eventually, he was no longer able to stand constantly looking over his shoulder and struggling to soothe his jackrabbit heart. He started scrapping further and further outside city limits, taking jobs by his lonesome that led him into the deep wild for weeks on end, where he could close his eyes and breathe in living air and feel truly, completely, utterly lost, in ways that even a city so large and grand and chaotic as Pearl Jin could never provide.

And for years, the untamed countryside was his best refuge from the sordid truth of who he was, what he was capable of, and what he had done. In the endless wild he was *small*, no different to the wild creatures than the drifting dust or the worried squirrel or long reaching river. In the wild, he was almost safe.

But now, his blissful refuge had been broken by two decidedly unwelcome presences.

Taein sighed as they came to a stop and looked to where Vince had dismounted and stood stroking the draft's pink nose. Taein got the sense that Vince was still disappointed that they weren't taking the kid where she 'belonged', and was giving Taein the corresponding silent treatment. But Taein also got the sense that Vince was more than a little afraid of the kid. The only time he'd addressed the kid directly was when she dropped a half-nibbled apple and Vince handed it back to her with a quiet *"um, you dropped this."*

"Dropped what?" Vince said.

Taein looked up. "What?"

"What do you mean, *what?* You were standin' there starin' at the dirt mumbling to yourself.'"

Taein blinked. "Uh..."

"It's alright, boss, you're always mumbling on. Now we headin' on, or is it lunch time? Please say it's lunch time."

"Guess we can break," Taein said, stuffing down his embarrassment. "You... ready for a break in the rain?"

Vince squinted up at the sky. "Don't care so much for the damp myself, boss. 'Specially this infernal mud."

"Rain does tend to make for muddy roads."

"Sure does. Just as hasty decisions make for a whole lot of regret."

Taein threw Vince a feral smile. "Easy now, Vincent. Nobody's forcing you to go with me."

"I ain't sayin' shit."

"Then keep it that way."

Taein squinted up at the sky and grimaced. He was due to look at the kid's wounds again.

He looked up at June. She was hunched forward in the saddle, silent. He couldn't tell whether or not she was asleep, so he tapped her knee. She just about bit him the last time he tried to take her out of the saddle without waking her up first.

June startled away, eyes flashing thunder and not softening even a bit when she recognized him.

Taein gave her the pretense of a smile. "Gotta check your wounds."

"And it's also lunchtime," Vince said from behind.

Taein nodded. "That too. Hungry?"

She shook her head and kicked her feet out of the stirrups to allow Taein to pull her down from Lorrin. As soon as her feet touched the ground she brushed Taein off and stepped over to the shoulder of the road beneath a grove of wind-swept trees, where she settled down and disappeared from sight amid the waist-high grass.

Taein took Vince's draft and Lorrin across the creek and to a knoll thick with clover on the other side of the road and tethered them there to graze.

"Didn't you already eat, Vince?" Taein asked absent-mindedly as he fetched his sheepskin and traipsed over to the creek.

Vince trailed behind, already pulling food from his pack "Just first lunch, boss."

"Ah," Taein said, crouching down to capture some water. The stream, swollen with ice-cold runoff from the mountains beyond, bit through his gloves at his fingertips. "And how many lunches do you usually have?"

Vince was still rifling through his pack. "Three, when I can get them."

Taein arched a brow. "And do you have three breakfasts and three dinners?"

Vince chuckled. "No, that would be ridiculous. I have breakfast and coffee, then first, second, and third lunch. Then there's midday snack, afternoon coffee, and then first dinner, second dinner, dinner coffee, and midnight snack. And midnight coffee, of course."

Taein nodded as he drew the water and hauled it back over to the horses, trying to fathom one man consuming that amount of food. "Sounds completely unsustainable."

Vince shrugged as he munched on a beef strip. "Well, I ain't following you all over hill 'n dale for nothing. Coffee's gotten too damn expensive these days."

"Don't even get me started on the price of pastries," Taein mimed.

Vince missed the jab and nodded enthusiastically. "I know, two whole marks for a dozen scones? It ain't like the flour's imported from the Outerlands." He paused, brushing crumbs from his lap. "What about you, Taein? How many lunches?"

Taein went from horse to horse, letting them drink, before spreading the sheepskin out to dry. "Whatever the normal amount of lunches is."

"Psh, all I ever see you consume is that cherry ale you down by the gallon—"

"It's white cherry *wine*," Taein corrected as he settled down on the damp grass beside June, tucking the long tail of his raincoat beneath him. "I'm too busy pestering Regor to worry about lunches."

"Busy? You don't do anything constructive in-city besides get your ass handed to you in brawls. Those bruises don't look any better, by the way."

Taein resisted the urge to touch his cheek. "As if you're any more productive. All you do is sleep and eat."

Vince eased himself down opposite of Taein and pulled out a quartet of biscuits and an accompanying pair of overripe nectarines, which infused the air with a bright, summery scent. "That ain't true, Regor kept me right busy. Or he used to," Vince muttered through a mouthful of food. "I'm gettin' poorer by the hour."

Tell me about it. With that thought, Taein turned his full attention onto the kid. She was hunched over, having busied herself with weaving strands of grass into braids with her blood-stained fingers. Her entire body was wild-cat tense beneath the spare cloak Taein loaned her. She'd pulled the oversized thing tight around her frame and was sitting there like a human loaf of bread. She looked and smelled worse than when he had found her, since they hadn't come across a suitable place to bathe. As such, her soot-stained face was still smeared with the dirt and dried blood Taein couldn't scrub away with a rag. But he wasn't too worried about it—the kid wouldn't let him doctor her for more than a moment or two at a time, anyway.

Taein couldn't hold it against her. If he was being honest, he was almost thankful for her mistrust. Even with the gloves, doctoring her made his stomach churn.

It's just too close.

He shoved his discomfort away and rummaged through his pack, searching for bread before starting the slow and delicate process of getting her to talk to them.

He produced the bread and offered it to her with a flourish. "Here you go, brat. Lunch first, or the wounds?"

After a pause for deliberation, June swiped the bread and gnawed on it sullenly.

Taein noticed that Vince had stopped humming and glanced back. The giant was staring at June with a tight expression, his brow pinched with concern. Taein followed his gaze and noticed the tiny white flowers sprouting up all around the kid, peppering the grass like fat flakes of snow.

Taein narrowed his eyes. How was she doing that?

He swallowed hard and decided to get her attention before she made Vince even more uncomfortable. Maybe if he got her talking, the flowers would... stop.

"How's your wounds doing?" he asked.

June didn't answer, and the little flowers intensified with a flare of life. She looked like a feral cat someone had dunked in the river. Damp, filthy, and in what seemed to be a permanent sour mood.

Taein sighed and tried for something more personal. "So... you like the outside world so far?"

Vince shook his head. "She don't like jack shit about the world, that much is for certain."

Taein glared. "Don't swear in front of the kid, Vincent."

"*You* swear in front of the kid."

"It doesn't count if she's passed out," Taein said as he turned back to June. Her eyes flickered up at him. She faltered before holding out her hand.

"What do you want? The pen?" Taein asked.

A nod. Taein dug through his pack before producing the near-ruined pad of parchment and pen.

Both he and Vince peered over to see what she wrote.

Everyone will be hunting.

Taein shook his head. "And somehow I'm still alive. Not *everyone* is hunting us."

Us? Also Anathema? She wrote, glancing between Taein and Vince.

"Not me," Vince answered a little too quickly.

Her eyes fell solely on Taein. *Which curse?*

Taein couldn't hold back a long sigh. He ran a hand through his hair, trying to summon all the patience he could, and met her unearthly gaze. "Lithriin."

June didn't seem to care. Her eyes darted over to Vince, and she stared at him down before resuming her scrawling.

Is he going to hurt us?

He looked over at Vince and offered the giant his best smile. "No, Vince would never do anything bad. Especially not something like selling me out for a fat stack of marks the second we're back in the Pearl. Right, Vince? Remember how we talked about that?"

Vince frowned. "Yeah, 'course I do."

Taein narrowed his eyes, trying to decide if Vince was deflecting. Vince looked right back at him, chewing away on another stick of dried beef, perfectly calm. He seemed so *genuine* all the time. Who from Pearl Jin was *ever* genuine?

Taein sighed before looking back at June. "He's safe, kid. He's decided by some small miracle that we Anathema aren't so bad after all."

"So far, at least," Vince grumbled through a mouthful of food.

"Now," Taein said, clapping his hands together, "back to the task at hand—"

June cut him off with a quick swipe of her hand. Something dark had come to shadow her face by the time she finished scrawling.

How do you control your curse?

Taein shrugged. In truth, he'd never even used it. He never felt the power, not once, and he didn't intend to ever go looking for it.

"Try wearing gloves. Ask for them at the orphanage. Tell them the only thing you're 'cursed' with is poor circulation."

But my hands are always sweaty.

"Well, that's something I didn't need to know." Taein shrugged. "Just lie."

Lie?

Taein nodded. "Lying is living for people like you and me."

June stared a moment longer before shrugging and scarfing the remains of her bread.

"May I check your wounds now?" Taein asked.

Another shrug. Deciding that a shrug would suffice as a yes, he scooted closer and rummaged through his pack for the strips of cloth he'd been using to bind the wounds. He unwrapped each and tossed the old, dirtied wrappings into the grass before taking out the bottles of medicine. The gashes on her neck and leg were healing decently, but the slice on her side was still oozing and raw.

Taein spent a while longer cleaning the gash before wrapping it back up. June remained perfectly still, eyes on the sky, simmering tension heavy on her little features. Taein tried not to look too close.

She wasn't going to last long at the orphanage if she didn't figure out how to keep a lid on it. It was more than likely she'd explode on some kid and show the orphanage what she *really* was, and she'd be imprisoned in no time, or hung, or dumped on the wrong side of the Southern Mists by the Enti Exchange.

She'd have a fighting chance if she got where she belongs.

Taein clenched his jaw. Once he got her to the orphanage, her life was in her own hands.

Right?

Hasty decisions make for a whole lot of regret.

Taein shook his head as he finished wrapping her side. Vince could go to hell—there wasn't anything *hasty* about his decision, because what happened to the kid shouldn't matter. *Didn't* matter.

Taein worked faster. He had to get rid of this kid before he went completely soft.

⸻

$$\text{🦋} \quad 22 \quad \text{🦋}$$

THE SHADE
VASILY

A day and a night passed by. The Enti came for Vasily in the heavy gray hours before dawn, as a thin pale mist curled over the snowy sands.

The soldiers spent the night before pulling the remaining prisoners from their cages and hauling them in varying degrees of distress into the largest tent in the encampment. Some struggled, kicking sand into spitting fires and cursing up righteous storms, while others went timid as mice before a barn owl. It didn't take more than a few minutes before each prisoner was drawn back out and either returned to a cage to face the coming dawn's execution, or set free.

That night fifteen prisoners entered the tents, and the five that fought the hardest went wailing back into their cages.

So when the Enti finally reached Vasily's lonesome cage, he knew better than to struggle. He clenched his jaw and let the soldiers rough him up onto his feet and march him through the mists toward the tent.

A soldier lifted the tar-colored entrance flap and shoved Vasily inside. Other than a pair of hanging lamps, the tent was largely bare of furniture. Blue smoke curled from an incense burner laid at the foot of a dark figure, smelling of cinnamon and cloves but not quite strong enough to block the scent of dust and something *else*, something sharp and alien and bitter, akin to a hard frost in the dead days of winter. A damp chill hung about the room, dense as the clouds that cloaked House Slate.

Vasily blinked in the dim light and looked around as a pair of Enti marched him up to Rafael, who was dressed in a heavy cloak almost as dark as the shadows beneath his eyes, and the murky figure sat in a high-backed wooden chair next to him.

The soldiers forced Vasily onto his hands and knees as soon as he neared the pair. He crouched in the position, digging his fingers into the white sand floor and trying to keep the tension brewing beneath his skin from boiling over.

Then came a voice like a shadow incarnate as the woman spoke, and all the rage drained from Vasily's body at once.

"Leave us."

The chill grew sharp. Vasily remained on his hands and knees as the Enti soldiers turned and hurried out, the sound of their boots padding away across the sand sending his heart into a slow-building panic. They hadn't left the other prisoners. Something was terribly amiss.

Silence hovered in the air, a tangible thing Vasily wanted to choke the life out of. Cold sweat crept along his brow. For a fleeting second, he was certain that he would throw up.

Again, the woman spoke. "Do you know who I am?"

Vasily kept his eyes on the ground. "No."

"I know who *you* are, Vasily of the High Mountain."

Vasily said nothing.

There was a creak as the figure rose from the chair and moved closer.

"Look at me," she said. "Get up."

She came to a stop before Vasily and he forced himself to obey.

The *thing* that loomed before him was not quite woman nor shadow but rather something in between, a grafted, ghostly figure, cloaked in darkness, intangible and yet so terribly real. A thin, unlined face that might've once been demure, girlish, and perhaps even pretty peered out from beneath a deep hood, punctuated by glittering eyes, dark as a well without bottom.

She spoke again, her voice the silken surface of an untouched lake after a deep freeze, and Vasily fought to keep himself still and patient. His heart beat desperately in his chest.

If this *creature* misdiagnosed him as an Anathema—what then?

"Do you understand why you were brought here?" she asked.

Vasily kept his eyes on the sand. "Whatever it is you look for within me, it is not there."

The corners of her lips curved. "You are not afraid?"

Vasily forced himself to keep her gaze. "I am always afraid."

She smiled again, the expression strange on her bone-white features, her eyes glittering obsidian in the yellow half-light. Vasily found himself looking a moment too long at the soft curve of that little smile and dropped his eyes to the floor.

"Then fear me, Lord of Slate."

She reached out a hand composed of long, twig-like fingers and rested it on Vasily's shoulder. Vasily flinched despite himself.

She spoke at length, meeting his eyes again, and he tumbled back into their unfathomable blackness.

"The light of your spirit burns clean before my gaze."

A weight slipped from Vasily's chest, and he breathed a little easier as the Shade withdrew her touch. Vasily could still feel the chill of her fingers searing through his cloak, draining into his very bones.

"Then why have I been brought before you?" Vasily asked.

The Shade ignored Vasily as Rafael spoke. "He is who he claims to be?"

"He is the Aal Salvara."

"And who are you?" Vasily demanded.

The woman faltered before Rafael stepped forward and laid a hand atop her shoulder. "She is of no importance to you, Lord Miinriel."

Vasily turned his gaze onto the commanding Enti and set his jaw. "You believe me now?"

Rafael smiled. "She cannot lie. It is but one aspect of many that make her of great use to me."

Vasily gritted his teeth. "Then you will move aside, Enti, and let me go."

Rafael clasped his hands behind his back. "I'm afraid not, *stajerno*. I have use for you, too."

Vasily stepped close, hungry for the familiar weight of his broadsword on his back. "Move," he growled, all the fear and anger from the last few days rising up in one great wave, "or I will move you myself."

"Quit toying with the man and tell him what you want." The Shade cut in.

The smile slipped from Rafael's face, and he looked to the Shade.

The commander's slip of attention was not lost on Vasily. He rammed his elbow into Rafael's face, hooked his boot around his knee, and yanked him crashing to the ground. Rafael stifled a howl, blood gushing from his nose, and Vasily placed his boot atop Rafael's bloodied breastplate and snarled into its owner's face as he retook his amulets.

"You have beat and caged me for three days straight," he growled, slipping his own amulet over his head. "If I let you leave this tent with all your appendages intact you will be the *luckiest* man ever to walk these accursed sands." Vasily leaned all his weight onto his braced leg. "Let me make this clear: *you don't get to want anything from me.*"

A violent shift stirred the air and the Shade's hand glanced Vasily's shoulder again, cold as the High Mountain wind. A sudden weakness flowed through him, sucking the fire out of his bones with the greed of starving late-summer earth stealing away morning dew.

Her voice was velvet death as she spoke. "Remove your boot, Slate."

Slowly, as if not by his own will, Vasily found himself lifting his foot. Rafael rolled away and stumbled back onto his feet, wiping away a spray of blood.

Vasily turned back to the Shade as he tucked Glass' amulet back in his pocket, ready to ask just what the *hell* she was, and instead found himself frozen to the spot the instant he met her gaze.

His heart slowed in his chest. The Shade held his gaze and swept back her hood to release a tumble of dark curls that seemed to float and wave in some intangible breeze as they hung down her back and shoulders, a girl underwater.

Beautiful. The thought flitted into his mind as if from the stars themselves, or perhaps the blackness beyond. Vasily hated himself for it, hated the way his limbs would not respond, hated the loveliness of her abysmal eyes, her porcelain skin.

What witchery is this?

"Do you remember," the Shade began, "those great plumes of smoke rising from the East some days ago?"

"Yes."

"There were six plumes, Lord Slate. One for each of Vandel's great cities, rising from the fires that consumed the bodies of the Anathema."

Vasily's breath caught as horror raked down his spine, sharp as the tip of some phantom icicle. He tried to look at Rafael, his heart gone suddenly still, and could not.

"How many?" he breathed.

Rafael wiped his bleeding nose on his sleeve and spat onto the sand, answering for the Shade. "Geiin forbid the Fathers to take wives, to bring forth children. Yet they did whatever they wanted, took women who whelped bastards, and now... here we are. On the brink of another crisis of Anathema. We burned *hundreds.* "

Vasily's mouth fell open. "Two nights ago he denied that Vandel would ever need help."

Her gaze was even, unwavering as her dulcet tone. "I convinced him otherwise."

Vasily scrambled, trying to understand, the only sound that of the blood dripping from Rafael's face onto the sand.

"You're lying. You must be."

The Shade *laughed* at him, and fear twisted like a knife in Vasily's gut.

"Why else would the mists be sinking?" she asked.

Vasily clenched his hands into fists, his mind spinning. "It isn't possible. It cannot be."

"But it is," Rafael cut in, coming to stand beside the Shade. He glared. "What the hell do you think the *raz-jyala* are? All sorts of things—*creatures*—are already slipping through the weak points. Coal-black wildcats bereft of eyes have been spotted along the Western Road. People talk of trees glowing blue against the night in Nown Jin, whole forests of them! The world is turning, Lord Slate, it is turning against us once again. If nothing is done to curb this collapse, all of Ieris will suffer, and the Vandel way of life will vanish." He smiled grimly. "There is no Enti or Mist Exchange without any *mists* in which to put prisoners, and where there is no Enti, there is no Vandel."

Vasily gaped, unable to think of a single thing to say above the swirling hurricane of thoughts battering about his mind.

Rafael stared before giving a huge sigh and brushing out the tent. He reappeared a few minutes later with a small, stooped man of middling years with small round bifocals and a pointed, graying beard. He looked up from a thick leather-bound journal rapidly snowing loose papers onto the sand and fidgeted a step closer to Rafael, whose face was still splotchy with the promise of coming bruises and splattered with red.

"Lord Miinriel, meet Medikolo Rodigis. I have enlisted him to monitor the mist's changes ever since I was made aware of the... phenomenon."

"*Bekko Dia*," Rodigis said, balancing the massive journal on one arm and reaching out a tentative hand. "Good day, sir."

Vasily looked from his bound hands to Rodigis' extended palm as it hung helplessly waiting in the air, and offered a grim smile.

"I would take your hand, *sir*, if I was able."

Rodigis flushed berry-red beneath his beard and awkwardly jerked his hand back, spilling more scribbled papers out onto the sand floor. "Yes, my lord, of course."

Rafael nodded to the journal. "This fool is slow to believe me, Rodigis. Show him your work."

"Ah, of course, of course." Rodigis shambled closer to Vasily, stooping to gather up only a few of the papers loose on the sand, and opened the book for Vasily to see. He was met with a scribbled, smudged collection of graphs, notes, charts, and sketches.

"As you see here, my lord, the mists have fallen some nineteen feet over the last week. The week before, some twelve. As time passes, the decay is only seeming to accelerate."

He flipped forward another few pages and came to stop on a collection of sketches portraying strange birds and animals. "I have also been charting the land's response to the decay. The variety of altered animals, birds, and even plants increases daily." He looked up at Vasily and blinked nervously. "I've managed to catch a few specimens, but they are rather hard to keep caged. Most do not respond to the laws of physics that bind ordinary things."

"Have you already lost the ones from last week?" Rafael inquired.

Rodigis snapped the journal close and hurried back over to the commanding Enti, pushing his glasses back up his nose with an alarming force. "All but one, my lord."

Rafael looked at Vasily. "Bring it, then."

Rodigis scurried back out of the tent and returned but a few minutes later with a single bird in an iron cage, its eye sockets strangely empty even as it fluttered against the bars.

"See here, my lord," Puffed Rodigis, "the only member of its flock yet to slip free. This one seems not to know it's any different from it ever was. See here."

See this, see that. Vasily hid his scowl and peered at the tiny dark creature.

"As you see, my lord, it has been touched by the Withering. Usually, marrow-birds such as this have a most pleasant white and green coloration, and the females mimic the red of arrinvale itself."

Vasily met Rodigis' eyes through the cage bars. "The Withering?"

"Yes, my lord. See! It is what we are calling the phenomenon that occurs when a small portion of the mist—or a creature once within it—detaches and creeps across the landscape, altering everything in its path. That's what's happened to this little fellow here."

"As with the shadow-dogs, I assume?" Vasily said.

"Yes, the *raz-jyala*."

"Tell our friend about the voids, the Witherings," Rafael said.

Rodigis glanced toward his commander. "Forgive me, but haven't you already?"

Rafael clenched his jaw. "My words seem to mean little to our *guest*."

Vasily met his eyes. "One's regard seems to slip when one is caged for days on end."

"You would know, Aal Salvara."

Vasily gave him a tight-lipped smile and said nothing, knowing full well what losing control would mean for him. Sooner or later, they'd have to cut his bonds, and then he'd have his *options* fully restored.

Rodigis shifted nervously before breaking the tense silence. "Ah, well, my lord," he stuttered as he flipped through his journal, "We've seen the most violent occurrences at dusk and dawn each day. The mists seem to decay faster during these changing hours, and the start and end of each day are marked by this low, crawling mist that now creeps among us," he paused to gesture at the faint gray matter swirling just above the sand at his feet. "This matter, we've discovered, has a most curious reaction to death."

Vasily raised his brow. "Death?"

"Yes." Rodigis nodded, stilling for the first time. "See, whenever a creature enters half-death within these faint mists, be it man or beast, or the mist finds a body, the land surrounding rather... erupts."

Vasily just stared. Rodigis fidgeted under his gaze and spoke faster.

"It's more of a riot, you see. The mist rages and wreaks havoc for miles surrounding whatever has died, drenching the world black, turning trees to char and sometimes infusing them with a strange light, altering any life nearby so severely the creatures are made beyond recognition. It's the most extreme natural phenomenon I have ever encountered. Or, well, unnatural."

Panic reared up like a spooked horse inside of him. "Why are you telling me these things?" Vasily breathed, "What are you asking me?"

Rafael spoke. "You are a great warrior, Miinriel, a hunter of men. I ask your aid in doing what must be done to secure my master peace and common men their mortal world. You waged war on the Anathema once before, I ask you to do it again. Help me destroy them." He stepped a fraction closer, trying to catch Vasily's eyes. "I ask for aid not for Vandel, but for myself. I need your guidance. I give you my word that you shall have your freedom in exchange for your wisdom, and your sword."

Vasily glared. "What right have you to bargain with me? I—"

"I am the commander of the Enti brotherhood, Slate," Rafael said. "All who trespass into the Wastes fall under my authority, and the authority of my Aal."

Vasily swallowed hard, thinking of the Enti on the block, the boy in the cage screaming, screaming, *screaming*. He thought of Efriel Shu's fall, the once-mighty warbands scattered, the Salt Watch devastated, the blood of House Glass on his hands, the blood of the House's defenders a red river following ever in the wake of his footsteps.

So much death, all for Babas. All for his family, his House, his country.

But this was bigger. *Ieris* was at stake. If Lithriin were to roam free once more, there wouldn't be a single space free of his corrosive touch. Mankind had waged countless wars for countless years in the age of the Long Night, throwing millions of mortal lives away to cage the fallen Father, all in vain. It had taken Geiin's own touch to finally raise a barrier between what was mortal and what was not in Ieris, to finally cage Lithriin once and for all.

And now that cage was collapsing, Lithriin's darkness once again spilling out into the world.

Still, something was caught deep in his chest. Vasily knew what it was, twisting there in his heart—he was *so tired.* He'd set out for Glass to at last end his long siege against the Anathema, to honor his father, return to Auryn, and go home. To find, at long last, what rest he might be entitled to after all this blood. All this suffering. To find what might be beyond, if there was anything.

"Please," said Rafael quietly. "I cannot allow our way of life fall to ruin no more than I can allow all of Ieris. We are Vandel, and we are strength from nothing. But you are *Aal Salava,* the great hunter of the Anathema. You laid siege to Efriel Shu and still it sits in isolation and despair a decade later. You, who alone broke the will of the Siou. You, whose grief was stronger." He shook his head. "Geiin withdrew his hand long ago, and Father-Graven beyond will not intervene. In the absence of the Celestial, we have only each other. My strength and your grief, which has toppled whole realms, ended whole bloodlines. Which can do it again."

Vasily drew in a shallow breath, growing unsteady on his feet as he thought of those six plums of smoke.

Hundreds of Anathema.

He looked back to the Shade, letting her take his eyes captive, forcing his mind to work through the lancing chill that followed. Who was to say she was even right? Who was to say *any* of the people falling upon the Enti block were cursed?

Vasily thought of the young Enti soldier, his little boy, and his stomach turned.

"You ask too much of me," he heard himself breathe as he looked at the Shade. He could not kill them all. The odds were impossible.

But he *could* catch Glass.

He raised his eyes up to the pair before him, steeled his voice. "No. I have already endured my days of bloodshed. All I want is to see those days end. You will find someone else."

The Shade looked back at Vasily. "You don't understand, Lord Slate. What is happening will soon turn the world asunder. If it is your family you are so desperate to protect, do so. Join us. The Anathema—"

Vasily shook his head, scrambled for words to affirm his resolution. "Need I justify myself to you?"

Rafael purpled beneath the crusting blood on his face. "Out, Rodigis," he growled low, and the little scientist scuttled out, spilling papers in his wake and muttering *"of course, of course."*

It was quiet for a long while before Rafael seemed to compose himself enough to speak.

"You are *Faeish*," he hissed. "What if the mists fall? How then will you save your precious house?"

Vasily straightened. "I'm only a man, Commander."

"A man who ended an entire realm!"

"Yes! I will go down to my Long Wait with a burden only the *Aal Salava* could recognize. Do you think my time in the battlefield was easy? A pleasure I long to recreate?" he found his voice rising with every word. "Find someone else, and *let me pass*."

Rafael stared him down. Red rose in Vasily's vision and he stepped forward.

"Send him to sleep, Shade," Rafael said.

Vasily hadn't the time to draw another breath before ice-like fingers touched his shoulder, and he pitched forward into pools black as a starless night, black as the witch's own eyes.

———

23

WHAT ARE YOU

Vasily woke once again to the cold press of bars against his back, a headache like a thunderstorm pounding against his temple. The sky was caught in the muzzy hours before another dawn and groups of soldiers were still clustered around fast-fading fires, drinking and laughing. He glanced around, his vision bleary, the dimming glow of the fires bathing the sand in a dancing sienna glow. An Enti brother said something and the group broke out in another burst of laughter, sloshing liquor onto the sand and slapping each other on the back and startling Vasily so badly he banged his head back against the bars. He slumped down and groaned as his head began to pound even harder, feeling as if he'd just been slugged in the face with a mallet. He fisted his hands in his hair and fought the urge to curse every living thing.

Locked up *again*, and with a skull-splitting headache to boot. Heaven and hell, what had the witch *done* to him?

"I did nothing to you."

Vasily startled, snatching at his amulet and opening his eyes to find the witch herself standing to the left of his cage, sheltered by the shadows and hidden from the laughing soldiers beyond.

Vasily struggled to gather his exhausted wits about him as he held the rosewood disc tight. "Who are you?"

The Shade stared at Vasily for a long while before moving closer and crouching down in the sand, her hair spilling out a black cloud tumble from her hood and catching the red light of the fire. She smiled and reached out with one scarred, twisted hand to grip the bars of his cage, and Vasily fought the sudden urge to move back. To get away from her fell air.

"Why do you want to know?" she asked.

Vasily stared as that same deathly chill swept through him. The truth came out before he even realized his mouth was moving.

"I've never met anything like you."

She smiled again, the expression a curious contradiction on the sharp planes of her features. "There are none like me."

"And just what, exactly, is that?"

"There are many other things I could tell you. The ages of the stars, the depths of the sea. The workings of a man's mind. How to kill an Anathema correctly."

Vasily scoffed. "They die like any other man, that much I know. What I don't understand is you."

The Shade just smiled. A long pause came before she spoke again. "If I tell you my truth, Slate, you will owe me your own."

"I think not," Vasily said.

She gave him a coy smile. "I could read your mind and pull out any answer I desire myself. But I think it might be more fun for me and much less painful for you if we share the simple pleasure of conversation."

Vasily looked at her, his head still pounding, his body tired and aching and sore, anger broiling in his bones and in his bloodstream. Still, he looked at her and for some terrible reason he could not fathom, he agreed.

"You have my word."

Her slight smile grew and she settled down on the sand, curls of shadow obscuring her small frame. She reflected a long while before beginning, her words falling from her lips like an invisible thread, reaching through the air to bind Vasily's attention.

"I am the root of the root, the murmur of the sea, the whispering of the oaken tree. I am a shadow brought down from the night sky above you. I drink of the dark and steal the light from the stars. I have been a spirit broken and reforged, a body turned to ash and back to life again. I am beyond your comprehension. But once, I was a girl. I was born into the Order Maage. Do you know what the Order Maage is, Slate?"

She spoke his name as if it belonged to a common simpleton, but Vasily didn't feel the same fire as when Rafael said it like that. The fire inside was rapidly settling with every word that dropped forth from her lips. He could hardly feel anything at all.

But Vasily *did* know what Order Maage was—stars, even a true simpleton was likely to recognize the name. It belonged to a highly prodigious order of magicians, alchemists, and necromancers, the head of which was traditionally the first advisor to the Aal of Vandel himself. Order Maage were the sole practitioners of 'the Lost Vein', as they called the supposed remnants of Geiin's touch. Ersii thought the Order a lot of heretics, Nown Jin upstarts, Efriel Shu extremists, and Faeriel idiots, but Vandel considered the Order to be of the highest and most sacred calling. And in Vandel, Vandel opinion was all that mattered.

Vasily nodded. "Of course I know what Order Maage is."

She quirked a brow. "Then you will know it was no small thing when I was ousted from their ranks."

"You must have done something terrible."

"I *was* something terrible."

Something clenched in Vasily's gut as the Shade's eyes turned to flint.

"I discovered I was Anathema very young, and when the Order did too, they *donated* me to The High Sect of Paragon, all the way in Nown Jin." She paused, her eyes darting away for only the spans of a breath. "Do you know that the Sect has been buying Anathema in secret for hundreds upon hundreds of years, Vasily? Do you know that the Sect experiments and operates on those Anathema, many of them young girls like myself, to seek a way in which they might *cleanse our spirits* by pulling the curse out from within?"

The chill in the air grew colder with sharp and pointed intensity. The Shade's gaze did not waver.

"Did they try to kill you?" Vasily found himself asking, his voice somehow steady in the early morning air. "Are you now free from the corruption of your body?"

Something feral curved the Shade's features, and she leaned closer. Every word was like velvet poison in the air.

"Their intentions are nothing in the face of such cruelty. You may say their operations were a mercy, but a curse is not so easily rooted out."

"So you remain Anathema."

She gave a shrug. "You cannot take up someone's soul like a rent pair of stockings and mend it with thread."

Vasily only dimly registered that he could not look away, not even if he wanted to.

Only dimly. The truth was, he didn't *want* to. There was a strange sweet sickness roiling in his gut that had nothing to do with her words and everything with the voice uttering them, the lips from which they fell.

"I escaped from the Sect after three years," the Shade said, "and ended up lost in the Wastes, where I was found by the Enti and taken in for trespassing. Rafael agreed to spare my life in exchange for my... abilities, when I learned of his quest to stop the mists from falling."

"So it's true, then?" Vasily asked. "The mists fall because of the Anathema."

A shadow drifted across her gaze. "It is possible."

Vasily stilled. "Only possible?"

She shook her head. "I said it *could* be true, Lord Slate, not that it wasn't."

Vasily ran a hand through his hair, trying to fathom her deceit. "But people are dying—*your* people are dying."

Her gaze did not waver. "People are always dying."

"But—"

She cut him off. "Compared to the fate that befell me, the block is the greatest mercy."

Vasily shook his head. "But they're your people, and yet you freely condemn them."

"It is not I who raises the sword, Slate."

"But it is you who delivers the sentence."

She let her eyes burn into Vasily's. "The world is not so black and white as you believe. You think me a monster and I think myself a survivor. What does it matter, which of us is right?"

All the difference, but Vasily couldn't ignore the twinge of guilt creeping into his heart.

He shook his head. "So what do you want with me?"

"Aha—not so fast. We struck a bargain, Slate. Give me your truth."

Vasily sighed. "Ask away."

She spoke without hesitation. "Tell me why you will not help Rafael."

Vasily thought of home, and his heart grew tight.

"I am hunting the Anathema who murdered my father, so that my father's lost spirit may be at peace, and I with him," he stated, as if he had said it aloud a thousand times before. "I am hunting that man for my kingdom, my house, my people. For my honor and my pride. For my family."

"But you don't want to."

"Don't presume you know anything about me," Vasily snapped.

"But I do. I know you just want it to be over," she said.

Vasily's protest died in his mouth. He saw something gentle the Shade's dagger-like features, easing away the sharpness, gentling the unnatural curves and planes of her face. For just a moment, he saw a glimpse of the girl she had once been, and she was beautiful.

"Forgive me" she said. "I don't mean to pry. Your devotion to your family is noble. But nobility is ground to dust beneath the wheels of necessity, and it is *necessary* that you help Rafael."

Vasily settled himself against the bars and tried to ignore the aching of his head. "Is that why you are here? He sent you to bargain?"

She shook her head. "I come on my own to offer you council. There is more to the lowering of the mists than the presence of the Cursed, this much I know. A thorn is rising beneath us, Slate. There are whispers of a force bent on resurrecting the power of the Four

Fathers in a new tetrad. But to do that, I suspect they would have to kill Lithriin first. That means they intend to collapse the mist in order to get to him, and if they succeed, Ieris will sink back into a desolation unrivaled. The world as we know it will end."

"Who is 'they'?"

"I cannot say anything for certain yet. It's all only a feeling."

Vasily remained still, a prisoner to her gaze. "So what are you asking of me?"

"Help Rafael. Help him until I know more, and I will come for you and we can destroy this 'thorn' before they have the chance to ruin the world once and for all." She leaned a little closer. "If you don't help Rafael, you will not leave the Wastes alive. He intends to take you to the mists at daybreak, where he will show you their decay and ask for your guidance once more. If you refuse him, he will have you sent to Sheffal to be sold as a fighter."

Vasily laughed before he could stop himself. "I'm Lord Slate, witch. That would be an act of war."

She smiled. "You don't understand. Sheffal is an ocean of human bodies in which the shield of your title is a frail thing, Slate. In the city, peasants and nobility alike are swept under and lost to the waves every day. Are you prepared to swim amid the driftwood?"

Vasily folded his arms and stared at her for a long time, unable to ease the smile off his face or tame his undeserved humor. "You know he's mad, don't you?"

She blinked, her eyelashes casting dark shadows on her cheeks. "Rafael? Of course. He has to be, to lead the Enti against the commands of the Aal."

"He lacks the Aal's support?"

She shifted on the sand and met his eyes. "The Aal is *old*, Lord Slate. Aal Selle has sat upon the Spice Throne in Aref Joula for the last sixty-seven years, his mind has gone to rot long before his body. His children do most of the ruling these days, but he still has the final say. Unfortunately, his final say is always to resist change with every last fiber of his decomposing being."

"A pity."

"It will be, if the mists fall. But that is why Rafael has led the

Enti out here, out against the Aal's wishes." She traced loops in the sand with a finger, the firelight illuminating the dark slender meshwork of scars wrapping around her ashen skin. "Rafael is the first commander to separate the Enti from the monarchy in two hundred and fifty years. But that madness doesn't make him entirely wrong."

She lifted her gaze from the sand and rested it on Vasily. "You must help him, Slate. If the Anathema are hunted from Vandel, it could slow the mist's collapse until we find the Thorn."

"But you don't *know* that."

"I know a chance when I see one."

Vasily shook his head. "Forgive me. I cannot understand why you so willingly condemn your people for the salvation of a world which has brought you nothing but pain."

Her eyes flickered. "Is it so hard to believe that I might want to continue living?"

Vasily smiled. "Rafael has promised you great things, hasn't you? In exchange for the betrayal of your people."

Her eyes went flat in an instant, and Vasily laughed a little.

"What is it, then? An estate with servants on the Ersiin coast? A hundred-thousand marks? The deed to a spice farm?"

"My life," she said. "Assurance that when this sordid affair has passed I will not be one of the Anathema on the block."

"Now I see you as you are," Vasily scoffed. "You speak of the killings of the Anathema as if death is a gift to them, yet you are here playing puppet for your own life. Some gift it must be, if you will not take it for yourself."

Her mouth set in a bitter line. "It is not for love of life that I fight to keep mine. In my world, Slate, there are things in motion so catastrophic they would break your mind. I fight for life that I may prevent the mass *extinction* of every other one."

Vasily shook his head. "Believe whatever you must. Your uses will run out their course and Rafael will turn on his word."

"Don't be so quick to judge, Lord Slate," she chided. "You are now in the very same situation, after all."

"But I am not Anathema."

"You trespassed on the Wastes. Some might say the crimes weigh equally on the Vandel balance."

"It doesn't seem I have much of a choice, then."

"You never have."

He stretched his legs and thought. "Alright, then. You tell your master I will speak to him again, if you answer me but one thing."

"Ask."

Vasily watched her. "What is your name?"

"I am the Shade."

"I meant the name given to you as a girl."

She looked right back at him for a long time, the fading fire reflected in those bottomless eyes, turning them golden in the graying light.

"My name was Aedya Drula."

Vasily's voice softened even in the strange chill of the air. "And what are you now, Aedya Drula?"

She stared at him for a long while and her eyes sought out the bloodstained block before the cages. When she looked back at Vasily, that soft amber light had vanished from her eyes.

"What are you?"

Before he could answer, she was gone.

24

THE GIANT

Wherever Vince went, music followed.

Not *literally*, of course. But music was always there, no matter the dirty joints he frequented or the bloody jobs he took, an instinctive, intangible sort of thing that lived inside and colored the whole world differently. Notes trailed after him like stray puppies. He couldn't watch a sunset or hear the laughing rivers without thinking about what notes he might use to transpose them into music. Music was everywhere, in everything.

He was born Vincent St. Jame'Estain, a very fancy name for a very *un*-fancy fellow in a family of modest means and honest intentions. Vince's family spent the first twelve years of his life in the service of some benign, obscenely-wealthy lord's house in the comfortable domestic countryside of Nown Jin, where Vince helped his older brother Alles chop wood and deal with cattle by day and played piano for old Lord Muey himself by night.

Life was good for a long while—a simple rhythm of honest work and sheet music read by candlelight. A life where his only true concern was finishing work on time and keeping his gifted fingers clear of sheers, scythes, and axeheads.

Then came a broad sweep of the Grey Lady that managed to drag the entire household under, plunging Vince's settled rhythms into a dark, long-simmering silence broken only by the rattling and raising of tired coughs and drowning lungs.

In the end, Vince and his littlest sister were the only ones to ever resurface.

So Vince found himself packing the two of them up and trekking to the nearby city of Pearl Jin, where he was told he could find Kassie treatment.

What he *wasn't* told was just how much that treatment would cost.

Vince, just short of his thirteenth birthday and already taller than most grown men, went looking for work. It didn't take much time to discover that the bars and taverns and hotels in Pearl Jin that did possess some form of a dilapidated piano were not keen on having a hulking giant play it, no matter how lovely the music he conjured forth truly was. Their appreciation for his talents lay in other areas, and if they wouldn't pay well for a youngster-musician already too big to fit on their piano benches, they were certainly keen on the *other* things he could do with his hands. Namely smash faces and crunch bones.

So Vince set his musical ambitions aside in the name of caring for little Kassie for however long her expensive treatments might last. Long years crept by, Vince callused his knuckles and gained scars into the name of 'workplace experience'. He rose in Regor's ranks, became the old-man's go-to. A woman came and went in his twenties—not just any woman, either. There were women all over the city to entice and entertain, women who taught you to be guarded, who made you cold. Not her. In a city where strength was survival, she made Vince weak. Her name was Jeaney, and she was a healer and an artist and gave Vince every tattoo he had, and she got tired of waiting around for Vince to leave the city that was rapidly becoming less of a prison and more of a home. Work was good. Kassie had her treatments. There was no real reason to leave, so he didn't, and Jeaney did, and the nights were long and lonesome for a while.

But time heals all wounds, especially the inside ones. Things were never good, but they were stable. Kassie had her treatments. They began when he was thirteen and she was six, and he was forty now.

Kassie grew weaker with every passing year and the treatments more expensive by the month.

And Regor, being mad at him, hadn't paid Vince for several of those months. Any savings he managed to rat-hole in the name of one day retiring and resuming his career as a musician were well-past long gone.

But then came an old man with a thick Faeish accent and a bag of marks that jingled with just the merry melody Vince had been seeking.

That happy little bag came with a price, of course. An admission that burned as he gave it voice. But Vince still said it without a second thought, no matter the sting. And for months after, there hadn't been a consequence in sight.

He was still desperate for money. And though Taein was right—selling the little rat outright *would* bring a handsome price—he needed more than that. He needed something sustainable. He needed to get back on Regor's good graces, and if following the distractible little Siou across the countryside was what would do it, then Vince was happy to put on a good face.

But that was before Taein pulled the little girl from the rubble and told Vince the truth.

Anathema.

The very word sent a bolt of unease slithering up his spine. Vince fiddled with Maple's reins as he snuck a glance at Taein. They'd been on the move toward the orphanage for about three full days now and the midday sun was bright on Taein's youthful face, highlighting the old smattering of bruises and cuts. The deep one on his cheekbone looked particularly painful, even by Vince's standards.

Vince's gaze left Taein's face and drifted down to rest on the lad's gloved hands as his personal unease grew. Following Taein around Ieris was one thing. Finding out he and the child were Anathema was another. But going to Efriel Shu itself? How could Regor expect that of him?

Vince looked away from Taein and to the little girl riding atop Lorrin. She was awake, eyes roving from place to place, never settling anywhere for more than a few seconds.

Probably thinking about her mum.

Vince understood. He'd spent the majority of his life thinking about his own mum. Wishing she was still here, so she could look after Kassie while he was working. Because what if Kassie went to her Long Wait while he was away? What if she was alone when it finally happened?

But Vince was also terrified, in some small, dark way, that she wouldn't ever go at all. That he would spend the rest of his life working for Regor, making just enough to keep her going, his fingers straying along the chipped keys of some back-water tavern's out-of-tune piano on rare and aimless occasions, always hungry for the polished ivory of a *real* piano, from which he could conjure melodies that might soothe the milage all these years working as professional muscle had carved into his achy bones.

But it was alright, really. It didn't matter that he had to set aside his dreams and spend his days working in Pearl Jin's hovels thrashing fellow gutter rats and gallivanting around the countryside protecting thieves and various other criminal entrepreneurs, or that he had to smile and pretend for Kassie that all the *imaginary* concerts he played and *imaginary* orchestral pieces he wrote in his *imaginary* free time were reality. It was alright, because he knew that she would do the same for him.

Vince snuck another glance at the little girl and found her eerie green eyes looking straight back at him.

She reminded him so much of Kassie—all wire-like limbs and mousey brown hair. It was easy then to put aside the kid's curse and remind himself that he was doing this heart-attack of a job for Kassie, that it was just another means to pay for the treatments and possibly a few replacement keys for the dilapidated piano lingering in a dank corner of the scrapper house he'd claimed as his personal refuge, back when he had enough marks left over to pay the rent. But then the kid —*June*—would look at him and he'd catch sight of those eyes, and *sweet Geiin*, they were terrifying. It wasn't even the color, though the pale green was certainly odd, but the expression. She seemed far too smart for a little girl. Far too old.

Vince dropped the kid's gaze, his heart picking up speed.

There's a hunter, Taein had said.

Vince knew. He'd known that, long before Taein. But he never thought *this* would happen.

Vince swallowed hard and raised his eyes back up to the sky, expecting to see the white bird still a far-away speck. Instead he nearly jumped out of his skin, startling his draft, because the bird was no longer way up in the sky but careening down at them, hurtling down toward the earth like a comet.

"Taein, sweet Geiin—*Taein!*" Vince stammered, pointing.

Taein shot him a glare before snapping his eyes to the sky as the bird came close enough for them to hear the wind rushing through its snowy feathers.

They watched, frozen, as the hawk suddenly flared its broad wings and slowed just enough to tear at June's shoulder. Vince swore as their horses startled away from the bird, which flapped back into the air as June and Taein both frantically smacked at it. The bird whirled around with a quick swoop and, near as quick as it came, bounded back into the air.

By the time Vince was able to rein in Maple, the hawk was far off. He shook his baffled head and looked at Taein.

"Do you think it was trying to snatch the kid—" the sentence fell dead in his mouth as he focused on Taein and June.

Taein was standing on his toes to steady June, who was glaring up at the sky with murder on her face, those green eyes glinting like the white-hot center of an overfed fire. Little leafy sprouts were curling up around Taein's boots and Lorrin's hooves, growing. *Growing.* The kid wasn't even touching the ground and yet things were growing up out of the dark spring soil because of her.

Vince toyed with a lock of Maple's thick mane and shifted in the saddle, already weary, until Taein got Lorrin moving again.

No one spoke.

They're just people, you podge, he told himself. *Only human.*

When he raised his eyes back to the sky, he could still see the tiny pale spot that was the hawk as it flew away, the slightest glint of blue fabric clutched in its talons.

There's a hunter. Vince lowered his eyes.

Sometimes the marks talked louder than his loyalty, especially when Kassie's doctors needed money and Regor was sitting on jobs. Sometimes, he couldn't afford to let his conscience win over reality.

And he could comfort himself with all the '*you only do what you have to*'s and the '*Kassie needs her medicine*'s and the '*you're not a bad man, you're still better off than all the liars and thieves and crooks out there, at least you're still trying*'s, and the '*at least you don't steal from orphanages like that rat bastard Taein*'s he possibly wanted.

But Vince knew the truth. When the chips were down, *really* down, he wasn't any different from the rest.

When the chips were down, he was just like Taein.

———

❧ 25 ❧

BURNING

June watched the falcon fly away with a piece of her sleeve in its talons, her blood boiling.

Why should that stupid bird be free to fly wherever it pleased, to *find* whomever it pleased, when she was still very much stuck to the ground, her heart on fire and the Raincloak Man still unpunished?

She glared at the sky until the bird was no more than a speck. Then she looked back down to the saddle horn and resumed tracing the engraved silver embedded atop the pommel with her eyes. She knew the engraving—a rose, with each petal terrifically detailed—by heart at this point. It was all she could do, as night and day kept up their relentless looping, to stare at it.

It was that, or think about Mama. She was awake now, and for good, it seemed like, and the darkness held no refuge any longer. Whenever she thought about Mama, that *thing* that'd come to live inside her ever since the Raincloak Man ruined everything would rear back up and start harrowing at her insides again.

But June was starting to get bored, and she was tired of the pain. The shock of it all was wearing thin and now something had to be done. She forced her eyes from the saddle horn and glanced around her surroundings. Their little group was cutting through a farmer's lush green field, a morning mist thick in the air and cloaking the rolling hills ahead.

Her heart sank. The strangers, the Idiot and the Giant, were taking her to an orphanage, where she would be *'safe'*.

June scoffed. The word felt the same as 'fairy' or 'bog goblin'. Silly and imagined and old-world. Something she believed in when she was a little kid. She knew better now, that was for sure.

The horse stumbled and sent June flopping forward in the saddle. She struggled to correct herself, but a hand pushed her upright before she had the chance. She glimpsed the Idiot himself, his frame made blurry by tears.

June blinked hard and glared. He had a strange face, not at all similar to Mama or Gram, and June had more than enough time to study what made him so different.

His features seemed very foreign, with a gentle slope to his nose and eyes the exact color of the rich dark coffee Gram drank on cold mornings. His hair was pitch-black, curly and very messy, shadowing his gaze and that odd, too-sharp grin he used whenever he seemed nervous. His skin was bruised in deep shades of purples and greens, especially on his face—how had he gotten so beaten up? One cheekbone bore a gash so deep it hurt June's stomach just to look. The stitches were good at least. June knew a good row when she saw one— Mama made her practice stitching wounds last year when they studied herbs and medicines.

June's eyes were drawn down to the Idiot's boots—lavish leather things with elaborate gold scrolling in shapes of ornate roses and tiny birds in flight and small long lines of pine trees. Who was he trying to impress? Nothing else he wore was of much interest—just a dark, weathered raincoat, trousers, and a white shirt speckled with old blood. But a glimmer of silver reflecting the gray sunlight kept catching June's eye. Some sort of charm was dangling from one of the Idiot's ears. Did it hurt to poke a hole through the lobe?

Hurt. June blinked as the pain from her wounds reclaimed her attention. Sometimes she forgot about them, too distracted with thoughts of the Raincloak Man and this strange new Idiot. Other times, she felt all her hurts at once.

This was one of those times, it seemed. June closed her eyes again, lights dotting the newborn darkness. She had never felt so horrible in all her life.

June's gaze drifted back toward the saddle horn. She felt her eyes glazing over again, her mind slipping back into that endless cycling rage, before she forced herself to look at the Giant. He was scary in different ways—where the Idiot was slight and sharp the Giant was blunt-featured and, well, *giant*. His face was more familiar than the Idiot's—he had plain, rough features beneath his shaggy hair and half-braided beard. He was tan like Mama and Gram, and his friendly eyes told June he probably really *was* kind beneath his massive appearance. He had tree-trunk arms covered in strange, intricate black tattoos, wore thick, coarse pants and a great big green jacket, and carried a beat-up guitar on one shoulder that he played quite nicely by the fire at night. June liked that. She liked the way the firelight would catch the plethora of rings the Giant wore—silvers, golds, bronze. Turquoise stones and dark obsidian. Smooth bands, some fully engraved. Where had all these rings come from? Why did he wear them? Her hands twitched, but she knew he wouldn't understand if she tried to ask.

The horse took another bad step and sent June slipping in the saddle again. She bit her lip to keep from crying and ignored the Idiot's concerned glance.

She hurt *so much*. How was it even possible to feel this much pain at once?

June gripped the saddle horn a little tighter. If only she could just fall back asleep... back to peace and quiet. While sleeping, she could try to figure the Giant and the Idiot, plan her escape, fester her thoughts on the Raincloak Man. Weather this new incredible ache, the emptiness and enormity of all these nameless feelings. She could think about House Light and the Lady Marguerite woman she'd never met and never wanted to.

She could think about the Raincloak Man, and just how much better she'd feel when she was finally able to make him understand the *hurt* he put inside her.

June remembered Mama telling her about the Four Fathers. Remembered listening to the story and not even being able to imagine that sort of evilness. Well, she certainly could now. *Evil* was what took her Mama and burned down their home. *Evil* was the cause of all this pain, the kindling to the inferno in her heart. *Evil* was the Raincloak Man.

But June would set things right. She would get her knife back and find him and make him *pay*. And then, and only then, all this pain would go away. She was sure of it.

There was no other way.

<hr>

❧ 26 ❧

HONOR HIM

Vasily awoke in the darkness of the next morning with that fell rumble echoing deep through the earth once again. He sat back against the bars of his cage and peered out his cage at the few patrolling soldiers. No one else seemed to notice the way the earth seemed to slightly shift, so Vasily just sat and watched the quaking as it knocked the little drifts of packed sand from the slats of his cage, his heart going tight, sinking ever lower.

Mari sensed this darkness brewing and yet Vasily had just brushed her off. But she was right—the old roots of fallen Fathers and lost specters seemed to be pushing up new, unwanted shoots.

And here he was, expected once again to fix it.

Vasily shivered as the groaning died down. *How can I ever stop this?*

Hours passed without an answer. When the faint morning bled into a bright clear day, Vasily received who he knew was to be his final visitor.

Rafael approached Vasily's cage, his cloak brushing atop the sand, and folded his arms.

"Did the Shade speak the truth?" he asked.

Vasily fought back a glower and just nodded. "Yes."

Rafael's eyes narrowed with unchecked skepticism before he

187

whirled around to the pack of Vandels standing behind, flung out his arms, and bellowed, *"Vjarfalla!"*

An uproarious shout arose from the Enti and the cage door was flung open and Vasily was hauled out and shoved onto his unsteady, sleep-dulled feet. He found himself passed from brother to brother, slapped on the back, shook by his shoulders, kissed on both cheeks and sometimes his forehead too, and crushed in so many iron Enti embraces he thought his bones might crack as the brotherhood seemed to congratulate him all at once.

What have I just agreed to?

By the time the outburst mellowed, Vasily's head was spinning so wildly he could hardly see straight as Rafael stepped forward with a bowl tucked in the crook of his arm. He grasped Vasily with one hand and smiled broadly despite the bruises peppering his face.

"Ave hala en guarenta Enti," he said warmly, as if Vasily hadn't assaulted him only a night before, "Welcome to the brotherhood Enti."

"Wait—" Vasily said, alarms blaring in his head. He'd only agreed to help them, not *join* their entire order.

The protest died on his lips as Rafael dipped his finger into the bowl and smeared the left side of Vasily's cheeks with a burning red powder that seared his nose and stung his eyes.

"Arrinvale," Rafael said, "the mark of the Bavarti, the Vandels of the Wastes."

Rafael dipped another finger in the bowl and smeared the right side of Vasily's cheeks with a line of pale blue powder.

"Dust of gorrinfish scales, the mark of the Jal, the Vandels of the Nujin Valley and the Great Marsh."

Rafael rubbed a black powder onto his own forehead, then Vasily's.

"And charcoal," Rafael said, "to mark the Enti, who ride upon the Wastes and go down to our Long Waits for both."

He tossed the bowl down, grasped Vasily by both of his shoulders, and kissed both of Vasily's cheeks. It was all Vasily could do to stay still and bear it with the most carefully composed expression of neutrality he could manage.

At last, Rafael let him go and addressed the Enti again.

"Oen marayeliousa kan Enti bayja Aal Salava!"

He didn't bother translating as the Enti cheered, and instead took Vasily's arm and began barking orders to the men at his heels. Instantly, the throng dispersed and returned leading horses, among them Vasily's own bay mare.

Vasily's heart leaped when he saw her. *Stars above*, if he could only get on and be done with this whole sordid affair—

"We will now ride out to retrieve the body of a fallen brother," Rafael said as he pulled Vasily toward the waiting horses, "and you shall see the Withering at its most harsh."

Vasily most certainly had questions, most all of them summarized by a brisk *what the hell is going on*, but Rafael barked *"As haunya!"*, and the group set out at once. Vasily was left following atop his bay, bonds cut, head whirling, heart hammering, trying in vain to catch up.

THEY RODE FOR SEVEN HOURS WITHOUT STOP.

The sun was bearing down with an oppressive heat by the time midday arrived. Vasily himself was sweating like a pig atop the bay while the twelve mounted Enti around him in their sweltering leather breastplates and thick tunics seemed perfectly content. But Vasily didn't have to suffer much longer; soon a thin gray mist came into view, curling just over the white sands, leaching color from the landscape, sucking away the heat, a stern silent warning.

With the curling mist came other strange indicators—blackened sage snowing flakes of papery ash, clusters of bloody arrinvale lit through with a dark, pulsing crimson, flocks of jaybirds turned a sooty black as if scorched by some great invisible fire.

They arrived, and Vasily saw the mists up close for the first time since his boyhood.

The wall reared high into the sky; imperious, proud, and alive. Their group stopped some hundred feet away and still the mists stole away the sun and drained every hint of warmth from the air. The mist itself seemed to move and churn from where he sat atop his mare, a swirling, swaying, stalking thing, an impassable wall that looked from this safe distance as traversable as passing through heavy rain.

Vasily stared at that churning silver fortress as the veiled afternoon sun refracted through the mists, illuminating the dark silhouettes of the strange shapes sailing through the sky beyond. He twisted the mare's black mane through his fingers and waited for the fear to come, but it didn't. The waiting was somehow worse.

Rafael reined his destrier over and leaned down. "Do you see how the sun brightens the sky just above the top?"

Vasily raised his eyes to the highest point of the mists and nodded.

"A week ago, the sun at this time of day would've been covered twice over."

A rock sunk hard in Vasily's stomach. Rafael kicked his horse back into a canter, and they rode on along the mist to the West and deeper into the Province. Vasily held on, forcing his body to move with the bay's quick strides as he tried to think.

It'd taken weeks to hunt down the bloodline of Glass, and even then he still missed one. How would he ever rid the entire province of the Anathema?

Did it even matter how long it took, if he was keeping his family safe?

The ground blurred beneath the mare's rolling strides and for just a moment Vasily saw his father's face again, saw the frozen horror etched into Babas' features as he grayed into ash and crumpled to the ground. As Vasily lurched forward to steady him, too late to make a difference.

Vasily's palms were sweaty that night. He was so afraid of the future, even before he had reason to be. So nervous to be among the royalty from all four houses, to be toted around behind Babas as the *heir of House Slate.*

I'm not enough to take his place.

And that sweaty-palmed young man of twenty was right. Vasily was not enough to fill Babas' void, and he never would be, because he *failed,* all those years ago in the snow. Because a Prince of Glass still lived, and Babas didn't.

Just like that, the old fire awoke again.

No. He could not do this. He couldn't. How could he rid the world of Anathema, when one of Babas' murderers still roamed free? This was not more important. This was not his burden. This was not his way.

A sudden burst of desperate energy coursed through Vasily's limbs, and his gaze went once more to the sands flying by below. If he turned the bay, it wouldn't take the Enti more than a second to realize and knock his head from his shoulders before he could so much as get three strides away. But if—

His line of thought was cut abruptly off as the sands below turned from white to a soot-stained black. Vasily blinked. Surely, he was seeing things. But when he opened his eyes again, the sands below were still colored the lifeless, charred obsidian of a burned-out mountainside.

Dread crept through his veins with arachnid precision. Vasily reached out to take up the saddle horn as he grew suddenly weak, his eyes fixed to the black sands blurring by below.

The mist rages and grows strong... drenching the world black.

Vasily forced himself to look away from the sands and immediately wished he hadn't. Rodigis' voice was still circling in his mind when the first of the Waste's rare *jaleno* trees came into view, twisted branches burnt to coal and stripped bare of their usual olive-green leaves and fire-hot fruits.

He stared as the tree went by, a blur of soot still somehow standing.

No.

He forced his gaze down to the saddle and held on tighter to the horn, squeezing his eyes shut.

This cannot be.

They rode deep into the heart of that blackness before the Enti slammed to a halt and Vasily slid from the saddle on board-stiff legs and hurried onward with the rest of the Vandels toward something lying broken and gnarled atop the black surface as the chill of the sand ate through his boots and froze his toes.

It was quiet as they jogged toward the lump. Vasily trailed between two Enti, their somber eyes fixated on whatever lay in the sands ahead.

Vasily looked to the horses standing ground-tied some twenty feet behind. Twenty feet and fading.

He slowed his pace a little more, relentless desperation poisoning his bloodstream, very much aware that what he was about to do was certain madness.

He didn't wait another moment, and instead tripped up the nearest Enti and snatched the soldier's knife before the man so much as hit the sand. He whirled around, ready to meet the second Enti, and found himself a second too late. Before he could draw a half-breath the soldier had him knocked on his back and the knife snatched away.

Vasily heard the uproar of the other Vandels, felt their footsteps as they pounded across the sand toward him, and braced.

Geiin help—

The thought was cut off by a fist to his gut. Vasily choked on a rush of blood, stars flashing before his eyes against the harsh glare of the mist-dimmed afternoon light.

There was a sudden pummeling and a sudden stop, and Vasily was jerked to his knees in front of Rafael.

The commander just glowered at Vasily. "What the hell, Slate!"

Vasily's head lolled as he tried to settle his gaze. He couldn't.

Rafael cuffed him. "What the *hell*, Slate! You gave your word to the Shade!"

It doesn't matter anymore, he thought blearily. The words didn't make it out of his mouth.

Rafael gripped Vasily by the cheeks he had only hours before smeared with spices and forced Vasily's lulling head still.

"You're *Faeish*, don't you remember?" Rafael snarled. "Your word is supposed to mean something!"

It used to.

"Why are you running?"

Vasily forced his eyes to focus on the commander. Hot blood oozed out of his mouth, down his chin.

"I have to... find Glass."

"What does that even mean? How could that *possibly* be more important than this?"

Vasily shook his head, trying to break free of Rafael's grip. "You don't even know if any of this is real."

Rafael stared Vasily down, his brothers behind him silent, the only sound that of the deathly wind stirring the cobalt sands at their feet.

Disbelief contorted Rafael's face. He barked out a word and instantly two brothers jerked him up and hauled him the rest of the way to the dark lump in the sand.

Vasily's legs were kicked out from beneath him and he was shoved onto his hands and knees as they reached the shape. An Enti forced his face closer to what lay in the sand and Vasily drew in a panicked breath, smelling charcoaled-flesh and something else; something alien and incredibly bitter.

It took him several heartbeats before his startled eyes finally comprehended just what it was, lying there.

A body—or what had been one. Twisted skeletal remains charred to the point of crumbling lay half-buried in the blackened sands, still smoldering with weak puffs of ash-gray smoke.

Vasily made out the cracked remains of what was a skull and forced himself backward against the Enti. The soldiers went to shove his face right back at the skeleton before the commander stopped them with a clipped word.

Vasily scrambled back from the body and sat in the sand, only dimly registering the Enti looming behind him. He looked into Rafael's face as the commander strode his way, pausing just before the corpse.

"There. What is it that you see there?"

Vasily kept his eyes on Rafael. "A body."

"Real enough for you, Slate? That body belonged to a living man a mere week ago. Is the week-old corpse here in a correct state of decay? Is the skeleton before you a natural thing?"

Vasily glared and tried not to gag on the blood congealing in his mouth. "It seems your mind is already made up."

Rafael clenched his jaw and spoke between flattened lips, his eyes glinting in the falling light. "That corpse was our *brother*. We left him here to rest his wounds with three other Enti. He succumbed and when we returned we found his body alone. The others were ashes."

Ashes.

A chill crept up the back of Vasily's neck. Still he kept ahold of Rafael's gaze, the sand cool beneath him.

Rafael stabbed a finger at the dark curling mists around them. "*This* is the withering. It is destroying the land, eating away natural things one plant, one animal, one man at a time. It is causing this sick decay wherever a man dies inside. Whatever your distraction, it does not matter. You must help me stop this."

Vasily looked at the mists beyond for a long time before returning his gaze to Rafael. "Why is it that your own people are not fighting this? Your own Aal?"

Rafael's lips mashed even tighter, and Vasily bared his teeth in a smile. He then let out a bark of laughter and clambered onto his feet as a dry wind began to pick up, carrying with it the winter-time scent of the mists.

Vasily straightened and looked Rafael in the eye, unable to bar his scorn any longer. "Rafael. My *brother*. I'm sorry."

And he meant it. He really did. But something inside him was broken, all his usual restraint and long-suffering patience ground down to nothing and stomped away, and before he could stop himself and think through a better plan, Vasily threw a fist into Rafael's face.

Rafael stumbled, and it was just enough for Vasily to land another punch and pluck the commander's knife away before Rafael had the time to draw a single stilted breath.

But blood was pounding loud in Vasily's ears, and he only felt the barest disturbance in the air behind him before he was tackled by a pair of Enti and found himself on his back as two pairs of fists raided down with such a vengeance he couldn't make out a single coherent thought until a bellowing roar ground the assault to a dead halt.

"*Enough!*"

Instantly, the Enti were off of Vasily and hauling his battered self back onto his knees. Blood dripped from Vasily's temple and bit at his eyes with such ferocity that he could hardly make out Rafael's looming shadow before he felt the commander's fist collide with his temple.

Pain splintered through his brain and blackness descended a heavy dropped curtain, only to be yanked up when someone pulled Vasily's head up by his hair and threw some strong fiery liquid into his face. The liquid found its way into Vasily's mouth just as Rafael clamped a hand on his jaw and forced Vasily to meet his infuriated gaze.

Red oozed from Rafael's nose. He leaned down close to Vasily's own face and snarled.

"You just threw your life away, Slate. And it's a damn shame, because you could've saved the whole world. *We* could've saved it."

Vasily spat blood into Rafael's face and hardly felt the blow when Rafael retaliated with a savage kick. His cheek met the sand and his body slipped from his grip, and for one terrible second, Vasily felt himself slipping back into the abyss. Binds tightened around his body like a noose.

That's when he heard Rafael's voice cut through the haze of pain and fading consciousness. Heard the creak of leather as the commander mounted his horse.

"Let the Withering do it for us... flee this place before the decay... *Aref Joula*... When it is finished, retrieve his corpse. Bring it to..."

Vasily ground his fingers into the sand, searching for something to hold onto, a way to make sense of the words. His body just screamed for him to stay still.

"But he will be unrecognizable, my lord, after it is finished. Why not draw him out of the mists and kill him in safety?"

There was a long silence. Vasily struggled, trying to haul himself away from the blackness sucking him down.

"It would be war, Imaan. A war we cannot afford, not while fighting this. Leave him... when he has withered, take his amulet now as proof."

"But he..."

Vasily dug his fingers into the sand and groaned, trying to get up, *get up*.

He heard Rafael scoff. He heard his own blood dripping onto the sand, running into his mouth, his eyes, his ears.

"Look at him, Camain. He is nothing more than a broken little boy playing pretend in the shadow of his father. Fear nothing."

He lives in you. Mother's voice came to him like the sweetest touch of rain. Vasily saw Babas' face somewhere in that blackness, if only for the barest breath of a second.

I'm not worthy, Mari.

Mother spoke again somewhere in that fast-fading darkness as every breath Vasily took became a deliberation.

Honor him.

Somehow, it was enough. Vasily kept her voice close as his battered body returned to him, bruised and bleeding, full of pain to the point of delirium. The small thunder of Rafael's horse cantering off swept the echo of mother's voice away. All was quiet for a long while, save for the wind stirring the sand.

At last, an Enti spoke. "Get it over with, then."

"Why me?"

There was the sound of boots scuffling and assorted grumblings before many saddles began creaking as their owners mounted. Horses stamped and swished their tails, eager to leave the desolation behind.

Vasily listened and kept still, his body bobbing up through that black fog and returning to him pain-shocked and angry, and heard only one pair of boots padding across the sand.

Honor him.

He waited, counting those steps. He waited until he was sure, and he threw himself up with such violence that all he heard was the disjointed shout of surprise from the Enti before Vasily tackled him, took the young man's knife in his own bloody hands, and stabbed the Enti through the heart.

Honor him.

The soldier toppled, Vasily with him.

He regained his footing and jerked the dead soldier's second dagger from its sheath only a second before the mounted Vandels came flying back to trample him, spear tips glinting in the sinking half-light. The sound of the Enti shouting and the thousands of pounds of muscled horse mass shaking the sand mere feet from Vasily drowned out every other sense. It was all he could do to keep scrambling away from hooves and spears and swords until the earth gave a riotous heave and the Enti's uproar came to a crashing halt, their horses rearing and shying as if they already knew just what was coming. As if they understood.

Vasily whirled around with the sword at ready, desperate to keep all the Enti in his sight at once, blood in his mouth and in his hair and dripping into his eyes, his heart hammering as a strange desperate iciness took the world captive.

Vasily felt that chill rising in time with the darkening of the sun as it fell well below the gray wall beyond, as that thin intangible mist curled low around his boots. He felt the chill in the air and understood himself.

The withering.

His eyes slid to the dead Enti bleeding on the sand, and his heart fell to his toes.

It worked.

It was still for a long moment. Then the earth shuddered and heaved, and the Vandels' hold on their horses slipped beyond repair at last. Vasily watched as the horses, fighting the bits in their mouths and the men on their backs, bucked and bolted. A horse reared up in the air and fell over, crashing down on his rider and snapping the rope that once tethered it to a struggling bay mare.

Vasily's bay mare. He forced his stiff legs into a shambling run toward his freed mare, praying she would hold still for just a little longer.

Please.

The thin mist all around sharpened to a needle-point the time Vasily reached the bay's side and vaulted up onto the saddle, flailing for the short rope connected to her halter. As soon as his weight came down on her back she flew into a gallop. He looked down, hardly able to feel his face, and saw the sands below flare with pulsating crimson veins of unnatural, *cursed* light, the glow a red fiery blur beneath the mare's pounding hooves.

Hundreds of feet flew by and still the chill in the air grew fierce, cutting at his skin, sucking the warmth out of Vasily's very bones, draining his cheeks of feeling.

Vasily gritted his teeth and held on as his legs went dead in the stirrups.

Another second ticked by, then another. He could no longer move his arms, his neck.

Tears pricked behind his eyes. Vasily felt his mare begin to slow even as her sides went dark with panicked exertion, he felt himself growing weak with terror.

Surely, this could not be it.

His mare continued to struggle, fighting for ground, her hooves scraping at the sand. A horrific cacophony of screams split the world in two behind them, and a terrific flare of red light exploded the way they had come.

Vasily didn't look back, he couldn't have if he wanted to. He forced his failing legs tighter around the mare's side and prayed she would keep running.

THE BAY OUTRAN THE WITHERING. VASILY DIDN'T UNDERSTAND how. By the time he finally drew her to a halt her sides were black with sweat and her legs trembling, but they were near the blessed northern border some fifty miles away from Nown Jin, so close to finally regaining the right path.

Vasily slid from the saddle and landed awkwardly on his own shaking legs.

"Good girl," he soothed, giving the mare a pat and smoothing her forelock. He fetched his canteen from his saddlebag and found it half-full of stale water. He poured some into his hands and let the mare drink, alternating sips between them until the canteen was empty.

He returned the canteen to the saddlebag and stilled as a familiar presence drew near. The hair on his arms rose at the whisper of feathers displacing air, and Vasily turned to spy his bloodhawk curling slow loops above.

He raised his arm and called for her as relief swept through him. But Bellan didn't come closer, instead swooping down and releasing something from her talons. Vasily stumbled forward to catch it and opened his palm to reveal a blood-stained stroke of fabric dotted with faded yellow flowers, the cloth itself once a pale, happy blue.

Vasily stared. His heart faltered in his chest.

This cloth was familiar. He'd seen this pattern before. Vasily squinted up at the bloodhawk before studying the fabric again. He had sent Bellan after Glass, but this fabric surely belonged to a woman.

Or a... girl.

A memory shifted into hazy focus, and Vasily's jaw clenched tight.

Not any girl. *The* girl, the tiny raging one from the Jinian valley. Vasily blinked hard, his fingers curling tight over the fabric. The little girl he *killed*. Why would Bellan bring him this when he'd specifically sent her after Glass?

Vasily looked up at the bloodhawk, who'd perched upon a scraggy jaleno tree and sat watching him with patient amber eyes. He and Babas trained Bellan exceptionally well. She understood Vasily's wishes better than most men did. She wouldn't bring him back a piece of fabric belonging to a random person, much less a Sleeper.

Vasily drew in a ragged breath and sank slowly to the ground.

That meant the little girl was... how could it be possible? He burned her little valley to the ground. He burned *her*.

He turned the fabric over on his palm, brushed off crusted blood. Bellan had found Glass, that much was certain. She wouldn't have returned until she located him.

But she'd also found the little girl again, and alive. Could she and Glass be together? Had Glass found her and resurrected her with his sorcery? Was he capable of such a feat?

Honor him, came the whisper.

Vasily sighed, got to his feet, and swung back into the saddle with bones grown weary. Bellan swept off the branch, flapped into the air, and circled above until Vasily coaxed his mare into a plodding walk. He leaned forward in the saddle, letting Bellan lead them onward, and curled a lock of the mare's cobalt mane around his finger.

Honor him.

There was no other way.

27

THE PARTING

Mid-afternoon.

They'd been traveling abandoned smuggler's routes—narrow, rain-choked trails of mud that would eventually turn into sun-baked paths once they got close enough to Ersii to escape Nown Jin's perpetual rains—for three days. Taein knew they were due to reach the tiny village surrounding *Myrtle's Home for Children* in an hour or so, which meant that today was the day he could finally wash his hands clean of the kid.

As such, today was downright *obligated* to be a good day. And so far, it was turning out that way. Pale morning sunlight peeked from behind the usual cloud cover above, stealing glances at the meadows sitting on either side of the trail. The left-side meadow was occupied by a long-abandoned barn, the dilapidated structure well on its way to being completely devoured by blackberry brambles and moss as thick as Vince's beard. A mild wind ruffled the leafy heads of the beech trees lining the trailsides. Between these trees sat clusters of pomegranate-colored foxgloves and cliques of yellow dandelions. The air was thick with the heady scents of spring; fresh rain on soft grass, hardy apple trees dense with sweet, snow-white blossoms, the honeyed perfume of clover. Life was everywhere, made gentle by the sun.

Taein batted away a honeybee and peered at the kid. She stared straight ahead, arms crossed tightly over her chest, sullen as ever, reflecting only thunderstorms at the merry spring day.

"We're only about an hour off, brat. You doing alright?"

No response. She'd never come around to them and kept her responses minimal to none. And when she needed looking after—which was *all* the shanking time—she squirmed and flinched at every touch and refused to talk to him altogether.

Taein sighed and waited. He'd always thought were children impossible, and the little brat in his saddle not only confirmed his suspicions but exceeded them with flying colors. He repeated himself, and at last June shook her head. Taein knew full well that she was probably lying, just like she did every other time he asked, before deciding he didn't care. Only an hour more, and she was someone else's problem.

The day wore on. As they neared the settlement they left the smuggler's trail and found a main road. Soon they were crunching over coarse gravel into a scattering of rough-hewn wooden houses. Taein led them straight through the settlement and up a hilly side road that took them right to the orphanage's twin oak doors.

Vince held the horses in the yard while Taein helped June down. She slid off the saddle and landed awkwardly on the uninjured leg. Taein offered his hand, but she batted it away with a glare. For a moment they stood side-by-side, surveying the house.

Myrtle's orphanage was an impressive structure for the poorer countryside of Nown Jin. Nestled snugly in a grove of alders, it looked to Taein some four stories tall; a long, rectangular building of white-washed wood lined with many windows; each of which were bestowed a small window box filled with yellow-and-black pansies, who peered over the edges of their boxes like tiny suspicious wardens. A sign hung above the door, reading *Myrtle's Home for Lost Boys and Girls.*

"Well," Taein said with a nod to June, "off you go. Just knock."

June looked up at him with something other than disgust for the first time in days, her features pinching.

"What?" Taein asked.

No answer. Her eyes were strangely void of their usual glassy hate and filled with something that looked almost similar to fear.

Taein looked up at Vince, who was already glaring at him with a certain level of disdain Taein hadn't anticipated.

"What?" he asked.

Vince arched his thick brows as if he thought Taein should already know the answer. "Walk her to the door, you rit-headed little podger."

Taein narrowed his eyes. "She's got legs."

Vince leaned back on his heels, closed his eyes, and hurled a sigh at the clouds. "Sweet Geiin, you're *impossible*. Look, Taein, she's just a kid. She's probably scared," he said, looking at June. "Are you scared?"

She didn't answer, eyes darting from the ground and to Vince and to the ground again.

"Ain't nothing to be ashamed of," Vince said. "I get scared, too."

June looked between the two of them before giving a little nod. Taein bit back a groan and shook his head. *Sweet Geiin indeed.*

"Alright, then," he sighed, nudging her forward. "Let's get this over with."

She stared at Taein, as if asking if he really was going to abandon her here.

Taein offered a tight smile. "Day's not getting any longer, brat."

She snatched her gaze away, shoulders sagging, and hobbled toward the door. Taein followed and hesitantly offered a hand so that she might better steady herself, which June promptly smacked away.

They reached the door and Taein knocked briskly before June had the chance, which incited a terse hiss and a glare.

"Oh, be nice," he murmured, stepping back and brushing mud off the front of his shirt. "Little girls that hiss at people stay in orphanages forever."

Another glare. He forced himself to soften and at least attempt to be understanding.

"Look, this is just how it has to be," he said. He fished for her knife and offered it to her in its leather sheath. "Don't use this unless you have to, yes? And don't let anyone know you have it."

She swiped the knife and stood there clutching it to her chest before Taein grabbed it back and stuffed it up her sleeve that hadn't ripped. She jerked away from him and pointed at the horses.

"You'd rather go with us?"

She shook her head, eyes narrowing.

Taein struggled against an eye roll. "Right, because I've horses to spare."

She nodded. Taein had nothing to say that he hadn't already, so they waited in silence as the sound of shuffling inside grew nearer. The steps finally closed in on the door, so Taein straightened up and tried to make himself look at least a little presentable (if that was ever even possible).

The door swung open and a small, shrew-faced woman shaped rather like an old laundry bag and clothed in a drab black dress peered out, blinking in the cheerful afternoon light.

"Yes?" she inquired.

"You must be Myrtle?" Taein asked, flashing his best smile.

Her eyes narrowed as she looked between them. "That depends on who's asking. What business?"

Taein didn't answer and instead asked, "May we come in?"

Myrtle scrutinized them again for another agonizing while before peering over their shoulders at Vince, who waved. She looked back at Taein, a question in her watery old eyes, and opened the door a little further.

"I do believe that's blood all over the little girl, isn't it?"

Taein nodded, clasping his hands behind his back and offering another winning smile. "Yes ma'am, but it's her own."

The woman pursed her lips. "That's very reassuring, master..?"

"Jean Kinsten," Taein supplied.

She looked him up and down once again before settling on his face. "You're Siou?"

He swallowed a choice oath and supplied another smile. "Half, ma'am, but grown up here in Nown Jin."

She hesitated before looking back at June, who wasn't looking at Myrtle with her strange shamrock eyes but rather at the ground in an exceedingly pitiful and much more constructive manner.

Good girl, Taein thought. *Tug those old heartstrings hard.*

Taein watched with silent glee as the old woman softened, then moved aside. "Well, come in, then."

Oh, sweet victory.

Taein nudged June forward and they climbed the step and entered a narrow, dimly lit hallway lined with faded rugs. The woman led them into the cramped, circular room that was probably once a well-adorned parlor but was now spectacularly jammed with a collection of antique, well-worn chairs, carved, scuffed-up end tables, and crooked, dust-coated paintings.

"Well," Myrtle said as she threw open sun-bleached curtains that Taein guessed might've once been a deep crimson, "Whatever sad tale you wish to spin for me about the little girl's origins, make it quick or make it the truth. I haven't the time for anything else."

Myrtle turned around and gestured for Taein to sit in a green velvet chair. "You can sit there if you please, but the girl must stand. I cannot have her soiling my sitting room in the state she is in."

Taein wasn't sure that June could manage to stand much longer, but before he could interject the kid sat herself on the floor, crossed her legs like a boy, and set about staring out the window in a pointedly disinterested fashion.

Silence hung about the room before Taein remembered himself and spoke.

"My companion and I were traveling from Pearl Jin and along our way we found her," he paused, gesturing at June, "in a ditch, all alone. Quite unfortunately, she's mute, so we weren't able to find what had happened to her or whether she belonged to anyone nearby. And she was hurt so badly we didn't feel it safe to leave her on her own, so we decided to bring her here and see if you would be so kind as to look after her."

Myrtle arched a brow, clasped her hands tightly in her lap, and smiled at Taein. "Aren't you the lad who stole my D'artigan?"

Taein froze before furrowing his brow and looking her dead in the eye. "I'm not sure I'm following."

She stared at him before nodding. "Yes, you *are* the lad. You got in through my chimney and plucked my painting off the wall, then went right back up. I remember you."

Taein sat back and laid on another smile. "Ma'am, I am most certainly no thief—"

She touched a finger to her earlobe, eyes still trained on him. "It's the earring. I remember."

Taein folded his hands in his lap and bit back a colossal sigh. "If we could get back the matter at hand—"

She picked up a chipped teacup from the end table and sipped. "Certainly, but I do hope you got a good price for it. I enjoyed having it on my wall, to be sure."

Taein narrowed his eyes. "Did you know what it was worth?"

"You concede to the crime, then?"

"No—"

She set the teacup down without noise. "Eighty-three years have not dulled my eyes nor my wits, lad. I watched you from the hallway. Good work, I must say. Mighty clean and quiet. I never would've known how you lifted it, had I not watched you."

"Thank you?" An awkward pause ensued. Taein tried another smile and posed his question again. "So will you keep the kid?"

Myrtle's gaze drifted to June and remained on her. "I wouldn't have let you in if I didn't intend to. Is your story true?"

Taein toyed with a thread poking out of the armrest and met her gaze. "Every word. Where are all the rest of the children?"

"Upstairs with Sister Agatha and Sister Farla, doing lessons. We have fifty-eight children right now. I never have room, and yet we make do." She squinted at him. "Are you in a hurry, Master Kinsten?"

Yes. "No."

"Then would you like to stay for tea?"

Taein stared. "I'm absolutely sure you're going to poison me if I say yes."

She chuckled. "Oh, heavens, no. It would be far too much work to dispose of your corpse for a woman of my age."

Taein's overly honeyed smile grew tight. "I see. I'm afraid I'd better be off, thank you. Wouldn't want to keep my associate waiting."

Myrtle nodded to June, who had not moved an inch but sat still, watching the window with her hands folded and resting atop her blood-crusted skirt. "How old are her injuries?"

"Maybe a week. The travel hasn't been kind."

"And what is her name?"

Taein hesitated. "June."

June didn't respond at the mention of her name, but a sudden pang tugged at Taein's heart, which he immediately stomped down with vigor. He didn't have time for this. Not now, and not ever.

"Would you like to say goodbye?" Myrtle asked, turning her sharp black eyes onto Taein.

"I—no, that won't—"

Myrtle rose from her chair with ease unnatural to her age. "Take your time."

Taein watched her walk out of the room, her gray bun bobbing atop her head, before looking at June.

She was already staring at him, eyes bright with betrayal.

Taein sighed. "Don't look at me that way, kid. This is for the best, remember?"

No response. Of course.

Taein got up from the chair and crouched before her. "I'm sorry I couldn't get you to where you really belonged. Maybe one day, when you're well and grown, you can do that for yourself. But for now... just be nice, alright?"

Her eyes were narrowed. She gave a begrudging nod.

Taein stood and turned to go before thinking better of it and looking back. As soon as he did, he regretted it.

Twin tears carved white paths through the grime on June's cheeks. As soon as she saw him looking she turned away, wiping her face on her sleeves and stifling her sniffles.

Taein blinked, trying to understand. Why in all of Ieris was she *crying*? She'd expressed nothing but contempt for him and Vince the entire time they'd taken care of her. Now tears? For what?

Taein dragged a hand through his hair. "This is how it has to be, alright?"

She turned all the way around. Unease crept into the pit of Taein's stomach.

"June?"

She shook her head.

"Please promise that you won't run after the Raincloak Man."

She shook her head, the action smaller this time.

Taein sighed and pinched the bridge of his nose. He waited a minute more, but she refused to turn back around, so he went for the door.

He found Myrtle out in the yard, talking with Vince and stroking the draft's nose. His boots crunched on the gravel as he walked over.

"Ah," Myrtle said, "said your goodbyes, then?"

Taein nodded. "Thank you for taking her."

She looked him in the eye. "What *really* happened to her, Master Kinsten?"

"I haven't a clue. We found her in a ditch, remember?"

"But your kind *associate* here says you found her in a burned-out settlement."

Taein bit the inside of his cheek to keep from glaring at Vince. "Yes. We found her in a ditch running through the settlement."

"He said she was beneath a pile of rubble. That a man had attacked her."

"Well, obviously *someone* attacked her."

Myrtle crossed her wispy arms. "Should I be concerned about that certain *someone* finding her here?"

Yes. "No."

"He must've had a strong motive, to be sure." She tsk'ed. "To attack a little girl of all things, the Celestial be good."

"Can insanity ever be rationalized?" he barreled on before Myrtle could reply. "Thank you, again. I wish I had the means to repay you."

She sniffed. "Restoring my D'artigan might suffice. But I can't imagine you held onto it."

Taein swung into the saddle. "I still haven't a clue what you're talking about."

She nodded. "If you fancy coming back here, I would advise you to use the front door, lad. Otherwise I may have to introduce you to Rowley."

"Who's he?" Vince asked before Taein could.

"My mastiff." Myrtle smiled at Taein. "He's a nice boy. He keeps my children very safe. I purchased him after your *first* visit."

Taein felt Vince's stare and smiled anyway. "I do appreciate the warning. For now, though, we'd better get going."

"Thank you for the muffins," Vince said. Taein noticed the basket he was holding and fought back the urge to knock it out of his hands.

"You're very welcome. Goodbye, lads! Come back soon!"

"Unlikely," Taein murmured, turning Lorrin around and setting him off down the path at a brisk trot.

When they were well out of her earshot, Taein swiveled back and glowered at Vince. "You've got to throw those away."

Vince, bouncing awkwardly in the saddle as his draft kept time with Lorrin, looked aghast. "Taein, she gave us *muffins*."

"She probably poisoned them, you imbecile," Taein hissed.

"Why would she do that?" Vince asked, fumbling to keep a hold of his reins and manage a pair of blueberry-dotted muffins at the same time.

"Because she knows I'm the one that stole from her, years back!"

Vince paused before popping an entire muffin into his mouth. "You're far too paranoid, Taein," he said as he chewed. "These are *blueberry* muffins. Suit yourself, but I ain't throwing these away even if they *are* poisoned."

"Well, don't go blaming me when you keel over. You were duly warned."

"*Me*, paying recompense for *your* poorly-executed crimes? When has that ever happened?" Vince chuckled. "Now, what do you say we crash in this village tonight?"

Taein frowned and peered at the horizon. "It's only sunset. We could probably ride for a good two hours more."

"Sure. Or we could call it a day and sleep in real beds and have a real meal for a change."

Taein wilted. "I won't be able to talk you out of this one after the Farthing incident, will I?"

"Exactly right," Vince said, slowing the draft to a walk. "You owe me."

Taein didn't bother with a response. They navigated the village in silence for a few minutes, working their way toward a little inn they had passed when they first arrived, when Taein looked suddenly at Vince.

"Vince, she cried when I left. The kid. Why on earth would she cry?"

"I dunno, ain't that just what kids do?"

"But we aren't her family. We aren't anybody to her."

Vince shrugged. "We saved her. That amounts to more than you might think."

Taein frowned and looked away, his chest tightening. There wasn't anything else to say. The sounds of the horses' hooves clopping over the gravel road and a calm whispering breeze filled the coming evening and did nothing to ease the sharp twinge of guilt in his heart.

28

TEA, BISCUITS, & THE GRUDGE

As soon as the Idiot left, the old woman turned to June with a withered finger set against her whiskery chin and sent her upstairs for a bath. June spent the next hour in a round tub, trying not to wince as a younger caretaker scrubbed the filth from her skin and hair and worrying her knife might be discovered where she hid it under her old dress. Her gashes still ached like clusters of bee stings even with the caretaker's fussing and medicines, each wound a stubborn reminder of what had happened—and who she should be hunting.

After the bath, the caretaker spread a sharp-smelling salve on June's wounds and wrapped them in soft, clean cloth. She was then given a too-big dress and left alone to change. June re-hid her knife, this time tying it to her waist beneath her new clothes with the dirty ribbon from her old dress. Then she was sent downstairs again for tea with the old woman.

June found this Myrtle lady in the same cramped sitting room, still nestled in her high-backed chair. But this time she had a platter of golden biscuits, a jar of honey, and a pot of tea on the table in front of her. An intoxicating smell, something sweet and warm and buttery, hung about the room like a golden cloud.

June's attention was lifted from the spread of food and back to the old woman—Myrtle—as she spoke.

"My," she said with a smile, "don't you look better. I'd imagine you feel much nicer now, don't you?"

June looked back at the spread, her mouth beginning to water. What kind of tea was there, in that pretty little pot? She could almost smell it—crisp and spiced and fruity.

"Would you please sit, June? I would like to ask you some questions."

June glanced over at her again. Hadn't the Idiot told this Myrtle creature that she couldn't speak?

The woman seemed to read her mind. She leaned forward and set a piece of paper and a pencil onto the table. June looked between her and the writing instruments.

Another smile. June might've been soothed if the woman's face didn't resemble an overly-ripe peach, all wrinkled, withered, and fuzzy. She'd never seen someone so old. Even Gram had still looked like a *person*, at least.

Myrtle gestured toward the biscuits and tea. "Go on, then, have some. You look half-starved, child."

June gingerly lowered herself onto the little stool opposite of the woman as she poured some of the tea into a china cup. The liquid was a faint purple in color, like the lilacs in Mama's garden. June gave it a sniff, then a sip.

"Rainberry tea," The woman said with a nod as she settled back into the chair with her own cup. "Very soothing for rattled senses. I can only imagine yours are of the sort."

June ignored her and sucked down the tea before cramming as many honey-drizzled biscuits into her mouth as she could fit. *Beetles and bird feathers,* food had never tasted so good. The Idiot's food was all boring, dry travel fare and she had mostly been too angry at everyone and everything to stomach it. And she still was angry, of course—right down to the marrow, a sort of blazing, burning anger she didn't think would ever really go away—but these were exceptional biscuits, and they, at the very least, were mellowing that fire inside.

"Where did you come from?" Myrtle asked. "Do you know how to write?"

June just nodded and stuffed another biscuit in her mouth.

"How old are you? Ten summers? Eleven?"

June didn't bother answering. It wasn't her business. As far as June was concerned, Myrtle didn't need to know a single thing about her. She'd be leaving soon, anyway. She wasn't sure she could relax in a place like this. It seemed quiet, but on the way to the bath, she'd seen a whole throng of children stuffed in a room, listening to a different caretaker drone on from a book. The sight of that many people, all clustered together, made her stomach churn. She started on another biscuit to settle it down.

"Who hurt you, June?"

June felt her face flush as that fire leaped up. She kept her head down and just kept eating.

"Was it either of the men who brought you here?"

June shook her head. The only thing those imbeciles hurt was her chances of finding the Raincloak Man within the month and making him pay so royally as he deserved.

"Who was it, then?"

June shrugged.

"A stranger?"

She didn't bother nodding. This woman was getting on her nerves.

"Did he kill your parents, June?"

June froze as heat shot through her veins, a half-eaten biscuit falling out of her hands and back onto the plate with a dull *thunk*. She looked up at the old woman almost involuntarily, surprised tears biting at the backs of her eyes.

Myrtle smiled in just the sort of way Gram would when she talked about her stillborn baby, resting one gnarled finger against her near-nonexistent lips.

"Right on the mark, aren't I?"

June scowled, she couldn't help it. Her lips were trembling and her blood felt incredibly hot but also so cold and the food in her mouth tasted like ash and she very much wanted to throw the plate of biscuits at Myrtle or the teacup at the wall or run away and run forever and not ever *ever* be found.

Instead, she just swallowed the food in her mouth, sat back, and hugged her knees to her chest.

The old woman's voice was soft. "I am sorry, my child. All I can offer you now is the safety of my house."

June refused to look at Myrtle and she refused to let the tears searing her eyes fall. She blinked them away and wiped her nose on her sleeves and glared at the floorboards. *Safety*, ha! Mama had said they were safe in the valley. She had been wrong. If their valley wasn't safe, nowhere was.

The room was quiet for a long time. June looked at the floorboards and felt the old woman's gaze resting heavily on her. The scent of the biscuits and tea was suddenly nauseating.

"Look at me, June."

June didn't look. She fought against the sobs snatching at her breath and stared at the stupid floor.

She heard the chair creak as the woman stood and shuffled over to June. To her surprise, Myrtle stooped down before her, bending those brittle old legs until she was crouched down at June's level. She slipped her fingers beneath June's chin, ignoring how June flinched away, and tilted her head up so that June had no choice but to meet the old bat's gaze.

The woman looked deeply into June's eyes before tsk'ing her tongue. "You are very angry, aren't you?"

June glared and pushed her hand away. She looked back to the floorboards.

"Why are you so angry?"

The absurdity of the question made June look up again. Why was she angry? The Raincloak Man had burned her house and killed her family. The Raincloak Man tore everything good away and tried to kill her. *Why* was she angry? What *else* was there to feel?

It was quiet for a moment. June clenched her jaw and tried to stop breathing so hard.

Myrtle nodded and sat back. "Let me tell you a story, then, of a little girl who was hurt very badly by the world. So very badly she wanted to burn it all down."

June couldn't help but look back at her.

The old woman rubbed her whiskery chin. "For many years, the little girl had a family with brothers and sisters and even both parents, a loving mum and pa. She lived in a village surrounded by fields of flowers and in the summer she would play with her siblings and the little bees in those honey-soaked meadows. Her entire world was warm and safe."

June dropped her eyes. This old bat was manipulating her, and she knew it. But still... that sounded a lot like her own home.

"One day, a hard winter came. It snowed for months and months and desperate men came to the little girl's home, stole everything from her family, and took her mother and sisters away too. Not long after, her Pa died, and so did her brothers, and she was left all alone."

June scowled. Now it was *really* sounding like her life.

Myrtle continued. "For years, the little girl was angry. Her heart hurt, and she wanted to hurt others in order to mend it. But years of cruelty did not fix the things that were wrong inside. She only ever felt better, when she finally let it all go. When she forgave."

June had almost calmed down when Myrtle spoke again, her croaking voice somehow gentle.

"Anger is a poison, June. Do you understand what I am trying to tell you?"

Anger flared back to life inside of her. June did nothing to stop it. She thought about her knife. Thought about how she might escape this place and put it to use against the only person who deserved it.

If the old woman detected the rage roaring up inside of June, she did not give up. She continued, her hands folded primly in her lap.

"Anger, in some form, is what made the man who hurt you do what he did. "

Obviously. And now she had to hurt him back.

"Do not let the sickness that ate him eat you as well, my child. It is a rot that will consume your whole life, if you let it."

She glared up at Myrtle, just as one tear managed to escape her and go slipping down her cheek. She swiped it away and dropped her gaze.

The look in the old woman's eyes made her uncomfortable. Something like pity and understanding.

You do not understand.

"It was hard for me too, June. Forgiveness is never fair. And I know it seems as if you will never feel whole again." Myrtle reached out to touch June's cheek and didn't seem the least bit offended when June jerked away.

Her decrepit voice was still kind despite June's glares. "Your winter cannot last forever. The sun will come again, if you let it."

June curled her arms around herself and stared at the carpet, hating the old woman, this old house, herself for the tears still escaping her stinging eyes.

Quiet came for a long while. If the old woman had more advice to give, she kept it to herself.

"Would you like to rest a little, June? Before you meet the other children?" Myrtle asked at length.

June nodded. Myrtle offered a hand, surprisingly strong for her brittle frame, and helped June to her feet and up the many flights of creaking stairs. She showed June into a long rectangular room filled with windows and lined with beds, most of which were occupied by stuffed animals or different blankets indicating their status as taken. Myrtle showed her to an unclaimed bed wedged beneath a window and against a wall, and left her alone.

June waited until the old woman shut the door to look around, imagining what it would be like if all these beds were occupied and the room was full of children. How many kids slept in here, perhaps twenty? Did the boys and girls share this room, or were they separated? She'd shared a room with Mama before, but that was *Mama*. How could she ever sleep when there was a whole mess of strangers around?

And what if they realized what she *was?*

June blinked, remembering the Idiot's warnings. He said she wouldn't last long, if they found out. That she had to be a liar just like him.

Heat shot through June's face. But what if he was right? What if she did lose control? Would they really throw her out? Send her to some prison? Burn her alive?

She sucked in a jittery breath and settled gingerly onto the bed. She'd just have to leave on her own before it happened. Tomorrow, maybe.

And go... where?

June dismissed the nagging thought with a little scoff. It didn't matter where. She belonged nowhere and to no one. She'd wander wherever she wanted until she found the Raincloak Man and made him pay and then...

And then. She blinked, startled by the enormity of the thought. Just what would she do? There would be no one there. She would be alone, truly, for the first time in her life.

She *was* alone.

A hard lump wedged itself in her throat as that too-familiar heat bit behind her eyes. June scrunched her brow, trying to stuff the bad feelings swarming inside down deep.

She'd find something else to do, once her debts were settled. In a world this big, surely it couldn't be that *hard*.

June settled down, her heart still hammering with anxiety, her insides all aflutter at the horrible newness of the room and the house and her life. The give of the mattress felt foreign after a week spent sleeping on the grass and she hated the strange scents of the room, how they all made her heart ache and her chest tight with tears and a wild panic she could not show.

June closed her eyes. She wanted to roll over and face the ceiling, but the wounds on her neck and side wouldn't allow it.

But sleep came in time with the pattering of rain on the roof overhead, and that solved almost everything.

❦ 29 ❦

LEFT BEHIND

When June opened her eyes, she expected to find the Idiot waking her up. But he wasn't there, of course, because he'd left her behind.

June hated the pang of unease that rippled in her stomach as her eyes searched the empty room, especially since the Idiot had done nothing but get her off course the entire time she'd been forced to travel with him and the Giant.

But the Idiot... *Taein*. He was like her. Anathema. Cursed, and yet alive. There was no one else in the world who could understand what she was going through besides him.

And he didn't even care enough to stay. He left. Disappeared into the countryside.

Disappeared.

June laid in bed for a long while, the scratchy, unfamiliar blankets heavy and warm against the drafts of the room, and thought about that.

Taein was Anathema, and yet there he went flitting around the countryside anyway, free as a lark. *How?* Just by being a coward and running away? Was he to run away from everything and everyone for his whole entire life?

She sat up, blinking away the heaviness behind her eyes. The room was still dark. The gray, rain-soaked light that'd come slanting through the many windows had vanished and a deep, pervasive blackness hung about the room, which was still empty of its occupants save for herself. The darkness hid the strange windows and the strange beds and the strange *vastness* of this home that wasn't her own and never would be.

She was just about to close her eyes and search for more sleep when something broke the darkness.

A shimmer of orange, flickering just beyond the window.

That was when June noticed a whiff of smoke about the room, faint, barely tangible, but present all the same.

June smelled the smoke and stilled.

The smoke. A memory, sharp and stinging as hate itself.

June smelled the smoke grow stronger and decided it was time to get out of bed.

She crept over to the windows, bare feet padding over rough floorboards, and peered out. It was still pouring, and the raindrops streaking down the window panes blurred the wavering orange glow beyond.

Orange. June furrowed her brow and pressed her face to the glass, trying to see better, to understand that strange light.

Then she realized. The first floor of the orphanage was on fire.

June stared dumbly out the window as the smoke grew stronger, feet rooted to the floor, head beginning to swim, hardly able to believe her eyes. Fire.

Fire?

A scream that was not her own ripped through her memory, and June drew in a sharp breath.

The memory of Mama's body, facedown on the grass beside Gram's half-filled grave and so terribly still. June touched a trembling hand to the window, trying to get the ugly sight out of her mind. The glass was warm beneath her fingertips despite the rain and spring chill. Warmed by the flames below.

She closed her eyes and felt the bite of the Raincloak Man's sword. Relieved every ounce of the pumping rage that propelled her to attack, to fight, to live. It wasn't enough then but it would be next time they met. June was sure of it. She knew it in her bones.

He burned my Mama.

June opened her eyes as a terrible clarity flooded her body.

He *burned* her.

June felt someone's hand clamp down on her shoulder and haul her off her feet. She didn't struggle. She didn't have the strength. She let herself be hauled down the stairs, out a doorway, and into the gravel yard amongst all the other children she'd yet to meet. The caretaker carried her to the edge of the group, sat her down, and rushed off.

June heard all the screaming and crying like she was underwater, drowning in the furious foaming sea of her own bloody rage.

The fire roared as it consumed the orphanage, a cracking, rampaging thing, a thief that would not stop following. The slow pound of her own heart was a war drum in her ears. She could do nothing but stare, the rain hissing as it argued with the inferno, everyone around her wailing and scrambling like rats running from a swooping barn owl.

June stared. Every nerve was sharp and searing beneath her skin, needles heated blue in the furnace of her hatred.

Anger is a poison, June.

For barely an instant, June heard Myrtle's voice in the back of her mind, a soft rain against the roaring heat burning her alive. For just an instant, her heart stilled.

Forgiveness is never fair.

But then June saw *him*, and the world snapped into perfect focus.

The Raincloak Man was behind the house, standing next to that same bay horse, watching the orphanage burn.

June saw *him*, and the whole world went white, bleached not by the inferno consuming the house but her own fire inside. The old woman's words weren't enough. Nothing would *ever* be enough.

Without another thought, June was on her feet, struggling for her knife and scrambling toward the Raincloak Man.

The sea of fire inside raged.

THE CHOICE

To Taein's complete and utter dismay, the inn had just one open room. This meant that not only was he to sleep in a building full of strangers, but he also wouldn't get any space from Vince. However, this sorry turn of events was amended for by an excellent dinner consisting of roast chicken, buttered bread, honied apples, and some sort of sweet, mulled wine that Taein downed with a vengeance while Vince guzzled his preferred mugs of frothy dark beer. If Taein was to be condemned to sleep in a strange inn full of strange folk whom he most certainly could not trust nor relax around, he intended to be drunk off his socks for it.

By midnight, the wine had done an excellent job of awakening his good humor and putting to sleep his anxious nerves, so he felt a bit more settled when he and Vince holed up in their room.

If he looked at the situation with a charitable gaze, he could say that their room was the size of a large closet, filled almost entirely by a cramped bed covered in a moth-eaten blanket, which Taein offered up to Vince. The remainder of the space was occupied by a little chair and circular table, both of which were boxed into a corner by an equally small window. Taein settled himself there after opening the window and propping his boots up on the table. He sat back and listened to the tranquil night breeze in one ear and Vince's rumbling snores in the other.

He gave up on sleep after ten minutes of half-hearted searching and just listened to the world beyond the window, the darkness of the night held at bay by the dim light of a half-used candle. The night grew old and rain drummed its too-familiar cadence atop the roof.

Taein drew the silver chain from beneath his shirt and turned the bounty disc over in his palm. On the front, Regor had engraved the words *Prince of Glass*, and on the back, their return date. Which they were set to totally blow.

"I'm making two of these, Taein. One for you... one more for me to give to our associates. If you don't get the kid to the Outlander safe and sound, your life is forfeit."

Taein shook his head and stuffed the disc back beneath his shirt as Regor's voice echoed in his head. *That stupid kid.*

And just like that, she was back on Taein's mind before he had the chance to get her out of it.

Why the tears? What did she care for him or Vince? And better yet, why was it *bothering* him so much? Children turned into orphans every single day. So what if she lost her mother and her home? By the looks of it, she'd been blessed with a happy and uneventful childhood beforehand, and that was more than most kids were ever allotted in the first place.

Her mother was murdered in front of her eyes, came that damn whisper. *Don't be so callous.*

He shook his head. Probably shouldn't have given her that damn gaudy dagger back considering the strength of her vendetta, but it seemed wrong to leave her with nothing to defend herself. It was only a matter of time before trouble found her again.

So it goes, living as an Anathema. Taein shifted in search of greater comfort. *Focus.* So many days lost... Taein cracked his knuckles, looked at the floorboards. They had a long road ahead of them, and *Geiin above,* did he want rit.

Taein stifled a groan as the wanting hit him like a brick to the face. It'd been a while since it flared up like this.

He'd walked into rit at sixteen. Or rather, he walked into *crystelin*, which was objectively very, *very* much worse.

Taein only got his hands on the richer's drug once, a thin glass vial of ice-blue liquid lifted from some daft blonde theater girl hanging off the arm of a RAC captain. A little research revealed that the vial was indeed crystelin, an opiate made from local Cryer's Weed and sacred silver-water smuggled from the deepest mountain ranges in Faeriel.

So Taein gave it a go. And Sweet Geiin above, was it *wonderful*. He spent that day elevated far above the claws of the past and the sordid present. Everything was very quiet.

All of the sudden, Taein understood the street poets who prattled on about true love and clandestine passion and soulmates divined by the stars themselves. He understood perfectly the Cathedral charlatans and their pamphlets on Geiin's boundless love, he understood Contentment, Happiness, and Peace. The drug hit so hard it knocked his body back against a brick wall and the impact felt like a kiss.

Here and now, high as a kite, Taein was touching fingertips with his lost life. Everything that'd once slipped away was back. The life he was destined for now held him cradled like a babe. The unnamed everything kissed his mouth. No one had ever kissed him before. No one had ever loved him like this. There was an incredible warmth everywhere, and forever. Taein felt, for the first time since that cursed day in the snow, unconditionally and totally loved.

He didn't even think once about Ruein the whole day, not even once did he feel the ache.

You can never leave, came that whispering warning voice. Taein laughed and laughed as he floated. Why would he ever *want* to? There was a cost, of course. This was Pearl Jin, after all, and nothing came for free.

To this day, Taein wasn't sure how long he was high, or how many days he went without sleep. But eventually he did pass out. When he woke up in an alley he was sober, crash-landed back into his damp and painful and oozy and hungry world. So he stumbled to his feet and set right out to get more crystelin, before coming to the swift and terrible realization that he would never in his life have the marks to get it, because crystelin was a richer's drug and notoriously impossible to make on the streets, and Taein was just an orphan rat with naught but a pair of precious boots to his name.

He was swiftly crushed beyond all belief, rattled and re-filled with what felt like more guilt than ever before. The only remedy seemed to be to do it again.

Because that's how all addictions start, aren't they? Like beautiful angels they come promising answers, healing, saying nothing of the cost.

But Taein had no idea, as he went searching for a replacement. They didn't have drugs like this in Efriel-Shu, just tobacco and *hitchka* leaves. The worst they could do was make you lazy and stain your teeth.

Taein's first hit of rit was sold to him as *'street crystelin'* for a fraction of the price, and for a while, it did almost the same thing. With rit, there was none of the bliss, the contentment, the *world* of Crystelin. There was nothing to be felt at *all*, only a state of floating and empty space. It felt like drowning in a thick fog, like falling forever and ever with only the far-away jagged beat of his heart for rhythm, and you didn't care if you ever landed.

Taein only ever felt that laboring pulse when the withdrawals came and he went crashing back to earth again. And that shuddering heartbeat *scared* him, it really did. It was just that the whisper of ash in his mind scared him more, so he kept seeking out rit until he couldn't even find his way out of a rit-house anymore, let alone handle jobs or pull off schemes, until the word became one gray-blue blur of breathing *in-out-and-in again*, awash in a haze where everything, for once, was perfectly still.

It stayed that way for a long time. Life was a slurry of dull colors. Drugs brought out all the worst sides of him, made him mean. Made him even more of a liar, made him even more selfish, made him even more lost. Taein tried to tell himself that the addiction never was *that* bad. He hadn't pawned off his boots, had he? It couldn't have escalated *that* far. But in foggy glimpses, he could remember the things he said, the things he did. And he felt bad about them. Felt bad about the addiction, which only made the addiction the worse, because half the fight of getting sober is reckoning with the fact that you need to, the fact that you're no saint to be around when you're not.

That being high doesn't make a thing better. It just makes you blind to the bad that's still there.

Slowly, when he was awake, Taein began to realize everything he felt the first times was a lie. He saw it for what it was, now.

But he couldn't stop.

And it stayed like that for a long time, until Regor found him and the bargain was struck.

And now here he was. Regor had kept him away from the stuff for years, giving him a reason. Taein knew that even if that reason was the promise of some mystical violence that could theoretically knock the bad out of him, there was something else that kept him off it. He didn't mind Regor's threats, they meant nothing. But in some odd way, he didn't like the thought of disappointing the old man.

"You gotta think it's worth it," Taein blearily remembered Regor grumbling to him, all those years ago. *"You'll never quit unless you think it's worth it."*

These days Taein's bones were still full of the old aches, arms still full of those pin-prick scars, mind still starving. He'd awakened a sort of hunger that never really goes away. No one was there to tell him the cost when he took his first hit, and even if someone had tried, Taein knew he wouldn't have listened. Because when did he ever?

Now was the sort of situation where the ache came back full force. Taein shifted, trying to puzzle out the exact reason why he knew he wouldn't go searching, why he hadn't for all these years.

The reason stayed murky, but at least it was there.

Taein blew a lock of hair off his face, just beginning to sweat, and squinted out the window as a flicker of light captured his attention. Was someone walking about, at this hour?

Somebody who had rit? *No—stop it, you irrational little podger.* He gripped the arm of the chair till his nails bit the wood. There it was again—a flicker of orange coming from beyond the distant tree line. Taein could barely make it out over the rooftops and through the trees, but it was there.

A prickle of unease ran down his neck. Taein leaned forward and scanned the treetops. It was then that the orange light reared over the tree line once again, this time hovering above, dancing and waving against the deep night, and Taein finally realized just what that light was.

Fire.

Coming from the orphanage.

Where they left the *shanking kid.*

"Oh... no," Taein breathed. He sprung out of the chair, knocking the table over and waking Vince up in the process. "No, no, no—"

"Bl-ARGH!" Vince shouted, bolting upright and smacking his head on the ceiling.

"Geiin alive, Vince! There's a fire!"

"A fire." Vince sat up and rubbed his head before comprehension hit him. He swore and stumbled out of bed, scrambling for his boots. "Where, Taein?"

Taein was frozen where he stood. His back was turned from the window but the orange light was growing larger, bright enough to loom on the wall before him, cut only by his shadow.

"Taein?" Vince questioned, tugging his last boot on. "Get your stuff, man. Where the hell is it?"

"Just over the tree line," Taein answered softly.

Vince paused. "By the orphanage?"

"We're safe here." Taein fought to keep from shriveling beneath the weight of the giant's stare. "We're under no obligation—"

Vince threw his hands up. "There are *children* in danger!"

"But I gave her dagger back—"

"What good is a blade to a fire?" Vince sputtered. "Geiin alive, man!"

Dread flooded Taein's body, and before he knew it he was shouting. "If we go back, we're going to get stuck with her again!"

Vince stopped short, blinking with uncertainty in the wavering orange light. "What?"

Taein ran a hand through his hair, heart hammering, and searched for words. "I—I... oh, shank this." He dropped his hands from his hair, looked Vince dead in the eye. "If we go back for her, she won't want to leave again. She didn't want to leave us in the first place."

Vince stared. "*You* didn't want to leave her in the first place."

Taein took no care to mask the venom in his voice. "Careful, Vincent. That is *not* what I said."

Vince shook his head and tossed Taein his coat. "We can talk about this later. We need to go help."

"Vince—"

"Well, *I'm* going. You can stay here and mope for all you want, but I'm going."

"Vincent," Taein snapped, finally getting his attention. "If we get the kid again, we're going to have to take her to *House Light.* You know that's how it'll end up. We'll throw the job. It's over."

That got Vince to pause. A shadow crossed his blunt, bearded features before he shook his head and met Taein's eyes.

"I'm still going."

With that final proclamation, Vince swung his own cloak over his massive frame and disappeared out the door in a hurry. Taein flinched as the door slammed shut and he was left to stare at his black shadow against the reddening wall.

A second passed. The flames grew taller above the tree line. His heart beat slow and hard in his ears.

Taein sucked in a breath, drumming his fingers against his leg. He knew what was at stake; his survival, his identity. A whole fortune, a life of leisure and peace, and maybe even relative safety. He might even get crystelin back, if he was lucky.

He knew.

Taein stayed still for a long moment. Each breath felt like thunder in the quiet of the room.

He closed his eyes against the red light, and just like that—a whisper of Ruein's voice. The barest memory of his laugh.

No.

Before Taein even knew what was happening, he was pulling on his boots and shouldering his coat and he too was out the door, running after Vince, running after the kid and away from every single thing he'd hoped for.

Taein found Vince in the stables, struggling to saddle his sleepy draft. To his surprise, Vince already had Lorrin out of his stall and cross-tied. A miserable groom still in his nightclothes was bustling about with Lorrin's tack, trying to dodge Lorrin as the stallion made sport of trying to knock the groom over with his head. Taein paused to take in the situation before the growing unrest in the village brought him to his senses. He took the saddle from the groom and finished tacking Lorrin up himself, avoiding Vince's gaze.

The silence was a tangible thing. Taein fumbled with the clinking metal buckles of the cinch and swore silently to himself.

"I knew you'd come," Vince said softly.

"Shank off, you didn't."

"I—"

"Shut up, Vince."

Vince shut up.

Minutes later they were mounted and flying down the road toward the side street that led to the orphanage. It'd taken thirty minutes to get to the village from the orphanage at a trot, but now they pushed the horses and got to Myrtle's in what felt like but a few breathless seconds.

Taein knew they were getting close by the heat. The inferno hit him like a wall as they rounded the bend. The towering whitewashed house was engulfed in orange flames, which reared out of broken windows and danced madly on the roof. Smoke was blocking out the stars, wafting across the yard, billowing out of the burned-out door. The moon, tinged a filthy soot-stained yellow, cast an eerie, too-sharp glare over everything, lining the edges of the roiling smoke, the streaking rain, and the hissing flames. Children and caretakers alike huddled together in the gravel receiving yard, screaming and shouting and praying and pleading and doing absolutely nothing to help themselves.

Taein shoved memories of old fire down deep, his heart tight in his chest, and kicked his feet free of the stirrups. Before Lorrin could slow to a walk he swung down and hit the ground at a run, Vince close behind.

Taein struggled to keep breathing. *In. Out. Again.* Looking for June's fierce green gaze among the soot-stained faces. *Sweet Geiin*, what if she was still in the building? He threw his hood back, turning wildly in circles as the deluge pelted his face. Vince's hulking silhouette loomed across the crowd as the giant searched the throng of children for her.

They couldn't beat the fire back. If she was inside the burning house, she was long dead. If she was out here among the other screaming children and flustered nurses, she was safe. Wasn't she? But Taein knew the answer. There was a reason the orphanage was on fire, not because of some knocked-over candle or log strayed from the fireplace.

He was here. The hunter had realized his error and found her. Taein was sure of it. He could *feel* it, right in the depths of his bones— nothing else on earth made his heart panic like this.

How the hell did he find her?

Taein froze as the brush of heavy wings cut through the roar and hiss of the fire. He looked to the sky, legs rooting to the ground, just in time to spot the dark silhouette of a white bloodhawk swooping low around the inferno and heading behind the house.

The same hawk that had snatched a piece of fabric from June, when they were traveling days ago. He'd almost forgotten about it. But now the pieces snapped together and Taein found himself shoving past kids and caretakers alike, running after the bird and screaming curses.

And sure enough, the hawk led him straight to her.

June was beneath a tree a few yards off, alone but for a caretaker who was trying to pull her back toward the group with all her might while June clung to the tree, that stupid knife in one hand, and snarled at the woman like an enraged badger. Taein skidded to a stop between the caretaker and June, scaring both.

"I got her," he gasped out through the smoke.

The woman looked between him and June before bursting into tears and running off.

Taein turned and grabbed June, yanking her away from the tree with one swift pull. She made a strangled noise and turned on him, green eyes bright with fury.

"I told you to be *nice*," Taein hissed as he picked her up and tossed her over his shoulder. He looked out into the darkness of the backyard and spied movement.

Sweet Geiin.

Taein stared. His heart shuddered to a stop. There, swallowed by the darkness and rain, illuminated ever so faintly by the eerie glow of the inferno behind them, was the hunter himself.

The screaming and chaos all around dulled as if Taein was slipping underwater. All he could hear was the reluctant shudder of his own pulse as the world seemed to slow, every shadow lengthening, pulling toward that broad-shouldered figure looming just beyond.

The hunter wore a dark raincloak and held the reins of a silent bay horse. His eyes, dark and proud and Faeish, met Taein's.

Taein was frozen, trapped by fear and memories as the world around fell farther and farther away.

And just like that he was thirteen again, and he was cold, desperate, and afraid, and there was blood in his mouth as snow fell like ash from the sky.

June, thrashing on Taein's shoulder, kicked him hard in the chest and so jolted him back to awareness. He tore his gaze from the hunter, pulled his flintlock from his hip, and blindly fired before turning tail. *Vince*. He had to find Vince and they had to go and—

"Taein?"

Taein stifled a scream and whirled around to find the giant standing behind.

"You found her!" Vince bellowed over the clamor. Taein didn't miss the bright smile that lit the giant's blunt features.

"Run!" Taein said, breaking back into a run toward the horses. He leaped onto Lorrin and fought to keep the panicked stallion still as Vince handed June up to him. Holding the kid tight, Taein booted Lorrin around and let the stallion spring into a gallop.

The horses thundered down the road, hoofbeats growing louder as the noise and chaos of the fire faded behind. The smoke-stained moon seemed like a giant torch reaching down to illuminate every stinging raindrop, to lay bare every shadow and every hiding place. There seemed to be no safe place in all the world.

Taein bit back an oath and booted Lorrin faster. The hunter had *seen* him. He *knew*.

Taein's luck had finally run out. He felt a wild laugh tear from his mouth. Deep down, he'd always known he couldn't hide forever, that it was bound to come to this one day. But he had never guessed it would be like *this*. For a kid who meant nothing.

Nevertheless, Taein found himself holding that accursed kid close, leaning forward to shelter her from the rain, to keep her from slipping from the saddle. They raced on, dark shadows in a too-bright night as the rain poured down to wash the earth clean. Taein gave Lorrin full rein and let the racehorse *fly*.

The hunter was near. Taein could feel it growing even with every striking hoofbeat he put between them—the needling, the pressure, the remembrance.

The ache where a heart used to be.

———————

31

RETURNING

Rain fell from the sooty heavens in torrential sheets, soaking June right through her new clean dress and down to the skin. The Idiot held her tight as his black horse flew down the road, one arm looped around her torso, the other clutching the reins. The horses were *galloping*, a speed June had never experienced before in her whole life, so fast it sent her head spinning. When she peered down, the road beneath them was but a dizzying black blur.

She shut her eyes tight. She didn't feel good and her wounds hurt more and more with every jostling stride the horse took, but in some tiny grateful scared space inside of her, she was glad the Idiot was here.

He came back for her, saved her from the fire.

He came back.

But on the other hand, he just stole her away from the Raincloak Man again. June had *seen* him, felt the fire roar inside of her louder than ever before. Her knife was at her ready, the emerald-crusted hilt pressing sharp into her palm. And at that moment she felt *alive*, so terribly ready to cut that evil excuse of a human being into pieces, to shove him into the fire, to hack at him until there was nothing left to hack at.

Would Mama be ashamed of her?

The rain lashed at her cheeks, stole hot tears from her cheeks. June drew in shocking bolts of icy air. Her throat was tight and raw. Her body ached.

June felt like a hole, not a person. A great big oozy, abscessing, hate-filled hole. She pressed her face into the Idiot's chest to hide from the rain and cursed every living thing beneath the raging gray sky.

Especially the Idiot, even if she knew in her heart that he didn't deserve it.

32

WHAT ELSE MATTERS
VASILY

Vasily hunched over the bay, her rain-soaked mane slapping him in the face as they raced down the road after Glass and the little girl. The off-kilter pound of his heart was still and a singular, burning focus now rested over him. Bellan flew just ahead, a lance of white against the clouded cobalt sky.

He'd tracked the Anathema girl to an orphanage and done the only reasonable thing to do—light it on fire. He lingered in the backyard, watching as the terrified occupants poured out, coughing and shouting and wailing, and waited. And kept waiting. It didn't take long before one of the women dragged a skinny, scruffy-haired girl bearing several bandages out of the building and set her down at the base of a tree a little aside from the group. The bandage around the little girl's neck was a bright, stark white against the darkness and downpour of the night.

Vasily had watched as the girl's gaze shifted, as she sought him out in the darkness like they were bound together by the fibers of their souls. He watched as those inhuman eyes lit with the very same anger he held in his heart. He watched as she struggled to her feet, fighting the next caretaker that came for her. He watched as someone else stopped her, snatched her up, and stole her away. A dark, scrawny figure with a too-familiar head of unruly curls.

The man reached for the little girl, sleeves shifting, and the golden light of the inferno behind illuminated the mar on his skin. The tattoo of a fern wrapping his forearm, precisely where the simple ceremonial tattoo of House Glass would've once been.

The man glanced over at Vasily, and time stood still as the orange light bathed his Siou features.

That man was Glass, Vasily *knew* he was. He hadn't got more than a few second's glance, lit only by those furious dancing flames, before Glass pulled a device from his hip. There was a burst of light and something grazed Vasily's shoulder as Glass turned and ran away.

But where was there to go? Glass was going to *die* like all the others, and there would be no Long Wait in the realm of spirits Between, no half-death to hold onto. He had a head start, but Vasily was gaining. Soon, Glass would be dead. Soon, it would finally be over. Soon—

"My lord!"

Vasily startled as a too-familiar voice roared over the rain. He hadn't a second to decipher how he knew that voice before his mare jolted to a stop, throwing Vasily onto her steaming neck as a trio of riders darted out of the forest and cut in front of them. He shoved himself upright and jabbed his heels into the mare's sides, but she refused to push through the wall of strange riders.

Vasily uttered an oath, blood still trickling from his shoulder, and swung out of the saddle.

"Get out of my way!" he bellowed, ripping his sword from its sheath.

"Thank the stars we've found you!"

Vasily stopped short as he recognized the slight figure hurrying forward. Sweet Geiin, it was *Nuest*.

"What the hell are you doing?" Vasily asked, throwing back his hood and letting the rain drench his sweat-slick forehead. "I've found him, I've found Glass! Clear this blockade at once!"

If Nuest heard Vasily, he made no indication. Instead the old man drew closer, his frame shaking with the force of the rain. "We've been chasing you nearly since you left, but your trail was almost completely indecipherable. Whatever brought you to the Wastes—"

"Nuest!" Vasily gripped the old man by his shoulders. *"I found Glass."*

Nuest shook his head. "No, Vasily. This *obsession* no longer matters."

Vasily sputtered, casting a sideways glance at the two soldiers standing behind Nuest with their horses. "Nothing else matters, not to me."

"I am calling you home." The iron edge in Nuest's voice forced Vasily's mouth shut. The old man looked deep into Vasily's face, old eyes strangely bright.

"My lord, the queen is dying."

❧ 33 ❧

A RIPPLE OF THE PAST

A few hours after dawn, the rain finally slowed. Taein spread the map out on a damp roadside shoulder the moment they were forced to rest the horses and set to work trying to find any possible outcome that didn't call for a total and complete loss of money.

"Whatcha looking at, boss?" Vince asked as he eased out of the saddle and landed on the ground with a *thud*.

Taein didn't look up. "Map."

"Well, obviously. Can I borrow an apple?"

"It's not borrowing if you're going to eat it, Vincent."

"Fine, got an apple I can *eat*, then?"

"Help yourself," Taein answered with a shake of his head as he turned back to his map. *Sweet Geiin alive.* His heart hadn't stopped ramming around in his chest since the moment he found June and spied the hunter. He hadn't a prayer of calming down without at least six consecutive hits of rit, and since he didn't have an icicle's chance in hell of getting even *one*, he was currently trying to accept the fact that they were just totally and irrefutably shanked.

"'*Irrefutably*' is quite a word from the likes of you."

Taein blinked. "Stuff it, Vince."

236

"Quit mumblin' and I will."

Taein gritted his teeth. Vince hadn't said a word about the kid since they found her, but Taein knew what was coming.

House shanking Light. There was just no way. It'd only been a few hours since they entered Crooked Warden's Way—a secluded thief's route that connected through all three standing realms and the Vandel Province—and already they were at an unfamiliar road. The path had split too soon—all dark looming firs and identical meadows on either side. Taein knew the way back to Efriel Shu, but he did *not* know the way to House Light. He could send a raven to that stupid Arvin bloke Regor kept sending on the Ersiin jobs and ask for directions, but he'd have to be as good as dead to suffer that level of embarrassment—

"Hey, Taein?"

Taein glanced up. "What?"

Vince nodded to June, lowering his voice. "The kid's acting weird."

Taein went right back to the map. "She *is* weird."

"Well, yes. But she's sleeping a hell of a lot more, and coughing, too, have you noticed that?"

Taein shook his head. "Can't say that I have, Vin."

Vince was quiet for a beat. "You don't suppose she's getting sick, do you?"

Taein dragged a finger along one penned path to another. "Nah, she's fine."

Quiet.

"So... where are we going?" Vince finally asked.

Taein looked up at the giant and straightened. "To Efriel-Shu, remember? Outlander—"

"Efriel-Shu ain't no place for a kid. Neither is with the Outlander."

Quiet again. Taein and Vince avoided eye contact.

Vince spoke first. "It's the right thing to do—"

Taein groaned and spun in a circle before throwing his hands in the air. "Oh, who gives a rat's ass about the *'right thing?'* Since when has that shit mattered to us? We're scrappers! We're paid to *steal* stuff, not babysit—" Taein trailed off. Vince wasn't even paying attention, his gaze stuck on something in the sky, his brow heavy. Taein followed his line of sight and spied a dark spot circling amid the clouds.

The world around them seemed to grow very shy—the birds ceased their chirping, the little mice and burrowing creatures went deadly still. Taein stared up at the dot, confused at the surge of unsolicited dread welling up inside him, strangely able to perceive the slightest sound. Air displaced. A ruffling of feathers.

Feathers.

He watched that dark spot grow closer. Watched it swoop down on them *again*.

That same white bloodhawk that tore a piece of June's dress and flew off with it. *That was how the hunter found them in the first place.*

Taein cursed as the pieces clicked together and he scrambled for his flintlock. He got it loaded, whirled, and shot just as the sound of wind rushing through feathers grew sharp. The hawk let out a piercing cry and fell flapping and squawking to the ground, startling the horses and waking the kid.

Vince went to settle the horses and Taein stalked over to the hawk, reloading the flintlock as he went. The bird was still, but he shot it again for good measure. Feathers puffed into the air and floated lazily down around him.

He turned and found Vince staring at him, his brow bunched. "That the same bird that attacked the kid before?"

Taein nodded, tucking the flintlock into his waistband. "Yes. That's how the bastard found her again." Taein spit on the pile of feathers. "This will slow him down at least."

"Him?"

"The shankin' hunter."

Vince looked at him. "I thought birds of prey were sacred to the Siou."

Taein bent, ripped a snowy tail feather from the corpse, and twirled it between his fingers. "Well, well, look who reads so much."

Neither spoke. Taein sensed Vince's unease and let the quiet rest heavy until the giant chose to break it.

"What are we going to do with her, Taein?" Vince asked.

Taein dragged a hand through his hair. "Drop her off at another orphanage."

Vince shook his head. "The hunter will just find her again."

Taein gestured to the bird-corpse. "I killed his bird."

"He'll still find her. He's the hunter, right?"

"That doesn't mean—"

"He will."

Taein knew Vince was right. "So we just dump her off here, then," he offered. "She wants to find him anyway."

Vince glowered. "He'll kill her in a heartbeat."

Taein returned the glare. "Sure he would, but she'd get what she wants."

"That's not what she wants, and you know it."

"I know that *I* want to get back to the path that leads to wealth and peace and quiet. Does it matter what *I* want?"

"...Could you live with yourself?"

Taein gritted his teeth. Dug in his heels. Fought the welling self-hate back. Still, all that came out was a tiny "...No."

Vince flung his arms out. "Then why are we having this conversation?"

Taein exploded. "Because we already gave up the biggest score any scrapper has ever heard of, Vincent! For some random *kid*! If we want to keep doing good shankin' deeds there's a thousand more kids in worse spots than here when we go home! But we need *money*!"

"Why is money more important—"

"Because *you* don't even have money to feed yourself back in the Pearl," Taein said, stabbing a finger at Vince, "and I want to be done with that shankin' city forever! I want to be free, Vince!"

"But you said you couldn't live with yourself."

"I—"

"You *said*."

Taein sputtered.

"So we take her to House Light, then." Vince said. "Drop her off where she belongs, and start over fresh on our get-rich scheme."

Taein pinched the bridge of his nose. "He'll kill us, Vince. The hunter won't stop with her. Not to mention what Regor will do when he realizes what we've done. Not to mention the shanking Outlander!"

Vince shrugged. "That's always been an occupational hazard."

"This is different."

It was a long time before Vince spoke again, his voice soft. "But this is the right thing to do, Taein."

Taein didn't lift his head from his hands. "Sweet Geiin, when did we get so soft? We're giving up being rich for altruism. *Altruism!*"

"Well, let's get this done and you can go back to being an asshole for the rest of your life. It'll be over before you know it," Vince said with a snap.

Taein looked away, his stomach tight. He wanted to scream. He wanted to vault onto Lorrin and leave all this Geiin-forsaken nonsense behind. He wanted to look Vince in the eyes and tell him that he couldn't *do* this, that there was a terrible rock in his stomach and a panicked catch to every breath grating through his claustrophobic lungs, that every time he looked over at that stupid kid he was *scared*, right down to the very marrow of his bones. Scared, because this journey wasn't about cargo and marks anymore, it was *familiar*, it was a ripple of the past, the wailing echo of a life he'd spent the last ten years trying to kill and bury down deep. And if it hadn't ended well then, how the ever-loving hell was he supposed to pull it off now?

And it *wasn't* going to be over in a snap, Taein knew that, and he was pretty sure Vince did too, and neither of them spoke for a long time.

———

THE WAY IT WAS

The night beat down from a moonless sky. Taein gazed at the fading fire, his coat pulled tight around his shoulders, sleep set far out of reach. The world was still, save for the quiet crop of the horses grazing, Vince's snoring, and June's soft, sleepy breaths. The kid was curled in on herself, wrapped tightly in the extra cloak Taein loaned her.

Taein sighed and folded his arms, his gaze drifting right back to the kid the minute he tried to look away. If he was being *objective*, she wasn't half-bad, despite her sullen silence and simmering green gaze. She could be as nasty as she wanted, for all he cared. At least she wasn't trying to stab him.

Yet.

Taein shook his head and brushed away the thought as he lit a cigarette. As far as kids went, he'd been around worse. But June wasn't much of a kid, not really. Taein watched her as she slept, studying the tension between her brows, the grim line of her mouth. There was an oldness to her, an isolation he felt mirrored within himself.

Taein settled back against the tree and pulled his coat tighter as he puffed away. That isolation hadn't always been with him. For a while he might even say he'd been *happy*, back when Ruein was alive and his world was whole. But that all fell apart the day Ruein bit the dust and ever since then, that damn *hole* inside had come back to stay, resuming its hungry, stubborn residence, rooting deep right where his heart should be.

Taein had felt inklings of that same hole as a child, during the long lonely days before he met Ruein. The first six years of his life were spent largely alone while his father the king and two of the elder princes were away keeping the warring Rhro-Rrimriden from tearing the realm apart. The only family members left at House Glass were his sort-of mother, Torien, and Laufein, who weren't keen on going out of their way for a bastard son so far from the throne it might as well go without saying.

The only one who made any effort at all was Laufein, the middle prince who at least *attempted* to forge some sort of alliance between himself and Taein. Laufein would invite Taein into his study and show him his many leather-bound books and read to him from *the Fables* and *Arboyl's Folly* and sometimes even *the Charter,* which documented the changing positions of the stars, and Taein would try to pay attention and almost always end up looking out the window with that persistent ache gnawing away at his insides like an over-anxious rat.

But then the father Taein had never before met returned home from his six-year quest to re-tame the horse lords, and he came home with his two favorite sons in tow.

When Taein met his father for the first time since he'd brought Taein to House Glass as a tiny bastard babe called *Mikhael*, his first impression was *tall*. And Lord Jaefin surely was—he presented a towering figure, strong, weathered, and lean, with a short beard and glittering eyes that roved from face to face with little pause.

Lord Jaefin bent down, studied Taein, and shook his hand like Taein was not a lad of six but another warlord to be negotiated with.

"What a fine lad you're growing up to be, my son," he said. "You have your mother's eyes."

Taein still remembered the way the scattering of people in court chuckled at his father's jest, and how his mother's face shriveled as if she'd smelled something foul.

Lord Jaefin moved on and Taein met Willaen. The crown prince of

House Glass was fair-haired like his mother and every bit as cold. He wore an embroidered tunic with their house crest on the chest, somehow clean despite their journeying, and brushed right past Taein as if he wasn't there at all.

Taein stared at the wall across from him, trying to hide the bitter disappointment eating him alive.

At least I have Laufein and his books, he thought.

That was when the final member of the newly-returned party stepped forward, and Taein met Ruein.

That very same instant, the hole inside was filled.

Ruein was still a boy then, no older than fifteen, all raven hair and roguish winks. He smelled of leather and horses and the wilderness beyond the valley. He looked and acted like everything Taein had ever wanted to be.

Ruein looked at Taein for a moment, *really* looked. Then he reached out and took Taein's hand and pinched Taein's cheek with the other.

"Why so glum, little brother?" Ruein asked. Then he opened his arms for a *hug*, and Taein's whole world fell into place.

From then on, they were inseparable. Ruein was the master of all things improper, unruly, and rouge, and Taein his willing pupil. If Ruein got it in his head to compete with the others for his father's favor and bat around for the throne, Taein was right there in the melee with him. If Ruein decided on a whim the next day (as he often did) that the throne and the whole house could go to hell, Taein was right there to wholeheartedly agree and suggest they go steal eggs from the kitchen for no particular reason other than the thrill. Ruein taught Taein how to climb the trickiest of trees, how to creep up on deer and sometimes even rabbits, how to catch a horse that didn't want to be caught, how to ride bareback and race the wind. They spent entire summers in the wilds together, inventing whole new personas like Ruein's Jinian mob boss *'Taein Tore'*, a man who spoke with his marks (even if those marks were acorns), and Taein's Vandel warlord *'Jean Kinsten'*, a man who spoke with his sword (even if that sword was a whittled stick). Ruein taught Taein to shoot a bow, wield a blade, and manage the court proceedings during the winter holidays. He taught

Taein what fashion was. He bought Taein his first pair of good leather boots for Festival Farrael one year and then decided to make it a tradition.

Ruein bought Taein every pair of boots he ever had, up until Vasily killed him. And now Taein had to make do with just one pair of boots for the rest of his life.

The fire hissed and popped, struggling to stay alive. Taein prodded the coals with a stick, which sent a shower of sparks up into the black sky.

Vasily.

The hunter–June's Raincloak Man–had known what he was doing when he burnt down the kid's settlement. Each house had been scorched to the foundation, almost meticulously so.

Taein's mind flashed back to June's wounds. Each one was the obvious result of a blade, likely a broadsword.

For a minute, Taein wondered if Vasily got Ruein with his sword, or the bow.

Taein waited for the thought to create some sort of discomfort, but it didn't. Thinking about all his losses was like dropping a tenth-mark into a dry well. He waited and felt nothing, not even when the thoughts kept coming.

The first time he witnessed Vasily go about his work was directly after the fall, which had been on Midsommer's Hallow. All four realms and even leaders from the Vandel Province had gathered at House Glass to celebrate, to work toward continuing a fragile peace that had lasted for decades. A peace that probably would've continued, had not Ruein broken their sacred rule and ditched his gloves for the night. Had not Ruein shook the King of Faeriel's hand.

In the chaos of that long night directly after, what was left of House Glass turned against its ruler. Their father was the first to go, then mother, killed by her own handmaidens. Servants, soldiers, courtiers... all people who moments before groveled at their feet were now either running away or trying to kill them.

As if it'd save them from the hunter. As if he cared. There was a line drawn the instant Ruein turned the King of Faeriel to ash, a mark smeared onto each and every Siou soul.

The line of Glass was *Anathema*. And in a few short months, every Siou would suffer for it, be they cursed or not.

Somehow, Willaen, Torien, Laufien, Ruein, and Taein all made it out, cutting down men who had moments before been their friends in a mad dash to reach the panic tunnels. When they got out and far enough away that the burning House was but a small, flickering yellow dot amid a sea of grass, Willaen insisted that their best chance at survival was to flee in groups. They would meet again at a later date, hastily agreeing on a forgotten boarding house in a forgotten village along a forgotten logging road deep in the Iri Mountain ranges. They didn't have time to argue with Willaen—he was the oldest, after all, and the only responsible one among them. He'd just led a slaughter to get them out alive. They trusted him.

So Taein and Ruein went one way, Willaen and Torien another, and Laufien not far behind on his own.

It took a few days. Maybe a week. Taein and Ruein were just nearing the promised boarding house when it erupted in flames. They crouched down along a line of fir trees and watched as the hunter chased down Willaen and Torien as they tried to flee and slaughtered them both.

They watched as the hunter dismounted his horse, the lodge behind belching fire and illuminating up the field with an eerie orange glow. He stood over the distant, shaking lump. Willaen. Two arrows protruded from his back like unruly spring twigs jutting from a fallen branch.

Taein and Ruein watched, rain dripping down on them from the low-hanging fir branches overhead, as the hunter decapitated him.

Willaen was always the favorite—he was a shadow to Lord Jaefin, a mirror image to his mother, confidant to both. No matter that he was cold and quiet—Taein knew he would've made a good king. A damned good one.

The hunter then moved to Torien.

Torien was nearing twenty-five when he died that night. He was strong and handsome, a favorite in the eyes of every girl he ever met.

As Taein watched the hunter approach, he didn't find himself wondering if Torien regretted spending his whole life in a saddle or in the bottom of his cup, if he felt sorry for calling Taein a bastard so often, if his mind was racing full of things that he should've done. If that was how Taein himself would one day feel, if—*when*—the hunter finally got to him.

Those thoughts came later. All Taein remembered thinking as the rain came down and the hunter got close, was *get up, get up, get up.* But Torien didn't get up. Torien was already dead, the single arrow Vasily embedded in his back claiming his life before Vasily could take it with his sword.

The hunter beheaded him anyway. And Taein watched, the ground cold beneath his body, his breaths fogging in the night air. He and Ruein watched as the hunter took their amulets, lit their brothers on fire, and then burned the rest of the village, too.

They watched Vasily disappear into the night. They knew they were next.

This prompted the desperate race to track down Laufein. They found him dying in a field a few days later, half burnt and stuck through with arrows, because apparently the hunter hadn't stayed to make sure his fire finished what his arrows did not.

Laufein, who was interested in science and the epics written by dead historians. Laufein, that harmless reed of a kid who looked younger than Taein himself, with soft brown curls and star-spattered freckles, who squinted because his eyes were poor, who sometimes forgot to eat because his books were so much more important.

Laufein's amulet was missing, so Ruein took off his own and gave it to him as Taein stood there and stared. Ruein held Laufein as he drifted off, so much blood oozing from their brother's charred mouth that they couldn't make out his last words. Taein remembered how it was only *then* that Ruein finally wept, cradling Laufein's body to his chest as fat ugly tears rolled down his cheeks. Taein stood to the side, unable to cry just like always, and watched as Ruein choked on his grief and heaped upon himself all that black-tar blame.

They buried Laufein beneath a fir in the same forest that the hunter murdered him in.

Then they kept moving, because Vasily was still coming. The days blended together in a haze of Ruein's grieving silence and Taein's own stubborn numbness. They found another amulet for Ruein somewhere along the line, but he never put it on. The rosewood piece lived in his pocket alongside the gloves he'd taken off and never put back on again.

Maybe it took three weeks, maybe even a month and a half. But the hunter *did* find them.

Taein's body was a distant thing as the memories flashed behind his eyes, the soft glow of the dying fire far away.

He was there again. He never really left. The snow was always right there. It lived in the space behind his eyes. Ate at him. Festered.

Taein heard the crunch of snow beneath his boots, felt the chill in his bones, his blood. A cold like that was felt everywhere, the kind that lives in you. Snowflakes stung his eyes, caught in his hair. They clung to his clothes, obscured the darkness all around, blurred the world into a haze of white.

Ruein was running behind. Taein heard the heavy fall of his steps, the rough grate of his breaths. They were exhausted.

Vasily had flushed them out of one of their hiding places in the mountains. He lit the forest around them on fire. He chased them through the winter deluge and into a wide, snow-choked meadow.

Taein could hear Ruein's footsteps again. He never stopped hearing them. Every footfall was a blow to his heart.

Ruein was a bigger man than Taein. He was tall and dark-haired and muscular. He was slower as they ran through the snow, heavier. His footsteps sunk in deeper.

Naturally, the hunter got to him first. And Taein just kept running.

Taein opened his eyes when the memory finally receded.

Slowly, his bleary vision refocused and the world turned from white back to the hazy orange glow of the dying fire. He stared into the smoldering coals, the stick he'd used to stir the fire back to life minutes ago now half burnt.

The hunter found him and Ruein all those years ago no matter how hard they tried to escape. He found them and somehow Taein was left behind to keep on running with all these memories locked inside, no matter how much rit or booze he dumped in his system, no matter how far he ran from House Glass, no matter how many nights he spent sleepless and suffering. The memories were here to stay and so was that Geiin-forsaken hole inside, now grown into a great, gaping maw that couldn't be filled by all the rit or all the marks in all of Ieris.

They stayed, the hole and the memories, and the hunter with them.

Taein shook himself a little and snuck a glance at June. She hadn't moved, still sound asleep. He thought back to the smoking heap that had been her settlement, thought of the cuts on her neck and the Faeish king who dealt them.

Yes, he had a pretty good idea of just who June's *Raincloak Man* truly was. He'd known since the second he first laid eyes on the kid's burning home. There was no doubting it. He and Vasily had even met eyes, felt those old shared wounds stir to life again.

The urge to run hit harder than ever before. It hit him like a brick to the face and took every ounce of decency left in his whole frame to stay where he was. Taein dug his fingers into the dirt and gritted his teeth and tried to think about anything other than his frizzing nerves and the panic that was rising, rising, *rising*, a starving wave seeking to suck him under and never let him surface again.

He ran away like the coward he was all those years ago, and most days it felt like he'd never stopped. So why bother now?

Taein stifled a groan, slumped down, and dragged a hand through his hair.

He couldn't think of a single answer that made a lick of *real* sense. Vince kept prattling on about 'doing the right thing', but what the hell had that ever meant to Taein?

But then June sniffled in her sleep, and Taein knew the answer.

He just didn't have the guts to think about it, so he settled for wrapping his arms around his frame until the freneticism bled from his bones and he was left drained and unsettled and sad. Ruein's lopsided grin burned in his brain as his gloved hands itched for a bottle, for a needle, for the worn leather of Lorrin's reins, for freedom.

This hurts.

He opened his eyes as the thought rattled about his brain and breathed out a strangled sigh. His cigarette had burnt down to nothing.

Taein knew at that moment he'd give anything to run, and keep on running until his legs failed and his lungs gave out and his body broke into a thousand pieces.

Instead, he did the impossible, and stayed still.

❦ *35* ❦

THE LAST STORY

The night was still untouched by natural light when June awoke.

She looked around with bleary eyes, unsure of what to do with herself. Both the Idiot and the Giant were asleep. For a short while she tried to fall back asleep too, but her mind didn't want to quiet back down and an unwelcome cough had made itself resident in her throat. So June eased herself upright, choking down her coughs so that she wouldn't wake the others, the night air cold and biting all around as she gazed across the dying fire.

The Idiot—*Taein*—was sprawled on the other side of the coals, his marble features faintly illuminated by the fire's fading, once-cheery glow that made every stray scratch and spare bruise on his strange skin stand out like the over-obvious smudges made by some worn-out sculptor scuffing up what could've been their masterwork. A frown tugged at her mouth. If she left, the odds of surviving long enough to find the Raincloak Man were less than good. She might even admit that they were downright bad.

But the Idiot and the Giant were intent on taking her to *House Light*. To hell with the House and this Lady Marguerite-whoever. They

250

didn't matter when the Raincloak Man was still roaming and free and unpunished. Nothing mattered. She had to fix it.

June was to be the Raincloak Man's reckoning, just as the myths Mama taught her went. In all those old stories, the robbed hero never stopped until they got their vengeance, until they made things right. Surely that was why she was still alive—she was to be the direct answer to every life the Raincloak Man ever stole before her, an echo of their suffering come to turn that same suffering back upon him. Just like in the stories. That could be the only reason. Nothing else made a lick of sense.

Mama certainly wouldn't approve, and June knew it. Mama taught her those myths—warriors whose wives were killed, so they burned the world down for them, women whose children were stolen so they stole all the beauty of the world in return, made-up gods whose creations hated them, so those made-up gods in turn hated them back—as cautionary tales. Mama would recite myth upon myth and ramble about how *pointless* they all were—none of the warrior husbands ever got their wives back. The mothers never found their children again. The gods razed their worlds of ungrateful creations and were left alone again in their eternities. Mama would rage about the futility of it all, the silliness. Mama's way—the right way—was to love everything and everyone, and that's what she taught June when she got caught swearing at the hawk that stole rabbits out of their meadow or said she hated the raccoons that kept spilling their garbage everywhere.

No such thing as hate without love first, little, she would chime, and June would roll her eyes and sign her secret swears at whoever and whatever irked her.

June had never really listened to Mama's preaching back then, and she sure wasn't now. Because now there was something *alive* inside, and June knew it was not something silly like the *absence of love.* Those myths might have been cautionary tales to Mama, but Mama had never been angry like this before. June was sure of it. Because if she had, Mama would've done something about it, just like June intended to.

June *hated* the Raincloak Man, and it didn't matter if Mama would be disappointed. The Raincloak Man was the reason Mama would never be disappointed in her again.

June rested her chin atop her knees and felt her heart beat slow in her chest.

Alive.

There were things alive inside June's heart that Mama would truly hate, if she knew. And Mama *always* knew. She could read people like books, just by looking into their eyes or at their hands.

The eyes speak the truth the soul knows and the mouth won't utter, June could hear her say, *and the hands tell the history. They are the only two things a man can't use to lie.*

June looked over at the Idiot again. He'd stirred and was now sleeping with one arm cast over his face, a worn-out leather glove covering his hand.

The hands tell the history.

June frowned. She'd already made up her mind about the Giant, and from what she'd seen of his hands and his eyes, her instincts weren't wrong. The Giant's eyes crinkled at the edges when he smiled, and although his hands were as big as boulders and she was certain he could crush her with one blow, he was always gentle when he patted his big red horse. When he picked a flower for her yesterday, he did so with such care that the stem wasn't even bruised. The Giant was *obviously* kind. And if he was kind, he certainly could be trusted.

But the Idiot... he had secrets. June could feel them hovering unsaid in the air all around, see them in the careful way he walked, hear them in the lilt of concern always tainting his words. His eyes were soft and dark and contradicted the sharpness of his smile. But there was still something else; a promise, a whisper. An unsaid history.

The hands tell the history.

Without any further deliberation, June eased herself upright, biting her lip against the pain, and crept past where the Giant lay snoring toward the Idiot. Mama never got around to teaching her how to read a person's hands, so June would just have to teach herself. Besides, if she couldn't kill the Raincloak Man on her own, she needed to convince the Idiot to help her do it. And if he was going to be the one to help her, at least she should know if he was trustworthy.

The Idiot didn't stir when June settled next to him. He was still, one arm still flung over his face, the rhythm of his breaths gentle. If it weren't for the half-healed gash on his cheekbone and the fading black eye, she would think him a statue of some fallen saint, a creature straight from Mama's bedtime stories. One of the heroes. She kept her eyes on his face as she reached for his glove, gripping the tips of two fingers with the same care she used to handle meadow butterflies in late summer.

June pinched the worn leather fingertips and tugged.

The glove slipped off without any real fuss, easy as shelling peas. June blinked, a little surprised, and squinted as she turned her full attention onto the Idiot's exposed hand.

His hands were even paler than his face, the color of fresh milk, of new snow. Despite the scruffy state of his worn-out gloves, there wasn't so much as a speck of dirt beneath his nails, but his fingers were covered in scars, just the same as the ones on Mama's fingers. Frostbite.

June looked down at her own hands. They seemed so filthy in comparison to his, despite the bath she endured at the orphanage. She had dirt under her nails and creased into her hands and scars from climbing and falling out of lots and lots of trees. Her hands looked like they had seen a hundred more years than the Idiot's, but *she* was twelve and *he* was an adult.

June frowned, turning his hand back over to examine his palm. How was she supposed to learn of his past when his hands betrayed hardly any sign of life at all? So he got frostbite, what could that tell her other than he'd once been very, very cold? Just how long had he been wearing those scuffed-up gloves?

June's eyes drifted to his other, still-gloved hand. Maybe she needed to see both before she could read them like Mama talked about. Maybe it was this was just like their mysterious power over plants that seemed to come and go as it pleased, and she just needed to—

June's thoughts faltered as the Idiot, ever so slowly, curled his long unmarked fingers around June's.

June went still as her heart grew unsteady in her chest. Surely, he was going to wake up and get *mad*. June saw the way he flinched at the slightest touch, how he shuddered beneath his coat when he doctored her wounds. He didn't seem to want anyone near at all and yet here she was, trying to read all his secrets like the gloves were what hid them.

"That ain't a good move, kid."

June looked over to the Giant and froze. He was awake, looking at her with wide eyes.

She furrowed her brow. What was his real name? Finch?

June waited. The Giant just stared, his tanned face gone white beneath his beard.

"Let go of his hand, kid," he whispered. "Now."

June narrowed her eyes. Why should she? Who was this guy, to tell her what to do?

He held up a hand and moved closer. Unease ran sharp down June's spine like the bite of a thistle.

"Go on, kid. Drop it."

Vince, June remembered. She looked away and begrudgingly set about dislodging her hand from the Idiot's. The Idiot wasn't exactly holding onto her, not *really*, but his hand had still closed over hers as if on reflex. She was almost free when the Idiot's slow breathing finally caught.

June stilled. *Please don't wake up.*

"What?" he mumbled, not quite awake yet.

June's heart slowed in her chest. She still had ahold of his hand.

"Taein..." Vince said, voice low and warning.

Warning of what?

June watched as the Taein's eyes cleared, then snapped to her hand.

He remained still for a sliver of a second, and June watched his face drain bone-white. She opened her mouth to say something and rammed right up against the old barrier.

Oh, forget this. June sat still, and waited. And for an agonizing half-breath the Idiot was still, too.

The next instant he *exploded*, springing onto his feet like a spooked rabbit and clutching his bare hand to his chest like it might fall dead from his wrist. He sputtered for words before bursting out only one.

"*Shit!*"

"Taein—" The Giant tried.

"Holy *shit!*" The Idiot was almost shouting now, still grasping his bare hand and looking with huge eyes between said hand and the Giant. "How—I—where the *shanking hell* is my glove?"

June didn't know what to do. She sat just staring at the Idiot, the abandoned glove lying in the dirt next to her like a dead animal.

He followed her gaze and sprang forward to snatch the glove before reeling back again. He stilled only after replacing the glove, then fisted his hands in his hair and flew into a tirade of foreign profanity.

"I'm cursed, you stupid little girl!" he said, pausing his rant just long enough to shout at her in Jinian.

He launched straight back to swearing and pacing before June could ask for the pad and pen to explain, so she just sat and watched as her chest grew incredibly tight. She'd never seen anyone as angry as this. The Idiot was acting just like how she felt inside as he paced around with his hands in his curls, oblivious to the coals he sent scattering toward June and the glare she shot back.

She remembered Vince and looked to him for answers, but the Giant had gone every bit as white as Taein.

Why is he mad? She wrote in the dirt with the tip of her finger. Vince squinted at her words, his eyes darting between her and the still-ranting Idiot, and just shrugged.

At long last, Taein stopped pacing and dropped down a few feet in front of her. He dragged his trembling hands across his face again before clasping them together. He looked to Vince as if asking for help, but Vince only shrugged.

The Idiot looked back at her. June looked back at him. She didn't feel like writing any words and he didn't speak. He just stared, his eyes full of a strange sort of terror she couldn't make sense of. What was so wrong with his gloves?

The sky began to gray at the edges. June closed her eyes, feeling every ache in her tired body.

Should've just gone back to sleep.

She snuck a glance at Vince and found him still staring at Taein with those wide, frightened eyes so out of place on his kind scruffy face.

What did he have to be afraid of?

June shrugged the thought away and kept waiting for Taein to say something, anything. To explain. He seemed even worse at giving answers than Mama.

More long minutes ticked by. An almost pleasant sort of fog inside was just beginning to dull her senses, promising sleep, when Taein finally spoke.

"Listen here, brat."

She opened her eyes. Taein was looking at her again, the kind of exhaustion that has nothing to do with sleep heavy on his strange foreign face.

"Sweet shanking hell, kid," he said, sounding far older than he looked. "Surely you know the story. I'm *Anathema*. Not the nice, neat kind with special powers. I'm the kind that ruins things. My-my hands, they—no, *I*..." He gave up, dropped his head back into his hands, and heaved a long sigh.

June traced letters in the dirt. She wrote the word *story* and placed a checkmark next to it, and then wrote *me too*. Then she tugged on the Idiot's pant leg to get him to read it. He did, and that terrible silence came back for a long time. When he spoke, there was a hard bite to his tone.

"No, kid, not like you. I'm descendant of Lithriin."

Lithriin... June frowned. It felt like a hundred years had passed since Mama told her the story.

The last story.

A sudden wave of heat sprung up behind her eyes and before June even knew what was happening, her face was crumpled and tears were streaming hot down her cheeks and a terrible force was pressing down on her chest and driving her heart into a frenzy and she couldn't breathe.

I can't breathe, she signed. But of course they didn't understand.

June sucked in strained hiccuping gasps and curled her arms around her frame as her chest kept lurching and her lungs kept on searching for air that wouldn't come. Waves of anger converged upon her like an angry sea and that was all she could feel until a pair of lean arms scooped her up.

The Idiot.

June buried her head in Taein's chest and let herself sob until air finally flooded her lungs again. She sobbed until all the anger and energy left her wilted and tired in the Idiot's arms and only then, when her tears faded into tired sniffles, did he boost her back into the saddle.

"Hey, look at me," she heard him say. But June didn't want to look at him, not when all she wanted was to go to sleep and sleep forever.

"It'll be fine," Taein said even when she didn't look, his voice soft again. "You'll be fine. I promise, brat."

I don't believe you, June wanted to say. But she settled for holding onto the saddle horn instead as Taein coaxed Lorrin to walk on into the murky dawn, still choking on her breaths, tears still stinging down her cheeks.

Things would never be fine again.

36

DEAD MAN WALKING

The world was terribly quiet.

It had been hours since they started the day's walk, and June had long since fallen asleep in the saddle and Vince into his own world. But the uninterrupted silence hadn't stilled the terror in Taein's heart like he hoped—he couldn't stop seeing the kid, her hand clutching his own.

He'd been dreaming some nonsensical caper when it happened—such visions always occurred when he finally let himself sleep; his starved subconscious unleashing torrents of nightmarish nonsense upon him as if making up for lost time. He was so held down in that mental deluge that he hadn't the slightest idea what was happening until he heard Vince's voice. Too tight, too pinched.

If Vince hadn't noticed... Oh Geiin. Taein squeezed his eyes closed and shook his head. It wasn't enough to clear the image from his mind — ash, raining down onto Ruein's boots.

It could've happened again.

The look Ruein wore as he watched the king of Faeriel dissolve in front of him. The horror smeared all over his face.

It could've happened to you.

Taein reached up and curled his fingers into Lorrin's mane, trying to find something tangible, something of the real world where nothing bad had actually happened.

Not yet, at least. And that thought alone was more than enough to send the terror rearing right back up.

Afternoon arrived, and along with it came a mandatory pause to examine June's wounds and have lunch. They drew the horses to a stop and Taein helped June down from Lorrin while Vince busied himself with lunch.

"You know," Taein said, his voice tight, "I'm genuinely shocked that he hasn't caught up with us yet."

"Who?" Vince asked, not looking up from his pack.

"The hunter."

"Ah. He's gotta be lost without the bird."

Taein shook his head and tried to stop scanning the road behind. "I doubt it."

"Huh." Vince chomped into a thick piece of bread. "Well, maybe he got mugged."

Taein sighed. "Wouldn't that be nice. How's our pantry looking?"

Vince glanced up as he tossed a sack over one intricately-tattooed arm. "Not too good, boss."

Taein pawed through his own bag. The contents of his pack yielded only a single mushy apple, Lorrin's half-emptied bag of grain, and a few slices of dried beef.

He looked up at Vince. "We're miles off from the nearest post, Vince."

Vince pulled a near-empty packet of dried fruit out of his own pack and commenced munching. "Probably should go kill somethin', I reckon."

Taein took a few pieces of the fruit without asking and nodded. "You stay and watch the kid, then."

Vince froze in the middle of trying to smack Taein's hand away from the rest of his fruit. "Look, Taein, my buddy," he stammered, "I think it'd be better if I went. Much better."

Taein plucked his pistol from Lorrin's saddlebag and tucked it into his shirt. "I'd like to be alone for a while, if it's all the same to you."

"It's really not."

Taein stared the giant down. "Between the two of us, Vin, *you're* her safer companion. I think last night more than proves it."

Vince frowned and looked at June, who sat silent and sullen in the grass a few feet off.

Taein heaved a sigh. "Look, Vin, she's not going to eat you. Just share your little fruit slices and make sure she doesn't wander off. That's all I'm asking."

"That's too much."

"Well, you know the way back to the Pearl."

Stiff silence for a minute. Then Vince gave a begrudging nod. "Then see that you come back with something tasty to roast."

Taein gave him a weak two-fingered salute, then struck out on his own.

A long walk through a maple grove, a lot of festering thought, and a crossed path with a wild boar later, and Taein found himself with enough breakfast, lunch, and dinner to last a good while.

The boar had made an incredible fuss on his way out, thrashing around in a mucky carpet of last year's fall foliage and squealing loud enough to raise the half-dead before Taein finally got his throat slit. Now he stood at the carcass with his chest heaving and breath clouding in the cooling spring air. The afternoon was getting late. He needed to get the boar butchered and head back.

Still, he just stood there, staring at the pig's glassy eyes. His body felt locked up, even with the receding adrenaline.

After butchering, he'd have to go back. And he didn't want to. Not one bit.

At last, Taein managed to wake his limbs and crouch down. He placed a hand on the boar's muddy hide, the body still warm beneath his glove. Memories of hunting parties long forgotten surfaced from the dimmer corners of his mind, and his heart stirred toward home; toward those endless yellow fields and blue mountains, where horses ran free on the plains and eagles cried in the blue open sky. Back to a place where the wind had a voice and spoke through every wild thing. Back to a place where the wind guided lost things home.

The longing came and went, withering away almost the same moment it took root.

Home? Taein scoffed, brushing a chunk of mud off the boar. When had Efriel Shu ever meant *home?*

Still, he couldn't bring himself to butcher the boar until he had said the rites.

Taein eased himself down on the grass next to the carcass and sighed. Animals like this poor bastard were the lucky ones. For them, death really *was* the end, and not the first of many stepping-off points, each one more broken than the last.

His chest felt especially heavy as he began the rite, searching for the once-familiar rhythm in the ancient words.

"*Aisha, non christja parfel soja ocre...*"

Ruein had been the one to teach him those words. The rite was a sort of farewell, a means of offering any felled creature's lesser spirit back up to the Celestial who first lent it breath. But animals were not the same as men, their dumb spirits always innocent in the eyes of a Celestial who knew their only crime was that of a life spent in a world man and Mithre alike had ruined.

For the men themselves, returning to the maker was not so easy. That was where the rosewood amulets were supposed to come in. They were a pledge of faith—and what else does man have to offer the Celestial, but his faith? But all the same, Taein hadn't worn an amulet since the day Ruein took it from him, all those years ago in the snow.

The feel of the pig's cooling body beneath grew more distant as the rite pushed Taein deeper into his thoughts.

Plenty of people asked questions when they noticed he went without an amulet. And Taein understood their bafflement, really, because why the hell *wouldn't* he wear his amulet? It was the first thing placed upon any newborn child, even before the cord was cut. That thin wooden disc was the only thing guaranteed to stay with a man from his first breath until his last, a tether to Geiin himself. They were a promise, meant upon death to drug a man's stranded spirit into that long, final sleep toward a supposed eternity, should Father-Graven ever find it pleasing to set right the world his son's own creation had so terribly skewed. A last gift to a race of men who did precious little besides scorn Geiin's holy name and then hold out their hands for favors.

Where the hell is your amulet?

It was a question even the worst bottom-barrel slime-ball scum-rat would ask Taein, eyes all wide, mouth agape. They would stand and stare, awaiting an answer that wouldn't come, and one they wouldn't have even the *slightest* capacity to understand if it did.

I don't have one.

And Taein hadn't so much as touched one with the intention of making it his own, not since Ruein, not since that night in the snow where he should've turned to a Shallow once and for all.

I don't have one.

He certainly could if he wanted to. Why be a dead man walking for no reason? There were plenty of tiny churches scattered across the countryside that gave away amulets for free, as the Monastery in the Windaerwood so fiercely (and sometimes violently) insisted. Wars had been waged over possession of the amulets yet none had ever taken control of them from the Monastery. There were monks whose sole purpose was to distribute amulets to all the world's people, sounding endlessly their singular rule: *Wear it, wear it, and wear it always.*

To take off an amulet was to be forsaken of the Celestial. Taein understood. The rule made sense, even to those who hated Geiin. Amulets turned the half-dead into Sleepers, and Sleepers could be embalmed and placed in the crypt-citadels made up of endless worming stone labyrinths beneath each Ierisian city, the resting place of millions. Sleepers could be cremated with their amulets, their ashes forged into hard gray gems and strewn in the wild ocean, where they would stay as silent dark pearls to rest in the deep until Father-Graven called them home. Sleepers could be stacked and stored, hauled away or buried in earthen graves, entombed among mountains, or dissolved into precious metals. Sleeper spirits were quiet, they were controlled, and they did little more than clutter up the dark underground. Those who were once the unwanted or the perverse could even be carted off into the Southern Mists and tossed in. They were sleeping, after all, so what would they care?

But Shallows could not be controlled so neatly. Really, they wouldn't be controlled at all.

Shallow spirits were restless, drifting, starving things, prone to growing so desperate for relief they learned to stir their rotting dead bodies back to movement. And when their bodies *did* finally salt away, ground back into the dirt from which they came, their spirits lived on. Awake. Growing wild and dangerous, cut off from the goodness of Geiin. Shallows could then roam the world with one foot on either side. Restless. Angry.

Taein had never seen one in real life, only heard the tales, heard the discussions. A few of the boldest thieves in Regor's service had made a career out of Shallow-hunting, and a lucrative one at that, despite the sky-high turnover rate. Taein wanted no part of it—Shallows were one of the only things around that still scared him more than himself.

But beside it all, still no amulet. It wasn't that Taein didn't *believe*, because he did. But what was the *point*, when Taein's sorry excuse of a soul wasn't *worth* the fleeting mercy of eternal sleep? What good was wearing another amulet when the last time one hung from his neck, Ruein himself was the one to take it away? And really, what could life as a Shallow possibly bring, that he had not already brought upon himself? What all did it matter, when he couldn't ever really die?

When Taein opened his eyes he was still sitting there like an idiot. The boar's body had gone cold and yet still he was murmuring the rite over and over as if he had gone senile.

...I send your Breath back to Geiin and your body to the Earth, which we all become, and where I one day will join you...

If only it was that easy.

Taein stood and stretched, the bounty disc around his neck still foreign, still heavy. He was debating taking it off and stuffing it in his pocket when an arid howl pierced the air and sent a cold wash slithering down Taein's spine. He froze, watching as a pair of wraithlike black dogs loped like living shadows out of the forest, beelining right toward his kill.

Right toward *him*.

Taein's heart faltered in his chest. Coyotes? No, these were bigger. These were unlike anything he'd ever seen. They moved like water, as if unfettered to the ground.

Run.

But Taein was morbidly fascinated. More and more dogs came

creeping out of the woods into the sunlight; dark, phantasmal, eyeless creatures, floating along as if they weren't made of blood and bone and the salt of the earth, but something of the dark crevices beneath.

Taein remembered Venny's shrouded corpse, saw Ka-el sitting on his bunk with those pathetic tear-stained cheeks, and gasped.

He was right. Ka-el was right.

Taein's legs finally uprooted and he sprinted away, the boar left behind and flintlock clutched in one sweaty palm. He didn't dare look back as the shrieks grew frenzied, mixing with the snapping of bones and wet severing of flesh as the pack did his butchering for him.

Taein could hardly see straight. His whole world narrowed to only the blurry grass beneath his boots and the roar of his own pulses. Every time he blinked he saw Venny. Saw the unnatural shape of her ravaged body beneath the white shroud. He *had* to get back. The dogs might not be able to kill him, but they sure at hell could get to Vince.

And the kid.

———

37

FLICKERING INNOCENCE

Vince and June watched in twin silence as Taein disappeared over a grassy knoll. A long, tense moment passed before the kid turned to face Vince with those alien green eyes. Vince stared back, still clutching his bag of dried fruit, and shuddered despite himself. For a long while, neither moved. Sweat beaded on Vince's forehead despite the cool afternoon. He swallowed hard.

Now this is just embarrassing, you milksop.

Vince steadied his hands and held out the bag as a peace offering. The kid's cemented-on glare softened, and she accepted the handout, chewed thoughtfully for a while, and crawled closer. Vince's every muscle tensed—was she going to use her witchcraft to bind him with vines and light him on fire? Or skewer him with a blackberry branch? Or—

The kid just pointed at the fruit.

Oh.

Vince handed over the whole bag, which she dumped out onto the grass and began sorting into neat piles. They sat in silence for what felt like an age. June munched on the fruit, making a priority of the pear slices before moving onto the apples, then the strawberries, and finally the figs. Every now and then she would offer up a piece, but Vince declined. He'd somehow lost his appetite.

"I'm not much for figs either," Vince said, nodding at the few remaining stragglers that June sat playing with.

She looked up with those horrible eyes and Vince stayed as still as he could and fiddled with each of his rings.

She's just a kid. So what if she could make things grow? She was still little, and by the looks of it didn't even know how to use her powers. And so what if she *did* know how? He'd seen far worse on the city streets. Roughed up and *been* roughed up by much worse.

Still, Vince nearly jumped out of his skin when the kid reached over and tapped one of his rings. She gave him an odd look and then made a few swift gestures with her hands.

Vince stared. "I don't know what you're saying."

She sighed and looked down, but they were sitting in the grass without any dirt for her to write in. She pointed to one of her hands and scribbled on it with a finger.

"The paper? I don't know where Taein stashed it."

Her little face wilted, and Vince found his own heart unexpectedly sink.

"Gimme a second," he said, going for his own pack. A little riffling produced a half-used pencil and a leather-bound book engraved with old Ersiin script that read *Pax Parcem,* or 'day of peace'. The journal was already half-filled with little sketches and unfinished sheet music, but the kid had something to say, so who was Vince to keep her silent?

"Here, kid," he said, handing her the book and pencil. "Best get it out if you got somethin' on your mind."

She looked between Vince and his journal before giving him a real, honest *smile*—no more than just a wee little grin, but the sight warmed Vince's heart right through. The kid flipped through until she found a blank page to begin scribbling. Vince had to squint to decipher her stick-like handwriting when she held up the page.

What're those for?

Vince read the sentence three times before he realized what she meant.

"Oh, these?" he asked, holding up a hand. "I wear all these beauts for work. Say... you wouldn't happen to still have that dagger, now would you?"

No, she wrote before scribbling some more. *What's your job that you gotta wear so much jewelry for it?*

"Well... golly." Vince tugged on his beard, trying to figure out how to explain his occupation somewhat nicely. "I'm what folk in the Pearl call *muscle.* I beat up... um, bad guys." He held out a hand. "These puppies make punching a lot more effective. Saves my trick shoulder."

June took his hand and launched a meticulous inspection of each ring; copper, silver, and gold alike; lingering on the engraved rings and especially the one studded with a trio of diamonds.

"I call that one Ripper," he offered as she admired the way the gems flashed in the sunlight. "Pretty, huh?"

That earned him another smile, which Vince couldn't help but return. June raised a hand and, resting her index finger atop her thumb with the rest of her fingers tucked against her palm, quickly twisted her wrist. Then she wrote the word *cool,* tapped the word three times, and repeated the gesture.

You try, she wrote.

Vince looked between her and the book before holding up a hand, mimicking the gesture. He must've done it right, because yet *another* smile broke across her face, a flickering innocence, and all the tension inside bled away before Vince even knew what happened.

June picked up the journal and wrote again. *Can you teach me to punch better?*

"Well, sure." He held up his hand. "Show me how you punch."

She settled in front of him, suddenly very serious, and gave his palm two quick jabs.

Vince laughed again, then took her hands. "No tuckin' your thumb into your fist."

She watched him, listening with serious focus, before nodding and signing something quick, then writing what it meant.

Vince squinted. "Ah. *Show me again?*"

She repeated the gestures and he mirrored her. Again came that sunlit smile. Again, Vince's heart melted.

June nodded, pointed to herself, and repeated the signs.

At last, Vince understood her sign *I want to try again*. He held up his palm and grinned. "Alright, let's see it."

She hauled her fist back and let fly.

"Nice!" he said, even though the punch was no different. "Wait, no." He awkwardly-signed her *cool*, and the kid beamed before dissolving into a coughing fit. Vince's heart sank. Day after day, she kept coughing like this. Nothing good could come of her getting sick, especially if they had to stop and let her rest up for a few days. And Taein... he didn't want anything to do with the kid in the first place. It seemed like every hour spent trekking toward Ersii ground down the thief's short supply of patience a bit more. If the kid got sick, *really* sick, would Taein even stick around?

Vince shook his head. Taein wouldn't leave them, surely. He'd always been the type to spout off nonsense he didn't really mean.

But he was still *Taein*, after all, and he meant it when he said he hated having people around. Vince saw the way he flinched whenever someone got too close, saw the effort it took him to doctor the kid's wounds, saw how his gloved hands shook all the time now. Vince knew there was a reason for that barely-concealed terror. And he knew full well that Taein's always-scant patience was already nearly out as things stood.

Vince offered June his canteen as her coughs wore on and paid close attention as she proceeded to teach him how to sign *thank-you*. Her coughs finally gave way and she sat hunched over, cheeks flushed and eyes gone bleary.

Vince drew in a long breath, wiggled his smallest ring off his pinky, and offered it to her. June took the silver band without a word and set about trying it on each of her fingers. It dwarfed even her thumbs, which made her laugh, and Vince couldn't help but smile.

Vince and June were both well-settled into the drowsy afternoon, with himself plucking on his guitar while the kid drew stick figures in his journal. The sun was still shining warm when Vince heard the slightest hint of a ruckus, rising the way Taein had gone. And of course, because ruckuses had nowhere to originate, if not Taein's direction.

Vince turned, squinting against the brightness of the fading day, and caught sight of Taein himself hauling ass down the hill, waving his arms like a mad man and shouting something incomprehensible at the top of his lungs.

"What?" Vince hollered. "You're too far away!"

More yelling. The stupid scrapper just out of range for Vince to understand a word he was shouting.

Dogs. Dogs?

Then Vince felt all the warmth drain from his body. *The dogs.*

He got to his feet in a hurry and had just hauled the kid up and gotten her into Lorrin's saddle when Taein came to a skidding stop in front of them.

"We gotta go. I have no idea if they followed," he puffed, face beet-red.

"Did you catch anything?"

"Does it *look* like I caught anything?" Taein snapped. "They ate my kill!"

"They?"

"Ka-el's magic monster dogs, what else?"

Damn. "Better our dinner than us proper," Vince said with a grimace.

Taein vaulted up into the saddle behind June and gathered Lorrin up. "Get moving, Vince! Worry about your stomach later!"

Vince didn't argue, slinging his guitar onto his back and clambering into his saddle. Before he could even get his ass in the seat Taein had Lorrin trotting off. Vince cursed and tapped his heels to Maple, who, sensing something was terribly amiss, stepped off quick. They hadn't gone more than a few paces before Taein spurred Lorrin into a breezing gallop and Vince had no choice but to loosen his trembling grip on Maple's reins and let the draft chase after them.

They went dashing through the Jinian countryside until Taein finally brought Lorrin down to a walk. Vince straightened in the saddle, forced himself to let go of Maple's blond mane, and gave the horse a few unsteady pats. But dread was still souring his stomach, and it only worsened when he saw the kid tucked against Taein's chest.

Stop it, she's just a kid. He looked back down at Maple and sighed.

First all this Anathema business with Taein and the kid, and now...

Ka-el had never been off his rocker. There was no way Taein would panic like this without having seen what Ka-el and Venny ran into. Something dark, something unnatural, something... old. A breath of the way things were before.

And the way things were before... the old world had been very, *very* dark.

Vince snuck another glance at Taein and June. Taein had dismounted and was leaning against his sweaty horse, his head in his dangerous gloved hands, his slight frame shaking like a sapling in the face of a strong gale. The kid still sat atop the horse, her back ramrod straight as she looked back the way they'd come, her eyes hunting the landscape for any sign of the dogs.

She wasn't afraid, Vince realized. She was *searching*. Looking for a fight, and that was almost worse than her being all terrified and pathetic.

Vince looked back at Taein as the scrapper gave Vince a half-hearted smile that ended up more of a grimace, and tugged Lorrin forward.

Vince coaxed Maple into a walk after him and shook his head, his hands still trembling around the reins.

They're only human.

❧ 38 ❧

WHEN IT IS FINISHED

When Vasily approached his mother's room for the last time, there was no soft voice to beckon him through the whitewashed doors. When he turned the knob and stepped inside, the once-gentle quiet of her abode had grown deep and heavy; Mari's fountains all silenced, her plants growing wild and unchecked, her windows to the valley below enclosed by thick curtains that banished any hint of daylight. The space was dark as a moonless night, save for a few candles set on either side of her bed.

The room used to be a sanctuary, but now it felt rather like a tomb.

It was a pale morning beyond those curtained windows, a week from that fell night when Nuest finally intercepted Vasily on the hunt, and the first day Vasily had spent in House Slate's towering reach in what felt like a hundred years.

There she lay, just a tiny gray figure amid a fleet of blankets, furs, and pillows. Vasily crossed the shadowy room, his steps muffled by dense woven rugs—rugs she had woven herself, back when Babas was alive and she was well—and eased himself down in the creaking chair beside her bed.

Mari didn't stir, the blue veins spidering across her closed eyelids standing out harshly against the pallor of her skin. Her face was hollowed out like the carven marble visage of some eternally-suffering saint in an Ersiin cathedral, devoid of any rosy pigments or false hues that might cast a semblance of health over her wasting skin.

She looked *old*. Old as Vasily felt inside.

He looked from her face to the candle flickering a weak yellow light over her bed, looked at the drenched handkerchief forgotten atop the end-table. Yena's, he realized. Vasily wasn't sure how long he stared at it before Mari stirred at last.

"Alaskie?"

He looked and found her eyes open and blessedly unchanged—still that light, pensive blue, the color of a bashful dawn, the color of a clear winter stream, the color he had seen a hundred thousand times before in his mothers face, the same color he saw reflected back in Auryn's gaze.

Auryn won't get to say goodbye.

Vasily brushed away the thought as soon as it came. He wasn't strong enough to face it.

"I'm here, Mari," he said, almost surprised by the stability in his voice as he reached out to take her hand. "I've come back to see you."

"Stars, whatever has happened to you? You look—"

Vasily squeezed her hand. "I'm here. Let that be enough."

Mari's face softened, and for the briefest moment Vasily saw her as she once was, as the woman Babas loved, the mother Vasily lived to protect. And she was beautiful; her face unlined, eyes merry, hair a tumble of black. But a shuddering cough lanced through her frail frame, and just like that, Mari was gone and this stranger's shell come back to replace her.

"Did the doctors—"

"Don't start on all of that, Vasily. Be kind to me." She tried to smile again and almost succeeded. "Have you seen the girls?"

"No, not yet."

She nodded, her sunken lips tightening. "They've taken it badly. You must be here for them, now more than ever. There is a coming darkness, Vasily, a shadow that grows. Y-you *must* protect them. You must bring Auryn home."

Vasily nodded, a sudden heat biting behind his eyes. Mother had never approved of his decision to send Auryn to House Light all those years ago, but what else was he to do? If he'd let Auryn stay home he knew she'd *still* be down in the crypts, reading against Babas' empty tomb by candlelight.

And Vasily wanted more for her than that. *Babas* wanted more

Vasily drew his hand back as the first unshed tears grew fierce and Mari noticed.

"Come now, none of that. You will see me again," she chided, her voice growing so rough.

"I know." Vasily swallowed hard, his throat gone impossibly tight, his heart beginning to panic. "I—Nuest told me—"

Mari spoke when his words failed. "The Celestial draws me to the long sleep. To the stars, Vasily."

He couldn't keep his voice from cracking. "I just didn't think it would be so soon. I thought you had more time."

Mari looked bemused. "Is that what belongs to us, time? It is Geiin's own breath in our lungs, after all. And what the Celestials give, they call home."

"It is a selfish thing, for them to steal you from me so soon."

She tilted her face toward him, opened her eyes. "But we will have all the time in the world when we meet again. This is just a little... stepping-off point."

Vasily ducked his head, his body washing through with a sort of disbelieving terror he hadn't felt since he watched Babas disintegrate all those years ago.

"I will be with you, Vasily. Just as is Babas."

This can't be happening, not again, not so soon.

Silence swallowed the room again for a long while. Vasily listened to the rough grate of Mari's breaths, heard the slow, hungry touch of the candle's flame eating away at the wick. He listened to that abysmal quiet as the remains of his fissured heart broke open once more in his chest. How much more grief could one man hold? How much more, before the fissures would never knit back together?

Hours passed in that dark space.

It seemed as if time itself had separated from them, as if it'd become some strange, stalking creature Vasily had left behind at the door, a selfish thief he never wanted to find again. If time was a thing of flesh and bone he would've killed it right then and there, burned it and the whole world too for just another moment, for just another day to say all these precious unsaid things clogging his chest that he hadn't the courage to say in the rapidly-fading *now*.

But *now* was all they had, just the barest whisper of a few stray moments, all so quick to slip through his fingers and fall to the floor.

Now was not enough. He was not enough.

Yena's handkerchief dried on the table. The candles slowly chewed through their wicks down to nothing and their yellow glow grew dim.

Hours passed.

Vasily knew the time was near when Mari finally spoke again. He heard the call echoed in her voice with every word.

"Vasily. *Os alsfalla.*"

Never waver.

"*Mie durksil menwi tu son gaethoa,*" he said. Even still, his voice cracked like tinder as he drew her hand to his forehead.

She squeezed his hand tight with what little strength had yet to abandon her failing body, her voice gone impossibly soft.

"Why do you cry?"

Her grip gave out before she even finished speaking. Still Vasily held her hand tight, unable to lie any longer. Not to her, not when this was the last time he'd ever look into her pale blue eyes and feel that chasm of grief echoed between them. Not when this was the last time that chasm would ever be understood by another human being again.

"Because I am not strong enough, Mari," he breathed. "Not enough to weather this coming storm. I can't do it anymore."

"Look at me."

He looked. Mari held his gaze, drank him in, and smiled the littlest smile Vasily had ever seen.

"Vasily. You have *always* been enough."

He didn't know what to say, so he said nothing, and just held on tighter.

Her breaths grew slow, grew shallow. Vasily just held on, even as she stilled, even as her hand grew cold and stiff, even as his tears came at last.

VASILY'S BREATH FOGGED GRAY AS HE FOLLOWED THE DIM YELLOW light of Nuest's torch down the long winding way into the crypts.

A full night had come and gone, and with it three priests of the House Slate's chantry who took Mari away for embalming and her half-death rites. Vasily had stayed in her room alone, head in his hands, sobbing until there were no more tears left in him to shed.

Now his whole body felt worn and stiff, like rain-ruined leather, his eyes still stinging as he trailed behind Nuest. One step after another. Too soon the stairs emptied out in the abysmal stone space that was House Slate's crypts; an echoing room carved deep into the heart of the mountain upon which the House stood, held up by pillars chiseled with the names of each Slate member within and the dates on which they had gone down to half-death.

Nuest's torchlight came to illuminate Mari's tomb, situated to the right of Babas'. To the left was Vasily's own, where he would one day come to rest when half-death finally came to claim him.

Unless Glass got to him first.

Vasily stopped beside Nuest. Mari was already laid within her stone tomb amid a bed of fresh-cut fir bows and red snowmint blossoms. Her entire body, save for her closed eyes, was wrapped in white cloth and covered in a woven blue blanket embroidered with a bloodhawk, the bird's pale wings outstretched across her tiny frame. The room smelled of the white-tea incense, jasmine, and silver-water solution she'd been embalmed with.

Embalmed. The priests had embalmed her because she was gone. Because she was asleep, and she always would be until the Celestials finally decided to end the long slow decay of this fallen, forsaken world.

If they ever came back at all.

More tears came to prick at Vasily's eyes. He clenched his jaw, bent, and forced himself to look at her. Tiny pieces of minnows-fern had been placed over her closed eyes.

Look at me, one last time.

But the last time had already come to pass.

Vasily steadied himself, bent, kissed Mari's brow for the very last time. He felt the chill of her body even through the wrappings.

Now there were no more *last time's* to be had. Together, he and Nuest eased the engraved stone slab suspended by pulleys down into place.

At least I know that she is resting. That she is safe.

And just like that, Vasily's gaze was pulled to Babas' empty tomb the second he and Nuest finished sliding the stone slab over Mari's, and there his eyes stayed for what felt like a whole eternity.

He hadn't been down here in ages, not since he tore Auryn from her self-inflicted place of penance beside Babas' tomb once and for all and carted her down to House Light.

And by Geiin's own breath, that was nearly *eight years prior.*

Bring Auryn home...

Mari's dying wish. But how could Vasily bring her home, when nothing had really changed but for more loss? How could he bring her home, when the world was not yet made safe? Instead, it had grown even worse. His failures deeper.

Vasily's breath caught as Nuest laid a hand on his shoulder.

"My lord, we must hold council even before you see to the girls. The Rudgars are threatening to usurp House Slate again, and the valley clans are feuding with the mountain clans and withholding crops *again*, and these strange beasts have been terrorizing the silver water lines, and—"

Vasily shied from Nuest's touch, his eyes still locked upon Babas' empty tomb, the memory of Auryn sitting there, surrounded by books and illuminated by pale candlelight in this cold deep reach where their father should be resting, burning too bright in his mind.

"You will tell the girls what has... you will tell them about Mari," he managed.

Shock colored Nuest's voice. "But my lord, the realm is starved of your leadership. The land is *changing*, just as your mother forewarned, and I do not see how—"

Vasily turned and brushed by the old man. "Tell the girls, Nuest. I will return when it is finished."

39

THE LIAR

nother somber morning arrived and shed light on the mist crawling sluggishly across the velvet green countryside.

They'd finally felt far enough from the dogs to seek out a village between three and four in the morning. They made camp just outside, and Vince kept watch and Taein actually managed to sleep for once, blessedly dreamless and still with exhaustion.

But now it was morning, and they had to get on the move again. Taein knew it was only a matter of time before the dogs found them again if they didn't.

He pried himself away from the grassy knoll where he'd nestled himself the night before and blinked in the hazy violet light.

"Headin' in?" Vince asked from where he sat leaning against a tree with his eyes still shut.

Taein ran a hand over his face and glanced at June's mud-stained clothes. He imagined the orphanage dress was already well-worn when she inherited it, and layers of blood and grime from her half-healed wound and days of traveling had done the thin fabric no favors.

"Suppose so," he said with a yawn. He went over to June, steeled himself, and tapped her shoulder. He snatched his hand back as she startled awake, eyes flashing green lightning.

Taein held his hands up. "Time to go, kid. I need to look at your bandages."

June gingerly eased herself upright and gazed over his shoulder with a far-away sheen to her eyes as Taein crouched down to examine her wounds. The gashes on her shoulder and leg were well scabbed over, but the cut on her side remained angry. The skin around the wound was tight and inflamed, oozing blood where the cracked scab clung to her dress.

Taein grimaced, flinching himself as he pulled the fabric away from the congealing mess. June herself remained still and silent, only coming to life long enough to scrawl a short message in the journal Vince had given her.

Will the dogs find us again?

Taein faltered. "No," he said with a quick smile as he tightened the last bandage. "We're fine."

She wrote again. *I don't believe you.*

Taein looked up, met her gaze. "Try harder, then."

More scribbling. Taein dug deep for patience and found precious little.

You're a coward.

He shook his head, fumbling with a few spare scraps of fabric. "Sure, but I fail to see how my cowardice pertains to this particular conversation."

I can't trust a coward.

Taein scoffed before he could stop himself. "Easy now, brat. Everyone is a coward, it's just some people are better at hiding it."

Her glare deepened. *Not true.*

"Oh, but it is. Cowardice is the bedrock of human nature." He wound a strip of fabric around her twig of a leg three times, then tied the ends in a quick knot. "Cowardice is just deep-rooted fear, and fear drives every single thing humanity does. People love because they're afraid of being alone, kill because they're afraid of dying, hate because they're afraid of themselves. It's so very simple, June, a girl of your age should know these things."

She stared at him with that searing green gaze, brows pulled tight, before scribbling again.

Then why did you come back for me?

Taein offered her a hand. "Because Vince told me to, since Vince is more afraid of bruising his silly conscience than he is excited to be rich and happy."

She frowned and wrote again, ignoring his hand.

Are dogs coming? No lies.

Taein resisted the urge to walk away and instead just sighed.

"No, of course not."

To his surprise, June's eyes welled with a sudden onslaught of tears. What the hell did he say now?

"Hey, don't cry," he said, forcing himself to reach out and brush a tear from her cheek. He felt the heat radiating from her face even through his glove. "Dammit, kid, they're not coming back. Really."

She looked at him, her face scrunched up and a blotchy beet-red. *Are you going to leave me somewhere again?*

Taein blinked. "No," he said after a too-long pause, "Vince and I are taking you to House Light, remember?"

You promise? Her handwriting was so shaky he could hardly make out the letters.

He drew in a deep breath. "Look at me, kid. Look, there you go. See? It's not so bad." He laughed a little as her tear-stained cheeks bunched with a smile. "Everything is going to be alright."

She shook her head and scribbled. *But I have to kill Raincloak Man.*

Taein clenched his jaw. *Not this again.* "Well, we can talk about that another time—"

She scribbled again and shoved the book into his face. Taein pulled away and squinted at the letters. *I have to. And you have to help me.*

Taein shook his head and rose. "Sure I do. But for now, we just have to keep moving."

She tugged on his sleeve, forcing him to stop, and held up the book. *Promise me.*

Taein stilled. "Promise what?"

That you won't leave again.

Taein offered a little smile. "Fine, I promise. Everything is going to be just fine, kid. Now let's get going, yes?"

June took his hand after a long moment of stubborn, suspicious silence and struggled up to her feet. Taein hoisted her atop Lorrin and sent a grin Vince's way. Vince, who sat towering atop his draft, didn't return it.

The fog was just beginning to burn off and unveil the long lines of viridian firs it'd formerly cloaked when they set off. Soon June was back to softly snoring in the saddle, and Taein could relax again.

"You're awfully quiet this morning, Vince. Dog's still got you rattled?"

Vince shifted uncomfortably in the saddle. "Everything is going to be just fine, huh?"

Taein turned in the saddle to look Vince in the face. "And?"

Vince shrugged. "Wish you didn't lie to her."

"Isn't that what all good parents do?"

"But—"

"Forget it, Vince."

Vince resumed his silence. But Taein couldn't find it in himself to relax again.

They entered the village—one of the little sleepy route-side hovels made up of those tall wooden houses and steeply gabled roofs the people of Nown Jin seemed to hold so dear—and stopped at the nearest trade post. It was here that Taein found himself standing at the cluttered counter of said trade post with June hovering silent and dirty just behind. The kid was quite obviously overwhelmed, her eyes darting from the villagers clustered in the corner around a stove to the towering stacks of supplies stuffed haphazardly about the establishment, spilling out last seasons apples and cheaply woven blankets, dried orange peels and folds of tanned leather, loose piles of parchment and odd boots bereft of their partners.

She's probably never seen so many people in one place in all her life, Taein realized. He tried to focus on the storekeeper glaring at them from across the counter and ended up pulling the kid closer anyway. It was so easy for him to forget that she'd never really left the shelter of her home, when he'd been without one for the last decade.

"How much for a sack of apples?" he asked as rain drizzled softly on the tin roof above. June reached up to take his hand and Taein flinched.

If the shrew-faced woman noticed Taein's flinch, she gave it no mind. All her attention was now fixed on June, and Taein didn't bother hiding his grin. Vince was still outside with the horses, but Taein had brought June in with the hope that her absolutely pitiful state might garner some sympathy and slashed prices.

Taein followed the woman's gaze to June. The kid had been awfully quiet all day. She was always quiet, of course, but usually that quiet held a sense of sizzling contempt for everyone and everything. Today she had gone *silent*, the sort that lingers in an empty house or rings at the bottom of a dried-up well. A sort of vacancy had settled within her, and it irritated Taein just as much as everything else about this accursed job.

Taein glanced back at the woman at the counter, presumably Lottie, and tried to give her a winning smile. They had to get moving, and this woman was taking ages to so much as say hello.

"Forgive me, but how much for apples?" he tried again.

"For you, one mark two-tenths." She drew her brown shawl tighter around her shoulders. "What business does a man like you have on the road with a kid?"

He bit back an oath and tried to remain polite. "Business of my own. And one mark two-tenths is pure extortion."

Lottie's eyes stayed on June. "Now it's two marks, buddy."

A bolt of heat shot up his veins, but Taein took a deep breath, curled his hands together, and leaned on the rough wood counter. "Look, I mean no offense. My *ward* and I are just trying to get where we're going and we've had nothing but trouble. What I *need* is more food. What I don't need is a hard time."

The woman's sharp eyes snapped up to him. "Ah. So you want to die, then?"

Taein arched his brows. "Well, that escalated quickly. Do you?"

She stared. "I'm talking about the road. It's dangerous out, don't you know?"

Taein gripped the edge of the rough-hewn counter. Drawing on every ounce of strength he could humanly muster, he tried to smile.

"That's no new revelation—"

She cut him off with a surprised scoff. "Geiin's knees, you really don't know?"

It was Taein's turn to stare as he gripped the edge of the counter a little tighter. "Excuse me?"

The storekeeper laughed. "You must be an idiot. You ain't heard—"

Taein leaned forward and let a harsh bite overtake his tone. "Are you going to sell me some shanking apples, or are we going to have a problem?"

She snorted. "It's your funeral."

"It certainly is. Now, *how much?*"

She took up polishing a glass with a grimy rag. "For you, three marks."

"But you said—"

"*Three.* What else?"

Taein thought a moment on showing her where this sort of attitude in the Pearl would get her before just gritting his teeth and flashing another tight smile. Best not make a scene in front of the kid, she'd had her share already.

"Alright, then. I'll take the apples, forty portions of hard bread, a bundle of jerky, and salted beef." He glanced down at June. She was shivering beneath his oversized spare raincloak. "I don't suppose you have any clothes for little girls, do you?"

The woman gave him a dark glare and stood, her chair scraping. She rustled through a few of the shelves before slamming down a stack of rough fabrics.

"This is what I got," she said as she plopped herself back onto the stool. "Parkas, shawls, little rain cloaks and such. Choose and leave."

"With pleasure," Taein grumbled, flipping through the stack. "June, would you like to pick?"

She blinked up at him, so he repeated the question. She pointed to a shawl made of a soft rosy fabric.

"How much?" Taein asked.

The woman stared at June again before shaking her head. "Just take it and get her out of here. You can have another dress for her as well, the thing she's wearing is disgusting. What are you thinking, bringing a child so young to a place like this?"

Taein glanced around. "Pardon? I know the road isn't the best place for children but it's not as if it's unheard of—"

She arched her brow. "What about the plague?"

Taein's words turned to ash in his mouth.

Lottie looked him dead in the face. "Said you didn't want to know, but I don't see how you could've missed it. It's everywhere in Nown Jin. And I can't imagine you've had her inoculated. She looks sick already."

Taein stared. "There hasn't been a plague since I was a child, I would know. I survived it."

"As did I." Her gaze fell to June again, who was still staring blankly at the stack of clothes. "Suppose it's sprung up again, the Grey Lady. And not a damn thing our plank-shanker of a king will do about it."

Taein grew lightheaded as the woman turned and began to pull items off the shelves for him. "And do you know anything about a pack of dogs?" he managed.

"Oh, sure," she said without turning. "They got a villager last week. Can't kill the bastards." She gestured dismissively as she set down a stack of items on the counter. "Dogs, plagues. It's all a part of the tide of life, you know."

Taein gaped. "You're not shanking with me?"

She shot him a nasty look. "Do I look like the sort of woman to shank with you?"

Cold fear drenched him head to toe. "Well, damn," he breathed.

Lottie just piled the food onto the counter along with the whole stack of garments. "Twenty-seven marks, if you would. You can just take the clothes."

Taein fumbled for his coin sack and blindly counted out the sum. "Thank you."

"Don't thank me, just leave."

"Of course." He gathered up his things, balancing them against his chest with one hand and snatching June's hand with the other.

Plague. The word wouldn't go away as he sorted the food between their packs and hefted June back into the saddle, looming as a dark shadow and whispering *I told you so, I told you.*

He should've known better. He should've put his foot down when he had the chance, stood up to Vince and left the giant outright if he wouldn't back down about the stupid kid. He should've—

"What's the rush?" Vince asked, handing over Lorrin's reins. "Something go wrong?"

Taein shook his head, unable to tell him.

Plague.

Hell below, he couldn't remember a worse childhood memory than when he caught the Lady himself. He barely lived through the sickness even with the best of care and prior good health.

June had no hope of anything resembling 'good care'. All she had was him and Vince.

Taein snuck a glance at June. She's already fallen back asleep in the saddle, in which she always slept so oddly—slumped with her head bobbing but still somehow upright. She slept too much. Far too much for a kid of her age.

He looked away. He'd been telling himself that she slept because of the trauma, the pain. Because that was how all children deal with their hurts. But her wounds were healing, and they were weeks away from the ruins of her home.

Children fall asleep to escape many things—fear, hurts. Sickness.

He glanced at her again, at the dark circles beneath her eyes and the pallor in her skin.

Geiin above, he couldn't afford this. Vasily was on the move, he was roving, his terrible eye would find them again somehow, that much Taein was sure of. There were two ends to this path. One ended with a clear conscience. The other ended red.

It's happening again...

Taein gritted his teeth and cued Lorrin into a trot. No need to finish that thought.

Not yet, at least.

❧ 40 ❧
EVERYTHING IS ABSOLUTELY NOT FINE

Vince narrowed his eyes at Taein as they hurried down the road. Something had happened in the trade post, and Taein wasn't letting him in on it.

It wasn't an unusual occurrence for Taein to forget to verbalize whatever flurry of malevolence was batting around in his head and it'd never been, but his silence still irritated the hell out of Vince as minutes oozed into hours and hours trudged into half the day. Vince drummed a tune on his thigh as that knot of suspicion grew tight inside.

Just tell me what's happened, you lying asshole.

But Vince couldn't say that, because Taein was more *withholding information* from Vince than really *lying*. And if Vince was going to sit there and call *withholding information* the same as *lying*, then he'd have to sit there and admit to himself that he'd been lying to Taein for months. And that was *not* on today's docket.

Vince remembered the first time he'd seen Taein lie. It certainly wasn't the last, because Taein lied all the time, especially when he was drunk—he lied about clothes, the weather, food, random facts that meant nothing to nobody; anything to breed chaos or mess with folk. But he lied about the important stuff, too—names, ages, dates, jobs, where he'd gone for an entire month some years back, that shankin' Blackblades tattoo... his whole entire history could be rewoven on a whim. Vince once watched the idiot drunkenly convince some poor sap new to the city that Regor was a loansman down on his luck and looking for new clients, and when they saw the poor lad's hand on Regor's infamous table the next day, Taein just laughed.

Taein lied as easily as breathing. He lied so much that Vince didn't even think the little scrapper realized it anymore. And Vince didn't mind it so much, really, because he knew Taein's tell—he always looked someone dead in the eyes when he was lying, and drew a little closer. And maybe for a normal man that might've been a sure sign of honesty, but when Taein closed that signature icy distance just a hair, Vince knew he was up to something absolutely rotten, because Taein would never draw near to anyone he didn't mean to hurt. He learned that the first time he saw Taein lie—*really* lie.

They were on a joint job lifting vintage Dobbiae portraits from a little vendor in the Black markets when the dealer himself wandered in, having distracted Venny, (who was *supposed* to be on lookout) and caught him, Ka-el, and Taein right in the midst of hauling a quartet of canvases up through a hole they'd cut in the ceiling of his five-story tent. Vince was handing off the paintings to Ka-el, and Taein, who'd only been off rit for four months and on their crew for a matter of weeks, was just beginning to stitch up the hole in the tent when they all spotted the dealer. Vince looked down to spy that poor sap frozen in place, gaping up at them like they were the biggest, hairiest spiders he'd ever seen on his ceiling and not a lot of scruffy thieves intent on making him their latest pigeon.

There was silence for a moment too long before Taein dropped down from the ceiling, landed nimbly on the floor, and stood with a flourish and that too-sharp grin.

As soon as Vince saw that grin, he knew trouble was coming. Taein had two smiles—his sweet, accidental, genuine grin, and the one that looked like blades.

"How're you on this fine afternoon, sir?"

"I—you can't—those are my life's work, I—"

Taein's voice scraped dangerously low as he stalked forward. Closed the gap. Melted his icy distance.

"Easy, old man. Everything is going to be just fine."

The dealer, for whatever reason, thought then was the proper time to pull a garden knife on Taein in some futile attempt to defend his *life's work*. This ended with Taein slipping to the side, tripping the old man up, and shoving him out of his tent and crashing down to splatter on the swarming Sheffal street below.

Then he went right back to helping Vince and Ka-el load up those Geiin-forsaken paintings, the hole in the ceiling forgotten and the trader sprawled on the uncaring streets below.

Everything is going to be just fine.

Taein was a liar, and he had been since the day Vince and Regor first saved him from the rit-house. And the further he got from the substance the less he did seem to lie, at least about the insignificant, nothing-stuff he'd always construed just for the hell of it.

Now he just seemed to lie about the important stuff—or at least as far as Vince could tell. But he still sat there in Maple's saddle thinking about the stillness of Taein's gaze as he shoved the dealer, his eyes dark and flat as the dead waters of an undisturbed lake, that void Vince glimpsed every time Taein got into scuffles or stole or lied or took a life a huge gaping abyss, and decided that it would probably best if he kept on lying himself just a little longer.

Everything is going to be just fine, kid.

Vince flinched at the memory of Taein's voice and hurried Maple onward.

Just a little longer. Once all this was over and the kid was where she belonged, he could come clean and Taein could just learn to deal with it.

After all, who was Taein to judge him?

PART III: SICKNESS

❧ 41 ❧

THE GREY LADY

Once he was back on the road, Vasily spent two days riding aimlessly around Nown Jin as he called for Bellan. But no matter how many times he sounded the horn, the bloodhawk never returned. Vasily didn't know why. There was only one real answer—something was stopping her from coming back. And very little could stop a bloodhawk's loyalty. Precious little indeed.

Now Vasily missed her shadow every time he looked to the sky. It was as though a piece of himself had gone missing.

Please come back.

He couldn't understand—didn't *want* to understand. He could stomach no more loss. All Vasily really understood anymore was that he was dangerously behind, wandering about bereft of his bloodhawk and with yet another colossal hole burned into his heart.

Why didn't you try, Mari?

Vasily clenched his jaw and cued his mare into a trot. He'd stayed away from villages for as long as possible, but now he was almost out of food and hadn't a single lead to follow. Now he didn't have a choice. So when a little village situated by the road called Pearish came along, Vasily didn't go around.

He rode into a quiet main street, a horrible tightness in his chest

290

he accredited to how long it'd been since he stepped inside any true civilization. Never mind that the feeling had been there ever since he realized just *what* the valley settlement woman and her daughter were, all those weeks ago. Never mind that the feeling had *always* been there, just sometimes stronger, since Babas first turned to ash before his helpless eyes.

Vasily rode through the rows of houses lining the main street and up to a steeply-roofed building made from thick logs and punctuated by little shuttered windows. Beneath each window was a small flower pot filled with wilted daisies, their mournful white heads bent beneath the weight of clinging raindrops. A moss-eaten sign read *Salty's Inn* over the doorway.

Vasily dismounted and waited for someone to stable his mare, but no grooms appeared. It occurred to him then that he hadn't seen a single face since riding into the settlement.

Strange, he thought as he settled for tying the mare to a holding post. For such a trade-driven culture, they were doing nothing to solicit his business. Was the settlement abandoned?

Vasily shook off his rain-drenched cloak, opened the heavy log door, and stepped inside. The hallway was strangely cold and dark, unlit but for a few small candles lining the walls.

"What business have you here, stranger?" Rasped a voice.

Vasily glanced up, and his heart stopped dead.

The innkeeper sat behind a half-melted candle, yellow wax pooling on his desk. Vasily stared at this withered husk, this *man* shuddering beneath layer upon layer of grime-coated garments, face ashen and shining with sweat despite his shivering. The innkeeper's eyes were nearly black, the whites gone so dark and blood-shot Vasily thought the man more dead than alive.

Vasily recognized the marks pocking his face right away—the way the innkeeper's ruined skin seemed to be pouring off of his skull, his flesh charred, sagging. Those oozing red welts.

All Vasily could do was stand and stare, unable to tear his eyes away from the sores coating every inch of the stranger's face, his neck, his hands. The way his body seemed burnt and blackened where the sores had 'healed'. The *reek* that hovered around him.

The hallways were silent but for the sound of water dripping from the cloak held in Vasily's now-shaking hands and the rasp of the innkeeper's breaths.

"Plague?" he dared whisper. The word cracked through the silence with a terrible finality.

The innkeeper swayed in his seat, his eyes floating toward Vasily but seeing nothing.

Vasily tried again. "The Grey Lady. Is it... you?"

The man bobbed his head, tufts of his thinning hair waving faintly in the dim light.

"You really ain't from around here, I reckon."

Vasily turned and bolted out the door.

YOU ARE NOTHING

They managed a full day of travel before things really started to fall apart. In a mere hour the kid's sickness set fully in, the dogs started howling in the distance, and it began to pour.

The sky was split open by flocks of heavy clouds, which let down a continuous and unrelenting deluge of fat, malicious raindrops. The downpour churned the path to a mud-choked mess, with some places virtually underwater.

These miserable circumstances found Taein squelching through the muck as he tugged Lorrin along, trying not to think about his poor beautiful boots as his frustration edged toward his breaking point. They'd been having to pull off to the side of the road for days now to make way for carriage upon carriage of the wealthy, fleeing their filthy cities to make for the fabled safety of the countryside. *They'd simply lost so much time.*

Taein glanced up at June and immediately looked away, the pallor of her skin sending his stomach back into knots. He remembered the Grey Lady. A little too well, if he was honest.

The plague struck when he was just six. He spent the next month and a half in confinement with only a nurse, his face ashen and full of welts. He remembered sleeping and sweating, remembered a constant chill leaching through his veins. Remembered how his mind seemed to spin out of control even when sleeping. Remembered drowning beneath the weight of the fluid in his lungs, how the quiet, rattling coughs never brought relief.

When he was finally well enough to be admitted back to the society of his family, he could still see how his father had gaped.

"It seems little Mikhael has some strength, my Lady," his father had said to his mother. *"Look at him, he's not even scarred from the welts! Good blood indeed."*

His mother had frowned and looked away, and from that day on Taein always wondered if she would've *preferred* that the plague had done him in. So she wouldn't have to look like she smelled something rank every time he came into the same room as her or laughed too loudly with Ruein or teased Laufein.

But none of that mattered *now*. Now, all Taein wished he could remember was how his nurse treated him, because that same plague was certainly making an unwanted reappearance, and it had found a home in June.

So their breaks went from taking ten minutes to a half-hour, and from three times a day to six.

And bit by bit, June began to turn gray.

They were just a week or so from the Fendall crossing by Taein's reckoning when the kid really started to cough—a heaving of her chest, that frail, familiar sputtering for air. A silent muffled racking of the lungs as the Grey Lady's voice took root.

But the Fendall River made up the Jinian/Ersiin border, and they were almost *close*. If they could just get out of Nown Jin, he could breathe a little easier.

But that hopeful estimation didn't account for the plague. Or if she...

Or if. He shook his head to clear the thought away and looked up at the kid as they trekked through the mud. "So, how do you like the new clothes?"

She just nodded. She'd chosen a heavy gray dress and a pink shawl from everything the shopkeeper had given her, but still insisted on wearing his extra raincloak over her own new blue one despite how badly it fit.

She lifted her hands and made a sign Taein knew referred to the Raincloak Man on account of how often she used it. He turned away instead of answering and got Lorrin moving faster. He couldn't deal with that right now. Not with sickness and the dogs behind.

There was a moment of silence, then a tap on his shoulder. He looked back at her with an inward groan.

Sweat was beading on the kid's forehead, her skin ashen. He could tell she was struggling to focus on him.

"What?"

She repeated the Raincloak Man sign, her brow bunching.

"I don't understand," he lied.

"Taein—" Vince tried to interject, but Taein silenced him with a wave of the hand.

She glared before reaching for her book. He didn't stop so she could write, letting her struggle with her trembling hands and Lorrin's lurching steps as she scribbled.

Another tap on the shoulder. He bit his lip and read.

I HAVE to find the Raincloak Man. <u>Help me.</u>

"You're sick, kid."

She blew a hot breath and trapped on the page, beneath the word *have*.

"Nope, sorry."

She kicked him, and it was then that Taein finally stopped. He took a step back and glared at her.

Vince was quick to speak up. "I'm sure that was an accident."

Taein didn't look away from the kid, nor did she from him.

"Well, June? Was it?" he asked.

She signed *the Raincloak Man* again, slowly, and then balled her fists together.

Taein closed his eyes, drew in a deep breath, and tried not to scream.

He offered a tight smile when he opened his eyes. "Stop talking about him."

He turned to get Lorrin moving again, and that was when she

chose to dismount. June bailed off Lorrin, still clutching her book, and landed in a heap in the mud.

For a long while, all Taein could do was stare. He looked to Vince, but all the giant offered was a baffled shrug.

"What are you doing?" Taein asked. "You're going to trash your new clothes."

June didn't so much as look at him and instead fought to her feet. She clutched the wound on her side with one hand, and he could tell that she had strained the scab. His patience was fizzling into nothing.

"June?"

She started walking in the opposite direction, hobbling through the ankle-deep mud, trying to clutch at her side and hold her book and lift her skirt out of the mud. The tail of his spare raincloak trailed pitifully behind her, the weathered green now mud-stained.

"June, you can't leave. You physically can't."

She made no indication that she heard him. Instead she slipped, nearly dropping her book, and landed hard with one knee in the mud. A tight squeak of pain escaped her, and she went terribly still.

He could see the dark blood beginning to stain the side of her dress, and something hard dropped in his stomach at the same time as heat flooded his veins.

"You're going to find the Raincloak Man on your own since I won't help you, then? Is that what this is?"

She looked at him, her face tight and eyes glassy, and nodded.

"Taein—" Vince warned, but Taein had way past enough. He laughed before he could check himself, and the glassy look fled from the kid's eyes. It was replaced, just for a moment, with pure hate as the strength of her anger beat back the sickness.

"I don't think so, brat," he said. "You're not going to make it two miles down the road whence we came. And you want to know why?"

She made no answer but just kept struggling to stand.

"It's not because you're still hurt, because I believe you're mad enough at this sorry son of a bitch to hunt him down even if you had an arrow in your heart. And it's not even because you're sick, either— it's because you're a *kid,* June. You know nothing of the world. You are a child and children don't kill monsters. They are killed by them."

Her fists clenched at her side. Still, she did not turn to face him.

"That's enough," Vince whispered, nudging his draft closer.

But Taein wasn't done yet. "Don't believe me? That's fine. You'll believe me if you're lucky enough to live through this plague and manage somehow, against *every* possibility, to find that bastard. The Raincloak Man will bend to his knee and hold you away from him with a single hand, and thank you for making his day so easy by removing your head from your shoulders before you can so much as land a single blow. And you know what the best part is? You don't even have to worry about finding him, because he's *chasing us!*"

She looked back at him. Tears were sliding down her cheeks.

"You are *nothing* to him, June." There was an emptiness in his voice, a chill. Taein didn't even try to change it. "He doesn't even know your name. You are an inconvenience. It doesn't matter if you don't want to hurt anyone. The mere possibility is enough. That's why he killed your mother and burned your home. That's why he tried to kill you. That's why, if he ever finds you again, he will."

June faced him, her entire body struggling with the effort to stand, clutching her book to her chest as tears continued to spill from her clouded green eyes. She was looking at him again like *he* was the monster that had burned down her home.

Taein moved a step closer. "All we have left is our lives. And if you and I can keep those, then we've done enough to spite him, to have our stupid shanking revenge. Because hunting him down and seeking justice and all that glorified horseshit is nothing but a good way to get yourself killed. We are not the storybook heroes your mother might've told you about. We are survivors, *nothing more*, and there are some things that happen in life that you can't ever make right. They just happen."

She tucked the book under her arm and made a sign with shaking hands. It took three times before he understood.

My mama.

She was struggling to sign, struggling to make him understand, hands shaking and face clouded with sickness and anger.

I want...

Taein hugged his arms across his chest and waited, trying to comprehend from the little she taught him by writing in her book and repeating the corresponding hand gestures.

I want...

"You can't have her back."

She choked on her breath, tears and snot running down her face.

I want my mama.

He raked a hand through his hair. "Most of the time nobody gets what they want."

Something cracked in June, and she threw the book in the mud and launched into signing with a force he didn't think she was capable of. He knew that if she'd been screaming at him if he could.

"I don't..." He drew off as she dropped to her knees in the mud, picked up the book, and scribbled. She tore the page from the book, scrunched it into a ball, and hurled it at him. He stepped forward to pick up the paper, brushing away the mud and creases.

Then what is the point? She had written. Her handwriting was so shaky he could hardly make out the words.

He looked at her. She was still in the mud, waiting for his reply, her chest heaving. He let him really look at her then, at the dark stain growing larger on her side, at the grayness of her face, at how hard she was working to breathe. How much fluid was already pooling in her lungs? And yet she was *still* fighting for her mother?

He met her eyes again. She was still expecting an answer.

"That is my revenge, June. Staying alive. That's all I have."

The book's cover was slammed open and the pen was stabbing at the page again. She held it up.

What did he even take from you?

"My home, my family, my future. My brother."

The words felt empty as they passed off his tongue. It just *was*, all the death. Just things that were and were no longer. Things he could do nothing about but carry on without.

June stared, her face clouding and eyes welling with fresh tears as she tried to understand. Again, she wrote.

You're letting yourself forget.

Taein gave a dry laugh. "That's the problem, kid. I'll never forget."

Then you are a coward.

"That's exactly what I am." The breeze tickled his face, toyed with his earring and his hair. Next to him, Lorrin stomped a hoof. "Just get back on the horse, kid. Please."

She didn't move.

"At least let me look at your side. I can tell it's bleeding again."

She looked away, out at the grassy hills that were beginning to give way to flat open fields and little forests and silver rivers of Ersii. For a long time, the only sounds were the birds chirping their hesitant morning calls in the distance and the stir of the wind. No one passed by.

"Please, brat. You know we can't... we don't *want* to leave you."

"C'mon, kid," Vince added softly.

The road was empty and time was slow. Taein kept his arms hugged to his chest and waited. There was nothing more he needed to say. All the words were spent.

Still, he couldn't leave her. He wasn't sure why.

Vince slid off his draft after ten long minutes and sloshed through the mud over to her. Taein watched the giant bend down and say something to her, watched as June reached out her arms. Then Vince scooped her up and carried her sloshing back through the mud to Lorrin.

Taein checked on her wound through the little hole he had cut in her dress. He got her secured in the saddle, placed some more salve on the gash, and hoped for the best.

Then he got Lorrin moving again. They hadn't gone more than a few paces before June was flopped over, asleep again in the saddle.

Taein looked a little closer and saw the signs of the first few sores brewing beneath her skin, the too-bright outlines of her swollen blue veins.

He looked away, back to the road. He could see the point where all the little streams came to an end so far in the distance, the Fendall River stretching out horizontally along the green horizon like a great silver thread. Beyond that was Ersii, and eventually House Light.

If the kid would just live long enough to see it.

<hr>

❧ 43 ❧

ASTRAY

Rain pitter-pattered down from an ashen sky. Vasily kept his gaze on the tree-lined road curving ahead as the bay mare's hoofbeats squelched in the fetlock-deep mud and tried to ignore the steady haze permeating his mind. When his vision grew gray as the clouded sky above, he just blinked the fog away and gripped the reins a little tighter.

This was how it started, he knew. The Lady took hold of a person in the softest ways, a viper coiling with slow precision until the time of constriction was right.

But Vasily was not going to think about that, nor the innkeeper's oozing sores, nor the growing heaviness in his lungs, nor the tomb he'd closed over his mother, nor the way he'd made Nuest tell the girls she was gone like a damn *coward*. He was going on until he found Glass, and he would put an end to it, and it would at last be over. He knew no other way.

That was Vasily's *plan*, anyway. But then came the hiss of a bolt whizzing through the air, and said plan came to a swift end before the day had even truly begun as Vasily threw himself from the saddle.

He toppled into the mud, the world suddenly coming in shocks as adrenaline ripped through his veins—his mare's mud-caked hooves

300

flashing above as she tripped and narrowly missed crushing his head, the abysmal sky spinning gray above, a rider approaching.

A *rider*, dressed in Enti colors and thundering down the road on a black destrier, a red-tipped Enti spear strapped to his back, a bow in his hand, his tanned face contorted with rage, his mouth open and *screaming*.

A rider, coming to kill him.

Vasily froze, mud on his cheeks and in his hair. This had to be a hallucination. Surely, he was just far sicker than he first thought.

But the destrier kept pounding through the muck and the rider kept screaming, and Vasily suddenly found himself moving with a desperation he hadn't known for days.

He scrambled to his feet, mud sloshing everywhere, dove slipping and sliding off the road, and found himself on thick green grass growing past his knees. Vasily ran like mad, drawing his sword from its mud-caked sheath as he went, searching for a footing that wasn't going to get him instantaneously killed.

He heard the change in the destrier's hoofbeats as the rider drove the horse off the road to follow. Vasily counted the stallion's nearing strides as he willed his legs faster, his boots pounding on the cobbled ground beneath the grass, praying for level ground.

Four strides away. Vasily's heartbeat boomed in his ears, his breaths tearing in and out of his burning lungs.

Three strides. Vasily tore up a little rise in the earth as another bolt went whistling by to hit the dirt a mere hair to his left.

Two. The rise gave way to a pasture dotted by the distant white cloud shapes of sheep.

One. This pasture was level.

Level.

Vasily skidded to a stop, his sword flashing out in the gray light as he whirled, and slashed a hard blow into the slender reaching forelegs of the oncoming horse.

Vasily's sword bit into bone, and the colliding forces of his blow and the stallion's power knocked the sword from Vasily's hands and threw him backward. He gasped as he hit the ground and all the air left his lungs in a single *whoosh*. He just stayed there gasping as the stallion toppled with a terrible grating squeal, flinging the rider from the saddle as the horse was dragged head-over-heels by sheer momentum.

The destrier and the rider crashed through the field, spraying clods of dirt and scaring the distant sheep. When they finally came to a stop, the horse lay still.

Its rider, however, didn't.

Vasily swore as the rider stood, threw down his bow, and took up his spear.

The red tip glinted in the dull light as Vasily recognized the mud-streaked face of *Rafael*, and felt the little he'd eaten in the last three days rush up his throat at once.

He forced himself to settle as he recovered his sword and stood at the ready. Rafael swiped a clod of dirt from his face, stabbed his spear at Vasily, and shouted.

"I have found you, Slate! And you tried to run, like a coward!"

Vasily forced himself to hold still as Rafael stalked forward. "I have done you no wrong—"

Vasily was cut off by a wild burst of laughter. "Liar! You broke your word! You killed my brothers! You left them to wither like *dogs*!"

Vasily gritted his teeth, trying to settle his breathing, to get just a little more air in his lungs as his vision grew dark at the edges. If he lost consciousness now, there would be no awakening.

Rafael rolled his shoulders as he neared, his hair dampened by the pervasive wetness of Jinian air and clinging to his forehead, his bared teeth bright against the tan of his skin.

"Now it is my turn, Slate. I care not if you are a king. I will cut your corpse in two and feed half to the shadow dogs, and leave the other half wherever I can find mist to wither it."

"Then get it over with," Vasily gritted out.

Rafael screamed and came whirling toward Vasily, and the hair rose on Vasily's arms as he remembered just *how* the Enti fought.

Like dancers, fell creatures born of fluidity, spears lashing out like thorns, bodies twirling, moving, spinning shapes, impossible to pin down, to strike, to kill.

He held his ground as Rafael came whirling at him with his spear.

Vasily ducked and blocked the first few blows before catching the red-tipped spear with his sword and pinning it to the grass. Rafael freed his weapon with a twist and lashed out at Vasily's face. It was all Vasily could do to stumble backward and block, the poison-tipped spear slicing close enough that the spice of the arrinvale powder burned his eyes.

He threw off the spear and went to advance, only to be forced away by Rafael's wild strikes. Vasily backpedaled and frantically blocked as he slipped on the rain-slick grass.

"Do you really expect to kill without consequence? Without retribution? You murdered my brothers!" Rafael bellowed, his spittle flying into Vasily's face as he dodged a wild thrust.

Vasily shook his head, staggering back and raising his sword just in time to knock away a blow meant to skewer his stomach straight through. "You caged me! I had no choice!"

"We wanted your help!" Rafael screamed as Vasily stumbled and barely regained his footing in time to deflect the next blow upwards.

"I have none to give!" he shouted back as Rafael caught his strike and sent him skidding backward with a force three times as fierce.

"Then you are a *coward*!" Rafael shouted, landing a terrific blow atop Vasily's shoulder and deadening the limb.

"You are a *liar*!" He struck out again and Vasily knocked the blow away with his sword.

"You are a *thief*!" Rafael whirled through the air. "You stole the lives of my brothers! You left them to rot like dogs! *Like dogs*!"

Vasily hardly heard the words as the tip of Rafael's spear buried itself in his gut. White-hot pain flared to life inside like a spark to summer-dry tinder, tinged a torrid, searing red.

Searing. The arrinvale powder.

Something awoke inside of Vasily beyond the pain, beyond the sickness. Rafael drove the spear in further, trying to stab him through like a piece of meat, and Vasily brought his sword down *hard* on the smooth wood.

The length of the spear separated with a ragged *snap*. Vasily bit back a groan, staggered back, and ripped the tip of the spear from his gut before throwing it as hard as he could across the field. Then *he* lashed out with his sword, blood leaking warm from his torso, pain and anger fueling each step, and advanced like a madman.

Rafael blocked the first few of his blows with the severed half of his spear, but Vasily hacked *that* in half too, and kept going.

Or at least he *would've*, had Rafael not hurled the remnants of his spear at Vasily's head with such a force it knocked Vasily flat on his back.

Before he knew what was happening, his sword was out of his hands and somehow in *Rafael's*, and Rafael had straddled him and was raising that sword up high in the sky and was swinging it down hard enough to cleave Vasily's head in two halves like an overripe melon.

Vasily threw his left arm up at the last minute and felt his wrist shatter beneath the brutish force as his gauntlet caught the blow. Before Rafael could recover from the jolt and draw the sword up again, Vasily found himself moving on desperation and smashing his forehead into Rafael's nose.

The horrible *crack* was loud enough to be heard beyond Vasily's raging pulse as his skull caved in Rafael's nose. Blood poured down Vasily's face—from his own forehead or Rafael's crushed nose, he was not sure, but Rafael reeled backward with a horrible scream, and it was enough.

Vasily knocked his sword from Rafael's hand and threw his weight hard against the other man, forcing his body off. Vasily rolled away, jerked his knife from his hip, and slashed out just as Rafael tackled him again.

He fell back as all the air left his body in a great *whoosh*, the world spinning as Rafael fought to pin his arms down, blood gushing from his nose as he screamed incomprehensible obscenities. His knee jammed into Vasily's rent gut, and Vasily coughed up blood with a scream of his own. The pain came in such a great rush that Vasily couldn't feel his shattered wrist as he drove the knife into Rafael's own gut.

Rafael faltered, his grip slipping as his body froze with a shock of pain, and Vasily threw his weight against Rafael and flipped him back.

Suddenly, Vasily found *himself* on top. He punched Rafael's face with his half-dead hand as Rafael drove his own Venrian dagger into Vasily's side.

Vasily caught the glimmer of steel as Rafael drew the blade back for another stab. He felt himself move as if he wasn't all the way in his body anymore, as if he was instead watching from somewhere high above as his husk reacted like an animal driven mad by instinct, felt his half-dead arm grip his knife tight as he brought the blade down onto Rafael's right wrist and cleaved his tattooed-hand from his arm.

Rafael shrieked and spat blood into Vasily's eyes. Vasily jerked backward, the world suddenly torn from his vision, and gasped as Rafael shoved him off. He landed on the grass and wiped frantically at his eyes, only to be kicked back over not a breath later.

Rafael's weight dropped back atop him the moment Vasily tried to fight him off, the world gone blurry and stinging and red. He went to curse and instead managed only a whispered *Geiin* as Rafael's remaining hand clamped down around his throat.

Rafael slammed Vasily's head against the ground and darkness crept closer as the Enti set about squeezing the life out of him. Vasily flailed his arms, gagging and half-blind, Rafael's weight forcing blood from his gut, his fingers searching in vain for his lost knife, for a rock, for a stick, for salvation.

Seconds passed by like an eternity, and the darkness started to eat his hand. The black was almost complete when Vasily's fingers finally glanced steel.

There. Vasily drew the knife toward him, slicing his fingers in the process, the bone handle unfamiliar and blood-slick.

Still, Vasily took Rafael's knife in his hands and slashed the blade across its owner's face.

And *this* time, it truly was enough.

Rafael fell forward onto Vasily's chest with a strangled cry, clutching at his eyes, and Vasily, pain-shocked tears pouring down his cheeks, rolled them both over and straddled Rafael once again.

He pinned Rafael's arms with his knees, blood running down from his gut and peppering Rafael's face, and pummeled the soldier with a fury he formerly only felt when dealing with the sons of Glass.

Babas.

His knuckles were bruising, concussing against Rafael's temple, his chin, his teeth.

Babas.

Blood and spittle ran down Vasily's chin. He was cursing in a language he didn't even recognize.

Babas.

Vasily saw his father in his mind's eye, watching him as he beat the life out of this pulverized Enti beneath his fists.

Vasily saw his Babas. He felt his father's disappointment, a moving breeze against the emptiness rattling around his ribcage.

He rolled off Rafael with a gasping shout and dragged himself a few feet away on his hands and knees.

Rafael groaned, the bloodied fingers on his remaining hand twitching feebly.

Blood was dripping down Vasily's temple, out of his mouth, from his gut, from his side. He clutched his stomach, probing the wound, and found it to be a ghastly circle perhaps the size of a Jinian half-mark.

Geiin above and Mithre below—what organs had the spear punched through?

Vasily staggered to his feet, refusing to let himself sink into the unconsciousness he knew would accompany lying down, and stood over Rafael.

His pulse still raging in his ears, rain drenching him to the bone, Vasily dropped down on one knee and took up Rafael's collar with both hands, shaking the man until one mutilated eye rolled his way.

"Look at me," he bit out, blood misting from his breath to smear on Rafael's face. "Look at me, if you still can. You caged me when I trespassed on your land but did not kill me outright as your vile excuse of a *law* allows. You showed me that one small mercy and now I will return it tenfold. I will let *you* live. But if you ever—" He cut himself off to draw Rafael closer and snarled into his face, "*ever* come near my family, there will be nowhere to hide. I will hunt you to the end of the world and *when I find you,* there won't be a single grain of sand in the Wastes I won't salt with your ashes. And when I've done that I'll burn the whole province to the *accursed* ground, and burn what remains."

Rafael groaned in response, blood burbling out of his mouth, one eye nearly swollen shut, the other too bloodied to make out.

Vasily dropped him back in the grass and staggered to his feet, searching the grass for his own sword and knife.

The sheep were peering at them from a distant nervous cluster and he had just found his sword and was searching for a clean inch of clothing on which he might wipe the blade clean when Rafael spoke, his voice a choked rasp.

"You're still after him, aren't you?"

Vasily looked back. Rafael was still flat on his back, blood pooling next to him from his severed hand.

"Whoever you're hunting. You're still after him, aren't you? Even after all of this."

Vasily spied his knife and took it up. "After all of this," he said. "After anything."

"He wronged you, then," Rafael said, now struggling to sit up. He failed and flopped right back down.

Vasily faced him, blood leaking through his fingers where he clutched at the hole in his gut.

"He is cursed. Anathema."

"But he wronged you."

"Yes."

Rafael gave a strangled laugh, turned onto his side, and vomited. He flopped back down, still chuckling to himself, and wiped his mouth with the back of his sleeve, smearing his face red.

"You have gone astray from your honor, then."

Vasily didn't bother denying it. "I have no more honor."

"The world is so much bigger than revenge, Slate."

"And yet, here you are."

Rafael just laughed in response.

He was still laughing when Vasily staggered back the way he came, his left arm still half-numb and hanging like a deadened branch from the battered trunk of his body, his right wrist shattered, holes in his side and his gut and blood oozing everywhere. He passed the still-steaming body of Rafael's destrier and called for his own horse, and couldn't keep the tears from his eyes when she came trotting to him without hesitation.

He fished out some bandages from his pack and gingerly wrapped his torso.

There was gore and mud and probably even grass in that wound, he knew. Arrinvale, a poison withstood only by the Vandels, and it was *inside* of him.

And that foul concoction bred infection, and infection bred death.

Not yet. Geiin above, not yet. There is still work to do.

That familiar grumbling echoed through the earth again. Vasily stayed still as the earth shifted beneath his boots, his entire body afire with blood and pain, and waited until his left arm recovered enough that he might haul himself into the saddle.

The feeling returned eventually, and he clambered pain-shocked, sick, and desperate into his saddle. The rumbles dulled, then died altogether.

Vasily steered his mare the way he'd been going with his one good hand, his lungs heavier than ever, each breath a torment.

He closed his eyes, clutching the saddle horn, and gritted his teeth against the waves of pain threatening to suck him into an unending sea.

I will not drown.

Rafael was silent by the time he finally rode off. Vasily shuddered and let out a tiny groan. Each step the mare took was a whole world born of agonies.

Father, help me.

The blood was iron in his mouth, and the downpour continued. He bent his head, his whole body trembling, and held on.

❧ 44 ❧

DROWN

Something June had never felt before was trying to drown her from the inside out. There was a weight in her lungs, a silent rattle in her chest, a dark pool behind her eyes.

She was so, *so* tired, and the Idiot wouldn't stop talking about some sort of plague and just be quiet.

Quiet.

Every sound was a hurricane in her ears, every brush of the wind or touch of the horse's mane a burn.

Quiet.

She hated the rustle of the trees overhead, the whisper of the breeze, the laughter of the little rivers all around. She hated how catastrophically loud they were, all crashing and competing and colliding against each other.

Quiet.

Every breath seemed to shred her lungs. The air was too cold. So cold it burned. Every inhale and every exhale felt like winter was trapped inside her. Like it wanted to get out.

But it wasn't just that—June could *feel life* dwelling in everything around her, from the tallest tree's deep thrumming to the little breaths of the grass to the smallest silent grain of pollen floating in the air.

Everything was so loud, so painfully noticeable. And there was that darkness beneath her eyelids. It wanted to suck her down, and she was so tired. She just wanted to sleep.

But... the Raincloak Man.

Something bit at the backs of June's eyes, the sensation so much further away than the feeling of the little dandelions growing all around. Is this what Mama felt? Is this how the world was to her, one great big sensory flood? Surely she must've known how to calm it all down.

Raincloak Man.

June tried to open her eyes and found it impossible. The sun was too bright. Instead, she let that dark pool pull her down. The Idiot's voice raised in tone, and she felt herself slide in her saddle. For a moment she tried to catch herself, but her limbs would not respond.

She found then that she could not open her eyes, not even if she wanted to.

Instead of falling, June felt the Idiot push her back upright in the saddle. The horse stopped plodding, and the Idiot seemed to try to talk. What was he saying? His voice was so far away, and yet the breeze so loud. If only the rivers, the grass, the trees... if only they would just be *quiet*.

The pool tugged at her. It eased the will from her limbs and soothed the grating of her breaths, the pain of the silent coughs. It took thoughts of Mama and the Raincloak Man and dulled them into distant, hazy musings. It made the pain go away.

Rest. Was this the way to find it? The Idiot would not let her hunt down the Raincloak Man, he was too stubborn and she was too hurt. Was this her only refuge?

The pool behind her eyes was safe. It took the white-hot aches and chills and trembles away. It brushed the icy beads of sweat from her forehead and soothed the aching of her joints. Down here, even the thrumming of the plants was quieter.

Quiet.

But no—she had to keep her wits about her.

June tried to stir, even just a little. If she could get well, then she could sneak away from the Idiot when he wasn't looking. Go find the Raincloak Man and make the pain in her heart go away forever.

But still. She was so, so tired.

❧ 45 ❧

UNRAVELING

Late afternoon and they were skirting along a quiet, abandoned orchard beneath a calm, white-cloud sky. To the left was the orchard in all its springtime glory, and on their right stretched a rotting, moss-encrusted fence which separated them from a line of alders and a stream dotted with rocks. The apple trees, their branches heavy with blossoms, bent over the path and reached toward the alders to form a green-and-white canopy that kept snowing white petals. This springtime deluge was encouraged by a whispering breeze that seemed almost desperate for companionship, as if the peace of the orchard, long independent from the management of mankind, had grown boring.

Taein would've thought the scene very pretty if it wasn't for the corpse of a kid lulling half-asleep in the saddle beside him.

He shook a few petals out of his hair and brushed them off his shoulders. Maybe he'd get bored if he was stuck in this orchard for a millennia, but at the moment boredom seemed a treat. Surely there was some sort of farmhouse, somewhere on the property, and he could renovate it into the palace he imagined. The property was far from any road stops or neighboring villages...

"Hey, it's time."

Taein looked to Vince. "It's really been two hours?"

Vince squinted up at the sky. "Roundabout."

Taein sighed and tied Lorrin to a low-hanging alder branch, then went to untie the ropes fastening the kid's legs to the stirrups. He'd given up on letting her maintain her own balance days ago.

"She looks pretty bad, boss," Vince mused, squinting against the dappled sunlight to look up at her.

Taein glanced at the kid and looked right away. Her face was as blue and gray as the sky above.

"I'm sure she's fine—"

"No, really. *Look* at her, Taein. It ain't natural to look that way in any type of sickness."

Taein lost patience with the ropes and broke out his knife. "Well, they don't call it the Grey Lady for nothing."

Vince gave a disapproving grunt as Taein finished untying the ropes and eased June out of the saddle. Usually, the kid just sort of let him guide her descent out of the saddle in a minimal-contact manner. But this time as Taein eased her from the saddle, something changed. She startled with a little gasp of fear and shrunk away from his touch, her eyes snapping open wide.

That was when Taein saw how *bad off* she truly was. Her eyes glinted with a pale wash of blue, her pupils unnaturally wide and dark, the whites shot through with flecks of black. Her skin was pocked through with sores, each of them oozing a clear, sick-smelling fluid.

"It's just me," he whispered. "Let me help you, brat."

June's eyes lulled uncertainly over to his general direction. Taein knew she wasn't really seeing him and tried to ignore the discomfort constricting in his stomach.

"June?"

She lulled a little in the saddle, as if trying to understand, and gestured with her hands awkwardly. It took Taein a minute to realize she was signing *idiot*. And *idiot* meant him, of course.

"It's me. It's Taein."

He wasn't sure if she heard him, but when he reached up to lift her out of the saddle once more she didn't flinch away. Instead she did something far worse, and as soon as he lifted her out of the saddle and set about carrying her over toward the shelter of an alder, she wrapped her arms around his neck and *clung* to him. And she kept doing it, skinny arms wreathed tight around his neck, her face pressed into his chest, her body quaking and limp, not letting go even when he tried to put her down.

She wouldn't let go. She was *holding onto him*.

A bolt of unfettered panic crackled right through him, and before Taein could regain control he dropped June and stumbled backward, heart in his mouth, vision spinning.

Oh Geiin oh Geiin oh Geiin oh—

"Taein!"

Taein whirled to face Vince, hardly able to see straight against the lights flashing in his eyes. "I'm sorry, I didn't—"

"Freezing hell, what's gotten into you! Is she hurt?" Vince said, dropping the horses' leads and hurrying over to June. Taein watched, rooted to the ground, his heart beating up his ribcage.

"I—dammit, Vince, she's fine!" he heard himself snap, stalking forward to push Vince away. "Look, there, she's sitting up, see? She's fine."

Taein instead found *him* shoved away as Vince extended one tree-trunk arm and brushed him off like a piece of lint.

"Vince, stop being an asshole and let me look at her."

Vince narrowed his eyes. There was a long, painful pause before he finally shook his head and, with a great sigh, moved aside.

"Thank you," Taein huffed, moving forward to crouch next to the kid. She was still halfway awake. Her eyes were open and roving around, at least, even if Taein didn't think she was seeing anything.

"Can you make some broth?" he asked. "If you're so keen on being useful for once."

He received another grunt in reply. Assuming it was an affirmative grunt, Taein turned his attention to unwrapping each of the old cloth strips binding June's wounds. He looked to the one on her neck—it was the trickiest to bind, and he could tell the scab had cracked open again by the flecks of dark red showing through to the grimy exterior of the fabric.

Maybe it had reopened when he dropped her.

Taein shook his head with a sigh. Her leg wound seemed to be healing the best. Perhaps he'd better start there, and work his way up to the hardest. Or should he start with the worse ones, since they might need a coating of salve, which would take more time? Or...

Taein realized how odd it must look to Vince for him to be sitting here, staring at her like the fretful little podge he was, so he decided to promptly busy himself by tearing off new strips of fabric from the spare shirt he'd been steadily dismantling for this purpose since they found her. He hurriedly tore off strips and coated the inside of two with a thin layer of that precious salve before dipping into Vince's pot for a bit of hot water, all the while trying to ignore the increasingly frantic beat of his own heart.

It'd been hard to bandage her wounds since June first came into his care. But ever since she took his gloves off and damn near turned herself to ash, it'd gotten so much harder.

Taein startled as an arid call pierced the stillness of the afternoon, his heart jumping into his throat and water sloshing from the little bowl all over his pants, before he realized it was *not* the dogs but instead a little golden bird perched on a thin alder branch above them, peering down with beady black eyes.

Taein breathed a curse, trying to force himself to relax and quit shaking and quit thinking about rit, and ignored the questioning look that Vince shot his way. This was getting ridiculous. He'd bandaged the kid several times a day ever since she'd come into their care. He'd probably done this over a hundred times by now.

It shouldn't be *getting* to him like this.

Taein took a deep breath, clenched his hands until they stilled, and set to work unwrapping the bandage on her leg. The fabric fell away and revealed an unbroken scab. Taein dabbed the wound with a wet rag anyway, cleaning off any dirt that may have slipped beneath the old bandage, and slowly set about rewrapping.

June began to stir. She eased herself upright on trembling arms and groped around in the grass for something.

Taein paused, watching as the grass flashed with brief, impossible flares of green-golden life each time her hand came down amongst the fresh spring blades. He turned back to Vince, acknowledging the uncertainty in the giant's eyes and challenging it.

"I think our friend June is looking for something, Vincent. Would you like to help her?"

Vince sent him a thunderous glare before looking back at the kid. He fiddled with each of his rings as he spoke, twisting them around and around his thick fingers.

"Whatcha after, kid?" he rumbled.

June's vacant gaze slowly drifted up and over to the general space Vince was occupying. She sat back, drawing her legs away from Taein, and thought for a while before raising her hands and making a few loopy, uncoordinated signs. Taein squinted, trying to understand.

"I think she wants your journal." Taein looked back to Vince. "Do you have it?"

Vince nodded and produced it from his pack. He glanced at Taein only once before handing it to June himself. She took it unsteadily and sat there with it, staring at the cover with those sick alien eyes.

Taein could only watch her a minute more before he turned to Vince and smiled with false cheeriness. "How's that soup coming?"

Vince kept staring at June, at the grass still flaring with unnatural green all around her. He looked like he might be sick. "Broth."

"Yes, right, the broth. Is it..?" Taein drew off, uncertain if Vince was even listening.

Vince seemed to come to himself and nodded, ladling some of the thin amber substance into another wooden bowl. "Here."

Taein took it without questioning and took his own spoon from his pack. He sat down in front of June again and stirred the broth before offering her some. But she wasn't paying attention to the food. She had her journal open, and she was writing something.

Writing? Could she even see?

Taein furrowed his brow. "Hey, brat. Eat this."

If she heard him, she didn't seem to care. Instead she produced a pencil seemingly out of thin air and began to scrawl. Taein watched her form indistinguishable letters before shaking his head with a sigh and reaching out to tilt her face toward him. She stared, blinking, and this time when he offered a spoonful of the broth she accepted before immediately returning to her writing. Taein pushed down the rising waves of impatience and waited for her to finish scrawling another incoherent word before offering another spoonful.

It went like that for a while—her scribblings, a single spoonful, repetition. The world grew ever quieter.

Taein was just beginning to think he might make it through lunch and be able to return to bandaging when she pushed away the second to last spoonful and shoved her book in his face. Taein leaned back, trying not to yell at her, a protest already forming when he recognized a word.

Brother.

Taein knew what she meant. He took the book from her on instinct and held it up, trying to make sense of the scrawls.

Your brother.

He read with a growing sickness, unable to believe his eyes as he made sense of her writing.

Where... is... your... brother.

Taein dropped the book as if it'd spontaneously caught fire, his gaze snapping up to hers as all the blood drained from his body. She wasn't even looking at him, instead picking at a fallen blossom with uncoordinated fingers.

How does she know?

Taein snapped the book closed where it lay on the grass and shoved it away. The sound scared June and her bleary eyes returned to his general direction. She reached out, looking for the book.

"No, kid," Taein said, startled to find that he could hardly whisper the words without his voice catching. "Just *eat*, alright?"

"Taein?" Said Vince from behind. *Dammit*, he'd already picked up that something was wrong.

Taein took the bowl back up and struggled to keep the spoon from clattering as June continued to blindly search the overgrown grass for her book.

"What did she write?" Vince asked.

Taein swore as he sloshed a spoonful of broth onto the grass and shook his head. "Nothing. Shut up, please."

He didn't turn to see Vince's expression. He could feel the giant's displeasure and concern burning into the back of his head. Instead, he struggled to get that last spoonful.

He'd just managed to steady himself enough to do so and was reaching out to offer it to June when the sound of Ruein's body hitting the snow ripped through his mind like an arrow to the heart. Taein jolted away, spilling the broth onto June and sending her cringing away with a little cry. Taein swore and scrambled to brush the broth off her dress and only ended up making things worse.

"Taein."

Taein didn't turn to look at Vince as he answered, he didn't have the capacity. "What?"

"Let me help."

This time Taein managed a glare. "No, I *got* this. Just watch the horses, alright? Can you please just handle that?"

Vince narrowed his eyes, but he didn't say anything.

Taein turned back to June, wiping his trembling hands on his pants. He had to finish the bandages, and *then* they could finally get moving and out of this cursed orchard.

He steeled himself, trying to shove away the tightness in his chest and stomp down the waves of panicky, disjointed thoughts. If he could get himself together for just *five* more minutes, he could get through this. Five more minutes. Two more bandages. He even had the new strips of cloth dressed and ready to go.

He sucked in a deep breath and moved closer to June. She had quit looking for her journal and was slumped down, her eyes half-shut and her little frame wracking with tiny, strangled coughs.

Taein waited until the bout of coughing had passed and she was still before reaching out and taking the edge of the bandage of her neck.

The second his gloved fingers brushed the skin of her neck, he went under.

Thud, and Ruein was hitting the snow again.

Before he knew what was happening, Taein was on his feet and stumbling backward, nearly colliding with Vince, hardly able to see. His vision was going white. Were those petals all over the ground, or snowflakes? He could smell the frost, so cold in his nose.

Thud.

That horrifically soft sound exploded in his brain once again, muffled, distant, *there*. He heard the crunch of his own footsteps, as he ran through ice-capped white powder.

Thud. Softly, he hit the snow again. Softly. How could a little noise chase him so far?

Taein tripped on the root-cobbled ground. Was that him cursing? He was underwater again, the only sound that of his own hammering heart, his running footsteps, and Ruein falling, over and over and *over again*.

Taein scrambled backward until his back hit rough tree bark, and sat there with his legs pulled up to his chest, lichen and damp moss pressing against his spine, until his vision finally began to clear and the frantic creature that had so suddenly replaced his heart began to calm in his chest.

For a long while he just sat, gasping in tight breaths of the misty air, feeling the dampness in his nose and clinging to it like a life rope.

Dampness. The dew-drop grass he was sitting on. The sighing breeze moving through the apple blossoms, perfuming the orchard with the sweet fragrance of new life. He clung to these things, eyes squeezed shut. Dug his fingers into the cool dark earth and felt the thick tops of tree roots resting just beneath the dirt. He breathed until he didn't have to think about breathing any longer.

When it finally passed and he was left shaking and aware, Taein opened his eyes to find Vince sitting with June. June was curled up against him, asleep or close to it, her head resting atop one of Vince's tree-trunk thighs, while Vince carefully looped a clean bandage around her neck. Taein watched as he finished tying off the bandage and eased away so that June was resting comfortably with her head on Vince's rolled-up cloak.

Vince met Taein's gaze and just watched. Then, with a shake of his head, he ambled over and stood looming over Taein, his iron arms crossed over his broad barrel of a chest.

Taein refused to soften his gaze. For a long while, the only sounds were that of the horses cropping grass and the gentle conversation between the stream and the breeze.

At last, Vince let out a long sigh and rubbed the back of his neck. "You gotta tell me what's going on, boss."

Taein set his jaw and looked away. He felt like socking Vince right in the face.

"Is this because of her being sick?"

Taein nodded. It was all he could manage.

"Or was all that because of this?" Vince asked. Taein looked up and came face to face with June's notebook once again, held open to her most recent scrawling.

Taein cringed away before he could make out the words again.

Vince shifted on his feet. "Look, Taein…"

Taein shook his head and pushed himself to his feet, a bolt of panic hitting him. He was not about to have a conversation, not now, not ever. "Is the kid alright?"

"Yeah—where are you going?"

Taein went to Lorrin and began rooting through his saddle pack for his pistol. "I need a walk."

There was a hard edge of frustration in Vince's voice. "I find that hard to believe, considering it's all you've done for a few…"

Vince drew off, his voice rising with a sudden uncertainty. Taein paused and looked up. Vince was staring out across the hills. Taein furrowed his brow, his heart skipping a beat, and followed the giant's gaze. Damn, was it the dogs? He scanned the hills for dark shapes moving through the grass and instead saw something far worse.

Two distinctly *human* figures were cresting the furthest hill, atop horses.

Men, heading straight toward them.

Taein looked to Vince as the giant breathed out a soft oath, and tightened his grip on his flintlock.

"What now, Vince?" Taein hissed.

Vince started edging toward June. "Get the horses. Maybe they haven't seen us. We can—"

A holler shattered the previous calm. Taein cringed, watching as the smaller of the two figures began waving wildly and kicked his horse into a canter.

"They saw us," Taein breathed.

"Well *obviously*," Vince said, "get your flintlock."

"I already have it!" Taein snapped, flying through the process of loading his pistol. "We have to hide her."

"I know!" Vince hissed, scrambling about wildly. "Where? This grass ain't tall enough!"

Taein jammed the flintlock into his waistband and darted over to scoop June up. He stumbled under a wave of panic and bit his tongue so hard he drew blood to fight it back. But it *worked*, and he managed to set June down amongst the tall reeds growing along the stream's steep bank. She stirred, eyes opening halfway, and Taein only had time to whisper a hissed 'be *quiet*' before the riders came to a stop, their horses sliding on the dewy grass, just in front of them.

_❧_ 46 _❧_

A BREAKING SHIELD

A pale morning came. For once the constant rain was light, and a thick mist had come to cloak the dark green hills in its place.

Vasily was sicker than ever before. The only other person he'd passed in the days since the fight was a farmer who took one look and declared he didn't want Vasily 'breathing on his beets'.

Whatever that meant, it made Vasily wonder just how poorly he looked. Because he certainly *felt* like death. His wounds wouldn't stop slowly oozing dark, halfway congealed blood, the smell of which seemed permanently burnt into his nose. His stomach hurt with a furious steady burning, and he hadn't dared eat a thing.

He had a *hole* in his gut. How could he?

His wrist hurt the worst of all. It'd swollen three times as large and forced him to cut away his sleeve to accommodate for the puffiness. He spent most of his time hunched over in the saddle steering the mare with just his legs, his right wrist cradled to his chest and the other clutching that pervasive, bleeding stomach wound, every breath that went scraping through his shredded, flooding lungs an agony. He couldn't stop thinking of that horrible tavern owner's face. The pockmarks, the black sores, the decay.

His one small comfort, of sorts, was that he had no chance in encountering his presumably horrific reflection. His vision had been blurry for days. Often he could not even distinguish the road from the fields. It was left to the horse to keep on in the right direction, and she seemed to be doing a good job.

It didn't matter that Glass' trail was next to non-existent, that Bellan was gone and so was Mari and so was near everything else. He had to keep going. He could not be sick. He could not be wounded. There was no time. If this path of blood he started all those years didn't end now, it would never.

Mie durksil menwi tu son gaaethoa.

Those ancient words. The first words Babas ever whispered in his ears as a newborn babe. The first thing Babas said to him in the morning and the last thing he said at night, his hello and goodbye, his promise. How old had he been, when Babas finally told him what they meant? Eight or nine?

'I was born a shield', Vasily. The words of our forebears. That is why I am here.

They were House Slate words. And that day, they became Vasily's. His father told him of his duty, as the firstborn son. How he was to always protect Faeriel and the House and his family above all. There was no greater honor.

But this did not feel like honor, nor great purpose. This felt like punishment. Vasily was neglecting the kingdom and the remnants of his family for a hunt leading him nowhere.

A hunt that was killing him.

Vasily bent over the bay's neck as a bout of silent coughs racked his entire body. He touched his mouth and his hand came away smeared red. He drew back on the reins a little and the bay stopped, shifting in the squelching mud. He wavered in the saddle, his vision swimming.

Red.

Stopping was not an option, because it did not matter if he was ill and maimed and lost. His father's honor was at stake. His family's *safety* was at stake.

I don't want to do this anymore.

A wave of resolve passed over him despite the thought. He touched his heels to the bay and she took a few steps forward before he keeled back over. There was a brief sensation of weightlessness, and then he slammed face-first into the cold mud.

He lacked the strength to right himself. For one terrible moment, Vasily wondered if this was *it*, if he was now to go down to his Long Wait as this suffocating, festering creature covered in mud, a strange fever ravaging his body and his life oozing ever out through a hole in his gut.

Mie durksil menwi tu son gaaethoa.

He ripped himself upright, gasping for breath, his father's voice so far away. He fell over onto his back, chest heaving, lungs grating, eyes swimming, and a different sort of sensation dropped over him. A hazy darkness swept down from the sky, heavy on his eyelids, easing the lurch of his chest, the dry, sucking grate of his breaths.

He was tired. Tired of being a shield. Tired of the hurt.

But he's still out there.

It was the last thought to enter his mind.

THE RATTLE OF A WAGON STIRRED HIM BACK TO CONSCIOUSNESS. Vasily struggled in vain to brush away the heaviness clinging to every cell in his body, struggled to open his eyes. Searched for any sensation other than the slow ache of his heart and the rattle of each breath scraping through his lungs.

Wagon. Someone was here. Someone... help.

Help.

He tried to speak, but the word didn't come out so much as a croak. The wagon wheels keep on rattling by, until—there. The wagon stopped.

Stopped.

Vasily willed himself to raise an arm, and when that didn't work, just his hand. No such luck. He focused on opening his eyes, focused on breathing, and succeeded in catching a glimpse of dark eyes peering out of a brown face. He had the vague impressions of a large straw hat. The smell of tobacco and sweat.

Tobacco. Father used to smell of pipe-smoke like that.

The face peered closer, and Vasily closed his eyes.

Where is Glass?

The sound of a wagon rattling down the road was now accompanied by a strange jostling. Vasily fought once again to open his eyes.

Grey sky above.

A coolness on his face. On his whole body. Chilling his veins.

Hoofbeats. A horse following behind a cart.

I'm not a very good shield, he thought. Where did the notion come from? He wanted to laugh.

I'm no shield. I'm only a man.

The dark pool sucked him down again, along with the notion of laughing.

Something was poking at his back. His weight was sunk down... straw. A blanket was covering his body. His veins were still so cool.

Straw mattress. Softer than any bed he had ever felt.

Where am I? Where is Glass?

The black pool rose up again. Vasily let himself sink down into it.

47

FAMILIAR FACES

"Vince! Taein! I can't believe you idiots are still alive!" Crowed a familiar gravel voice, and Taein wheeled around in the middle of trying to settle Lorrin, who was fighting his rope and nickering at the new horses.

Atop the smaller of these unfamiliar horses was a familiar face—a dark gaze shadowed by dark hair, fair skin scorched pink by the sun.

Ka-el.

Taein stared for only a split second before glancing at the other man, who he recognized after a moment of confusion as Bill, one of Regor's other muscles.

Taein left Lorrin to his own devices without another thought and came to stand next to Vince, taking care to keep from touching the gun in his waistband. He flashed what he hoped was a relaxed grin and waved.

"Good to see you up and functioning, Ka-el," he greeted.

A shadow withered Ka-el's smile as he swung down from his horse.

"Thank you," he said somberly, his gaze flickering between Taein and Vince. "I don't want to discuss it, if it's all the same to you."

Taein flashed another smile, this one far more genuine than the others. "Peachy."

Ka-el nodded before doing something immensely strange and hurrying forward to embrace Vince. The giant reciprocated stiffly, obviously surprised by the show of affection. Taein didn't think he'd ever seen Ka-el touch another human being outside of a fight, aside from that time Taein could tell he was secretly holding Venny's hand underneath a blanket years ago. It was one of the reasons Taein had allowed his company on occasion—he'd always been a low risk when considering the possibility of an *incident*.

Until now, apparently.

Taein plastered on that same relaxed smile and was busy thanking the Celestials when Ka-el didn't move to give him an embrace after letting Vince go. Instead, Ka-el stood between them, looking back and forth with his usual tight, thin-lipped smile and chatting with Vince about who even knew what—Taein could hardly process what was being said over the sheer panic shutting down his brain.

Instead of paying attention, Taein studied Bill. The bruiser still sat atop a black draft, scanning the orchard with bored eyes. Taein watched him as Ka-el and Vince continued exchanging pleasantries, tracking his every move. One flicker of alarm or suspicion on the bruiser's hammered face, and Taein was going to shoot him. No shanking around anymore, not after carting the kid this far. He was going to *finish* this.

He faltered as Ka-el turned to him and broke out in a cold sweat, nodding his head and smiling in time with whatever Ka-el was saying.

Finish this? When did he start caring? Since shanking *when*?

Sweet Geiin. The kid was getting *close.*

Taein shuddered as he violently dismissed the thought and forced himself to listen to Ka-el's prattling.

"...And I said to Bill, there was no way in hell you guys had gotten this off course, but look! Stars above, Taein! What happened? How did you end up here?"

Taein shrugged and adjusted his stance in a loose effort to veil the anxiety freezing up his body. "Oh, well, you know how my jobs usually go down. We ran into a few complications, you know. You know."

Very smooth, idiot.

Ka-el stared at him blankly. "No, I really don't."

Taein laughed a little as Vince shifted closer. He could tell the giant was sweating like a pig. "What do you mean, you don't?"

Ka-el's brow bunched. "I mean, *I don't know*. What happened? You guys are past return. Regor sent me out to retrieve your corpses. Why are you *here*, of all places?"

Taein, glancing at Bill, leaned toward Ka-el to create a sense of conspiracy. "The *dogs*, man. The ones that got Venny. They've been chasing us off course."

Something dark blistered across Ka-el's features with such a strength it chilled Taein. "Oh," was all the tracker managed to get out before Bill cut him off, his voice raised.

"Ka-el, what the hell is that *thing*?"

"Shit," Taein said through his smile, nudging Vince with the toe of his boot.

Ka-el glanced back at Bill. "What?"

Bill was leaning forward in the saddle, confusion all over his ugly face, pointing toward the bank of the stream. "Something's moving over there, and—hell, Ka-el! Shit's *growing*! The grass—"

This time a brisk *crack* cut Bill off as Taein fired a wild shot in his direction. It must've hit, because the bruiser shouted and bailed off his horse, swatting at his shoulder.

Taein whirled around to see June and felt his blood turn to ice.

She had crawled halfway up the bank toward them and collapsed into some sort of seizure—the earth around her was writhing with an explosion of growth. Flowers, grass, weeds, brush—it was all bursting out of the ground, lush, luminescent, glowing, *cursed*.

"What the hell is going on?" Ka-el shouted as Bill stumbled around, gripping his profusely bleeding shoulder.

Taein held up his free hand, stepping forward to block Ka-el's view of June as the wind began to rise. "Ka-el, I need you to stay absolutely perfectly calm or things are about to get real messy."

Vince was edging back toward Ka-el. "Listen to him, brother. We can explain this real well."

Ka-el blinked, stumbling for words. "I... I'll be damned... what did you *do* to her?"

Taein jammed his pistol into his waistband and withdrew his knife.

His shot was spent, his bullets were in the saddlebag. "Cool it, Ka-el. C'mon, man, you know us."

Ka-el looked rapidly between them and June before something like horror settled onto his features. Taein barely heard his whisper above Bill's frantic swearing.

"Anathema."

Bill must've heard it as well, because he stopped mid-oath and stared at June, blood oozing from between his fingers where he gripped his shoulder. Vince moved another step closer as Ka-el looked between them and the kid, baffled.

Taein saw it. The precise moment Ka-el realized.

"Sweet Geiin, I *touched* it. *Venny* touched it. And now you're protecting—you... we have to kill it," he stammered, his rock-salt rasp more frantic than Taein had ever heard before.

Then came something far worse. Ka-el looked at Taein's hands. At his gloves.

And the impossible thing happened, as Ka-el *knew*.

"You," Ka-el breathed. Taein felt his vision grow dim around the edges as blood rushed to his head.

"Vince, get him," he whispered.

Vince lunged just as Ka-el tried to scramble toward June. Taein turned to face Bill and found the bruiser already barreling toward him, a long knife in one hand. Taein braced, readying, before he understood what was really happening.

Bill wasn't attacking him. Bill was attacking *June*.

Taein ducked into Bill's path at the last second and tripped him, sending the bruiser sprawling. Before Taein even knew what he was doing, he ripped off his gloves, straddled Bill, and waved his naked hand in his face.

"One move, buddy—" he began.

Bill did the unwise thing and did indeed move, throwing a meaty fist up to cuff Taein smartly across the face. Taein felt blood gush from his nose.

Taein was not thinking anymore. He *knew* he wasn't thinking, because he didn't just *touch* Bill like he should've, even as the blow awakened something sharp and dark and long-since buried inside. He gave into the sheer fact that ashing Bill would send him into a panic from which he'd never resurface and also into that dark thing raging inside and brought his knife down—*hard*—on Bill's esophagus.

Blood, hot and sticky, splattered across Taein's face. He hardly felt it. Instead, he jerked his knife out as Bill convulsed, gasping and spraying more misting blood into Taein's face, and stabbed him again.

And again.

And again.

Something desperate and terribly afraid had taken ahold of him and it wasn't letting go. It was in his chest, in his heart, pounding like a drum, a wild animal brawling against his ribcage, trying to smash its way out.

And when Taein finally came back to earth and realized what was going on, he was still stabbing the *shit* out of Bill.

Taein heard distant shouting. He rolled off of Bill and onto his hands and knees, gasping wildly. After a second he realized Vince and Ka-el were both screaming, though Vince was screaming Taein's name at him in a *good-Geiin-stop-stabbing-the-man* sort of way while Ka-el was just plain screaming.

"Stop—stop it! Shut up, both of you! He was going to kill her!" Taein snapped hoarsely, hardly able to speak on account of the dryness of his mouth.

"You killed him!" Ka-el shouted, struggling in vain against Vince, who was holding him captive with just one arm. "You—"

Vince cut him off. "You killed him."

"So shanking *what*?" Taein snarled.

Vince blinked at him, his eyes wide. "That's... well..."

Ka-el, on the other hand, was not pacified. He was still shouting incoherently and struggling against Vince, stomping on his feet in a futile effort to get free.

Taein dragged over his face, smearing blood all over, and smiled a wild smile. "Yeah, I killed him! He was going to kill June!"

He must've looked like a terror, because Ka-el actually shut up.

"Now you ritheads *listen* to me," Taein snarled as blood oozed from his nose. "Because I am not shanking around. You see what happened with your little friend there, Ka-el?" He pointed to Bill with the tip of his knife. "He didn't listen to me. Learn from his mistake."

Ka-el stared.

"I'm going to go check on that kid over there and get my gloves. You are going to stay here with Vince, and he's not going to let you go until we have a nice understanding between us, yes?"

A nod.

Taein turned on his heel and trotted over to June, scooping his gloves up on the way. He didn't look at Bill. He knew he couldn't.

He slipped his gloves back on and scrubbed at his face with his sleeve to get rid of the blood, knowing full well he was probably only making things worse.

June was prone on the ground, surrounded by a dense, lush thicket of her own creation. The wind continued to rush around, pulling apple blossoms from their branches into thick, frenzied clouds, but the explosive growth seemed to have slowed. He pushed his way past flowers and brush, crouched down next to her, and cradled her head.

"June?"

She stirred the slightest bit, her breaths calming, but did not open her eyes. For once, Taein was thankful. He knew he'd scare her.

He waited until she was asleep and calm before rising and striding back over to where Vince stood with Ka-el.

"Let me make this absolutely clear," he said. "You will not hurt that kid, or myself, for that matter, or Vince. You won't, because I'll slash your throat and leave you for the shadow-dogs. Understand that, Ka-el?"

Ka-el nodded, his chest still heaving with panicked breaths.

Taein looked up to Vince.

"Well? What are we going to do with him?"

"Not kill him, that's for sure," Vince said, glaring at Taein.

Taein arched his brows. "Oh, are you *mad*, Vince? Was Bill your little tea buddy? Did you have ninth-lunch together every other Friday?"

"No, but—"

"No, you didn't! He was a threat!"

"I just—"

"Get over it, Vince. The fact that I'm still here ruining my life in the middle of happy-sack farmland-nowheresville is *your* fault."

Vince reddened. "Look here, you little shit, that ain't the least bit true. I ain't held a blade at your throat and forced you to do the right thing. If you want to leave, then do it."

Taein glared, Vince glared right back. Ka-el, clenched in Vince's white-knuckled fists, coughed between them.

Vince clutched the tracker closer as he struggled. "I'm going to let him go."

Taein laughed in Vince's face. "He can't go back and tell Regor about this! Or anyone, for that matter."

Vince narrowed his eyes. "Ka-el is our friend. We can't just kill him."

Taein glowered. "Ka-el is *your* friend. I don't *have* friends."

"Now what about *me?*" Vince bellowed, starting to squeeze Ka-el like a doll.

Ka-el stomped down hard on Vince's boot. "That's enough with your little domestic spat! Let go of me before I get squashed like that stupid diplomat behind the door!"

Vince's face was so red it was going purple. A vein was bulging out his forehead. "It was an *ACCIDENT!*"

Taein ignored Ka-el and kept yelling at Vince. "I wasn't even suggesting we kill him! That's never been on the table!"

Vince glowered. "Forgive me, it's just the fact that you're covered in blood that makes me a little nervous."

Taein gritted his teeth. "Now is not the time for blithering *morality*, Vincent. We can't let him go. If you do, I *will* kill him."

It took Vince a minute, but at last the giant gave a stiff nod.

Taein clapped his gloved hands together. Ka-el flinched.

"Excellent," he said, turning his full attention back to Ka-el. "Let's have us a little chat."

Ka-el wasn't even looking at him. Taein reached up, steeling himself for the touch, and tilted Ka-el's chin down, forcing the tracker to meet his eyes.

"Now, what have we learned so far?" he asked softly, taking care to smear Ka-el's chin with blood as he withdrew his hand.

Ka-el clenched his jaw. "You're not the stupid ritter I thought you were."

Taein felt the corner of his lip quirk. "Cute. I won't ask again."

Ka-el gritted his teeth a little tighter, and Vince, seeming to sense his growing agitation, tightened his grip.

"I'm not going to hurt any one of you," Ka-el squeaked.

"Good lad," Taein said, patting his cheek despite the chill it sent down his spine. "You're also not to run when Vince lets you go. You and Vince and I are all going to sit down, right here on the grass, and figure out a solution to this problem that keeps everyone alive and happy." Taein glanced up at Vince. "Because win-win solutions do exist, don't they, Vincent?"

Vince nodded. "Sure do, boss."

"Fantastic. Let Ka-el go."

Vince let him go. Ka-el stepped forward, brushing him off and messaging his arms. He looked at Taein and spat. And then he bolted.

Taein swore and lunged for him, his fingers brushing the edge of Ka-el's coat as he flew by.

"Oh, Geiin's thumb..." Taein hissed, watching as Ka-el hightailed it faster than Taein had ever seen anyone run, his dark form flying up the hills he had cantered down only some ten or twenty minutes before. "No, no, *no*." He jerked the flintlock from his waistband before remembering it wasn't loaded and gritting out an oath.

Vince took a few shambling steps after Ka-el before stopping and dragging a hand through his mane of hair. "Dammit, Taein, look at him go."

"Well, go *after* him!" Taein shouted, his heart hammering. "Vince, he's going to rat on us. Not just about Bill, but about June. *Everyone* will know!   I—" Taein cut himself off, jerking the bounty disc from beneath his bloodied shirt. "I have a bounty on myself, Vince! That's how Regor got me to take the kid in the first place!"

Vince swung around to face him. "A *bounty?*"

Ka-el was getting smaller. He'd almost reached his spooked horse.

"Yes! If we don't bring back a hell of a lot of marks, I'm forfeit. But not if Ka-el rats me out to the whole of the city first!"

Taein searched Vince's face, waiting for him to say something, *anything*, when a shriek pierced the air. Taein whirled around to spot Ka-el, now tearing across the field back *toward* them, as three dark shapes moved like shadows through the grass after him.

Dogs.

Hell and damnation. *The* dogs.

Vince scrambled to untie their already-frantic horses as Taein skidded down the grass-slick sides of the bank, grabbed June, and tossed her over his shoulder with an adrenaline-fueled burst of strength. He got her in the saddle and climbed onto Lorrin himself, barely able to wrap his arms around the kid to keep her from falling before Lorrin bolted into a canter.

They only made it three strides away before Taein realized that neither Vince nor his draft were coming after them. Taein, only half-conscious of the barrage of curses pouring from his mouth, wrestled Lorrin to a stop and booted the stallion around to spot Vince, who was not only running *the wrong way*, but was running after one of the frantic loose horses that Ka-el and Bill had ridden in on.

"What are you doing?" Taein screamed over the rising cacophony of howls and shrieks.

If Vince heard him, he didn't take any notice and instead kept chasing down the hysterical dark bay that Ka-el had ridden before. Taein fought to keep Lorrin still as the stallion pranced and threatened to rear, his neck already slick with sweat, eyes rolling.

"Easy, you ugly bastard," Taein soothed, allowing Lorrin just enough rein to pace in circles.

What is that idiot doing? What the hell did they need another horse for?

"C'mon, Vince..." Taein whispered, still struggling with Lorrin. He couldn't hold the stallion forever.

Vince, him and his draft looking almost normal-sized in the distance, finally caught the bay. Taein watched, his heart in his mouth, as Vince awkwardly turned both horses around and somehow persuaded them to run not away from the incoming dogs but rather *toward* them. Toward Ka-el.

Ka-el. *Vince was saving Ka-el.*

"Vince, you big dumb bastard! Leave him!" Taein screamed, booting Lorrin toward them. *"Leave him!"*

Vince didn't hear him, of course. The only sound to possibly be heard was that of the dogs and their screams.

June stirred, squirming in the saddle, and began to sob. Taein held her closer and continued to fight with Lorrin and curse with every fiber of his being.

By some miracle, Ka-el managed to vault up onto the bay. With that, he and Vince finally set off in the right direction. Taein held Lorrin until the last possible second before finally letting Lorrin whirl around and launch into a break-neck gallop. Taein held on for dear life, struggling to simultaneously keep the kid in the saddle and regain some semblance of control over Lorrin to keep the stallion from killing them both.

Because they'd come this far, *dammit*, and he'd just killed a man for this stupid kid sobbing into his chest and trying to squirm out of the saddle as they flew over the ground below.

Whatever came next could be dealt with, but he was not letting a pack of *shanking dogs* win.

❧ 48 ❧

COMING APART

Hours passed, and the dogs stayed just behind.

There had been three instances where the howls grew dim enough for Taein to wonder if they'd somehow managed to escape, but the damned things kept coming back. Exactly how close they were, and how many, Taein didn't know. But he could hear the howls, feel the way the land responded. Taein watched deer bolt and birds quiet their chipping as they ran through forests and rolling hills, the dogs always just behind. Even the trees seemed to shudder and turn away, the wind still and withdraw.

Taein twisted in the saddle, tightening his grip on a half-asleep June as she lulled forward. Vince, white-faced and obviously exhausted, kicked his equally-spent draft forward to get within hearing distance. Ka-el's horse could barely keep up and Ka-el himself was stone-faced, sitting rigid in the saddle.

"Do you know where we are?" Taein hollered to Vince.

Vince shook his head, urging his draft to hurry. Taein drew Lorrin down to a walk, ignoring the not-so-distant howl that rose up and split the evening air like a knife. They were in the depths of a dense, dark wood and Taein could barely see the way ahead, let alone identify where they were.

"What's the plan, boss?" Vince puffed, out of breath. He sat clutching his saddle horn with one hand and the lead to Ka-el's horse in an iron grip with the other, holding on so tight his tattooed knuckles were white. The reins to his own horse hung loose on the draft's neck; Vince had long ago given up directing the horse and had let his draft follow along behind Lorrin, a move which Taein thought very smart, considering *he* was the one guiding Lorrin.

Or it *would've* been smart, if he'd actually done some guiding in the first place and still knew where the bloody hell they were.

Taein dragged a hand through his hair and squinted at the sky. A heavy cloud cover had swept in.

We're lost. Unease slithered in his gut at the thought, and he startled with a curse when another howl pierced the momentary quiet.

"Let's keep going," he said, kicking Lorrin into a trot and adjusting his hold on June. She was fully asleep again, her shallow breaths catching with each inhale. Just how long had they been riding?

Lorrin drug himself into a trot upon Taein insistence, and the other horses followed suit, each heavy hoofbeat grinding despair deeper into Taein's heart. But what could he do? They'd been riding at a breakneck speed for hours. The horses were simply too used up to carry on at any real pace.

Vince seemed to sense it as well. "I don't know how much longer they're going to keep going, boss."

Taein glanced over to Vince's draft. The stallion's hide was drenched in sweat, his mighty head drooping and his flaxen forelock falling into his sad brown eyes, dragging his massive tree trunk legs one after another in a shameful shamble just to keep up with Lorrin. Taein knew the horse didn't have more than an hour left in him at this turtle's pace alone. Ka-el's bay looked to be in marginally better spirits, but was favoring one hoof.

"Just a while longer, Vince. They can do it."

More howls. The horses picked up the pace a hair on their own, but it was still so *slow*.

Something shifted in the night, and the pack began to *shriek* again; demonic, wild, and hungry, aware that they were gaining. Aware that the horses had passed a threshold. Taein pushed them onward anyway, holding his breath as he guided Lorrin through crops of dense trees and up steep rises choked with blackberries until they rode up to an ivy-covered barricade made of a nearly vertical embankment. Taein's heart plummeted as the rhapsodic clamor of the frenzied dogs reached new heights.

Trapped.

Taein dropped from the saddle, careful to steady June lest she try to follow suit, and hurried over to the dirt embankment. If he could just find some holds, they could climb.

And then what—run on foot? Outrun the dogs without their horses?

He gritted his teeth and fumbled through the ivy, trying to reach through and find the dirt wall beneath, his arm reaching, reaching, and grasping only air. He stepped forward, trying to push through, the dogs getting louder with every passing breath along with the memory of Venny's mangled body, her lumpy white shroud.

He was certain the dirt was just beyond when he finally lost his balance and crashed head first through the ivy into a void.

He toppled into a wide, vaulted cave and blinked in the dim light, freezing for a half-second before the noise outside reminded him of the present crisis.

Hope flooded through him. There wasn't a wall here at all. This was a *cave*.

Horses could fit in here.

The thought jarred him into action. He shoved back through the curtain of ivy and waved wildly for Vince.

"In here!" he shouted above the howls, lunging for Lorrin's bridle.

Vince nodded, dismounting and tugging his draft and the bay after him. Taein pulled Lorrin and June forward, somehow managing to persuade the stubborn stallion to plow through the ivy into the dim maw of the cave, which was illuminated only by a dappling of light filtering through hundreds of rounded holes in the crumbling ceiling. Taein hurried Lorrin, heart pounding, expecting at any second a horde of dogs to come bursting through the ivy and rip them all to shreds. But an uneasy quiet descended instead as the howls abruptly cut off.

After hours of listening to that accursed shrieking, it was finally quiet.

That was certainly... *suspicious.*

Taein clutched Lorrin's halter, murmuring softly to keep the exhausted, sweat-slick horse still. Once Lorrin had settled enough to be trusted, Taein let go of his halter and helped June down, barely managing to keep his discomfort at bay as she slumped into his arms and sagged against his chest. He carried her to a safer corner, away from the horses and their dangerous hooves. He realized she wasn't awake and swallowed the sudden knot in his throat as he carefully set her down on a moss-eaten floor against the rounded wall and tucked his old cloak under her head.

Taein turned and caught Vince's eye before holding a finger to his lips. Vince, still clutching his exhausted draft's lead rope like his life depended on it, nodded and swallowed hard. Ka-el, still atop his spent horse, stared unmoving at the veil of ivy. Taein walked over to them, the draft's massive frame almost blocking his view of the entrance, and laid a hand on the trembling animal.

"Move him over to a wall," he whispered. "And get him some water."

Vince nodded and set about coaxing his horse over to the support of a wall. As his form moved out of the way of the entrance, more gentle light entered from through the thick doorway of ivy. Taein crept closer and parted a few strands, the exact green velvet color as the hat Regor always wore. He peered out, unsure of what he might find. The quiet was dense and oppressive over him, charged with the violence of waiting. Surely, the dogs had seen them enter the cave. And even if they hadn't, they would follow the scent trail, wouldn't they? Those things were *relentless.* Why would a few strands of ivy deter them, after the pack spent so long driving them into the wilderness?

But when Taein looked out the little clearing before the entrance was empty, as was the forest beyond for as far as he could see. There was no sight nor sound of the dogs. Even the pervasive, subtle scent of ash that had dogged them since he first saw the creatures on his hunt weeks ago was gone.

Gone? It couldn't be.

He blinked, trying to clear his vision, certain that they would soon dart out again and that Geiin-forsaken demonic clamor would start back up again and be the last thing his ears ever had the privilege of hearing, but the landscape before him didn't change. His exhausted eyes *weren't* playing tricks on him for once.

After a long moment, he let the thick stands of ivy fall back into place and turned back around, surveying their situation.

Vince, obviously exhausted, had sunk down and was staring off into space next to his draft, who, finally bereft of his saddle and bridle, stood on unsteady legs with his head hung low, sides still heaving from the effort and terror that day had exerted. June where Taein left her, head lulling, little body shivering. The dappled light danced strangely on her gray face.

Taein looked up. The curved walls ended far above with a rough, stone-carved ceiling, dotted with those little holes to let in a scattering of soft light onto the crumbling floor and walls below. Before him, the cave stretched into a long hallway of sorts, strewn with toppled stone pedestals which once boasted the cracked remains of what looked like statues, dotted by patches of overgrown grass and daisies, growing lush beneath the biggest ceiling-holes. Water patiently dripped down the walls and pooled onto the floor. The lances of light were golden, brushed through with the fine dust they had stirred upon their entrance. The air itself seemed too-thick, almost *alive* in some strange way. A sort of indistinct humming filled the tunnel.

Taein squinted down the hallway, trying to see where it led. Trying to see what *else* might be here.

A sense of anxiety settled in the pit of his stomach, and just for a second, a sort of feather-light *beckoning* brushed through him, as if some intangible fingers had reached deep past his skin, taken ahold of his soul, and gave it the faintest tug forward.

Taein shuddered and took a step backward, snapping himself back to reality and forcing himself to look away from the tunnel. This place was ancient, in dangerous ways.

Taein shook away the thought and looked up at the final member of their party.

Ka-el was still atop his bay, who stood with splayed legs, head hanging.

Taein looked back to Vince and nodded for him to come over before taking the bay's bridle and snapping his fingers at Ka-el.

Ka-el jolted as if surfacing from a trance and glared down at Taein. Taein glared right back.

"Get off, please." His voice sounded wrong in the strange heavy silence of the tunnel. "Your loyal steed is about to collapse."

Ka-el looked between him and the ivy before booting the bay forward. Taein arched his brows, still holding the horse's bridle. The mare didn't so much as move an inch. Vince plucked Ka-el out of the saddle before he could try to boot the poor creature forward and out of the cave again, and set him roughly on the floor.

"Thank you, Vince. Since you went so unnecessarily out of your way to keep your *friend* alive, would you deposit him in a corner? A nice tight one we can keep him bullied in, if you please."

"Certainly," Vince grumbled, reaching out for Ka-el.

Ka-el uttered an oath and smacked Vince's hand away.

For a while the three of them stood, just watching each other, the only sound in the cave that of the horses' labored breathing and condensation dripping from the mossy, pocked ceiling and down onto the stone floor.

Then Ka-el tried to bolt *again*—but this time Vince was ready for it. The giant grabbed Ka-el before he could so much as move one strand of ivy and hauled him, struggling, shouting, and swearing, to a corner in which Vince wedged him like a slice of cheese.

"This isn't right!" Ka-el bellowed, his voice amplified by the high ceilings.

Taein kicked him. "Shut *up*, or you'll wake the kid."

Ka-el tried to scramble out of the corner. "This is ridiculous—" he broke off when Vince pushed him back down with one hand and shot the giant an accusatory glare. "Vince, I thought we were friends. Why the hell are you taking *his* side?"

Vince folded his arms. "Since you decided that killing children is acceptable."

"Killing *Anathema*, not children! Stars above, Vince! It's what anyone in their right mind would do!"

"I'm standing right here." Taein said, dragging a hand through his hair.

Ka-el glared, chest heaving. He was still for a second before lunging to his feet with a startling burst of desperation and tackling Taein.

Taein saw the glimmer of the stiletto in Ka-el's hand as he pitched backwards, his head cracking against the floor, and saw stars as his teeth clacked down on his tongue and his mouth filled with blood. He gagged, rolling over onto his stomach as Vince ripped Ka-el off of him and knocked the tiny blade from Ka-el's grip and onto the floor with an offensive clatter. Taein spat a mouthful of blood and resisted the urge to curl in on himself, his vision swimming and skull feeling as fragile as a dropped egg. He clambered back onto his feet and watched unsteadily as Vince, cursing to himself, set about restraining Ka-el and tying the tracker's hands together at the same time. Taein stumbled forward and took the rope from Vince, struggling to tie the knots and keep standing as his visions swirled.

"You're going to regret that, Ka-el," he hissed. "I'm famously awful to be around when I have a headache."

"Or any sort of ail. Or bad mood," Vince grumbled.

Taein ignored Vince and shoved Ka-el back into the corner as soon as he succeeded with the knots. He fought to keep standing, his knees trembling, his head beginning to pound with a vicious thunder.

"Look," he growled, "let's refresh our terms. You're stuck with Vince and I until we figure out how the hell to keep you quiet. If you behave, I'm sure we'll work out something mutually beneficial. But if you *don't*, I'll dump your flayed body in the nearest river no matter what Vince has to say about it. *Do you understand?*"

Ka-el nodded shortly with a glower.

"Good." Taein looked at Vince. "Fill him in on what's going on, I'm going to take care of the horses."

Vince nodded. Even in the dim light of the cave, Taein could see the dark circles beneath the giant's eyes.

He looked away and spat out another mouthful of blood, his tongue smarting and head aching, and limped over to Lorrin. He untacked and watered both his stallion and Vince's and was just caring for Ka-el's bay when he heard Ka-el's voice raise once again.

"...then why the *hell* don't you just ditch her?"

Taein paused halfway through removing the bay's bridle and listened, not quite able to catch Vince's demure response.

"Vince, that doesn't make any sense. She's cursed. How are you fine with that? With *him*, no less?"

Taein resumed unbridling Ka-el's mare, resting the sweat-slick headstall over his arm. The tracker *did* have a point.

When he was finished with the horses, Taein debated whether he should return to Vince and Ka-el's ongoing argument or check on the kid. Instead, he did neither, just lingering amongst the horses and watching June, from this safe distance as a too-familiar uncertainty took root inside.

June was still asleep, her face ashen. For a second, he didn't even think she was breathing. But then she lurched into another bout of dry, stifled coughing, and his heart clenched tight in his chest.

This whole job was a mistake.

He turned abruptly and strode over to Vince, who was still trying to convince Ka-el that the Anathema were not, in fact, demons incarnate.

"...I don't *care* that I've known Taein for years, Vince—"

Vince cut the tracker off. "But think about it, Ka-el. It's *Taein*. You've slept near him and ate with him and worked with him side by side, and he's had your back and you've had his. He's kin to you, by scrapper's honor."

Ka-el purpled, tense as a wildcat against the wall. "I don't give a *damn* what the history is, Vince. *He's Anathema.*"

Taein folded his arms and looked down at Ka-el. "And what are you gonna do about it?"

Ka-el looked up at him, stone-faced. "I'd skewer you where you stand, *Glass.*"

Taein dropped to Ka-el's level and looked him right in the eye. "You wouldn't say that if Venny was the Anathema standing here in front of you."

Vince's voice was laced with disapproval. "Taein..."

Taein looked up at the giant and scoffed. "Oh, I don't *care* if it's mean." He looked back at Ka-el, who was staring at him with red-hot rage in his eyes. "It's true, isn't it? You can't tell me you'd skewer your beloved *Venny*—"

Ka-el's voice was poisonous. "Leave her *out* of this. She was the worst mistake of my life, and I won't—"

Vince shook his head. "Don't say that, Ka-el, you loved Venny."

Ka-el exploded, practically spitting with rage. "*Yes!* And look where it got me! She's dead and so am I, only I still have to deal with you idiots!"

Vince sighed heavily and rubbed a hand over his face. "Look, Ka-el. We're not going to hurt you—"

"Speak for yourself," Taein interrupted.

Vince gave him a murderous glare and continued. "*We,*" he affirmed, "are not going to hurt you—"

"Unless we have to," Taein said.

Vince sighed again and rubbed his face. "You gotta work with us, Ka-el. We're trying to do a good thing here."

Ka-el gave a bitter laugh. "Sure, Vince! Getting some cursed kid from one place to another in the company of an even *more* dangerous Anathema is a wonderful deed for the good of the world! How could I have been so blind? Of *course* I'll risk my life for such a noble cause!"

Vince dropped his hands from his face, somehow able to keep control of his voice. "Saving a kid *is* a good deed."

"Since when does anyone in the service of Regor Snevets give a flying rat's ass about those?" Ka-el demanded, folding his arms.

Exactly my point, but here we are, Taein thought with some discomfort.

"You should just dump her in a river and be done with it," Ka-el said. He leaned forward suddenly, his eyes wide, trying to empathize with Vince. Taein watched, discomfort growing, and shifted his weight.

"Vince, please. Listen to reason. You don't even have to kill her. She's sick, isn't she? Just leave her and she probably won't even wake up to know you're gone. Leave, and we can go back to the Pearl and let

Regor decide what to do with Taein. You and I can wash our hands of this. I'll speak for you, I'll help you regain his favor."

Before Vince could answer, Taein heard himself speak on impulse.

"Maybe he's right, Vince."

Vince turned suddenly to face him. "You're kidding me, right?"

Taein looked at him, and then went back to Ka-el. "He's got a point. Not about me, of course, but the kid. She probably isn't going to make it. So why... continue to screw ourselves over like this?"

Vince gaped. "Because we care about her. *You* care about her."

Taein stared back at him, unflinching. *That's exactly the problem.*

Ka-el's voice took on the first hint of a hopeful note since Taein first killed Bill and sat up a bit straighter. "Vince, Vince, Taein is on board, this is how it's going to be. Let me out of this damned corner and—"

Vince slammed Ka-el back down the second he started up and leveled a glare at Taein so intense it could've ground mountains to dust.

"Taein," he growled. "We've been through this."

Taein shifted on his feet. They had, of course, but that was before, when he was still in control of himself. That was *before.*

He'd killed a man today for her. Now, he was getting *close.*

Taein dropped Vince's gaze, something burrowing deep into his nerves.

Not again.

A cold sweat broke out on his forehead as he took an involuntary step backward.

Sweet Geiin above, what had he done?

He swallowed hard and stuffed down the rising fear, refusing to look at June as another burst of her muffled coughing broke the newborn silence of the cave, and steeled himself to meet Vince's heavy gaze.

"Things change," he said quietly.

Vince turned his massive frame fully toward Taein and towered over him. His voice was a low growl.

"Could you live with yourself?"

"Who says I can now?"

Vince just glared. Taein glared back, refusing to be intimidated. Heavy seconds crawled by.

Vince shook his head. "C'mon, boss. Quit trying to fool yourself into thinkin' you could just walk away. If that was true, you would've turned tail the minute you found her in the ash. The minute you ride off you'd start killing yourself again from all the guilt."

Could you live with yourself?

Taein sputtered, for one at a loss for words. That was just the thing —he most certainly *could* live with himself and he had for ten years already, no matter how badly it hurt, but instead the horrible, damning, unexpected *truth* came out, soft as the whispering wind, the one hasty word all choked up and breaking as it fell from his mouth.

"No."

Vince stilled, and Taein realized he was actually surprised.

"But she's a monster!" Ka-el said from his corner.

And that finally lit something inside of Taein. He turned to Ka-el, but before he could say anything Vince beat him to it.

"That's *enough*," Vince said, stepping forward and slamming Ka-el back in the corner. "You quit it with that nonsense, Ka-el, because it ain't you either. You really tryin' to tell me that you could actually kill that sick little girl over there?"

Ka-el squirmed. "Taein killed *Bill* without a second thought, Vincent, you saw that with your own eyes and it doesn't seem to be bothering you any. We do what we have to. We do what it takes to *survive*."

Vince gritted his teeth, and for a brief moment Taein thought he was going to pummel Ka-el. But instead Vince took a long-suffering breath and continued on in a level voice, his hands clenched into fists.

"Bill was a grown-ass man and it was self-defense—"

"So is getting rid of the kid, or Taein."

"But they ain't threatening you."

"Their existence threatens *everything!*" Ka-el half-shouted, fisting his hands in his dark tangle of hair. "Why can't you understand that? Do I have to remind you what the Four Fathers did? Why we even *have* the Southern Mists? We're not even talking about our survival alone, but the worlds!"

Vince let out a frustrated growl. "Mithre below, Ka-el, she controls plants! Sure as hell it's freaky, but she's a kid!"

Ka-el shook his head furiously. "My whole life, no matter what country I called home, the Anathema have always been creatures of a sordid history to be feared. The emergence of the Anathema in the line of Glass caused the collapse of an entire country. How can I sit here and do nothing?"

"I thought the highest crime a Faeish man could commit was the theft of another's life," Vince said.

Ka-el, still squirming, clamped his mouth shut and went purple again. Vince had won.

"Stay in your corner, Ka-el," the giant said. "We'll talk more tomorrow."

Ka-el shrugged at length. "I give you my word," he said, so quietly Taein almost missed it.

Taein and Vince exchanged a glance before leaving the tracker to his corner. Those Faeish roots ran deep and held fast, and when Ka-el gave his word, he meant it.

Taein hugged his frame, smoked through the last of his cigarettes, and wondered what that was like.

———

❧ 49 ❧

BREATH OF THE FORSAKEN

Anathema. The cursed, the cast-outs. Creatures of a lost world where dragons once roamed and kelpies ruled the sea. Proof that Geiin existed, that magic, the essence of the Divine, once touched the face of the earth.

Anathema. The descendants of dead men made into Fathers by the Celestials themselves. The end-bringers of the Old World. The bearers of a long-ago apocalypse. Remnants of the way things were.

And here Vince was, trapped in a cave with *more than one*, and with Ka-el mad as a hornet to boot.

How the hell did I get here? He shook his head and walked over to the ivy covered entrance to the cave. His life began quietly in a countryside manor, his greatest excitement then whenever the piano tuner stopped by twice a year. In all his wildest childhood dreaming, he only ever imagined himself married to a pretty girl and building a little farmhouse with room for a piano of his own. Not this, not here. Certainly not lost in the forgotten reaches of Nown Jin, trapped in a cave with his only companions among the ghosts of the past world.

They're my friends, they're my friends, they're my friends.

Vince shook his head and looked out into the wooded area outside the cave. The growing night was eerily still—the tree clustered

348

together, casting long shadows on the overgrown grass, cloaking any sign of movement. Still, the night smelled of dew and spring growth, bereft of the reek of death and ash that followed those damned hellhounds everywhere.

"So the dogs are just gone?" Vince muttered, looking back. "That can't be. That'd be too damn easy."

Taein, who had settled himself in a corner opposite of Ka-el, didn't respond. His eyes had gone glazed again as he stared down the long, dark tunnel leading deeper into the cave.

"Taein? Why'd they just... leave?"

Again, no response. Taein's eyes didn't stray from that long cavernous hallway.

"Tae—" Vince was cut off by a distant shuffling some ways up the tunnel, an echoing thud, and a scream.

An uncanny smile curved Taein's mouth as the sound splintered the quiet. "Because they knew."

A chill ran down Vince's spine. The cave went still again, but Vince knew better. His fingers shook as they sought his twin knives.

Taein looked back, and Vince immediately wished he hadn't—the thief's eyes were a flat and miserable black, like a still and forgotten lake—the kind you stash bodies in, the kind that eats your secrets. Taein's eyes only ever went black like that when things were well and truly shanked.

"Get that creepy stare off me 'n prepare for company," Vince gritted out.

"Shallows?" Taein asked.

"Don't tell me you ain't never seen one before."

"I—"

Another scream floated down the hall, the sound echoing off the walls, clinging to the air. The shuffling grew, and so did the shrieking.

Sweet Geiin—

Vince cracked his neck, rolled his shoulders, shook his frame loose. He was unfortunate enough to know screams like these better than the back of his own shanking hand, thanks to Ka-el's brief stint as a Shallow hunter and his own brief stint as the stupid tracker's unlucky bodyguard.

Another assignment received while on Regor's bad side, only *that* one he'd survived. This one, though... Vince let out a low chuckle as the sound of many skittering footsteps grew. If this job wasn't the death of him, nothing would ever be.

"What are you *doing*?" Vince hissed when he realized Taein was still slumped in his corner, his eyes fixed on the tunnel. "Fire, you idiot. Get. Fire."

Taein looked up at Vince with the fear of death in his dark eyes, and Vince fought the sudden urge to pick the kid up and run right out the cave himself.

But Vincent St. Jame'Estain was *not* a coward, so he shoved Taein toward his pack instead and caught the first Shallow as it staggered rot-limbed and half-headed, smelling of decay and sulfur, out into their midst.

The Shallow was in relatively good repair, all things considered. Its body must've only been dead for some weeks, still good enough for Vince to tell that it once was a woman—her spirit certainly was *angry* enough to be, as the creature lunged at him with a grating shriek the moment she skittered out the hallway and laid her empty eye sockets on Vince. Vince cursed, feinted left, and snatched the stump of one wrist. His stomach jolted at the familiar contact of bloodless flesh, soft beneath his grip, but he turned his revulsion right off and snapped the Shallow's rotting branch of an arm from her shoulder as he swung her closer. She fell at him, gargling on words her ruined throat could no longer form, and clawed at his face with her remaining arm. Vince dropped his blade, caught it with his other hand, and stabbed clean through her ribcage. He gritted out another oath and drew upward with a jerk. The Shallow gritted out a few chitters and collapsed in two writhing heaps.

"Take that, you menace," Vince grumbled, stepping aside as her halves kept on convulsing.

The next few came in a pair—two slim Shallows, each one missing an arm, their bones jutting forth from sprung-open rib cages and decomposing clothes hanging off exposed hip bones, too far gone for Vince to have any clue as to what sort of people they might've been before their bodies failed them and disbelief or misfortune stole their half-deaths away. Vince immobilized their ruined frames for good by knocking their heads together until they just sort of... fell apart, and was just catching his breath when a huge, freezing, and *very* disturbed hand clamped down on his shoulder and hauled him right off his feet.

The next thing Vince knew, he was sailing through the air, light as a leaf.

Then he smacked into the opposite wall, suddenly feeling heavy as a whole mountainside again, the world spinning as if he'd just fallen out the sky and back into it. He saw the hulking shape of something huge waddling toward him and had just enough time to stagger onto his feet and step aside as that same massive hand went plowing through the air to concuss the wall where his head had just been.

"A torch would be real shankin' nice right now, Taein!" He hollered, scooting away and fighting back a stunned laugh as the Shallow giant's fist plain fell off his wrist.

"Thank Divine you ain't durable," Vince gritted out as he forced the Shallow back with a few blows. "*Taein—*"

Vince's words fell dead in his mouth as his fist plowed straight through the giant's rotted face. Vince froze, half-conscious that somebody was screaming *other* than the Shallows.

It was only after the rotting giant shoved him back into the wall that Vince realized *he* was the one screaming. He scrabbled against the Shallow's grip, kicking his gut, his brittle legs, his groin. The Shallow kept on squeezing Vince's neck anyway, his grip inhumanly strong for a *dead guy* with his face punched in, oblivious to Vince's blows even when Vince kicked both his rotting kneecaps into a mangle of shards.

It was only when a blessed amber glow came to life and Taein lit the stupid thing on fire that the half-dead brute finally shuddered, stumbled backward, and let go. Vince lurched away, coughing, and lopped his head off.

There were a few more minutes of blurry scuffling. Two Shallows, these ones small—too small—came hobbling in and Vince pummeled them into pieces and tried not to think about the people they once were.

The people they *still* were, trapped inside.

When every Shallow was in enough parts to have at last lost full animation of their corpses, Vince turned to Taein. The scrapper stood at the crumbled remains of a Shallow splattered between him and the somehow *still* sleeping kid, fixated on the body.

Vince wiped his blades clean and swore. His hands were still coated in gore. He smelled as if he'd just taken a bath in a butcher's week-old chop bucket.

"See, Taein," Vince said, "this is why we wear our amulets like good little children. That *thing* right there is why nobody, not even Regor, strips folk of their amulets. So wear one, or so help me—"

"Shut up, Vince."

Vince shut up. Taein had his liar's voice on, and he was looking up at him again with those dead-lake liar's eyes.

The scrapper's voice teetered precariously close to sounding as though he was fighting tears. "So this is what they're like, huh?"

"Don't tell me you ain't never seen one before."

"Of course I have."

Vince shrugged. "The more sentient Shallows like to hole up in dark places. Misery likes company, I reckon."

Taein prodded the broken corpse on the ground. "Gross."

"They just get grouchier the longer they're dead, too. And they hate noise." Vince turned to spy Ka-el still in his corner. "Hey, hey! Thanks a lot for your help back there, Master Shallow-Hunter!"

Ka-el glowered. "I'm retired."

"You were never good in the first place." Vince swiped a hand through his hair and swore as he remembered the filth coating his entire frame.

"Oh really, Vincent?" Ka-el's voice was rising. "Some *bodyguard* you were. I seem to recall a dent in my left arm—"

Vince whirled. "You just stayed in your stupid corner because you were hoping those things would kill the kid!"

"Oh, sweet disappointment," Ka-el snipped, "you got me there. No, Vincent, I was staying in my corner because you *told* me to!"

Vince gestured wildly with his blades, flinging bits of gore onto the opposite wall. "Oh, well *excuse me* then. Next time we're attacked by a bunch of monsters you have my solemn blessing to help out—"

"Shut up!" Taein exploded. "Shut up, shut up, shut up!"

Ka-el wedged himself even further into his corner. And June, lying where Taein had left her a whole hour ago, was still asleep.

Asleep, through the uproar of a Shallow attack and all their fighting.

That can't be good.

Vince shook his head. "Just help me clear these bodies so we can get the hell out of here."

Taein scoffed. "And go where? The only reason those dogs didn't mangle us is because they knew about the Shallows. I'm sure they're out there in the brush, just waiting for dinner to come waltzing out."

Vince drew in a deep breath of tainted air. "Just help me clear 'em, then. I ain't sleeping 'round this mess."

"Think we got them all?"

"They usually move in packs." Vince rubbed his neck at Taein's piercing look. "There ain't any stragglers, Taein. Why are you so scared—"

Vince stopped short, but the damage was already done. Taein's eyes went even darker, and before Vince knew it Taein threw a punch. Vince ducked on instinct and caught the scrapper's next blow with his palm.

"Taein—"

"Don't go shanking with me right now, Vincent." Taein's voice was a flinty rasp, harsher than Vince had ever heard it before. "Don't, or I am going to *lose it.*"

Vince swallowed hard, waited for Taein's gaze to soften. It never did, and Taein jerked his gloved hand away and shoved Vince a step back.

They cleared the bodies in silence but for June's rough breathing. When it was finished, Vince kneeled by a dent in the floor pooled with water and started ridding himself of Shallow gore.

This is why mum told you not to lie, you dumb podger.

He sighed and just kept on scrubbing.

SNOWFALL

Once the Shallows were piled in the deepest reaches of the cave, Taein settled down against the wall opposite Vince and neither moved nor said a word. Taein passed the hours watching June struggle to breathe, uncertain as to whether he wanted to check on her or bolt out the door and never stop running, while Vince stared off into his own little world. Ka-el remained in his corner, silent, sullen, and mad. The only noises in the cave for a long time were the horses shifting in place, June's thick, strained breathing, and the steady drip of condensation from the ceiling to the mossy stone floor. The tick, tick, tick of the water ground Taein's nerves down to nothing.

Better than the racket of the Shallows, though. Taein ran a hand over his face and sighed. Anything was better than that.

I can't turn into one of those things.

They were disgusting. What's worse, they were *sad*—it was almost as if they'd wanted Taein to kill them. As if they were desperate for release. And it wouldn't come, no matter how much he or Vince hacked them up. Those accursed things were just as trapped as they'd always been since their failed half-death, in pieces or not.

Taein ran a thumb over his opposite gloved hand. *I don't deserve any better.*

Still, the quiet soothed, and for a long while things were almost peaceful. But Taein couldn't relax, not when every breath June fought for came to rest upon him like a ton of bricks.

"I hate this place," he said at length, unable to stand the quiet anymore. Even at a whisper, his voice seemed too loud, too large in the tunnel.

Vince looked up, then away. "Know where we are?"

Taein stretched his stiff legs and dug the map out of his pack, trying to hide the way his hands still shook.

He rolled the map out onto the cave floor and pondered.

"I don't really know, Vin. The dogs drove us well off our path. I think..." Taein paused, tracing his finger along the map, trying to sort through any landmarks they'd passed. A forest this dense resembled the sort that closely circled Thieve's Post, which was... very well west of Ersii.

And Efriel Shu.

Taein leaned back, dropped his head into his hands, and stifled a flood of obscenities as their location resonated. They were in the *shanking Oldswood.*

There were only two forests in all of Nown Jin House Ring preserved; the Godswood, for harvesting the poisonous sap of the oak trees within to boil down and make into ink for their precious tattoos, and the Oldswood.

The Oldswood was one of the only pieces of nature in Ieris to escape the raze of Lithriin ages ago, and as such remained the singular place in Nown Jin where a soul could come into contact with Geiin's fabled touch. Many heretics and magic-fearers had tried to destroy the Oldswood over the long years, but the forest rejected their fire, axes, and curses with a resilience unnatural to the rest of the fallen world, and remained.

Such Celestial presence attracted a lot of activity—marriages and their consummations, as well as murders and their cover-ups, and pretty much everything else one might want done beneath the direct gaze of the Celestial-Creator himself, were all commonly conducted amid the sun-starved forests of the Oldswood. In a country where judgment was rare to be passed and most men were faithless but for the faith found in their amulets, the Oldswood was a way for men to bare their souls and seek atonement. It's never mattered how faithless a people become— guilt is guilt, and it aches and eats at your soul whether you believe you have one or not. And that's a feeling even the most cynical want to rid themselves of. A feeling that only the Oldswood could remedy.

Taein had done a few jobs that took him deep into the forests' sunless reaches before. His strategy had always been to stay in constant motion, to get in-and-out before a day could pass. He hated the Oldswood oaks, so tall they felt like mountains. He hated how they grew so close a man could hardly pass between them, hated the strange plants that clustered at their roots, hated how the trees leaned together and interlocked their canopies so that no light could reach the forest floor. He hated the creaking at night as the trees talked, hated the spookiness of the chilly, whispering air, hated the roving men always passing through, hated how in one night he could hear two wedding songs at opposite corners of the woods mingling with the screams of the dying in another. He hurried his way through whatever shenanigans Regor wanted conducted within its 'sacred' borders, less somehow the rumors be true and Geiin himself lay eyes on Taein's own rotten soul.

There's a guilt that even the eyes of the Celestial's can't soothe. That guilt lived in Taein. Festered in him. And the Oldswood only made it hurt the worse.

And now he was here once again, deeper than he'd ever ventured before, the path lost.

How could this have happened? He'd been too focused on running Lorrin from the dogs to even notice they were being driven in the *wrong shanking direction.*

"What now?" Vince rumbled.

Taein dropped his hands from his face and struggled to compose himself. "We've been going the wrong way, Vince. The pack turned us around and I didn't notice and now we're in the shanking *Oldswood* and

I have no clue how to get out and sweet Geiin, we've blown the job for good!"

"Well, that's alright. Ka-el will help us find our way out."

Taein glared. "If we would've just taken her to the Outlander—"

Vince shook his head and picked at a splatter of Shallow gore on his shirt. "Don't do that, boss. You made the right choice."

"*We* made the choice."

Vince folded his meaty arms and gave Taein a pointed look. "Look, Taein, *you're* the one in charge of this operation, I'm just your muscle. We'd likely just be reaching the Siou border now anyhow, and have a whole new set of trouble dealing with the Alliance and the Salt Watch and n' all that scuffling."

"But we would be *close*," Taein hissed, "hell, Vince, as we stand it might take another full month to both drop her off, get our shit together, and get back to Pearl Jin. Regor only gave me only a handful of *weeks*, not to mention this was a direct commission from the Outlander himself! And you were already on very thin ice."

Vince furrowed his brow. "But you–"

"I'm always on thin ice, Vince," Taein snapped, "it's how I live out my sorry existence. I'm on thin ice the moment people catch sight of me."

"But you're Regor's favorite," Vince argued.

"Only because I *always* get my score," Taein said, voice rising as he jerked the bounty disc from beneath his shirt and gave the chain a rattle. "Yet I still wear this. He puts up with a day or two off-schedule, even three if I'm really pushing my luck, but it's *Regor*, Vince. He—"

Taein forced himself to shut up, closing his eyes tight, his head spinning like an out of control top, and wrestled the panic back, shoving and stomping and stuffing it down inside, deeper than ever before.

Stop it, stop it, stop it.

His heart didn't want to listen. It wanted rit. It wanted silence. And there was no chance of either, so it continued to career around his chest.

Just stop.

He couldn't control his breathing. His breaths were coming in gulps, chest heaving.

It was happening again. *Again.*

Stop.

He forced himself to master his breathing first. The rest would follow.

It was minutes before he dared open his eyes to face Vince again, and as soon as he did, shame rushed in. Vince was watching, an awful, sickening concoction of concern and empathy plain on his features.

Taein worked on his breathing and wrapped his arms around his torso so that Vince wouldn't see how his chest was still shuddering up and down all out of control. He sent a glare Vince's way and kept his voice good and even when he finally dared speak.

"Like I *said*, I'm on thin ice, and you are, too. So let's come up with something that allows us the continued possession of our lives, since we are both in agreement that ditching her, as Ka-el so enticingly suggested, isn't a viable option. Sounds good?"

Vince stared before giving a sigh and tugging at his beard. "Sounds good."

"Fantastic." Taein slumped down, his heart finally beginning to slow down. "What are you thinking?"

"Well, first we take June where she belongs," Vince said slowly. He tapped his long tattooed fingers over his thigh in an intricate pattern as he worked through his thoughts. "So we get back on the right path, cross the Fendall, head north, and drop her off at House Light. Then... then we'll figure out the money." Vince drew off. "That would be where your expertise comes in. We'll cook up something good, pay the old man off."

Taein folded his arms. "Regor will take the marks and lop off our heads anyway."

"He won't be so hasty if we..." Vince faltered with a frown. "Hey, you ain't serious about substituting some kid in June's place, are you?"

Taein snorted. "Sure was."

"But what if the Outlander wants to kill Anathema, and that poor kid bites it for no good reason? I mean, what if he wants you to eat June's eyes or liver or something, and the substitute—"

"I don't *care*, Vincent," Taein snapped. "What choice do I have? I don't get back to the city soon, it's going to look like I dodged the bounty. And it won't be long before he's stringing my entrails around the city himself, *if* he doesn't hand me over to the Outlander for dissection first."

Vince stubbornly shook his head. "But you're an asset, Taein. That's why I'm on this job in the first place. Regor loves you like a son."

Taein laughed before he could stop himself. "Bullshit! Regor doesn't love anything except money and his horse, who I'm currently ruining."

"I *told* you not to—"

"I know you did!"

Vince shook his head, quieted. "You know, you were sick for months after we picked you up from the rit-house. Months of feedin' you, givin' you the good, spendy medicines. Regor... doesn't just *do* that. Nice things for random folk."

Taein blinked, for the briefest moment on the verge of tearing up. But he swiped the heat from his eyes and cleared his throat.

"The smart thing to do would be to get ourselves well and lost the moment we're through with this job. Disappear forever."

"Don't sell yourself short." Vince offered a tight grin. "If anyone can talk Regor out of delivering their death sentence, it's you."

Taein watched as the soft light from the cave entrance began to fade with the coming night, his mind working in overdrive.

Run.

He couldn't bear to leave the kid behind, but she would still have Vince, after all. Taein looked up at the giant. If he ran, Vince would pay the price. But what did it matter? The job was already thrown and June was dying anyway.

Taein looked back up at Vince, who sat patiently waiting for an answer.

"Let's carry on in the morning," he said, "and hope that Regor is feeling particularly charitable when we finally get home."

"Fine by me." Vince lowered himself onto his back and threw an arm over his eyes. "You should say a prayer."

Taein stopped short. For a second he thought he'd imagined Vince talking, but then the giant continued.

"I always heard that the Siou were very good at praying," He murmured. "That it was something of a skill to them. That they got Geiin to listen, most times."

"I wouldn't know," Taein said, stirring June. She opened her eyes and gave him a glower that lessened the weight on Taein's chest. Surely she wasn't too poorly, if she had the strength for such a glare.

"You should pray," Vince said. "For good luck."

"Well, *I* for one don't think Geiin works like that," Taein said, helping June upright and rooting through his pack. He produced a chunk of bread and his canteen, she took both.

"Even if I did," he continued, easing upright and heading back to his spot, "my praying days are long over."

He waited for a response from Vince and snores were all he got.

Taein lowered himself back down and pulled his coat tight around his shoulders. No matter how hard he tried to brush away the thought of his embarrassing little display in front of Vince or the strange humming in the air or the grayness of June's skin, sleep did not come.

Taein stared at the hole-pocked ceiling for hours that night.

You should say a prayer.

He almost scoffed. Vince should know him better than that.

He rolled over to face the wall. When *was* the last time he'd prayed? He prayed three times daily before the incident, as was their custom, but the House's collapse brought an end to every familiar childhood rhythm he'd ever known.

A memory surfaced—a cold night spent huddled beneath the snow-heavy bows of a fir tree, arms wrapped tight around his torso, torn gloves exposing the tips of two fingers, turning blue with frostbite.

A very long, cold night, spent *praying*.

The very air seemed to compress against Taein, suffocating, squeezing.

He spent days beneath that tree, hungry, cold, and numb in ways that'd never gone away. The entire time he'd been praying for Ruein—that he'd come back, that he was alright, that he was alive.

Such pleading had fallen on deaf ears, of course, because Ruein never came back, and Taein was left with unanswered empty prayers and the muffled sound of a body hitting the snow for the rest of his life.

Stop thinking, you rit-headed little twit.

He leaned his head back against the cool cave wall, curling his hands into fists, bouncing his leg as the energy inside swirled. The thoughts continued. His whole body grew tense as a wire.

Stop.

He couldn't. He wasn't in control. *Hell*, he'd never been in control. He'd spent his whole life since the incident keeping instances like these at bay or spazzed out of his mind, and sooner than later they always won, even with drugs, space, or silence. There was no escape.

It's just the stress of the job.

He knew it wasn't. It never was the stress. It was deeper than that. The forgotten, stomped down, suppressed things that surfaced to eat away any sense of momentary peace he found.

Which was well-deserved, he had to admit.

His whole body was quaking now, begging him to just get up, to move, because if not he was certain to fall apart in ways that could never be pieced back together.

He faltered. But *then*, would he finally feel something? Then, would the numbness finally give way to the grief that'd never truly come?

It should've been me.

He went still. There was a long, faltering pause in the rising panic as the thought sunk in, bite down, buried itself deep.

Of course, he'd encountered that same thought a million times before in the first few years after the incident. But it'd dulled away as time crawled by, as all pains do.

Now it was back, and with all its old agonies.

Why now?

He couldn't take another second. Taein sprung to his feet in a burst of desperate energy and set off at a brisk clip down the hall. Shallows be damned—he knew if he went the other direction, he would brush past that ivy doorway and never stop.

And he couldn't run. Not again.

The next instant, something shifted. He blinked, and suddenly he was no longer in the dark cave but a snow-choked field, ringed by frosted firs with branches hung low with snow.

Reality and memories merged into one. His body was a distant thing, his nerves frozen, his breaths delayed, the beat of his heart uncertain. He lifted a hand and it waved in front of his face like mist.

Taein drew in a watery breath, expecting a wash of terror, but for once it didn't come. Everything was still. Encapsulated.

That night—*the* night—was on the precipice of dawn. The still-dark sky, choked with cobalt clouds, was just beginning to gray around the edges. It was quiet everywhere, even the birds and snow rabbits had yet to wake up. The little creek running through the left side of the clearing was silenced by a layer of ice and snow.

The world was suffocating. Drowning in snow.

Taein's slow breaths fogged in the air. His heart fluttered, waiting. He knew where he was. He'd recognize this meadow any time of day, in any season.

Presently, he heard the first few faint footfalls. Boots, padding through the snow.

And heavier steps, just behind.

Taein knew what was coming.

He closed his eyes as the footfalls grew louder, closer. He could hear the third set, now. Driven by a righteous anger to shake the heavens.

He kept his eyes tightly closed. He curled his stiff fingers into fists as the three figures rushed by. He felt the air they displaced. It blew over him, feathered through his curls, so terribly cold.

There was a scuffle. A wet thump as a body stumbled and fell down in the snow, and someone else stopped short.

His head grew light.

One pair of footfalls now, running light and fast into the coming dawn.

A soft, brushing wind drifted toward Taein, pulled at the edges of his coat. It trailed invisible fingers over his cheeks, coaxed his eyes open.

Almost without knowing, Taein obeyed.

He blinked, snowflakes still caught in his eyelashes, as his surroundings were once again changed. The snow-smothered valley was gone, as were the hunter and Ruein. The empty throne of House Glass flashed before him instead, cast in a great shadow, the fires that always burned in great iron bowls beside the throne extinguished.

The scene shifted violently if the floor had fallen out beneath him. A flashing shadow of a person came, standing before the throne with his mother's circlet in his hands. The opals on her crown gleamed like white moons against the darkness, chasing him even as the vision slipped and separated.

The wet, mossy smells of the cave slowly vanquished the scent of frost and smoke. He blinked rapidly, felt tears on his cheeks, the way his hands were trembling as the vision receded like an ebbing tide.

He gasped and took an unsteady step forward. He smacked into the cold wall, looked up, and saw Ruein's face.

Those eyes. Taein's own eyes in a different face.

He threw himself backward and tripped with a muffled, tear-choked curse, his heart catching in his chest.

He hit the ground and a resounding *crack* exploded through his head as the vision ripped fully away, taking Ruein with it.

For a moment it was all Taein could do to lay there and breathe.

At last, Taein braced his palms on the damp, slick stone floor and heaved himself up, only to come face-to-face with a sleepy, thoroughly confused Vince.

"You don't look so good, boss."

Something like anger lit in Taein's chest. "I'm—"

Thud.

The words died in his mouth as the sound of Ruein's body hitting the snow ripped through his mind like a bolt to the chest, and he cut himself off with a gasp. He sunk down and fisted his hands in his hair, trembling, trying to beat back the images, the sound.

"Taein?"

Taein heard himself swear as he stood and shoved past Vince.

"Taein?" Vince called, hurrying after him. "Hey, what's going on?"

Taein ignored the giant and flung himself down against the gore-splattered wall.

He just had to finish the job.

Finish, and *somehow* get his promised marks, no matter what. And that would make everything better, and he could live on his own with no one and nothing to stress him out ever again, and then he could stomp all this nonsense back down where it belonged, and it would stay there.

He'd be happy then, wouldn't he?

Taein wiped his nose with his sleeve, drew in a shuddering breath, and wondered if it even mattered anymore. If something inside of him was too cracked for even barrels of marks or buckets of rit to mend.

❧ 51 ❧

THE TRUTH

Vince halfway-awoke to the fluttering of wings brushing through the air—birds. He'd been waking up to that same sound for weeks now, so it wasn't anything to be bothered with until he remembered that they were indeed sleeping in a cave in the freaky shankin' Oldswood, and those birds could very well be *bats*.

But when he jolted up with alarm, all he saw in the dim light of the cave were a pair of silver-winged sparrows diving in and out of the ceiling through those little holes, their wings skimming the rough-hewn stone as they darted about twittering to each other.

Vince heaved a long sigh and sunk back down again the wall of the cave. He hated bats.

He rubbed his face and looked blearily about the cave, trying to guess what time it was. His back hurt something awful, and his legs seemed more stiff and sore than they ever had in his life. He didn't think he'd ever been on a rougher trip in all the time he'd spent signed on with Regor.

Vince looked over to Ka-el with a sudden prickle of alarm, unsure if he'd still be in his corner. But the tracker was right where Vince left him, hunched over and staring at the floor with bloodshot eyes. Vince thought to wish him good morning but stopped short. Ka-el was more than likely to resume his rambling with Taein asleep, and Vince was nowhere near awake enough to deal with that nonsense again.

Vince looked over to Taein and found the lad facing the opposite wall, curled up in a tight ball. Vince didn't know just exactly what had happened to put Taein in such an awful mood the night before... or in general, really. He'd never seen anyone in such a state but for Ka-el after Venny went down to her Long Wait. But that was different, because Ka-el was in grief and grief made people behave in all sorts of spectacularly odd ways. Taein *wasn't* in grief, he was just spectacularly stressed out.

A sputter of coughs broke the silence, and Vince looked over to June. She was sleeping all curled up, just like Taein. He could see the grayness of her face in the spotty light, the dark places where sores were brewing, the blue of the veins spidering across her hollow cheeks. She looked just like Kassie had, all those years ago. Looking at June now made it all come rushing back.

Vince shook his head and looked away. He'd known for days that she was getting sick, that things were changing, but stars above, he hadn't imagined *this*. First the dogs, now the plague. What was the world coming to?

Vince sighed again. It'd probably be good to get up. Maybe he could get the horses fed and tacked up.

Before he could give another thought to the idea, he was back asleep.

The sun was fully up when Vince awoke again, and someone was swearing.

He opened his eyes just in time to spot Ka-el creeping toward the doorway, hobbling as if he'd just banged his foot and cursing with a muffled intensity. Vince muttered a choice oath of his own and hurried up onto his feet, nearly toppling over as his still-drowsy body struggled to accept the urgency of the situation. Ka-el caught sight of him and bolted for the doorway just as Taein stepped inside, a saddle under each arm, and tripped him.

Ka-el went sprawling. Taein stopped and watched him squirm on the stone floor, the tracker silent and seething, before looking up at Vince and arching a brow.

Vince glared, rubbing one sore shoulder, and hurried over to collect Ka-el.

"Don't look at me like that," he muttered as he hauled Ka-el up and dragged him back to his corner, "not everyone can go days without sleep."

Taein just shook his head and continued gathering up tack. Vince watched as he brushed back through the ivy and out to the horses, who were picketed and cropping grass just beyond.

Vince shook his head and stretched, stifling a yawn, and turned to Ka-el, whom he expected to see sulking. Instead, Ka-el was watching the ivy doorway with an unnerving intensity over his sleep-starved features. He looked up to Vince as if sensing his gaze, but the searing intensity remained. Vince braced, anticipating the onslaught, and he didn't have to wait long.

"That plank-shanking *idiot* is going to get us all killed."

Vince sighed. "Leave it be, Ka-el, you ain't getting nowhere."

Ka-el itched his scruffy cheeks, his eyes darting around the cave before settling on Vince again. "I could make it worth your while, Vincent. I heard Taein talking about how your job is getting thrown and I know you need the money."

Vince glared. "Somethin' tells me I wouldn't be getting it honestly."

Ka-el laughed. "Since when has that ever mattered to you?"

Vince shrugged. "It does when the marks come red."

"You must not sleep well at night, then."

Vince crossed his arms. "Dead thugs are different from dead friends. Real different from dead children. And that sort of thing used to matter to you, too."

Ka-el faltered. "Things were different."

"I know they were."

"It doesn't change the fact that dirty marks still spend."

Vince heaved a sigh and set about rolling up his sleeping mat and putting a few odds and ends into his pack, conscious of June's stressed breathing.

As if reading his mind, Ka-el spoke again.

"She won't last much longer, anyway."

Vince slammed his book of *Asha's Poems and Assorted Shorts* into his pack and glared up at Ka-el. "That's enough, Ka-el. If you know what's good for you—"

Apparently he didn't, because not only did Ka-el cut him off, but he kept on *talking*, and Vince knew he was real dangerously close to losing his temper for good.

"But I thought we were friends," Ka-el hissed, moving closer, "come on, Vincent, *please*. I have marks I've been saving, I could—"

Ka-el fell silent as Taein brushed back inside and strode over to June, his boots padding lightly over the cracked stone floor. Vince watched as Taein carefully maneuvered the kid into his arms and carried her out without sparing them so much as a side-way glance. June didn't wake.

As soon as Taein had exited the cave, Ka-el started in again.

"Vince—"

Vince glowered. "You're nearin' the end of my patience, Ka-el, and you of all people have seen what happens when—"

Ka-el plowed on. "I know where your sister is."

Vince froze as something cold curled down his spine. He looked at Ka-el, *really* looked at him for the first time since Ka-el made his decidedly unwelcome appearance. Ka-el looked right back, dirty and disheveled and nervous, his eyes darting from Vince's face and to the floor and to the doorway and back in a nervous loop.

Vince narrowed his eyes and felt himself take an unconscious step forward. "I want you to reconsider what you just said to me, Ka-el. Think long and hard before you open your mouth again."

Ka-el shifted backward, wringing his hands together like a sot, but the steel remained unrelenting in his gaze. He swallowed hard and spoke again with a surprising amount of confidence for a man literally caught in a corner.

"I *said*, I know about your sister, and I know where she is."

Vince felt all the blood rush to his face in a wash. Just as he was about to pull back his fist to pummel Ka-el, he heard a crash beyond the cave and a fresh burst of cursing. He looked over to see Taein struggling to keep hold of the horses while simultaneously trying to lift the very much unconscious June up into Lorrin's saddle and swearing up a storm. Vince mumbled an oath of his own and turned back at Ka-el, channeling all his anger into one murderous look.

"If you so much as move a damn *inch* from your corner, I'll turn you inside out."

Ka-el sat, his hopeful shoulders slumping back down, and Vince hurried out of the cave to go help Taein.

"Here, Taein, lemme help you," Vince said as he hurried into the daylight, reaching for June.

Taein shook his head and tried to heave her up into the saddle again. He managed to get her up, only to drop Lorrin's reins. Lorrin, sensing he was free, startled forward and dumped June before Taein had the chance to secure her in the saddle. Taein and Vince swore at the same time and dove for her. Taein, slipping on the dew-slick grass, tripped and managed to blunt her fall with himself. June, startled awake before sinking down with a stifled cry, clutching at her side. Vince stopped short as Taein scrambled over to her.

He watched as Taein froze just as he reached for the kid. As he paused, and drew away.

Vince fought back the urge to shout. Why did he always pull away like that? What if the kid was hurt?

And she *was* hurt, by the looks of it. June was crying, her fever-darkened eyes darting blearily around the clearing. She looked at Vince and he didn't think she even recognized him.

June tried to sit upright again and sunk back down, her breaths coming in little gasps, tears streaming down her blue-tinted face. She reached for Taein, fingers searching out something familiar, searching for comfort, and a lump settled in Vince's throat.

June reached for Taein again. Vince watched as Taein recoiled the fraction of an inch, his features blanching white.

Afraid? What reason did Taein have to be afraid of a kid like her?

June made a sound akin to a whimper, trying to talk and unable to voice a word. Vince fought to keep from going to the kid and picking her up himself. He knew she didn't want him. She wanted the one who doctored her wounds, who coaxed her to eat, who came back.

She wanted Taein, no matter how much Taein didn't seem to want her.

But no matter how he fought it, Taein *had* come back for her. Vince had left him alone at the inn, expecting Taein to leave for Efriel Shu on his own, but he *came back*. Taein had followed him there and found the kid himself. That had to mean something, didn't it?

Vince watched, fighting back a wave of tears when June, with the tight, strangled rasp of a half-drowned man, continued to try to voice some desperate thought. The sound of her voice was almost inhuman, a terrible thing to hear. It certainly shouldn't belong to a little girl such as her.

But then Vince heard it. A discernible word, just barely clear enough to make out.

"Taein."

Help her, you idiot, he silently willed.

For a long moment, Taein still did nothing. He stared at June, his brows pulled together, something deeply uncertain on his clouded features.

C'mon, Taein. Do the right thing.

But just when it seemed like Taein would never make a move, he reached out with his gloved hands and navigated June carefully into his arms. She clung to him instantly and buried her head into his chest. Vince could tell that she was crying harder now—scared, confused, lost to her delirium.

Vince just watched, uncertain of what he could even do, and Taein sat there with the kid in his arms, his face gone blank.

The clearing was quiet save for the sound of June's sobs, as Taein stared off into the distance and held her, his face impenetrable. At last June stopped crying, swept back into some fever dream, and Taein immediately eased her away and back onto the grass. He checked her wounds, covered her with his old cloak, walked a few paces off, and then sunk down in silence. He lay back on the grass and stayed there for a long while, eyes shut tight, the fading bruises on his face an ugly yellow against the pallor of his skin.

Vince waited for him to open his eyes, to get up, to start cursing, to do *something*, but the little scrapper remained silent and still.

"Taein?"

No answer. He was still breathing, at least.

Uncertain, Vince busied himself by catching the horses. He truly had no clue what to do. Was this a moment in which he was supposed to give some big, fatherly speech? What the hell was there even to say?

He waited ten minutes before walking over to the sprawled-out scrapper, the horses following behind, and nudging Taein with the tip of his boot.

"You alive there?"

Only then did Taein open his eyes and send Vince a look far darker than Vince ever imagined him capable of.

"Could you *please* shut up?" There was an unexpected venom in his voice.

Vince frowned. "No need to get so testy."

Taein sat up, dropped his face into his hands, and let out another monumental groan. He was still shaking.

"You ain't hurt, are you?"

The groan rose into a ragged scream. Taein struggled to his feet, looked down at June, fisted his hands into his hair, and began to pace.

That was when Vince caught the very unexpected sight of the tears pouring down Taein's cheeks.

He swallowed hard. What the hell was he supposed to do now?

"What's going on?" he tried, fidgeting with the lead ropes as the horses grazed.

Taein stopped short and stared at Vince, his brows pinched as if he was trying to figure out if Vince was being genuine.

Vince cleared his throat. Sweet Geiin, this was hard. "What are you so afraid of, boss? That you're gonna die? Because I don't think—"

Taein cut him off was a harsh laugh. "You're shanking with me, right? You can't possibly be serious."

Vince shrugged. "Well, you seem pretty upset—"

Taein scoffed. "*Upset.* Sure, Vincent, I'm upset. I'm very upset. We've lost the biggest score we'll ever have a chance at for some half-dead kid who I can't fix. Do you understand that?"

Vince reached out to pat Maple. "Sure, boss——"

Taein resumed pacing, dragging his hands through dark curls over and over. "Well, it sure doesn't seem like it, because every time I bring it up you just go on about how we 'have to get the kid where she belongs' because it's the 'right thing to do' and—" Taein stopped short again, whirling to face Vince, his eyes wide, his body shaking. "And I *know* it's the right thing to do, Vincent, you don't have to say it again. But she's going to die before we get there, so what even is the *accursed point*?"

Vince didn't know what to say. He stared at Taein, unable to get over how startlingly angry he looked.

"You don't know that she'll die."

"Look at her, Vince!"

But Vince didn't look at the kid, and kept his eyes trained on Taein instead.

"This has got something to do with you, don't it?"

Taein pulled at the grass. His eyes were dark. "Leave it the hell alone, Vince."

"I asked a question."

Vince didn't think he'd get an answer, but after several agonizing minutes Taein actually replied, his voice low and deadly even.

"I've done this whole thing before."

Vince furrowed his brow. "This job? How—"

"This *journey*. Trying to get somewhere safe with someone. And it didn't end well then..." He drew off, clenching his teeth to keep from crying again. "And it didn't end well then, so why the hell would I think I can pull it off now?"

Vince pondered, brushing off the urge to ask a million questions.

"Well," he began, treading very carefully, "sometimes doing the right thing ain't easy."

Taein rolled his eyes. "Oh, sweet Geiin, Vince, I *know*—"

"Now hear me out," Vince asked, holding up a hand. "When I was young, my mum..." Vince shook his head. "It was just me and my sister. I think I was about, ah, twelve at the time. But she wasn't the same from the sickness, ain't never been—"

"And you still take care of her. Congratulations, you're a better man than me," Taein bit out. "That's no high-fluting award."

Vince shook his head. "That ain't my point. What I'm saying is, it's never been easy to watch over her my whole life, and it won't ever be. But I sacrifice for her because she's my baby sister, Taein. And knowing she's safe makes it all bearable." He shrugged. "Sometimes doing the right thing feels wrong. Sometimes doing the right thing hurts, and it shanks you over, and you look back at your whole life and wish it'd been different. But you did the right thing, and that's what matters, at the end of it all."

Taein scoffed. "Bullshit. *Bullshit*, and you know it is. You spend your whole life fussing over right and wrong and morality and you'll still end up in a ditch with your brains oozing out your ear. This world, the *real* one we live in, Vince? It isn't built that way, and you know it. All you can do is to keep moving and *maybe*, if you're real damn lucky, you can look back at the end of it all and not be too ashamed of what you've done to get there."

Vince tried to meet Taein's eyes and didn't let himself feel the sting when Taein avoided his gaze.

"Good things don't come without sacrifice."

That got Taein to look at him. He stared at Vince, his mouth agape as if he couldn't even begin to fathom what Vince had just said, before stabbing a finger to where June lay on the grass, her chest rising and falling shallowly, her face blue in the brightness of the day.

When Taein spoke again, his voice was raw. "She's not going to make it, and you know as well as I that those shanking dogs are going to come back, and so will the hunter. And I can't even—I can't..."

"Can't what?"

Taein looked away. "I can't get her up in the saddle. I can't do this anymore."

Quiet, for a while. Vince unclipped the leads from the horses' halters to let them go back to grazing before settling on the ground next to June. He checked to make sure she was still breathing, then propped his own coat beneath her head. For a few more long minutes, the only sounds in the little clearing were the horses cropping at the grass, the wind rustling through the vine-encrusted hillside, and the ragged sound of the kid's shallow breaths.

When Taein finally spoke again, he seemed to have regained control of himself. There was a cold edge in every word he spoke.

"Ka-el is right."

Vince let the weight of the statement linger. He looked at June and brushed the hair off of her sweaty forehead, forcing himself not to cringe away at the eerie chill of her skin.

Surely, it was because she was sick, and not because of her curse.

"Look, I know it's hard, Taein," was all Vince could think to offer. The memory of his mother's body beneath a white sheet and how the sores had ravaged her once-pretty face beyond recognition was heavy on his mind.

"Especially with who... with *what* you are."

Taein didn't answer. He looked hard at Vince, hugging his arms around his torso.

"And I know this ain't the sort of thing we do, because we're not the good guys, and it ain't never been that way." Vince looked at Taein, looked back at him hard. "Because in our line of work, kindness is the sort of thing that gets you killed."

Taein glanced at Vince, sudden tears once again glimmering behind his dark eyes. He swiped away the first one to fall and looked down.

Vince waited.

"It's too close," Taein said after a long pause, his voice flat. "This whole thing. She's getting too damn close."

Vince tried to understand. He kept quiet and let the morning steal back in and settle his own nerves.

"This about somethin' you did, Taein?" he asked at length.

Taein clenched his jaw. Vince barely caught his reply.

"Yes."

Vince shook his head. "Well, maybe this is your chance to make it right."

All the fight was gone from Taein's face. His voice was quiet, beaten. "It's a little late for that. Really late."

Vince shrugged. "I don't think so." He eased himself up, ignoring the aches in his legs, and offered Taein a hand. "It's never too late."

"Things like this just don't work out—"

Vince cut him off. "Not often, at least. So don't walk away."

After a pause, Taein took Vince's hand and rose.

They finished readying the horses in silence. When it was time,

Taein awkwardly picked June up. Vince stepped forward and together, they managed to get her in the saddle.

The sun was high in the sky when they forced the ever-sullen Ka-el onto his own horse and set out to find a path out of the Oldswood and to the Ersiin border.

Hours passed before Taein spoke again, and when he did his voice was but a murmur against the spring quiet.

"What's your sister's name, Vince?" he asked.

Vince swallowed the lump that rose in his throat and smiled.

"Kassie."

❧ *52* ❧

TORN IN TWO

For once in the entire history of Nown Jinian weather, there was not a cloud in the sky. Taein's mood did not match the sunny day.

He trudged alongside Lorrin, doing his best to evade Vince's glances and the too-heavy silence that had fallen between them. He felt more than a prickle of guilt for how he'd been treating Vince, but he didn't know what to say to make it better.

A twinge of unease hit him, sharpening the minute he mistakenly caught Vince's eyes. He looked away, a foul brew of embarrassment and guilt swirling in the pit of his stomach and an apology he couldn't yet deal with resting heavy and unsaid on his tongue. Vince didn't deserve this coldness, but Taein couldn't handle any more encouragement.

Maybe this is your chance to make it right.

He kicked a rock out of the path. If only it really was that simple.

What are you so afraid of? That you're gonna die?

Taein bit back a scoff. He was still pretty sure, even after all they'd just been through, that he couldn't die. Because for that long year he spent chasing death, something had prevented it *every single time.*

It started after Regor saved him from overdosing in the rit-house—as soon as he sobered up, a curiosity took hold. Bit by bit, he started to

376

seek out danger. The first time he stood on the edge of Piper's Bridge over the city canals, a stray dog yanked him back by his pant leg. When he tried to turn a knife on himself, a fight inexplicably broke out in spite of the care he'd taken to be alone and he got caught in the middle of it. He climbed a granary tower and a city guard materialized out of thin shankin' air and got him in trouble with Regor. Even the Blackblades in all their bloody glory couldn't take him down, no matter how hard he tried to help their cause.

It didn't make sense. There was no possible explanation. It wasn't as if he healed in an instant or could regenerate or had magical blood, it was that he could never get *close* enough to the end. Something was always there to yank him back from whatever proverbial ledge he might seek out. It took the Blackblades herself, in all her dazzling carnal renown, for Taein to finally come to a startling realization: after all this time spent chasing a death that just wouldn't come, he'd missed the point. Dying would just give Vasily what he'd always wanted.

But living? Therein lay all the spite, malevolence, and revenge in the world.

So Taein stopped trying. He used petty fights and brawls to satisfy the destructive side of himself that still longed for the pure atonement of *pain* and smoked through a pack of cigarettes a day to stay off rit and dedicated himself to becoming the best thief in all Regor's service, because if he was going to live to stick it to the hunter then he might as well do it in style.

And for a long while, that had been enough. But the nights were still long and the city too crowded and the older he got the more the Pearl and her vices called out to him. He started taking longer and longer jobs that took him far from the city, spent as much time wandering the countryside as Regor would afford him. Bit by bit he started dreaming of a farm set far, far away where he could grow old in solitude, where the risk of ashing someone didn't exist and all his contradictions—the way he loathed to be touched but couldn't keep himself out of fights, the way he loved how the Pearl swallowed him whole and yet couldn't hardly sleep until he left her walls, how he wanted so badly to get what he deserved yet couldn't bear the thought of dying—all these things would finally fade to the back of his mind and stay there. They would collect dust and disintegrate once and for all, all those crutches and vices no longer necessary, because Taein Glass at last would be alone.

And it would be over, and he could finally rest, and cope with his guilt any way he wanted, and there would be no one around to get hurt.

But then came the kid. Then came something, at long last, to live for. That right there was the scariest thing Taein ever had to face, because all it took was another clash with the hunter and everyone around him would die and he'd be left living again. And that was a sort of pain he'd dedicated the rest of his life to avoiding. That was a sort of pain he didn't think he could survive again. But he'd be forced to.

Of that, Taein was absolutely terrified.

THEY MANAGED TO MAKE A MUCH-NEED FULL DAY OF PROGRESS without any sign of the dogs *or* Vasily. They made camp along a tree-lined stream near the tenth hour, where Vince made a vegetable stew, ate six bowls, and fell asleep within a half-hour while Ka-el sat at his side, staring at the fire and silently sipping from a silver flask he'd pulled from within his coat around midday and set about entertaining himself with ever since. Taein let him be. The quieter it was, the sooner Taein could think of a way to sort this mess out without anyone getting bloody.

But he was still distracted, even with Vince snoring and Ka-el silent. June was sleeping fitfully near the dying fire, her breathing just as labored as ever, forehead hot and body shivering beneath the cloak Taein had bundled her in. He was watching her struggle from across the fire, a bowl of half-eaten stew going cold where it sat balanced on his thigh, when Ka-el broke his long silence.

"I wasn't always like this, you know."

Taein looked up. Ka-el's dark eyes glinted with a strange light in the amber glow of the fire. He looked at Taein and a prickle of unease ran down his spine.

Ka-el nodded toward June. "I didn't always... I had a family, once. A little son, a good woman." A rueful smile split his somber face. "Then she ran away. And I... ah, I was nineteen at the time, stupid and angry and in love, so I ran after her and killed the bastard she was running to."

Taein stared, shifting a little closer to June as Ka-el wiped his mouth.

"That's how I got to the Pearl, all those years ago. I was supposed to go to the Southern Mists, being a murderer and all, but a gang got my prison wagon and sold us all to Pearl Jin. And eventually, Regor came along and made life much better for me."

His unsteady gaze flickered up to meet Taein's once again. "And then came Venny, on my crew."

It was long before he could continue. "Then there was Venny, and I..." Ka-el shook his head, clenching his jaw. "She got close."

Taein froze.

Ka-el took a long draught before he spoke again, his eyes flickering back up to meet Taein's. "This is council, Taein, from one... *friend* to another."

The intensity in his eyes scared Taein, but he found himself unable to look away.

"Don't make the same mistake as I did, kid. I see what you carry, how you flinch when people get too close. You're a loose cannon with gloves and you know it. And you got a good thing going, don't you? With Regor. Regardless of what *should* be done with you." Moonlight glinted off his flask as he gestured suddenly, his gaze searing into Taein's with a desperate intensity. "I say this as your friend. The convictions you have inside, those things you think will keep you safe... they're there for a reason. And if you let them go for the first sad sob that softens your heart... you're just going to get shanked again."

Taein stayed frozen until he realized that Ka-el actually expected a response.

"Thanks, I guess," he said as he shifted to block June from Ka-el's sight.

Ka-el lurched backward a little, losing his coordination, and snorted. "You're an idiot, Taein, and I don't 'spect you to listen to me. But it's just hard to keep on living when your life is composed damn near solely of..." he drew off, his brow furrowing as if he'd forgotten what he was trying to say.

But Taein knew.

"Of regrets," he supplied.

"See, you understand." Ka-el wobbled from side to side before sticking out the flask. "Here, you look like you could use a drink, huh?"

Taein accepted the flask and took a sip. The sour taste of mulberry ale scorched his tongue, and he took a deeper draught before handing it back.

Ka-el took the flask and grinned. "I think you and I understand each other real well, Taein. It's a terrible shame you're not human."

"I know," Taein said.

Ka-el swiveled so fast he almost pitched over. He stared out at the darkness before turning around.

"I thought I heard one of those dogs," he said with a strange grin. "It's awfully light out right now. And bad things only happen in the day, you know."

With that, he slumped over onto his face.

Taein watched Ka-el for a minute as the dying coals hissed and popped before sighing and shaking his head.

He laid down, nestling himself into the grass, and looked up. A thick cloud canopy hid most of the sky but for a few resilient patches of stars. They looked so small... just indistinguishable specks of white sprinkled onto an abyss of blue paper. Leaves rustled through the trees alongside the stream and as the tall grass whispered, and for once the whole world felt soft.

Taein closed his eyes.

Stay, Vince had said, *this is a chance.*

If he got June to Ersii, would that make things right? Would he finally be able to sleep again without his mind spiraling out of control?

Ka-el had spoken of a much harder sort of truth. The kind that made sense to Taein, that made sense in the real world.

Leave, this will only bring pain.

He knew which was true and which was delusion. He knew, deep in the hidden recesses of his heart.

Taein listened to June's rough breathing and reached out on impulse with one gloved hand to brush her own. He fought to ignore the wave of revulsion that rose from the pit of his stomach at the brush of her fingertips. She flinched away, her breath catching, before curling a tiny, twig-like finger around one of Taein's own.

It's alright, he thought as his heart hammered, squeezing his eyes shut tighter.

Slowly, the grip on his heart loosened, then settled.

It's alright.

He drew a deep breath, let it go, and forced himself to relax.

He lay awake for the rest of the night, listening to the soft midnight murmuring of the landscape and June's ragged breathing, his heart torn two ways.

✤ *53* ✤

BLACKOUT

Days bled by. If Ka-el remembered the conversation he shared with Taein that drunken night, he gave no indication.

Instead, the tracker sat sullen and continuously hungover as Taein and Vince broke up camp and saddled the horses day after day, drinking from dawn to dusk from a mysteriously endless supply of liquor. Taein drank with him whenever the flask was offered and otherwise let him be. He had more than enough on his mind to ponder beyond the tracker's mood swings.

Taein walked alongside Lorrin on a clear morning, still struggling to ease off that perpetual tension inside as June coughed away in the saddle. He forced himself not to look at her and instead tried to loosen his shoulders. He knew she was teetering on that very same edge he once walked along as a child. But the Fendall River—and therefore Ersii—almost *close*.

He knew it was naive to think that the hunter wouldn't just track them down in Ersii, or even the dogs for that matter, but the thought of leaving Nown Jin behind for a while was enough to give him a tiny shred of hope.

If they could just make it across, she would be safe.

Taein finally let himself look at June. Her skin was still blue, her veins dark against the pallor of her skin, hollows beneath her eyes where there hadn't been before.

He looked away, back at the path winding before them. The late afternoon sun was glinting through the cloud layer with a pale cold light. They were nearing Ersii and its blue skies and warm air with every step.

If she could just hold on. He really didn't want to dig a grave.

He looked around. The road followed along the bank of a large stream running toward the Fendall. Near the stream grew lush emerald grass almost half Taein's height—good grazing for the horses, and good cover for their little group.

Taein jostled the kid's leg. "June? Are you awake?"

No response, so he shook her a little harder. "June?"

She stirred then as if surfacing from deep water, looking at him with glazed eyes.

"Break? We've come upon a good spot."

She stared before giving a slow nod. Taein stopped Lorrin and eased her from the saddle with excruciating care. She flopped against his chest anyway and he cradled her with a sigh and walked down the bank after entrusting Lorrin's lead to Vince.

He set June down among the grass and dipped a rag in the stream, his chest relaxing the second he set her down. He dabbed the damp rag against her forehead as his mind began to wander, pacified by the familiar routine, when she stirred.

Taein faltered, water dripping down his arms, and stared as she began to struggle upright.

June, who had not signed nor written a word to him in almost a week, who was so weak she could not stay in the saddle without help or ties. June, who had been half-dead for days.

She was clawing at the earth, digging her fingers into the grass and mud, shudders wracking her frame.

"Taein?" Vince called from the road.

June kept struggling, flinching away when Taein tried to push her back down. "Hey now, brat, take it easy."

A rasp of a breath escaped her and she fought against his touch, trying to sit up like her whole world was depending on it.

Taein dropped the rag, his heart beginning to hammer. "June, you have to stop. June?"

Her eyes were open, dark and glassy and seeing nothing. This time she managed to pull herself to her knees before smacking back on her face. Taein sprang forward and rolled her onto her back. Blood leaked from the corner of her mouth.

She just bit her tongue, he told himself. But he had never been *that* good at lying to himself, and panic rose up like a black wave from the pit on his stomach.

Oh, Geiin. Was this it? Was it finally time?

"Taein, what's going on?" Vince hollered Taein could hear him starting down the incline.

"Just stay with Ka-el," he said, tapping June's cheeks.

She didn't respond.

"June?" he asked, his voice cracking as he shook her by the shoulders.

"Taein, you have to fix this—" Vince said.

"I'm *trying.*"

June still wasn't responding, her eyes fixed on the sky, arms flung wide, bloody fingers clawing at the earth.

The grass beneath her fingers flared a sudden unnatural green, the blades standing up pin-straight as if called to attention. Taein froze. Behind him, the wind picked up and rose to an angry roar.

The grass began to grow tall. Little flowers came crawling up where flowers had not been before, blooming in the space between breaths.

"Taein?" Vince's voice was growing panicked now. Taein heard rough scuffling and a muffled shout—Vince was restraining Ka-el again.

Taein ignored them and shook June, trying to snap her out of it. "June, look at me. Keep your eyes on me—"

Her palm snapped closed and curled right, and his breath caught in his throat.

She found what she was looking for. She was holding on tight.

All around them, the earth began to tremble.

384

❧ 54 ❧

RISE

When June was little still, afraid to go out in the woods alone or sleep in the dark, Mama taught her to swim.

June was afraid of a lot back then, and the river running through their backyard was certainly high on the list. She watched those moving waters suck down sticks and insects and autumn leaves with a wild current, drawing them away from their valley and Mama and safety. She didn't want to know where it led, didn't want to test its depth or challenge its strength, because June knew she was *small*, and small things don't best rivers.

But Mama didn't care if June was small or afraid—she taught June to watch for wild things in the woods herself, made her learn to listen with one ear even while sleeping so she could be safe in the dark, and as soon as June's fifth summer came she chucked June into that river and together, they went for a swim.

And it was terrifying, of course, and desperately cold and swift and deep. But Mama was there to keep June's head above water until she could do it on her own.

She was there. Mama was *always* there.

"Don't be afraid, little."

But I am so tired, June thought. She was in a different sort of river now, and the waters were dark and heavy.

"Don't be silly. You know what to do."

Each breath was a battle, and the darkness was so near.

I am so heavy.

"Then find the shore."

For a while longer, June was still. She let Mama's words echo in her head and the weight of her own lungs drag her down.

But then—

There was a *something* at the bottom.

June opened her eyes. A bolt of fear lanced up her spine, the first thing she had felt for a very long time that wasn't the overwhelming roar of nature speaking.

That something was hungry. It was not letting go. It wanted her and it wanted her *now*.

She looked up. There was a swirling glass ceiling above her now, but it had never been so far.

But still, June stirred. Felt something beneath her sluggish fingers other than the water all around.

She sunk her fingers into the cool, damp earth. She fought to tread water, to rise, and felt the first hints of the life that was all around her. Sought for those overwhelming waves of the living, for the brush of the pollen in the air and the persistent thrum of the growing grass, for the slow thoughtful rumble of the trees. She felt these things and took hold.

June held on tight. Struggled. These dark waters could claim her no longer, because Mama had taught her to swim.

"Find the shore."

Mama taught her to rise.

$$\text{\ding{*} } 55 \text{ \ding{*}}$$

THE CHANCE

"June!"

Taein screamed at the kid, barely able to hear his own voice above the roaring chaos. The wind swirled overhead with a terrible force, ripping leaves from the startled poplar trees and driving the grass wild as it grew skyward.

June's fingers were sunk deep into the earth, and it was responding —little saplings exploded up from the dirt, the stream choked on a sudden flush of dense green reeds growing as thick as a man's arm.

Taein heard frantic hoofbeats and whirled around just in time to see all three horses thundering away, Vince on his ass and looking dazed where he had presumably lost control of them.

Taein watched as Lorrin's dark shape dashed out of sight and felt all the blood drain from his body. *Sweet Geiin*—if he lost the stallion Regor really *was* going to kill him. There wouldn't be a single street in Pearl Jin that the old man wouldn't salt with his blood.

"Go after them!" he shouted to Vince. Vince nodded, barely on his feet, and took off the way they'd run, dragging Ka-el after him.

Taein struggled up himself as the ground began to splinter and crack beneath his feet, jutting upward and out of place. He toppled as soon as he stood and swore. June was just across from him.

"June!" he bellowed.

Her eyes were open wide, locked on the sky.

He dragged himself to her as the ground heaved and split, gripping her shoulders and shaking her with more force than he ever dared before.

"*June!*"

The grass was taller than he was, and the little saplings thrusting forth from the earth were no longer *little* at all, now rupturing from the ground as full-grown budding trees, unfurling long branches and rearing up busy green crowns with a terrible cracking. Branches crowded in on them, scratching at Taein's cheeks and tearing at his clothes.

"*JUNE!*" he screamed, but he could not hear his own voice above the roar of the earth and wind.

For just a second he thought to run.

But the thought was gone as soon as it came, and he covered June with his own body and held on tight as the earth broke apart with a deafening clap of thunder.

He felt the ground beneath them split and jut upwards, and in the span of a breath they were tossed violently through the air.

For a breath, all Taein knew was the thundering pulse in his own ears. He gripped June tighter and braced.

They sailed through the air for only a moment before crashing into a tree. Taein's back hit the trunk, his head colliding against rough bark, and the world went dark.

He felt June slip out of his arms as he toppled to the ground, and his heart rose in his throat.

He met with earth, felt his body roll, and tumbled headfirst into that darkness.

TAEIN AWOKE WITH A SCREAMING HEADACHE, STRAY LEAVES tickling his face and grass poking up his nose.

He rolled over on his back and gasped for breath before struggling to his feet. His vision wouldn't focus and his head was spinning like a top, but at least he was standing.

He took a stumbling step and caught himself on a tree as his back protested. Something warm was trickling down the side of his face from his temple,

But his legs. His legs were fine.

What just happened?

June. The riotous growth. He let go.

June.

Taein opened his eyes, still choking in tight gasps of air. It was still daylight, and he was standing amid a newborn forest.

Hundreds of trees had sprung up where trees were not before, tall and thick as if they'd been growing for hundreds of years instead of maybe an hour, bark gnarled and branches draped with moss, leaves fully furled and sending dapples of golden sunlight to the grassy knoll below. Leaves were still shaking to the ground from their newborn branches. Taein shook them from his hair and staggered forward.

A few yards away he spotted Vince, sitting up dazed next to an unconscious Ka-el.

But no June.

Taein scanned the trees, his breaths catching. Where was she? He tried to hold on, but who was he, to stand in the face of power like *this*?

"Ju-"

He cut himself off, catching sight of a blotch of pink amongst the green.

And there she was, sitting among the trees on the edge of the stream, her feet in the water and head bowed. Sitting upright, and conscious.

"June?" he asked. There was blood in his mouth, but he didn't care.

The kid didn't respond, of course. But Taein could hear her feet swishing in the water.

He stood there, watching, and felt something give inside as he took up a long breath, and let go.

When the lump in his throat finally softened he kept walking, weaving through patches of pushed-up earth as he made his way to the stream.

She didn't move when he sat down next to her and set about

gingerly pulling off his boots and socks. He brushed the mud off of the rich dark leather of his boots and checked to see that the gold scrolling hadn't become even *more* scuffed up before dipping his feet into the water.

"Cold, huh?" he asked, flinching at the spring chill. His voice seemed unnaturally large in the new silence of the newborn grove. There wasn't a single bird about, not even a bee. If it weren't for the noise of the reed-choked stream, there would've been total, anomalous silence.

"I'd wager it's still being fed by winter ice melts."

June was still but for her swishing legs. Her dress hung off the knife-like angles of her shoulders. Just above the collar, he could see the sickle-sharp bend of her spine. Taein followed her gaze down to her hands, sitting folded and motionless in her lap, and quickly looked away.

They sat in silence for a long time. She stared at her hands and he watched the stream flow around the new reeds, adapting to its new course.

When Taein couldn't stand it any longer, he reached out on instinct and felt her forehead through his gloves. June didn't flinch away. He wasn't sure if she even felt his touch.

But the fever. It had broken.

He looked at her then, at the fading gray of her skin and the new scrape on her cheek. He touched the mark with the back of one finger, a lump setting hard in his throat. She didn't recoil, and neither did he.

The fever was gone. He almost smiled.

He drew his hand away and relief bathed him like cool rain on a humid summer day.

Her fever was gone. Gone. Vince was right, she would *live*.

Taein stared at the water, his mind spinning. He wouldn't have to dig a nameless grave without a shovel. He wouldn't have to make the agonizing choice to leave her behind for the dogs and ravens, for the rot.

He wouldn't have to leave her behind at all.

Maybe this is your chance to get it right.

Taein drew in a shuddering breath, the water swirling around his ankles a welcome, shocking cold. He... he could actually do it.

He could finally make it up to Ruein. After all those years, he could finally take out those old hurts and let them go. Be a *decent man* again. Not a great one, not by any respects, and probably not even a good one.

But... but if there was any way at all to be good again, maybe it was this. Maybe Vince was right.

Heat bit the backs of his eyes, and Taein bit his lip to keep his face from crumpling.

The fever was gone. She would *live*.

Taein shut his eyes as something welled up from deep within. A long, shuddering sigh escaped him, and he drew his first real breath since they found her among the smoking rubble weeks ago.

He eased himself down, his back throbbing with a dull pain almost in tempo with the pound of his head, and held back a groan. He covered his eyes with his arm, feeling the fabric of his shirt as it stuck to a congealing gash on his head, and focused on breathing, on the sunlight warming his exhausted body.

For the first time in a long time, there was a hint of hope in his heart. Hope for something more than his spiteful, lonesome dream.

There is a way to be good again.

TAEIN WASN'T SURE WHEN HE FELL ASLEEP, BUT BY THE TIME HE awoke the sun was dimming, and both Ka-el and Vince were still gone.

Taein kept glancing at the spot on the hill the giant had previously occupied as he got a fire going, tension knotting in his chest.

Had Vince and Ka-el ditched him? It wasn't as if they could be blamed—the display June had put on in the throes of her fever was enough to scare even him.

But he really didn't want to do this alone.

Taein shook his head, settling down as his modest fire stabilized. Hopefully, Vince had just gone to find the horses and dragged Ka-el along.

June sat across the fire with her back to the stream, peering at him from beneath the coat Taein had draped over her shoulders. With Lorrin having left with pretty much all their stuff in his saddle packs, it was the best he could do to keep her warm.

"How're you doing, brat?" he asked to distract himself from thoughts of the dinner they had no chance of getting.

June considered before writing a reply in her book. She showed it to him, then demonstrated the corresponding sign twice.

Taein squinted, trying to understand. "Better?"

She grinned and nodded, the fire's wavering yellow light dancing on her features as she bent her head and once again commenced scribbling.

A moment later she held the book up for Taein to read. *Tell me about House Glass.*

"Oh, I don't think that's..." Taein faltered as her thin face fell. "What do you even want to know?"

Everything was her obviously emphatic response.

Taein arched his brows. "You don't ask for much, do you?"

Just tell me.

He looked down, his heart tight, but before he knew it he was describing House Glass in all its former rough-hewn, carven glory no matter how bitter or how hesitant the words fell from his lips. June listened from beneath her coat fortress with wide-eyed sincerity, and when Taein paused and asked, "isn't this boring?", June just shook her head and taught him how to sign *no.* So Taein found himself carrying on, going from the ornate receiving hall to the kitchens, courtrooms and stables, and even the throne room itself.

When he was finished, June sat there and stared at him for a long while before scrawling a quick sentence.

Taein frowned as he read, then looked at her. "When will I take what back?"

It took a minute to decipher her spelling before he finally made out *Efriel Shu. Isn't it your home?*

He chuckled before he realized she was serious.

"Taking back the House is pretty impossible."

What happened?

He looked up from her writing, met her eyes. "Well, the Raincloak Man waged a war. You know, as Raincloak Men do."

Did he win?

"Of course he won."

So what happened?

Taein wrapped his arms around his torso. "He banished Efriel Shu, set up a border watch called the Alliance that keeps anyone from going in or out. Stole my people's horses, burned their major exports so that none of the other realms could protest losing the realm for its resources. Took everything of value and sealed it off. That way Efriel Shu was... just gone. Wiped off the map."

She watched him, silent, and wrote again.

Does that make you sad?

Taein stared at the paper for a bit too long before giving a shrug. "That's what your heart's for, kid." He pressed his hand to his chest. "Can't change the past, but I can carry the way things were inside."

June thought for a minute. Then she wrote, crawling over to his side of the fire so he didn't have to peer over their fading fire to read her scribblings.

I miss my home too.

He found himself blinking rapidly to stave off the heat behind his eyes.

"What about you, brat?" he asked, wiping his nose on his sleeve. "Tell me about your world."

She looked at him for a long time before taking up her pencil and turning the journal to a new page. There, by the faint light of the fire, he read about June's Mama and her Gram, about the quiet hidden valley they lived in and all the ways June spent her once-endless free time.

Taein watched June as she wrote, this child with an ugly oozing grudge ripped through her heart who sat there scribbling about her old stuffed rabbit and wooden horse figurines and the little bird that visited their house for seeds each morning. This strange creature, not quite a child any longer but most certainly not grown-up, who wanted to find a murderer to avenge her mama and yet could hardly stay awake as she furiously wrote, more words spilling from her pen than Taein ever imagined her wanting to express.

Eventually, June nodded off with the pen still clutched in her hand. Taein let her sleep and watched the night sky above as June's breaths still struggled beneath the weight of her sickness.

Dread of her fever was gone, and something suspiciously close to hope had come to rest in its place.

Taein watched sparks rise and disappear against the black sky as the fire burnt down to nothing, and thought about home.

It wasn't House Glass that he carried with him, really. It was Ruein. And for years, Ruein's memory had been a corrosive weight over Taein's empty chest, a constant whispering reminder of just how much his survival cost. A reminder of what he really was *inside*, beyond his curse, beyond all his questionable dark deeds in Regor's sordid service.

Coward, that small voice whispered as the years crawled by. *Murderer*.

But now, sitting here in the red light of a dying fire with only June's little snores for company, that voice was silent. And Taein wondered if this was what peace really felt like—not a great, profound tranquility or knowing all the answers, but a sort of stillness. A sense of moving in the right direction.

He breathed in the cool night air, listening to the stream as it flowed ever on toward the Fendall.

There is a way to be good again.

TAEIN AND JUNE SPENT HOURS IN THE FOREST OF JUNE'S OWN making before Vince and Ka-el finally returned, bereft of their horses and in equally foul moods.

"Good morning, lads," Taein greeted, sitting up and ruffling grass out of his hair. "I wasn't sure if you would be rejoining me on our little trek."

Ka-el shook his head. "If it was up to me, we wouldn't have."

"But it wasn't," Vince grumbled, easing himself down against an impressive maple with a groan. "Good Geiin, my legs are sore."

"I'm sure you're glad to see you've come just in time for another morning departure, then," Taein said as he stretched.

"Overjoyed," Vince said with a shake of his head. "The horses seem to be on a warpath back to Pearl Jin and ain't nothin' slowing them down."

Taein scoffed. "Shocking."

Ka-el interrupted the brief pause by unscrewing his cap flask as noisily as possible.

"How is there anything left in there?" Taein marveled as Ka-el guzzled.

Ka-el glared and wiped his mouth. "There's not, unless you count water."

"Damn. What a fine time to run out."

"On that we agree," Ka-el grunted.

Vince nodded to where June was still sleeping. "The kid doesn't sound like she's dying anymore."

Taein grinned. "Her fever broke."

Ka-el uttered an oath and received a swift smack on the back of his head by Vince.

"Told you," The giant said with a smile.

Taein shrugged. "Guess you did."

Vince took a minute to survey their surroundings before he spoke. "Any idea what the fastest way out of the Oldswood and to Ersii is, then?"

Taein shrugged. "No clue. This forest could eat a whole army and no one would ever find the bones."

Vince looked to Ka-el. "Maybe this is a good time for you to make some of those helpful suggestions we talked about, hmm?"

Ka-el darkened. "Vince—"

Vince's elbow was quick to cut Ka-el off before his protest could gain any traction.

Ka-el gave a withering groan. "I suppose I could offer some... assistance with getting us out of these infernal woods and to Ersii."

Taein nodded. "If we get June there, we can get back on the job. Theoretically."

Ka-el narrowed his eyes. "But you're already past your return time, *theoretically*, which means you've officially blown off the Outlander. And we don't even have horses any longer, thanks to that miserable creat—"

Once again, Ka-el received a sharp jab to the side. After a long minute of steeling himself, the tracker finally continued.

"I'll help," he said, as if in incredible pain. "Just tell me where you want to go."

"Great," Taein said. "I need you to take us directly to House Light."

Ka-el laughed. "You're joking."

"Deadly serious, I'm afraid."

Ka-el quit laughing and gaped. "What for? The kid?"

Taein nodded. "For the kid. Not start mapping out a trail."

"This is insanity—"

"Sure is. But we're gonna make it." Taein took a deep breath, let it go. "I can feel it."

———

❧ 56 ❧

AWAKENING

Slowly, the pool behind his eyes receded, and Vasily's body came back to him.

He opened his eyes to a thatched ceiling, his body damp with sweat. He looked to his right and spotted a tiny man sitting in an armchair by the window, his nose buried in a book, little puffs of smoke from his pipe curling up from over the cover. A straw hat rested on the table next to his chair, the window beyond streaked with raindrops.

Vasily tried to swallow, his throat as dry as parchment. Disjointed thoughts flooded his mind—where was he? Who was this stranger? How long had he been out, how much time had been lost? Where was Glass?

Glass.

Vasily's breath caught. He had to get out of here.

He tried to bolt upright and only succeeded in collapsing right back down, a fresh wave of cold sweat breaking out on his forehead. His chest heaved with the effort and before he could try again to throw himself out of the foreign bed again, the stranger took notice.

"Easy there, buddy," he said, peering at Vasily from the top of his book. "You ain't got a prayer in hell of gettin' up."

Vasily gritted out something unintelligible and tried again anyway, and this time he succeeded in getting his head all the way off the pillow before collapsing back down, vision spinning and nausea somehow rising from the pit of his empty stomach. He heard the chair creak and suddenly the little man was frowning down at him, eyes narrowed behind his spectacles.

"I have to leave," Vasily gritted out.

The man chuckled and turned, pouring water from a jug at the bedside table into a small clay cup. He offered Vasily the cup and that was when Vasily discovered he could not lift his own hands, and the panic truly set in.

The man tsk'ed his tongue and waited until Vasily stilled before putting the cup to his lips. Vasily closed his eyes, shame and relief churning in the pit of his stomach as the water soothed his raw throat. How did this happen? How could he have grown so weak?

He tried again to lift his hands, willing his traitorous muscles to obey, and succeeded only in stirring a few fingers. His broken wrist was held hostage in a splint and layers of clean bandages.

His chest began to heave again as he realized he was completely helpless to any attack. A man could stab him to death right this instant and he'd be incapable to do anything other than lay there and watch it happen.

"Come now, settle down," The stranger urged, pushing Vasily down by the shoulders as soon as he tried to struggle upright again. "You're only makin' things worse."

"Who are you?" Vasily managed, his hair sticking to his forehead. He felt wrong in his own body, like he'd been pulled out and stuck back into a frame that didn't belong to him. His skin seemed to hang off his bones, the comfortable weight he'd known his entire life wasted away, a stiff bandage wrapped around his torso. Even his shoulders felt wrong, weak and narrow as a starved deer.

The little man spoke again. "Darley Schein, lad. Darl, to my friends. I ain't nobody to fear."

"A dangerous thing to admit in this country. What am I doing here?" Vasily asked, closing his eyes as the waves of nausea grew fiercer.

"I found you in the middle o' the road, lad. Off your horse, right coated in mud, and stuck in the throws of the Grey Lady with a poisoned hole in your guts. I find it a bit strange you're still alive, really."

Vasily groaned. "What of my horse?"

Schein puffed on his pipe. "I have her in a paddock with my own mare. Real quiet horse you got there, mister. Odd little thing."

Vasily waited till his nausea lessened before voicing his next inquiry. "Do you know who I am?"

"'Naw. We don't get many stranger 'round here." Schein answered as he filled the cup and helped Vasily drink again. "Who are you, then?"

Vasily latched onto the first name that entered his mind. "Terrin Westerly. Please, I have to leave."

Schein chuckled, hobbling back to his book. "Sure you do. Be my guest once you can stand on your own feet."

Vasily shook his head. "You don't understand. It's a matter of utmost urgency."

"I'm sure it is, Mr. Westerly. All the same, you ain't getting out of that bed even if you try. Now what can I do to make you comfortable?"

"You've done far too much already."

Schein shrugged. "Tis' nothing. We're all Countrymen out here, we do our best for one another."

Vasily scoffed. "This can't be Nown Jin, then."

"Ah, it is. But these are the river-lands, mister, you're right smack in the Fingerlinks. We's close enough to Ersii to behave a little like civilized fellows. Count your blessings you didn't keel over near the Sisters." He shook his head. "The Nomen would've stripped you for your organs and sold them for rit-money before you'd even gone cold, to be sure."

"Thank you," Vasily murmured. Glass had been spotted in such cities. How had the boy survived in a place like *that*?

"Don't mention it."

"I'll find some way to repay you," Vasily said, even as his mind began to fog with a coming weariness he was powerless to fend off. "Truly. I'll be on my way soon."

"It ain't nothing, mister..."

He said more, but Vasily didn't hear, his body slipping, slipping, gone.

WHEN HE WOKE HOURS LATER, THE LITTLE CURLY-HAIRED MAN WAS gone, his book resting open-faced on the arm of the chair. Vasily waited for the fog of sleep to fully recede before attempting to sit up once again. He didn't succeed and instead settled for looking out the window at the rain. From the window, he could see a little garden and a scattering of small, well-trimmed trees. This modest yard was surrounded by a short stone wall covered in moss, beyond which lay a pieced-together fence in which a pair of horses stood facing away from the rain beneath the scant shelter of a towering maple tree. He recognized his bay mare and felt a weight slide from his chest. He hadn't a chance to catch Glass without her, especially without Bellan.

Glass. How in all of Ieris was he to kill the creature in a state such as this? Nuest had built the man up as if he was practically unkillable, but Vasily knew better. Taein Glass couldn't be any more fearsome than his brothers, and he took each easily enough in his prime.

Glimpses of each kill drifted forward from the dark edges of Vasily's memory and he closed his eyes. Knife, arrow, sword, and one by one the sons of Glass had died at his feet. Not a single one offered a fair fight.

Vasily frowned. It'd been snowing the night he found the final two. The night was dark, thick with snow. Somehow he must've gotten confused, and the son of Glass he *had* caught must've been better.

Vasily scoffed. The one he caught that night was the easiest of them all. The fool simply stopped running and pitched forward into the snow like a sot. He *let* Vasily kill him. And for all these years Vasily had never given much thought as to why.

After the first one gave up it took time to track down who he then *thought* was Taein Glass—but he found the bastard all the same, huddled beneath a tree, bleeding, shivering, and sad.

Vasily hadn't stopped to find out *why* the creature was bleeding, not when his intention was to simply make him bleed more. He just went and got it over with, because stars above, how *badly* he'd wanted to go home.

But how... Vasily opened his eyes and stared at the ceiling, his mind beginning to work overtime despite the fog clinging to every thought, his hand straying to his amulet.

He took five amulets. Five from the sons of Glass. And yet... here he was. Trying to amend an impossible failure.

When he first heard that Taein Glass was alive, he assumed the bastard survived what Vasily was careless enough to assume were killing strokes. But when he thought about it...

His mind flashed back to Nuest's description of Taein Glass. Nuest described him as a *reed* of a boy, well on the small side, dark-haired and shadowy.

Not an imposing figure at all, but for his sharp little smile.

A few seconds passed, and Vasily understood.

He burst out *laughing*, the sound tearing loose from deep within the recesses of his soul. He laughed as his lungs ached and his chest spasmed, gripping the blanket until his nails bit through the fabric and into the bruised flesh of his palms.

The men he killed that snow-choked winter night were *both* tall, broad, and strong. Certainly imposing figures, almost identical in their strength, which is why he was so surprised that they were the easiest of the five brothers to do in.

"Oh, I must get well," he whispered to himself, his laughter dissolving into wracking coughs that sent the hot pain his stomach rearing into an agonizing inferno. "I must tell Taein Glass what his brother did."

Vasily felt the blood trickling from his nose, felt every pain shocked nerve come alight as that constant simmering anger rose up and boiled over. He wiped his nose with shaking fingers and smiled. Evidently, Taein Glass wasn't the only Prince of Glass fond of trickery.

Because on that cold snowy night some ten years prior, Vasily had stabbed the same man twice.

❧   *57*   ❧

THE TYRANT

Before, guilt was never something Vince thought much about.

Everyone was asleep, and the night was still. Vince lay still with a clump of dense moss for a pillow, eyes closed and mind wide awake. For once, there was no faint melody batting about his mind to distract from his tumbling thoughts. Everything was silent, and Vince was left to think.

Vince had seen guilt in many people over the years—in the harrowed lines on another scrapper's face or splashed bloody on a mark, saw it in the wide eyes of a failed sneak-thief in the streets too young or too stupid to know how to pull off his game properly. Vince knew that most people were familiar with the age-old tyrant, in some way or another. But it never stuck out much to him.

That is, not until he met Taein, and saw guilt come alive in the form of a walking man.

It had been just him and Regor, the first time Vince saw Taein. He met Taein's eyes in a rit house and stopped dead in his tracks—the kid's eyes were twin chasms—young, dark, and *scared*. Consumed entirely by rit.

Vince knew in that precise moment just what was alive inside Taein, and only came to learn more as the years went by and he saw

402

more and more of him. Guilt was what drove every step Taein took—it was in his every flinch, in the pallor of his skin when someone called him a slur. It colored his every lying breath, kept him up and sleepless on every joint job, no matter how long the journey. Guilt governed every conscious moment of Taein's life with an iron fist. Guilt kept Taein alive and also from ever really living.

Vince remembered meeting Taein for the first time, and the strange relief he felt. Sure, taking care of Kassie was hard and really expensive and sometimes even kind of miserable. But at least he'd never feel *that*. He went through life the same steady way the moss beneath his head might—slow, careful, consistent in his ways and routines. Sure, it meant being tied to the city and consistently bored and dreaming of something better, but a life lived quietly didn't create many avenues on which he might encounter that terrible ol' tyrant.

Or at least it *hadn't*, for some thirty years. But on a swampy night in Pearl Jin some three months ago, rent was due and Vince was broke.

It'd been a long while since he botched his last job by squishing his target, and his reserves were completely dried up. The rent-hag kept calling, Kassie's treatment center was haranguing him for money, and his pantry was well past empty. The rats darting in and out of the hole in his wall were starting to look appealing.

He was on his way to plead with Regor for the hundredth time, stomach empty and torrential rain pouring down, when he heard a strange voice filtering through Regor's tent walls. He hesitated, torn between waiting in the downpour and asking entrance, but Regor was never keen on interruptions and Vince was hoping to catch him in the very best mood possible if he had any hope of getting on an assignment.

So he waited. The rain soaked him right through and he stood there hovering by the entrance to the tent like a podge, water dripping from his beard and soaking through his coat.

Maybe a half-hour passed, the murmuring inside indistinct before it rose Vince from his stubborn daydreaming with a sudden burst of shouting.

"All I ask is that you keep one eye out—" came that strangely accented voice.

Regor spoke, and Vince winced. He knew that tone all too well.

"If you want to keep both of yours, I suggest you leave while I'm still in possession of a sliver of patience."

"But sir–"

"*Out!*" Regor bellowed, and Vince had just enough time to scuttle backward a step before the tent entrance was flung out of the way by a small, stooped-over, utterly peeved old man with dark hair shot through silver and skin bereft of the sun's touch.

The stranger stomped forward and bumped right into Vince before springing away with surprise. He looked up into Vince's face and that was when Vince realized just how *old* the man was; a slow-caving, grave-walking sort of ancient.

"Pardon me," Vince said, wiping away at the rainwater drenching his face and squinting to see the stranger more clearly.

The old man didn't acknowledge his niceties and instead peered up into Vince's face as if he was trying to look straight through him. Vince squirmed under the weight of his inspection.

"You're not the sort of fellow to lie, cheat, or steal, are you?"

Vince furrowed his brow, looking over the old man's shoulder at the glow of Regor's tent. "You do know you're in Pearl Jin, don't you?"

The man kept staring, so Vince relented.

"Well, I reckon nobody does 'till they have to."

And moments of *have-to* were more than abundant, in a city like this. But Vince kept that part to himself.

The old man drew Vince's gaze back and pinned him there. "Do you work for Snevets, son?"

Vince finally placed the accent as Faeish and nodded. "Sure do."

"Not a scrapper, though."

"'Naw. I'm signed on as muscle."

The old man nodded and thought furiously before looking back up at Vince. "Would you like a job?"

In retrospect, it was an innocent enough request, and a timely one, at that. Vince remembered looking at Regor's tent and back to the little stranger peering up at him with intense Faeish eyes, expectant, desperate.

Vince felt the sickening lightness of his pockets, the hollow in his stomach, the black-cloud pressure of those sinister bills resting in his little shared apartment with *Mary-Enn Rest & Healing Centre* stamped in swirling crimson ink on the front.

"I sure would," he said.

With those words, he opened the door to guilt and left it wide open. Unknowingly, of course. He didn't realize just what the job was, back then. But that's how everyone's worst mistakes are made, aren't they? After all, no one ever set out to a whorehouse intending to catch cleaver's rot or left for the alehouse looking to end up in the alleyway barfing their ever-loving guts out or hopped aboard a ship eager for its sinking. The worst mistakes Vince had ever made in his life all started with an innocent step forward, just like his easy little *'I sure would'*.

It just so happened that this was bound to be the crown jewel mistake of them all. Because that little job came with a little question Vince didn't think much of, standing there in the rain.

The old man looked at him with a gentle smile and asked whether he'd ever encountered anyone who looked Siou?

Perhaps it was the cold that numbed him to the obvious reality of the question, or the hunger gnawing in his stomach that blinded him to the questions' insidious insinuations. Whatever it was, it didn't matter *now*, because he looked right into the old man's eyes and nodded and said "Sure, Boss, but only a half-Siou. He's this skinny kid I work with, you probably know of him. The Unkillable Kid. You got business for him? He's out of the city for a while, but I can take a message."

The old man's eyes widened for a fraction of a second. "I may... he might be of the sort I am looking for. I'm a Siou scout, you see. Does he wear gloves?"

And that right there should've tipped Vincent off, but he was starving and his head was as addled as could be, and when all those years ago in the rithouse Taein said he was the last Prince of Glass, Regor had insisted he was lying and Vincent not take him seriously. So he hadn't.

"Oh, sure thing," Vince remembered replying, clear as a bell, "most scrappers 'round these parts do, though. Makes their lifts easier."

The old man smiled and produced a small burlap sack. "Five

hundred marks for you, if you will but keep an eye on him for me. I want to ensure... no harm comes to him."

"Ah, you want to be his Benefactor? I don't think he's got a record to pass the Council, much less why you'd want *him* for Right Society, but—"

"No, no, none of that now. Just take the money."

Vince just smiled, took the marks like a podge, and went out to Minjin's tavern for the biggest dinner he'd ever eaten in his life.

For months, he hadn't given the old man or his questions a second thought. Not until the kid, Taein's truth, and the hunter.

And now, here he was. Sitting atop a carpet of moss beneath the shelter of a decaying log, Ka-el scowling at one of his maps, Taein staring off into the distance with too much hope resting strange on his face, and the kid snoring away at his side. Vince swallowed hard. Things had taken a turn for the *better*, for once. It made the unease churning in his stomach hurt all the worse, because there was no way things could stay this way. Not after what he'd done.

Vince didn't want to live this way. He *liked* life living like the boring old moss beneath his head. He liked his boring honest ways and his boring consistency, because when it came right down to it, life as a lump of moss did more than keep him alive and content—it kept *Kassie* alive, and it had for thirty-some years now.

His quiet life had been generous, and it had been relatively kind. Vince knew better than to expect guilt to govern with the same mercy. He'd avoided the tyrant his whole life, done everything he could possible to keep his head above water, and Kassie's, too.

But guilt was a patient hunter just as it was an iron tyrant. It caught Taein early, and now it had caught Vince, too.

THE GIFT
VASILY

Time crawled by in a haze of sleep and small interactions with Schein. Day by day, the innkeeper spooned Vasily a thin broth and he gulped it down, shame squirming in his belly and souring his appetite. His strength crept back as the hours crept away, and eight days after his awakening he finally felt strong enough to get out of bed. Schein helped him down a narrow stairway and into the roadside tavern he operated below while Vasily counted his lucky stars that the only good Countryman in all of Nown Jin had been the one to find him. He settled on a barstool and Schein was quick to supply a chipped mug of warm, frothy beer.

And that's where Vasily spent half a week—slumped over the top of a polished bar beneath the soft yellow glow of the overhead lanterns as he drank himself into oblivion. Hour by hour, day by day. Schein supplied the drinks and Vasily kept him silent company as the little man tended to various passer-throughs and regular drunkards.

The time lost didn't matter. What did? He was without a trail, without a lead, and without the strength to find either. He could stay chained by his weakness while rain poured down atop the high-peaked roof and people came to and fro in a boozy tide forever. It didn't matter. Nothing did.

Day by Day. Waves of noise passed over Vasily, muted and blurred as though he was underwater. He would take out Glass' amulet, stare at the blood-stained circle, trace the horse engraved deep into the rosewood. He drank, drank, and drank some more, leaving only a few sober minutes to the day whenever he woke up from oblivion's claim the night before. These few moments of clarity were quickly burnt out as Vasily tried to raise his arms high enough to climb into a saddle, tried to walk across the room without gripping chairs and table tops for support. When he inevitably fell and was left biting his lip to keep from screaming, Schein was there with another mug of beer and a helping hand.

"Your tab keeps gettin' fatter, m'lord."

Day by day, Vasily would take the hand, then the mug. A long draught was necessary before he could summon the humanity to reply.

"Whatever my debt, it will be repaid."

Only good Countryman in all of Nown Jin, to be sure.

ONE RAIN-SOAKED MORNING, VASILY PEELED HIS HUNG-OVER HEAD from the bar and opened his eyes before the gray of morning had fully receded. Schein was not yet down to open his bar—the candles weren't lit, the oak log barricading the door still sat in place.

Usually, he was jarred awake by Schein slamming down mugs, or some drunk oaf shouting at another, or somebody throwing up whatever foul swill they'd just indentured themselves to the little man for. Vasily blinked in the dim and quiet, raised his arm, and stretched.

And it hurt. But it was *possible.*

Vasily's breath caught. Perhaps Babas himself had woken him up. Perhaps it was finally time to *finish it.*

The next moment Vasily's boots were on the ground and he was inching across the room, arms out as he walked the tightrope of this newborn hope and wavering like the unsteady wings of an eaglet taking its first flight.

And he made it. Stood before the opposite wall, breathing hard, sweat on his temple, his legs still under him.

His legs were under him, and he was out the door.

Nor Schein or the sun were fully up by the time Vasily made it to the corral out back. Vasily found where the little man had tucked away his things and tacked up his horse. His knees shook with the effort of standing and it took every ounce of strength to swing into the saddle and even more to keep from toppling right off. But he managed to nudge the bay mare into a canter, and soon the little roadside tavern was out of sight. He didn't worry about direction. A sign would come, a trail, a clue. Babas would help him. Babas would send him a gift.

He looked back only once, trying to memorize the little cropping of shacks and the two-story tavern. As soon as he had the opportunity he *did* intend to return, only this time well and with enough marks to keep Schein comfortable for the rest of his life.

Vasily didn't make it very far down the road before his mare tensed, her ears pricking forward and flattening as a riderless black horse, ugly as Mithre's own arse, came racing down the road straight at them.

"Shit," Vasily swore as his mare darted out of the black's warpath, the quickness of the movement almost throwing him from the saddle. But the black didn't collide with them, nor go racing on by. Instead it slid to a sharp stop, unrefined nostrils flaring and sides heaving, and stuck its face right at his mare's.

"Shit!" he said again as his mare let out a hellish squeal, scrambling to stay seated as she struck out with her forelegs.

The black didn't seem to get the message and pressed forward. Vasily drew up the reins and booted the mare to the side, fighting to reclaim her focus. After a second he succeeded in moving her toward the black and he snagged the new horse's dangling reins, his muscles trembling with the effort of keeping himself in the saddle, his wrist still immobilized by Schein's splint.

Good Geiin, I've gotten weak.

Vasily dismounted after a brief deliberation, leaving his mare to look after herself while he inspected the black.

It was a stallion, the color of burnt-out coal, sides darkened with sweat and froth caked around his mouth. Despite the ranginess of his build, the stallion's eyes held a sort of intelligence that made Vasily wary as he checked the packs hanging off its saddle.

Where was his owner? Vasily eyed the tack. Both the lack of bit and the fact that the saddle was still on the horse after the mad tear it just executed told Vasily that whoever rode this beast knew what he was doing. But if that was the case, how had he lost the horse in the first place? Had he been killed? Surely a man confident enough to ride without a bit wouldn't be simply thrown.

Vasily caught the black staring at him again and changed his mind. With a horse as wily as this one seemed, anything might be possible.

Vasily flipped open the first pack, searching for clues. Inside was a small collection of traveling food—dried meat, apples, a few hunks of bread, and a large canteen. He snapped it closed and moved onto the next one, glancing back at his mare to make sure she hadn't budged. He reached in, shooting her a dark look. She was trying to edge her way over to them, ears still pinned flat.

"Come over and squeal like that again and I'm going—"

The words died in his mouth as his hand probed a familiar metal shape. He withdrew it, felt the chill of the material in his hands.

A... what was this called? A *flintlock*. He had read about these—strange new machinery from the Outerlands. Something never before seen in all of Ieris, to his knowledge.

Vasily cradled the weapon, his heart stilling. The Prince of Glass had pointed this at him. There had been a flash of fire, the tear in his coat. The bite, as its arrow grazed his shoulder.

Vasily kept digging and produced a bag of small iron balls, and another of some black powder. He took out one of the balls, rolled it between his fingers. Not an arrow, then. The device must launch such orbs. This little thing was what bit him, that night there in the fire and rain.

Vasily threw back his head and let out a bark of laughter so sudden it sent the stallion skittering backward.

How could it be this *easy*? After all this time... first the Vandel cages and then losing Mari, all the wasted days spent wandering the countryside lost and sicker than a dog... *now* he was to find Glass? It must be providence. There was no other way. This had to be Babas, guiding him toward the last step.

He was still laughing as he struggled back onto the mare and urged her into a canter. The black wheeled around and ran after them. Vasily smiled as tears of joy threatened to spill. Just as well the stallion follow along.

Glass *had* to be in need of his horse.

PART IIII: BLOOD LIKE WATER

❧ 59 ❧

REMEMBRANCE

It was the kind of morning that waits for you.

Taein woke to the whispering of pines. He opened his eyes to a world cast in a gray-blue haze, wind drifting through the tall pines overhead. The trees speared up against the sky, dark silhouettes, tall, watching. The earth felt completely still, as if it had frozen that morning and saved it for Taein for a thousand years. Anticipating his presence. Like it was incomplete without him.

Taein went to stand up and found himself already on his feet, waist-deep in the tall yellow grass of deep summer. He brushed his hand through the grass, so heavy with seed heads, and drew in a breath as the wind grew, lifting his hair from his forehead, chilling his ears.

Summer, but not a Jinian summer. This was home. And even in the deep of summer, the air moved with a bite.

A sound pulled at Taein's focus. He lifted his eyes from the yellow grass and caught the distant sight of horses. Dapples, bays, chestnuts, and grays... each of them impossibly beautiful, half-obscured by mist, spirited in the cool of the new day. They moved like water, rearing and bucking as the mist crawled over the golden sea of grass. A palomino mare bolted and they all took off after her, slender legs striking the earth. The roll of thunder. Taein watched them gallop down the field, his eye drawn to the mare who outran the rest.

"I miss watching them run."

Taein's eyes slid from the horses and onto Ruein, and his breath went cold in his throat.

He caught only a glimpse of Ruein's eyes, just a sliver of his smile, before he snapped awake.

WHEN TAEIN CAME TO, HE WAS BACK IN THE MUDDY FOREST FLOOR of the Oldswood. Sat right down where he belonged in the back shankin' forty, sweating like a pig, freezing cold, and hardly able to breathe. He sat upright, gasping for air and digging his hands into the dirt. Where—how? What happened? He looked around. June, Vince, and Ka-el were all still asleep in their respective places. The leafy trees ahead were still and a heavy cloud covering was brewing beyond their scant cover. The gray of morning was fading away fast.

Taein blinked, and there it was again.

Dark eyes. The smile.

He flinched and stumbled onto his feet. Just for a few minutes. All he needed was a second totally alone to overcome the rock in his throat. He was just excited for once, and all this shanking hope in the world was making him miss Ruein, that's all. It was just a bad dream. It didn't mean anything more than that, it couldn't—

A rock hit Taein's back and he whirled to spot June, sitting up and glaring at him with bleary eyes.

"What?" he hissed.

She scribbled in her journal for a moment. He could barely make out her handwriting in the dim light.

Where are you going? Are you leaving?

"No! I'm just... scoping out the path."

She nodded and started up. *I'll come with you.*

Taein held out his hands as June came wobbling up to him on her weak legs. "Not a chance, kid. Go back to sleep."

She gave him that creepy smile instead, all the light-heartedness she had just worn the day before gone and replaced by something very empty.

Taein blinked. Why the sudden shift? "You have to stay here with Vince, alright? Promise."

June didn't bother writing out her next protest; it was a sentence she had signed so many times Taein knew it in an instant.

But the Raincloak man is near.

"We haven't seen hide nor hair of him for ages, kid. I wouldn't worry."

She started signing fast before giving up with a hiss and taking the book back up. More writing.

I can feel him near. The earth is telling me, in the dirt and the trees and even the birds. He's close.

"Even if he is, which he *isn't*, because we're in the *Oldswood*, and nobody can find anything in here. If we can't even find a way out, do you really think he's going to find us?" Taein said. "Besides, it's not your job to worry. Now back to your patch of dirt. Keep sleeping 'till your legs don't wobble around like that. You couldn't keep up with me right now if you tried."

She looked at him blankly, then wrote. *But I have to kill him.*

"What? Listen here, brat—"

She scribbled furiously and somehow managed to cut Taein off, shoving the book into his face.

He's close.

"Stop it," Taein said, "and go back to sleep before you wake everyone else up."

But the trees are only quiet when he's close by. It's our chance.

"No dice."

June stared at Taein, impossibly still, before punching him square in the chest. Taein recoiled before he could stop himself and the kid landed a few more shockingly-solid hits before he caught her fists and forced her still.

"What's gotten into you?" he hissed, trying to ride out the sudden wave of nausea roiling in his gut.

June stomped her foot and ripped her hands out of Taein's, then picked up her book out of the dirt. She stabbed at the page, then threw the book at Taein with a hiss of her own.

You think of me as a helpless little girl but I'm not, I am Anathema like you and I will show Vasily why he's right to be afraid of us.

She glared up at Taein. He looked between her and her scribbles before snapping the book closed, tucking it under his arm, and bending to rest on one knee. He looked deep into June's eyes, trying to look past the hate, past the hurt. To find the kid in there.

"That's what you really want? To make him hurt?"

She nodded, knocking a fist against her head as if to say *duh*.

"Is it what your mother would want?"

Doesn't matter, she signed.

Taein shook his head. "The Raincloak Man is right to be afraid of me, kid, but you. *I'm* the cursed one." He showed her a gloved hand. "All I can do is damage. But all you can do is bring life." He searched those pale green eyes, tried to make her understand. "You're not a weapon, June. You're a *gift*."

She scrunched her brows. But, she began to sign, but Taein batted her hands down.

"You have to let it go."

I can't.

"Don't be the monster he thinks you are." Taein shook his head. "You're meant for so much more."

The anger in her eyes quieted. She raised her hands to argue but they sank slowly back to her sides. The birds were beginning to stir and chirp before quickly quieting their morning conversations. June seemed rooted to the ground, so Taein gripped her by the shoulders, turned her around, and gave her a nudge. She looked up at him as he guided her wobbling back to her make-shift bed of Taein's old cloak and a nestle of leaves, her brows still tight and eyes gone bleary.

"Promise me you'll stay here," Taein said as she sat back down.

She nodded, but her eyes ran straight away from his and accosted a particularly-uninteresting leaf.

"Hey now," Taein said, holding out his hand, "you're about as good a liar as I am an honest man. You have to pinky-promise."

Her glare softened. *Do what?*

"A pinky-promise," Taein said. "Didn't your mother ever show you those?"

No answer.

"A pinky-promise just means your word is genuine. It's a thing friends do."

June relented and stuck out her hand.

Taein twined his gloved pinky around hers and shoved down a wave of nausea. "Excellent, I'll be right back. I'm sure you'll keep yourself entertained if you can't sleep and *stay put*. Draw in your book or stab beetles or whatever it is you find fun."

June huffed and looked away, and Taein couldn't help but hesitate. But there was something tight in his chest and the longer he looked the more that feeling spread, leaching into every muscle, locking his joints, stifling his breath.

He blinked, and there was Ruein again. Just a flash. Dark eyes winking. But it was enough.

Taein turned, heart in his mouth, and started walking.

Just for a minute. Just until he could breathe again.

THE HOLD ON HIS CHEST DIDN'T LOOSEN UNTIL HE'D WALKED FOR AN hour. The early morning was heating up, made muggy by the dense clouds, and he was starting to sweat, so Taein stopped at the first shallow river he found. It was a pretty little spot—the stream was perhaps twenty or thirty feet across, dotted with large rocks. Little yellow flowers grew in the tight crevices between the rocks, turning up small faces to drink in the sparse warmth managing to sneak through the cloud cover and dapple the stream. The trees on either side seemed to reach for each other, like old friends after a long separation.

Taein found himself wandering up the stream for maybe ten minutes before a structure came into view—an old hunting shack, three stories tall and half-eaten by wood rot, an infestation of ivy, and the stream it sat over. Taein sloshed closer. Had someone built the shack over the water on purpose, or had the stream come up after it was built and ate its way right through the foundation?

He came up to the door, held ajar by driftwood, and slipped inside.

The shack reeked of mold and algae. The stream really did cut right through the foundation, breaking up the floorboards and littering the place with rocks. The interior was all rotting, brittle wood walls, equipped even with a gaping hole in the roof that cut through all three floors and exposed the heavy sky above. Scattered about were animal bones and red-rusted butchering tools atop brittle, moss-eaten work benches and counters. A few decomposing pelts hung on the walls—a beaver, maybe that other one was once a coyote?

Taein moved about the room, boots splashing. It was a crowded space, filled with several work tables, benches, counters, and even a shanty kitchen set up along the far wall. A round table sat in the corner under a sagging stretch of ceiling still bore a set of chipped mugs, plates, and wooden utensils. A half-eaten meal had long-since turned back to dirt on one of the plates, covered in green fuzz. Taein opened a rusty flask, sniffed, and flinched away as the scent of Faeish *seer* alcohol bit at his nose. Whoever had occupied the shack last had certainly left in a hurry to leave such fine booze behind. He considered the flask, swirled the opaque liquid around, and promptly gulped it. The liquor burned his throat—it felt like swallowing a fireball, really—and warmed him head to toe. He couldn't help but grin. Not bad for sitting out for some-odd years.

Taein chucked the flask over his shoulder and set about rooting through the few cabinets still hanging off the leaning walls. Maybe they'd been drug or booze luggers. Maybe they left something more behind than half a flask of *seer*.

Maybe this was a stash house.

Maybe there was *rit*.

The base floor revealed nothing else consumable, so Taein tackled a ladder built into the wall. The second floor was empty, which left the attic. It was a high-ceilinged space, well-lit by the hole splitting open the center of the bowing roof. A support beam ran the length of the ceiling and crossed weakly over the hole, its length almost entirely eaten by moss and looking particularly frail. The roof's collapse had punched an equally-gaping maw into the floor of the attic, which buckled and moaned as Taein walked about. He came up upon an abandoned bedroll and pack in the corner beside a broken-out window.

Hope. He settled down, brushing away a leafy branch poking curiously through the window, and dumped out the pack. Nothing at first, but a little expert rooting for hidden pockets rewarded Taein with a musty pack of cigarettes. He fished for matches, somehow got one to take, and sat there puffing for a while. Cigarettes certainly weren't rit, but they'd have to do.

His mind drifted to June. After all of it—the bloodshed, the running, the loss—they were almost to the end.

There is a way to be good again.

Taein leaned his head against the moldy wall and listened to the stream flowing through the house below. He was halfway through the pack, smoke curling from his fingers and settling his nerves, when Ruein floated right back to mind. Taein lit his third cigarette, took another drag, and let him come.

Summer came with its challenges back during their boyhood. When the Efriel Shu sun returned and the grass grew tall and golden, assemblies from each of the roving bands of horse lords would journey to House Glass for weeks of negotiations, over which their illustrious father presided.

Naturally, Taein and Ruein made sure to disappear. They made a tradition out of riding to the Benson River, made tame by the summer sun, and spent those all-important weeks becoming as close to amphibious as a man could get. They'd spend the better part of a day at home in the water, not a single care in the world. But it'd always taken Ruein ages to actually *get in.* He was a wader, his relationship with water one of his few points of caution, and it drove Taein absolutely mad.

"It's all about acclimation, Mikhael," Taein could still hear Ruein say, though the memory of Ruein's voice had grown faded in his mind like a letter read and refolded too many times. *"But I'm only human, after all, and I'm afraid of the shock."*

"Milksop," Taein would call him, never thinking much about that criminal phrase, *I'm only human.*

Ruein quipped the phrase often back then. It never meant a thing, not until the incident, after which Ruein stopped saying much of anything at all. There had been times, during those silent weeks on the run, that Taein wanted to ask Ruein just exactly *what* they were. It'd become clear that 'human' wasn't exactly appropriate anymore.

But then... what were they? They lived and died near the same as any mortal man, that much became clear as Vasily made short work of their brothers. If they bled and died like any other man, was it their very spirits, then, that were broken? Had Geiin breathed life into them the wrong way?

Taein flinched as that hard lump slammed back in his throat. Sweet Geiin, was he really about to start *crying*? Over a few fond memories? He wiped his eyes and lit another cigarette. Took a long, deep drag, let the smoke out slow.

Breathe.

If there was a way to be good again, it had to be this. He'd finish the journey, and things would be made as right as they could ever be.

Breathe.

"May I have one?"

Taein froze. It occurred to him, as his heart stopped dead in his chest, that this was the first time he'd ever heard Vasily Miinriel speak.

***

❧ 60 ☙

THE KID TRIES VERY, VERY
HARD TO BE GOOD

June watched until the dense green brush swallowed Taein whole before wobbling back to her spot in the dirt.

The Giant and the stranger, the one called Ka-el, were still asleep. June ignored them both. She laid on her back, arms folded, and stared at the little patch of sky visible through the trees. The gray light of morning was quickly sweeping away the stars. A breeze hinted at a warm day ahead. A day to be spent getting closer to her safe place, where she could have a real bed again. Books to read and lots of paper to write on. Meals, and lots of them.

The thought did nothing to cool the burning inside her. June rolled over and frowned. The fire inside had nothing to do with her retreating sickness or her scabbed-over wounds or the fading bruises and everything to do with the wound in her heart that was very much still open, still very much bleeding.

The Raincloak Man was close.

June could feel it in the way the breeze seemed to hold its breath, in the stillness of the trees, in the dense crowding brush. Even the grass around seemed to press close, as if trying to knit together and shield her. June hated that. What right did the slow-growing things have to fear a man even she wasn't afraid of?

422

June rolled over, quieted the flow of her thoughts, and tried to listen to herself. Tried to peel back all the layers of discombobulated, half-formed thoughts and feel what was *really* there, beneath all the hate and longing and confusion and pain.

She listened. The sound of a distant stream rushing on seemed loud as a waterfall, her own bumping heart an earthquake. June listened and felt nothing. There was an abyss inside where fear used to be. But so *what* if she wasn't afraid of the Raincloak Man. She was still stuck here, bound by her stupid promise to hide like a coward. Like the Idiot.

June scoffed, flipped over again. All Taein ever had to say was *let go, forget, we can't change the past.* She scoffed. What a silly, muck-brained thing to say. Of course she couldn't change the past. June knew that, everyone knew that. If she *could,* she would've already brought her Mama back and gone home. She would've run straight to Mama and buried her face in her soft plaid skirt and cried until all this *hate* inside went away.

And Mama would fix it, and the world would go back to normal.

June could sleep again without seeing the Raincloak Man and his blade. She could sleep and not wake up with this horrible fire burning her alive. The voices in her head saying *you can't let him get away with this* would be gone forever. They could go together to visit the nice old woman at the Orphanage and June could eat her biscuits and drink tea without this hole gnawing away inside.

The sun will come again, if you let it, the old woman had said. If only she knew how to make that true.

The coming morning went blurry with tears. June let the first few fall hot down her cheeks and balled her hands into fists.

The old woman had also said that anger was a poison. But Mama was dead. There was no fixing it. There was nothing to do but try to fix herself, and how could she possibly do that without getting the Raincloak Man first?

So June did her best to stop thinking about *him*, and tried to go back asleep. She couldn't of course, because she wasn't tired, she was *mad.* Instead of sleeping, June found herself bracing a palm flat against the ground and concentrating. Trying to will life up into the grass like

Mama used to. Like she herself had, when she fought her fever and won.

But nothing happened. June closed her eyes and reached deeper, searching for the root of life itself, for the thrumming breaths of silent growing things. All she felt was the wet grass flattened and cold beneath her palm, felt the slow rising sun warm her face. The world just wasn't *alive* for her like it used to be when she was little, back when the days were warm and endless and Mama's ire at finished chores was the only danger to dodge. The world was dead to her right now, turned away and silent.

Just like Mama.

Heat erupted from June's heart and went oozing through her veins. She dug her fingers into the dirt like a falcon sinking his talons into a rabbit.

I miss Gram, she thought, and that heat only grew.

I miss our tiny stupid house.

I miss the lonely forests.

I miss the empty meadow.

I miss the bees and the hoot owls. I miss the bunnies and my reading log. I miss my dolls and my horse figures and my bed and my blankets.

I miss my Mama.

June's anger became a living thing again, hot and vicious and demanding. It flooded her body, tensing every muscle, lending an energy that didn't belong to her, blotting out every thought, every distraction. It surrounded and swallowed her all at once.

Grow, she demanded, and the earth listened.

The grass beneath June's hand shot up, wrestling out from beneath her palm. The blades grew tall and new and the tiniest bit sharp.

Sharp.

When Mama made grass grow, it was never cutting like this. It was always the soft, velvety, bluish sort of grass that was the best to take naps on.

June didn't care. She lifted her hand from the ground, watching as the grass came to a quick halt without her touch, and picked a blade. She ran the strand between two fingers and didn't flinch when its razor-edges drew blood.

He's close, the growing things whispered. They were frantic. They wanted her to save them. But June didn't *want* to save anything at all, she just wanted things to burn. Wanted *him* to burn.

June wiggled her toes to chase the cold from her bones. Flopped back amid her razor-tipped grass and stared at the brightening sky. Watched the tiny black silhouettes of birds flying high above. Felt the shadows cast by the trees above dance on her face.

But those awful feelings didn't close over like a cut left to scab. She'd pried back the layers and found a hole and now *it wouldn't go away.*

So June sat up. She snuck her knife from her dress and cut a few pieces of her sharp grass. Sat there and braided them into a crown, the little cuts they rent into her skin nothing but a welcome distraction.

Be good. Mama would want her to *be good.*

She ended up with three crowns and was halfway through braiding a necklace when that hole in her chest finally got the best of her, and before June even knew what was happening she was struggling to her feet again, weak as a newborn fawn, but *moving.*

A trickle of blood crept down her leg as a scab cracked open. Warm and stinging. But it didn't matter, because she was on her way. Knife clutched in her hand. Taking tiny footsteps toward the wall of brush that separated her from the Raincloak Man. She brushed aside the first of many branches, slipping into the wall of bushes just like Taein, and everything became perfectly clear.

She was going to find the Raincloak Man. He was close, and the earth was crying out to her, betraying his presence. June was going to find him, and he was going to pay.

You are not a weapon. You are a gift.

June smiled. Maybe Taein was right. But her power was not the same as Mama's power. And if this thing living inside her really was a gift, she was going to use it however she wanted.

I will make you hurt.

And this time when they met, June was going to show the Raincloak Man just how *right* he was to fear little girls like her.

61

THE RECKONING

"May I have one?"

The hunter's voice was nothing like Taein imagined.

Vasily's voice wasn't ferocious. Not gravely, dark, or deep. It wasn't even *angry*. His voice held the patience of a priest, the softness of a teacher, the gentleness of a father.

Somehow, that made everything worse. What kind of monster must he truly be, to warrant destruction at the hands of a soft-spoken man like *this*?

Taein, still wedged in the corner beneath the window, forced himself to stay still and silent as Vasily carefully crossed the attic floor and crouched down, the two of them separated only by the hole in the floor. An awful wash of relief coursed through his very soul, like rainfall washing away the dust of a long dry summer.

It was finally here. His reckoning.

After *all these years*—the awful culmination of a story his cowardice long since left unfinished. After all this time of inexplicably staying alive, no matter how badly he always shanked things up—it was for this. No atonement. No new life, no fresh start, no slate washed clean. Just his inescapable fate. Just the same story, finally set to end.

Here it was. Here *he* was—Vasily, the hunter, the Raincloak Man

426

himself. If nothing else in the world could kill Taein Glass, surely he could. He *had* to.

Taein hardly felt the cigarette singe his fingers as it burned down to nothing. The man crouching across the hole in the floor different from the young prince Taein had watched hunt down his brothers. His shoulders were the same—prideful, straight, and his hair the same wash of black. But where there had once been only a monotone look of intensity, Vasily now held something different. His face bore a few more lines than when they last met, and there were dark hollows beneath his eyes, fresh raw gashes marring his cheeks. He was thinner, his body tensed a little too tightly. He looked unbalanced, as he crouched there across from Taein. The hunter looked worn, he looked wounded, and he looked downright *tired*. There was a look in those once-gentle eyes of a pain like no other. The kind that eats you from the inside out. The kind that's not entirely of the body.

Taein stared Vasily Miinriel in the face, and realized he was finally about to die.

❧ 62 ❧

NO OTHER WAY

Vasily couldn't breathe.

Glass sat across a gaping hole in the floor, statue-still even as the shack swayed precariously in the wind and the clouds above grew darker. The world could've torn at the seams that very moment and Vasily wouldn't have noticed nor cared. His whole world sat in front of him, an amber-tipped cigarette clenched between two gloved fingers, a trail of smoke curling up to cast a thin veil over his features.

Vasily couldn't remember what the other princes of Glass looked like anymore—he felled each one in a haze of grief and rage, their gazes muddled by varying shades of terror, hate, and shock. Vasily appreciated that jumbling of their countenances—he carried the weight of their deaths with him every day, at least he could escape their faces.

But now, looking at this last Prince of Glass through his wall of curling smoke, Vasily knew without a shadow of a doubt he'd seen these eyes before. Glass' eyes were dark as starless night, devoid of all emotion, empty searching holes in a face that were looking right through Vasily, right to the core of him. Vasily looked back and found nothing. Just an abyss where Vasily usually found the core of a man.

He'd never seen a look of such absence like that before, but there was something else lingering in Glass' gaze that recalled another of the princes: the tall one Vasily killed twice, all those years ago. That one had dark eyes, too, but they were human-like, full of terror and agony and something else that Vasily had never quite understood. That same something was lingering in this Glass' eyes now, as he stared steadily back at Vasily.

Vasily drew a shuddering breath, his gut roiling. Silence reigned for a long while. The rain began to patter down on the remnants of the fallen roof, it fell through the attic and down into the stream below. Glass' cigarette burned slowly down in his fingers and Vasily finally realized what made him so familiar. There in those dark, soulless eyes, Vasily identified the look, that *something else* he never understood in the prince he killed twice.

Relief.

If Vasily hadn't been able to breathe before, he certainly couldn't now. The world had pinched, narrowed in on itself. After all this time —after all the bloodshed, the pain, the *loss*—the last Prince of Glass was finally sat before Vasily, pinned in the attic of a decaying hunting shack. Helpless, cornered. His to claim. It would only take a minute and it would, at long last, be *over*.

Vasily had expected the old, familiar rage in him to reignite at this moment, thought the starved honor in him would drown everything else and bathe the world red once again, make strong his body and steady his mind and turn to stone his heart. He thought in this precious, long-awaited moment he fought and bled and killed all the good in him for, the rage that never really left would come back effortlessly.

But it wasn't. The road had been long and the monster in him was spent. Vasily stared at the Prince of Glass, his heart eerily still, his body full of strange aches, and found himself paralyzed by dread.

"I said, may I have one?" Vasily tried again, barely able to steady his voice.

Glass extended the pack of cigarettes.

"Throw it to me."

Glass narrowed his eyes, took one more cigarette from the pack, and threw it over. Glass lit his with the stub of his previous, took a long drag and let it go slowly. Vasily settled down, the two of them still separated only by that abyss of a hole in the floor, and picked the pack up. He turned the half-rotted box over and over in his hands, unable to take one out, unable to tear his eyes away from Glass.

Nuest was right—the bastard Prince of Glass was just a reed of a man, lanky and thin and gaunt-faced, with a pallor to his skin and curly, unkempt hair that flopped somewhat comically over his face. He was cramped in a corner between a window and a wall, knees pulled up to his chest as a child might sit.

Glass didn't look afraid, and he didn't look sad. He didn't even look *angry*. Where was his terror? Didn't he know what was bound to happen?

When Vasily managed to speak again, he couldn't keep the emotion from his voice.

"Forgive me..." he managed, "It's just, after all this time... I'd begun to think I'd never find you."

The prince shrugged, tapped the ash from his cigarette. He took another drag before speaking. "When did you catch my trail?"

Glass' voice was rougher than Vasily expected. It had a rasp on the edges, a bite that betrayed the innocuousness of his features.

"Two or three months ago." Vasily shook his head. "The time all blends together. I... I thought you were dead, really. For such a long time."

A smile tugged at Glass' lips. "Forgive me if my enthusiasm seems lacking."

"I take no offense, Glass," Vasily said.

Glass declined to say anymore and just sat there, puffing away on his cigarette and looking unflinchingly back at Vasily.

Vasily was suddenly at a loss for words. Here was his ultimate quarry, the fabled, fearsome, last *Prince of Glass*, abomination of mankind and threat to all living things, and the boy was just... sitting there. A chill that had nothing to do with the bite of the spring air ran down Vasily's spine. What kind of monster was Glass, to just be sitting there with his cigarette, eyeing Vasily with that strange dead-eye gaze, as if he didn't care at all what came next?

"Well," Glass said, flicking his cigarette away, "not to escalate the situation, but I'm a little surprised you haven't tried to kill me yet."

I can't.

Vasily wiped the thought from his mind and instead withdrew Glass' amulet. He dangled it over the hole, waiting for Glass' expression to change. It didn't.

"Have... you a new amulet?"

Glass just shook his head. Vasily swung the rosewood piece in the air for just a moment longer, the horse engraved on the blood-smeared wood still frozen in its perpetual defiant rear, then let go. The amulet whistled through the air and hit the water with a *sploosh*.

It was then that Glass finally began to squirm. "Look, I–"

Vasily cut him off. "What of the child?"

Glass stilled. "What child?"

The corner of Vasily's lip twitched. So she was still alive, then. "I have to kill her, you know. The little girl."

"I'm alone."

Vasily looked deep into that bottomless gaze, trying to find the man in there. "We are both liars, you and I. It is the price of my honor and of your survival. But we need not lie to each other."

Glass scoffed. "That's the unfortunate thing about lying for a living, asshole. I wouldn't know the truth if it punched me in the face."

Vasily shook his head, dug for resolve, for anger. "It matters not. I know the truth. I know what I have to do."

Glass didn't answer, and the dread began to rise stronger in Vasily and began to smother him. His heart clammed up, palms sweating. He could only stare, powerless in his body, as Glass edged onto his feet.

Vasily's vision blurred at the edges, spun as though the world was tipping on its axis. Dimly, he heard himself speak.

"Do you understand why I must kill you, Glass?"

Glass almost laughed. "It doesn't matter *why*. Do you think you're special to me?" His face hardened. "You're just in my way. You're—"

Vasily cut him off, blinking rapidly to try to clear his vision. "But I *do* think I'm special to you, Glass. You're special to me."

Glass said nothing. Vasily dug down into the well of himself, grasping in vain for the monster who for once would not come out, and continued.

"Are we not bound together by bloodshed? You are more than a grudge, Glass. You are an obligation. You are the ultimate threat."

"Or maybe men like you are, Vasily," Glass retorted. "Killers of children."

A pang pieced Vasily's heart. "No—"

Glass tried to cut him off. "Yes—"

"No!" Vasily steeled his voice. "In Faeriel, we have many sayings. One of them is *love conquers all*."

Glass had shut up, so Vasily continued.

"No other realm understands our ways," he said, "they think we are honor-bound, that we live and die by the way of righteousness. But we are governed by the law of *love*, which transcends all other laws, which has no mortal bounds. No wrong thing can be done in the name of love."

Vasily held Glass' gaze as that terrible intensity inside him flickered back to life and went to war with his dread.

"Love conquers all," he said. "That is how I will conquer you, Glass."

Glass just stood there with his mouth agape, his back against the open window, the wind tugging at his hair. For the first time, Vasily caught a glimmer of fear in those impassive dark eyes.

"You're not even going to try to run away?" Vasily asked.

Glass shook his head.

"Don't you want to live?"

Another smile cracked Glass' face in half. "Do I finally have a choice?"

Vasily didn't understand, but Glass shook his head, his eyes gone glassy.

"That night, in the snow..." He stared at Vasily with a sickening intensity. "This time, Slate, I need it to be me."

Vasily's breath caught. "Then it seems you know what you are."

Glass went silent, remained perfectly still. Vasily found it in himself to stand.

"It seems you know what you've done."

Glass just looked back at Vasily, unshaken. All the years melted one by one from his face, and suddenly cornered there with his back against the window stood the same thirteen year old boy Vasily had mistakenly let live all those years ago. And he was *ready*.

Heat pricked behind Vasily's eyes. A rock settled hard in his throat. He forced the feelings away, deadened his heart. He could hardly feel his breath as it grated in and out of his lungs.

"You know you cannot be remade."

Glass' eyes fell slowly down to the floor. Vasily knew it was time. *Glass* knew it was time.

Vasily's broadsword went sliding from its scabbard, his grip on the hilt somehow became firm.

He looked Glass dead in the eyes, and whispered.

"Then you will forgive me. There is no other way."

❧ *63* ❧

THE REASON

"There is no other way."

Taein could barely hear the hunter as he stood across the hole, broadsword glinting in the gray light. He took a step around the hole, then another. The distance separating them like an ocean began to close. Taein expected some terror to rise and instead found only a relief he'd been thirsting for all his life.

It's finally over.

Vasily was going to kill him. If anyone in Ieris could kill him, it had to be Vasily. After all this borrowed time, Taein Glass was finally going to *pay*.

"You cannot be remade," Vasily said again, nearer now, the knuckles of the hand gripping his broadsword bone-white.

I know.

But before the thought could cement in his mind Taein saw *her*.

There was June, comatose in her blue dress beneath the blackberry bramble that saved her life. He saw her looking at him, those unearthly green eyes searching out answers, trying so hard to understand just what had happened to her life, tearing right through his pretenses and seeing him for the fool and the coward he truly was.

You are not a weapon, June.

All the feeling drained from Taein's body. He stood a dead man pinned against the wall and saw June in his mind's eye. Felt the way she made the earth shake, the struggling joy in her tiny, muted laughs, felt the pain and hate and fear and that tiny, desperate *hope* with which she looked at the world, somehow still alive within her no matter what they weathered through, no matter how hard Taein tried to discourage it.

You are a gift.

Taein's breath caught as he flicked his lit cigarette away, the wind pulling hard at his back. Rain continued to patter down through the hole in the ceiling as he looked Vasily in the eye. The hunter stalked ever closer, his good nature shedding with every step he took, that thin princely guise slipping off to reveal the predator beneath. His broadsword gleamed bright and savage in the gray morning light, and Taein thought about how it had fallen in its lethal arc after each of his brothers, all those years ago. Thought of the deep cuts still slowly healing on June's little frame.

There is no other way.

Taein's heart shuddered in his chest. There were no safe places for a man like him. He'd had his chance, and he squandered it.

But for June. For her, he would make a safe place. For her, he would live.

Taein whirled just as Vasily lunged and threw a leg over the ledge. He pushed off of the window and just barely felt his stomach drop as his body went weightless, when—

—all the air left his lungs in one swift *whoosh*. Vasily caught him by the collar, hauled him back into the attic, and slammed him back onto the floor with an astounding savagery Taein hadn't thought he still possessed. Stars flashed in his eyes and he rolled left just as the hunter's broadsword bit into the floor where his head had been and lodged there. Taein got to his feet and threw himself onto Vasily before the hunter could rip his sword from the floor. Taein punched Vasily in the face and scrabbled for the knife at the hunter's hip. His fingers barely grazed the hilt before Vasily threw him off, but Taein still had his sticky thief fingers and a touch held true. He slammed back into the floor with the knife in hand, got back up in time to get out of the way of a sword stroke meant to spill his guts, and kept moving around the hole. Vasily was blocking the window, so that left the ladder.

The sky began to pour harder. Taein kept scrambling and Vasily kept after him. He could barely see with the amount of adrenaline coursing through his body. The world was coming at him in shuddering bursts of motion.

He'd just taken ahold of the ladder when the attic floor gave way with a *crack*. A bolt of lightning broke the sky in two with a flash of brilliant light as the floor collapsed and the remaining roof along with it, exposing the shack to the whole of the crying sky.

That weightless kiss of air Taein wanted from the window escape now came in a rain-streaked blur. Only for a moment. He smacked against a rotting countertop before slapping face-first into the rocky bed of the stream.

After that, just dark.

❧ 64 ❧

MONSTER WAKING

Lightning cracked, bleached the world white, and broke it apart.

Vasily tumbled through open space and crashed into the stream. He felt his mouth part as he screamed. The sound was so far away. Darkness descended to eat his consciousness whole, only to be swiftly beaten back.

Something else prevailed. Shocked his eyes open, infused his limbs with that old familiar rage. Something stronger than pain. Something stronger than the weakness of his heart.

Rain caressed Vasily's cheeks as the monster inside finally woke up.

❧ 65 ❧

THE GRAVE

Facedown. Bright lights. Water holding him like a child.

Taein tried to suck in air on reflex and only received a gush of water straight to the lungs. He reared up, coughing up and choking and scratching at his throat, before pain knocked his body right back down. He clutched his throat, his head only a few inches below the stream's surface, eyes wide open. The world was just a flare of white above the dark and rippling surface. The water was closed around him like a silver, rippling coffin. The knife was still clutched in his other hand, but what good would it do him now?

Moving colors, bright lights in the back of his eyes.

Get up.

The water was like a kiss. His eyelids fluttered, their weight suddenly too heavy to bear. He let go of the knife.

Get up.

Taein's head hurt something terrible. The world above was getting further away, dappled by the pouring rain. He could barely feel his hand at his throat, clawing for air. He could glimpse a shape struggling.

Get. Up.

Taein's eyes were almost shut when a different sort of darkness shadowed the world above. Growing fast. Falling at him, like the sky

438

had snapped the threads by which Geiin had once sewn it onto the heavens, detached, and was racing down to crush him.

The support beam.

Animal instinct sent Taein thrashing to the side just in time to escape the beam as it crashed down, taking most of the second floor with it and sending chunks of wood splintering everywhere. He struggled onto his hands and knees and crawled, dodging pieces of floorboards and hunks of moss and shards of glass. The raining debris nicked and slashed at his face and hands. He got up, tripped on a rock in the water, got up, and fell again. This time he stayed down, crawling until he'd taken shelter beneath the table, which was still somehow set with its chipped tableware. He hugged his knees to his chest and tried to catch his breath as he hacked up more water, barely able to see over the wall of rubble the support beam had created between him and Vasily.

A few long seconds passed. Taein heaved in breath after breath, head spinning and blood trickling down his forehead from where he'd bashed his head, every inch of his body throbbing. The only sounds were the downpour and the groaning of the shack as it fell apart.

Then—just as Taein began to hope that maybe, just *maybe*, Vasily had been crushed in the roof's collapse, he caught sight of the hunter's silhouette rising up through the wreckage. Taein could make out the set of his shoulders and head above the divide. Vasily seemed dazed, lurching around, head swiveling. He faced the pile and started rooting around. Taein took the opportunity and slunk toward the back door that stood by the shack's kitchen-space.

Sparks rained from the ceiling as another bolt of lightning slammed into the shack. The walls around them were beginning to crumble when Vasily spoke.

"I thought you wanted it to be over, Glass!" he bellowed.

Taein kept quiet, kept dragging himself sloshing through the stream. What felt like a thousand miles of detritus, overturned work tables, and scattered hunting paraphernalia lay between him and survival.

"I thought you understood!"

"I changed my mind, shanker," Taein hissed under his breath as he crawled over the snapped pieces of a workbench.

"*Love conquers all, Glass!*" Vasily shouted. Taein doubled his speed as Vasily clawed and crashed his way through the wall of wreckage, suddenly aware that the hunter wasn't looking for anything but a way through. "I will conquer you!"

Taein made it onto his feet and started dodging obstacles in a fast-shambling hurry. He wasn't angry. He wasn't sad. He was shanking *terrified*. And that was good, because terror was what had kept Taein Glass alive for the last ten years, and he was sure terror is what would keep him alive now.

And maybe it would've, if the blood dripping into his eyes hadn't half-blinded him to the boulder sitting just a few precious steps before the door. Taein tripped and fell knee-first onto an overturned board, and a rust-eaten nail longer than his index finger gored straight through his kneecap. A scream he hardly registered as his own ripped through the shack as pain went cracking and blistering through his knee.

Taein heaved in a breath and punched the floor, tears streaking down his cheeks as more blood laced from his forehead into his eyes. He tried to stand and couldn't. His knee was refusing to move, to straighten. He made another frantic attempt to get up, pale lights flashing in his eyes, certain that at any second Vasily's sword was going to lop his head off, and instead just caused himself so much pain the world darkened at the edges. He collapsed back down, snapping the board, rolled onto his back, and ripped the nail out.

His knee made the ugliest sound he'd ever heard. Another scream. His world dimmed dark at the edges. Blood in his mouth. Was there any part of him that wasn't bleeding?

Taein focused on breathing as his stomach turned, and tried to listen above the cries of the disintegrating shack. The sound of Vasily ripping through the debris was gone. It was too quiet. He dragged himself to the back door, turned the handle, and pulled.

And the door didn't budge.

Taein threw his entire weight against the exit, hammered himself against it. It didn't move a hair, blocked shut by something outside. He slumped down, his heart hammering so hard he thought it might burst, and waited.

Then—there. A figure looming. Vasily was separated from Taein now by only a few destroyed work benches. No broadsword in his hand, instead he'd picked up one of the corroded butcher's cleavers, and was staring Taein down with a certain disbelief.

"Nuest told me you were dangerous," Vasily said, "but I have yet to strike you and you've already broken *yourself*. I heard the sound your knee just made."

"*Shut up,*" Taein croaked, dragging himself backward and using the wall to shove himself back onto his feet, almost buckling back over as soon as his weight even hinted at resting on his newly-ruined knee.

"There is no conceivable way you'll escape me. Not with what you've just done to yourself."

Blood trickled from Taein's mouth. "But that's the thing," he said as he spat, "nobody shanks me up more than myself, and yet here I am, *still alive,* after all these years. Do you think I can even die, at this point? Much less fight fair? I don't even know how!"

Vasily smiled tightly. "You scorn my honor again, Prince of Glass, but it's the only thing keeping you alive."

"Right now your precious honor is just wasting my time," Taein said, "so let's finish this."

"Very well." He stepped forward and Taein clocked him with a rock and *moved*.

He shut away the pain in his leg and darted along the wall and into the area of the shack that had presumably once served as a kitchen. Sheets of rain hammered the shack as he threw open the cabinets lining the wall and middle counter space, ripping out pots and pans and hurling them at Vasily. Taein hobbled over and around wreckage, trying to make it back to the front door which he *knew* would open. He swiped a long fileting knife and chucked that at Vasily, too, then threw himself over a table. He landed hard on his punctured knee and collapsed for the spans of a breath before he was back and in maddened motion.

He *had* to get back to June.

Taein had just about hurled every kind of rusty knife and corroded tool at Vasily before the hunter caught up again. Vasily shoved Taein forward and he fell over a chair, rolled, and crawled away. Taein made it to his feet just in time to clock Vasily with a rock. But Vasily just shrugged it off and when Taein feinted left, Vasily blocked him with a swing of his cleaver. The blade skimmed the side of Taein's arm, and his mind scrambled for a solution. Vasily's cleaver bit into the side of his good leg, and Taein found an answer.

Rather, he found a *stupid* answer, but he'd never been one to think twice before, and he certainly wasn't about to change now. Because he was *still* Taein Glass, after all. And learning from mistakes would never, *ever* be his specialty.

Taein stopped backpedaling and launched himself at Vasily. He grabbed the arm with which Vasily held his cleaver and bit down as hard as he could. Vasily snarled, dropping the weapon on reflex, and punched Taein's face. Taein wasn't sure whose blood went splattering across his vision. Vasily threw Taein off and he doubled over, his knee almost giving out again.

Vasily whirled, blood gushing from his arm as he looked for the cleaver. Behind him was that same chair Taein had tripped over. Taein threw himself at Vasily, knocking the hunter over the chair and onto his back in the water. He clamped his hands around Vasily's neck and slammed his head down. The stream was shallow here, but it was enough. Vasily's head barely dipped under as he clawed at Taein's face, his eyes wild beneath the churning water. But Taein was half Vasily's weight, and in a matter of seconds Vasily breached the surface, got into a choking breath of air, and threw Taein across the stream.

Suddenly they were both wallowing like wounded animals through the stream, Taein scrambling for the door, Vasily right behind him. Vasily grabbed ahold of one of Taein's boots and yanked back.

It was the foot attached to his newly-shredded knee. Vasily dragged him closer and Taein screamed so hard his throat stung as his knee shattered even further. Vasily flipped Taein over, straddled him, and this time it was *Taein* who was getting the life choked out of him, it was *Taein* whose head was dipping underwater. He started drowning, unable to make out Vasily's face through the filthy rushing water. Vasily pinned one of his flailing arms, just one hand on Taein's throat. It was more than sufficient to choke the life out of him. Taein kept scrabbling with his free arm, but the world was dimming, getting darker and darker by the second. Vasily's shape was blurring by the second. Taein's eyes slipped shut, burned by the water, tired of staying open. His arm went limp, fell to the side. Grazed something sharp.

Sharp.

Taein's eyes snapped open. His body seized with desperate hope. The edge of a blade slit his fingertips—it was the cleaver Vasily dropped. Taein curled his stiffening fingers around the hilt, drug it closer, and then *swung*.

The cleaver buried itself in Vasily's arm and the pressure on Taein's throat vanished. Taein reared up, vomiting water, nose burning, vision swirling, and crawled frantically away. He threw up blood and water again, and clambered slowly to his feet.

Taein turned. Why was Vasily even allowing him to stand? But the hunter was still on his knees in the stream, blood gushing profusely from his upper bicep as he desperately tried to hold pressure on the wound.

Taein stared at Vasily, hardly able to stay on his feet, and suddenly got very, *very angry*.

He lunged at Vasily with a feral scream and knocked him on his back. Vasily's head hit the bed of the stream hard and he made an odd noise, hardly fought back. Taein just started beating his face in.

Blow after blow. His knuckles split open. Blood and spittle fell from his mouth as the shack continued to crumble. Lightning seared the air and rain poured down, washing the world in blood and water. No feat of nature could falter Taein's sudden, vicious, long-coming hate.

He was going to kill Vasily. Taein was going to kill the hunter, and then it would be *over*.

He took the butcher's cleaver back up, Vasily's face turned black and blue, his eyes swollen shut. Taein raised the blade over his head, screaming in a language he didn't know, and was just about to hack Vasily's face apart when a glimpse of pink caught his eye. He froze, the cleaver hovering in mid air, and looked with horror back at *June,* who was standing in the doorway he'd been trying so hard to reach, her mouth poised in a shocked *o*, her eyes filled with tears and hands clenched in fists at her sides.

June.

Just like that, the cleaver toppled from Taein's hands and splashed uselessly into the stream.

"June, wait—" Taein tried, but June's green eyes had gone a flat and terrible black, her hair hanging drenched into her face, dirt on her cheeks, a wordless cry clenched between her teeth. Before Taein could say another word, she bent and touched the earth.

The world convulsed and Taein found himself sailing through air again and smacking into the rubble. Thorny blackberry stalks jutted from the earth before he could get back to his feet and wrapped tight around his frame. His vision spun as the thorns bit into his skin. It was all he could do to watch, while bright lights flashed behind his eyes and his mind grew dim, as June stepped slowly into the collapsing house toward Vasily.

Lightning shocked the gray sky again. The hunter lay totally concussed where Taein had beaten him, the stream pulling ribbons of blood from his broad, broken frame as it flowed away from him. Vasily didn't move when June crept toward him.

"No!" Taein shouted, his voice swept away by a clap of thunder.

June looked his way for but a moment, rain and tears dripping down her face, before turning her back to Taein. She sank down on her knees in the stream and raised something over her head—not the rusted cleaver. The emerald-crusted dagger Regor had given her. The dagger Taein didn't know she still had. Polished steel glinted in the downpour.

Taein threw himself against the blackberries, thorns tearing at his arms, his legs. He watched the kid hesitate and suddenly all he could see was himself ten years ago, huddled under the bows of a snow-heavy fir, knees clutched to his chest and hunger clawing apart his belly as he waited for Ruein to come back. Waiting for someone to save him from the life that lay waiting.

But no one ever came, and his path led to a city that swallowed him whole, and bit by bit, Taein Glass became the coward, thief, and *monster* he was always meant to be—but not a heartless one.

If the kid killed Vasily, Taein knew what would follow. He knew where this path led, because no one ever came to save him all those years ago beneath the fir tree. But the suffering that followed wasn't without purpose. His suffering made him a man strong enough to fulfill a purpose, strong enough to save *her*.

"No!" Taein screamed as he thrashed against the thorns, the harsh copper smell of his own blood growing heavier in the air.

He had to get free. He was the monster, he was the curse, he was the one left alive to finish this once and for all and die trying, *not her*.

"June!"

But Taein's voice was erased again, this time by another crack of pure, blistering energy. Taein's hearing snapped out as the shack split once and for all, brought down by a bolt of white light. It was brighter than the sun. It ate the whole of the world.

Yet again, Taein felt the sensation of flying before the world was swallowed by total darkness.

HE LAY IN THE DARK FOR A LONG, LONG TIME, BEFORE SOMETHING —intangible, unwavering—pushed him back into the world of the living.

Just as always.

Taein woke up to a clearing grey sky as the wind pushed the purple thunderheads east in a hurry. His body was covered in debris—broken wood, shattered clay, dirt and muck. Blood oozed from his head, stung his eyes. He couldn't feel his legs. Not his arms, either. All the hate had dissipated from his body like a morning fog, leaving emptiness in its place.

His head lolled on his shoulders as he searched for the kid. A glimpse of pink—there. She'd been thrown a good ways away from the shack and was crumpled in the stream. Taein sucked in a deep breath, tried to say her name. He couldn't make out a single word.

He groaned, fought the feeling back into his hands, then his arms. Dragged his limbs around to shove off chunks of plaster, pieces of flooring. Found his way clawing and climbing up onto his one good leg. There wasn't a single sensation in his other.

Step by step. The world was a dark narrow tunnel pulling him to her. He paused at the edge of the rubble and looked back only once.

If the hunter had survived the lightning strike, he was buried alive in the wreckage. Taein was not strong enough to root around and find out—he needed help. He needed help *now*.

Taein found June a few paces away from the wreckage, the dagger still clutched in her hand. She was unconscious, soaked from the stream and covered in little gashes and cuts. He sunk down, navigated her into his arms, and fought to stand again. Wrenched the dagger from her grip and left it in the dirt where it belonged.

Back to camp. Help. He clutched the kid in his trembling arms and limped away.

Help.

Taein was bleeding in ways that no man could sustain for long, but he had a job to do. The path ahead had to be finished, before all this blood like water ran out and the grave closed over him at last.

❧ 66 ❧

THE FAILURE

There is a place men go to, when pain has eaten all other things.

There is a hole that arises in such moments, when you have succumbed to your agony. When all the blood has been spilled, all your resolve gone with it. You have sweated out your life. You have wielded the white sword of defiance against the great Reaper, and been found wanting.

You are just a man. And the tide of life has beaten you.

This place, this in-between, is where one meets the animal inside. This is where a man decides just who he is going to be, if the Celestials find it amusing to allow him reentrance to the world of the living.

It is a rare privilege, granted to few. This resetting that comes up in a place between life and death, governed by those beings of stars and light and immaculateness. And who really can understand their ways? Their plans are fickle and odd and careless, to the minds of men. Yet their plans are always true. Yet their plans are always, somehow, good.

We know the plans of the Celestial are good because we cannot understand them. We know their ways are pure, because they cannot be fathomed. Surely anything set beyond the understanding of men is holy enough to be good.

Yet how fickle it all seems—this place where men go when their pain has drowned them. This moment of divine reckoning. This gift to choose again. To be reborn.

For some reason, Vasily of House Slate, murderer, war-bringer, son, brother, and king, was granted such privilege. And while he did wake up to face himself again, he did not choose shadow or soul.

He did not choose at all. And in that, he chose both.

When Vasily drifted back to consciousness, he knew he was alone.

For days since he found the black stallion, he'd felt Glass' presence in his heart like a beacon to guide him. He felt Glass' fear, stronger than any feeling he'd ever felt before, stronger even than Vasily's own hate.

Vasily had followed that fear deep into the fabled treachery of the Oldswood and all the way to the hunting shack, where he made up his mind to give this Prince of Glass the honor he never even considered offering to his brothers. He wanted to look Glass in the eye before he killed him. He wanted Glass to know. That even with all the hate, all the malice, all the *loss*, his death had a purpose. That it was the only way to fix things, the only way for Vasily to regain peace. To make things right. He wanted—he *needed*—Glass to understand. He needed Glass to forgive him for it, before the deed could be done.

That was his first mistake. Looking for forgiveness where there was none to be found.

Vasily tried to open his eyes. Only one cracked open, just barely. The world was a dark blur. He was still in the stream, the hunting shack a smoking, blackened heap all around and all over him, laid out on his back with his head barely above water. Dirt and boards covered every inch of his body. Somewhere above the debris he caught a glimpse of the dark night sky, dotted with a trillion tiny white stars.

Night. How long had he been out?

Vasily forced his frozen muscles to stir, shoving off pieces of shattered cabinetry, his limbs barely responding. The water was a cocoon of ice all around, tugging back at his every move as he struggled up. His head pounded so hard it felt as if his brain might burst inside his skull. Perhaps it already had. The only thing that felt truly real was the cuff on his wrist. The silver was so cold it burned.

He groaned, feeling for the gash Glass had rent into his bicep. The bleeding had slowed immensely, thanks to the chill of the water, but blood still oozed through his fingers. Vasily climbed gingerly onto his feet, his legs aching but still sturdy, and stumbled out of the stream. He got a few paces away from the rubble before sinking down on the riverbank. A glimmer caught his eye. He lifted an emerald-crusted dagger from the silt.

Glass hadn't brandished such a weapon, had he? Pieces of the fight came back in little fractured moments, but he didn't recall such a fine blade.

No matter. Vasily slipped it into his belt. Tried to whistle for his mare and found he couldn't. His face was too swollen to move.

Vasily hissed in pain as he tore a strip of fabric from his shirt to tourniquet his arm. If his first mistake was offering Glass decency, his second mistake was expecting Glass to be finished after the bastard shattered his own knee. But *any* man should've been finished after suffering a wound such as that. How did he keep going?

Just the same as I, after Babas died.

Vasily forced himself back onto his feet with a growl. He waited for a rush of rage to propel him forward that didn't come.

He took a few staggering steps before his legs gave out and he was forced to brace himself against a mossy rock, chest heaving with the effort.

He was still so weak from the sickness, from his brawl with the Enti commander. And now with all this new bleeding... his body was shutting down again. He couldn't afford more days of rest. Glass had gotten away, yes, but there was only so far he could go on a shattered leg. Vasily was weak, but he knew Glass was weaker. All he had to do was carry on just a little further and then he could truly rest for the first time in a decade. And it would be over.

Vasily clambered onto his feet and pointed himself toward where he left the horses, praying Glass hadn't found them first.

The horses were just as Vasily left them, his bay ground tied and the black too busy pestering her to wander off. Vasily struggled up onto his mare, his body protesting every motion, and took up the stallion's lead rope.

Help me, father, he prayed. *Give me the strength to finish this.*

Vasily waited a minute, looking for some sort of resolve, perhaps even hope. He glanced up at the deepening sky. The rain was gone and a clear inky darkness stretched out all around. But the moon was hidden and Babas was far away, and Vasily was left feeling the same old emptiness.

He spurred his mare forward, clutching the saddle horn as her every step sent waves of pain crescendoing through his body. He was failing Babas. His father would never speak to him until it was finished. He was even failing his sweet Mari. What would she say, if she could see him now?

I will not fail you again.

Vasily pressed his hand to his bicep. His palm came away glistening red again.

No hesitation, not this time. No honor for a creature that couldn't even comprehend the meaning of it. If he had to kill every last ounce of weakness inside himself, he would. It was the boy inside of him that questioned. It was the *boy* inside, cringing at what needed to be done.

Weakness. Vasily gripped the reins tighter, booted his mare into a canter. Disgust and dread roiled in his stomach even as he forced himself to find resolve. He would burn himself on the altar of his father. Make a stronger man out of the ashes.

I will bring you honor, Babas, or nothing at all.

❦ 67 ❦

OUR BEST DAYS

There was a day in Vince's mid-twenties, a good day. The best day.

He and Jeaney were in that happy stage of a romance—everything was new, their respective flaws no more bothersome than a fly easily brushed away. The days were warm despite the autumn storm clouds that'd taken residence above the Pearl. The sun was golden up there somewhere behind the clouds. There was a world out there beyond the city where things were green and people were happy, and Vince and Jeaney lived there together even in the mucky midst of the Keenween District.

It's amazing, what love can do. The places it takes you.

The best day started like any other September day; Vince picked Jeaney up from the cramped stoop of her little shack in Regor's square, and hand-in-hand they headed out for their day's assignments: Vince had a couple beatings of higher-ups to take care of, and Jeaney was to come along with him to patch the victims up afterward. Regor didn't want them dead, exactly, he just wanted them scared, and that was Jeaney's job in their terrible business: she was a healer of the old ways, a practitioner of old-world magics, and that made her very unpopular with the regular, magic-scoffing blokes of the Shardain District she

451

grew up amongst. But Jeaney was good for quick stitches if Vince's rings cut a little too deep, good for bringing the lights back on if Vince knocked them out a little too hard. They were an excellent team, and made excellent marks at it.

But instead of singling out their pigeons for the day or asking to practice another tattoo on him, Jeaney turned to Vince with those devastating green eyes of hers and smiled her devastating crooked smile.

"What if we go on a little adventure today?"

"Shouldn't we get this done first? Regor—"

Jeaney scoffed. "Regor-shmeegor. The day is young. I want to show you something."

So she took Vince by the hand, hers so soft in his own, and led him crossing side-streets and cutting down alleys toward the better part of town. Vince followed. What else could he do? If she told him to jump from Shrine's Tower or throw all his rings into the city dump or swim in the canals, he would've. That was how he loved her then: with the death of himself, without qualms or questions. She was his world, plain and simple. That was how he always should've loved her.

Their trek ended at an old granary on the edge of the city walls that'd burned out the spring before. One of the mill towers was half-way standing, and Jeaney led him climbing, crawling, and shimmying through the wreckage to get to the top.

They stood at the very top, the tower so high it swayed in the wind, and there it was—just out a small, narrow window was the countryside of Nown Jin, rising and rolling and slanting ever on down toward the green oasis of Ersii, cut through by the broad watery gash that was the River of Coins. Just beyond the last stretch of land, following the flow of the river, was a distant silver shimmer. A glimpse of the sea.

Jeaney tucked herself into Vince's embrace, looked up at him. Her cheeks had a dusting of freckles beneath the scald of dirt and smog the Pearl plastered onto everyone's faces. Those freckles made her look so innocent compared to the washed-out haze that bleached the life from everyone else their age. Jeaney was one of the few girls that wasn't high or boozed out of her brains or hazed to death by drumweed. She didn't even smoke. Her eyes were the same every day: never blurred, never darkened. Her eyes were clear and green like the hills of the better world beyond the city. Those eyes felt like the only spot of innocence in all the world. Those eyes felt like hope.

"Let's go to the sea," Jeaney said.

"Tomorrow?" Vince asked, even though neither of them had horses to their name and they both had work for all the foreseeable days in the foreseeable forever.

"Tomorrow."

Vince kissed the top of her head. "We'll go. I promise."

Vince barely remembered the view anymore, could barely remember how he'd seen the world through that golden-yellow haze of first love. But he remembered Jeaney's hand in his own like it was still there. The feel of her beside him: there, anything was possible, and the future was their own, and there were endless new things to be learned about each other and treasured for life. The little bad things—like Kassie's sickness, her treatments binding Vince to Regor and all Regor's endless bloody jobs, or Jeaney's restlessness, her ill-fitting in a city of violence in which she was the only spot of sunlight to ever make it through the clouds—all these things were just flies. Things to be brushed off. Things to be conquered tomorrow.

Well, not tomorrow. They had an ocean to see. A happy day ahead. The best day.

But the seaside never came, and the years crawled by and took with them all the reasons they worked and made monsters out of the reasons they didn't. Jeaney got tired of waiting for their best day to come and left to find it on her own. That September day at the top of the granary became Vince's best day; not because anything especially perfect or divine had happened, but because it was *theirs*, and it was full of endless possibilities, and they had everything ahead and not a thing in the world to lose, except each other.

And in those happy golden days of early love, 'losing each other' is something that will never happen, because it only ever happens to people who can't work things out, to people who can't come together and make a future that's good for two. Better days—best days—were always just ahead.

But all those years ago atop the granary tower, they were just kids.

Vince kissed Jeaney in the light of the little window, the outside world but a painting hung in their little burned-out palace, all the 'need-to's' a blur in the back of his mind. Vince kissed her, held her close, felt her hand in his own, and knew that *this,* his very own place of innocence— this was forever, and everything would be alright, and nothing in the world could separate them. They would head north to the seaside tomorrow, and losing each other was a thing that only ever happened to other people, to quitters. It was a thing Vince and Jeaney were safe from. It could never come to pass.

Until it did.

When Vince awoke the first time, the sun was just creeping over the horizon, and Taein was gone.

Vince stared at the empty spot where Taein had previously nestled himself, blinked twice, and decided Taein probably just went on one of those personal walks he was always taking.

As if we don't do enough walking these days, the idiot.

And Vince fell back asleep without another thought, a pile of dense moss and a rolled-up saddle blanket making for an excellent pillow.

When Vince awoke the second time, the sun was high in the sky, the birds loud and chirping, Depheche's *Eighth Symphony* playing on a lazy loop in his head, and Taein was *still* gone. And then Vince realized that June was gone, too.

It was then that Vince began to worry. He shook his head and rose, peering about the clearing. Where the hell was he? He woke Ka-el up in a hurry, packed up all there things, and had just headed out of their little knoll and down the trail when Taein himself came staggering up on one leg, soaked in water and blood and looking thoroughly trashed, with the kid clinging at his side and clutching his coat like the earth might swallow him if she let go.

"What the sweet hell happened *now?*" Vince said, hurrying over just in time to catch Taein as his mangled leg gave out.

Taein stiffened as soon as he fell into Vince's arms and shoved him away, only to crumpled back down like a squashed leaf. Vince rolled his eyes and bent to haul Taein back to his feet.

"Taein. If it's even possible, stop being difficult and talk."

"What's going on?" Ka-el hissed from behind Vince.

Taein shook his head, his face white. "Hunter," he rasped, pushing Vince away again and started hobbling down the trail. "We gotta go."

A rock settled in Vince's stomach. "He got to you?"

Taein dragged a battered hand through his ragged hair. June was still clinging at his side, hanging onto Taein's coat with a death grip. "No, Vincent, I fell off a cliff."

Vince blinked, expecting a surge of adrenaline or desperation. Instead, he found himself getting *mad*.

"Oh, you just *had* to wander off," he snapped. "You *idiot*! You knew he was close!"

"C'mon, I need you to help me. And thanks for making sure the shankin' kid didn't wander off, by the way," Taein hissed, stooping below a low-hanging branch.

"Sorry," Vince, following close behind, stepped on said low-hanging branch and snapped in two. Taein flinched at the noise and looked back to glare before dropping his gaze onto Ka-el, who was still hiding behind Vince.

"And you weren't any help, Ka-el," Taein said. "Sleeping as well?"

Ka-el scoffed. "No."

Taein stopped short, then slowly turned back around. "So you just *let her go?*"

Ka-el glared back. "Well, it's not as if I'm keen on keeping her around, Taein. One would think you'd have realized that by now—"

Taein lurched a step closer and Vince reached out to hold him back. "Easy, boss."

"She could've gotten killed, asshole," Taein whisper-shouted. "Or me, for that matter! Some of us actually *enjoy* staying alive."

Ka-el flushed red and stammered before turning his gaze up to Vince. "And have very important things to live for, evidently."

And that was it. Vince officially had enough. Before he could take a deep breath and consider, he threw a punch and Ka-el was on his ass in the dirt.

"I *told* you," Vince growled, squatting down to shove Ka-el onto his back the second the tracker tried to scramble onto his feet, a massive bruise already beginning to flower on the right side of his face. "I told you, Ka-el. Trashed. You leave my sister outta this."

"Brawl later," Taein said. "We seriously need to finish this. He's dead, but—"

June smacked Taein. The scrapper fell silent, looking down at her. "What?"

She shook her head, then signed slowly, repeating her motions until they all understood.

He's still coming.

Taein just stared at the kid, his shoulders slumping lower and lower, a look deeper than exhaustion settling on his features.

"Are you sure?" he said quietly.

Hate bleached all the youth out of June's features. *The earth is crying to me.*

It was quiet in their camp for a long time before Taein slowly turned back to Vince.

"We need to go," was all he said.

Vince turned around, mad and without his breakfast and tired of being worried and confused and lost. And maybe that's what finally did it, maybe he just finally surpassed his tolerance of their sweet *hell* of a journey. Or maybe it was the bloodless white of Taein's bruised face, or his mangled, blood-soaked leg, or the wild-eyed kid glued to his side. But whatever it was, it rammed into the dam Vince had built up around all that pent-up guilt and washed it right out, and before he knew it, out spilled the terrible truth.

"Dammit, Taein," Vince heard himself say, "I sold you out."

Taein stilled, his eyes going completely blank. The world went silent. Taein blinked, still looking Vince right in the eyes with that hollowed-out stare, and sweat began to pour down Vince's face.

Oh, sweet Geiin.

"You *what?*" Taein hissed, a hint of red flaring in his pallid cheeks.

Vince scrambled. "I'm sorry. It was a few months after the accident with that stupid diplomat and the door and I was broke and I *needed* the money—"

Taein's eyes narrowed as he bristled. "*That's* why you wouldn't let me ditch the kid. Not because you're some saint but because you're a guilty son of a bitch! Because *you* put the bastard on my trail and *she*," Taein stabbed his finger at the kid, "got caught up in the shitstorm!"

Vince wrung his hands, his heart in his throat. "Taein, I'm so sorry. I never meant for this, I–I never thought anything would come of it."

Taein gaped. "How did it even happen?"

"An old man asked if I knew any Siou."

Taein's brows flew up. "And that didn't tip you off as maybe just *maybe* even a *tiny bit* suspicious?"

Vince shrugged. "All I was really thinkin' about was my bills."

"Your *bills*. You're shitting me, *your bills!* And I'm sure a big old dinner at Kaljen's was also the last thing on your mind! What'd you get, the crab platter? Torta's Special? Extra lamb sauce on the shankin' side?"

"No, but I did get—"

"I knew it. *I knew it,* I..." Taein drew off, choking on words as he fisted his hands in his hair.

"I'm sorry, Taein." It was all Vince could think to say. "Suppose I wasn't really thinkin' much at all, was I?"

Taein stared at him for a terrible moment before Ka-el broke out in a burst of hoarse laughter.

"This is a hoot, you know that?" Ka-el said, clutching his pack with white knuckles. "You two are going to get us all killed!"

Taein was still staring at Vince when he turned back to face him.

"You know what, Vince?" Taein said softly. "I don't care. All that matters now is we move."

Vince rubbed the back of his neck. "I'm still sorry, though."

"Then help me. I–" Taein looked down at his blood-soaked leg as a little more color drained from his face. "I think I just royally shanked myself over for the last time."

Vince's stomach clenched just looking at the mangled leg, held together by only a dirty strip of fabric. He looked back up at Taein and steeled himself. "What do you need?"

Taein collapsed down on the side of their tiny make-shift trail and set about fashioning two sticks into a brace. June sat down next to him, her eyes glued to the ground. She seemed almost oblivious of them, her mind a million miles away. The Oldswood oaks loomed overhead, their dense canopy seeming to reach down and wait for their plan.

"Somebody's got to stay and meet Vasily head on," Taein said, "because we're sure as hell not outrunning him. I'll— "

"I'll do it," Vince said without another thought.

Taein scoffed. "Vince, I'm half-dead already. You take her to House Light, and I'll finish this."

"No dice. Ka-el can lead you the rest of the way out and to House Light. He knows the best shortcuts."

"*No—*" Ka-el and Taein both in unison.

Vince silenced them with another shake of his head and bent to grasp Taein by the shoulder. "Just look after her for me, alright? My kid sister."

"Look after her yourself—"

June cut Taein off, tugging sharply on his sleeve.

You come with me, she signed.

Taein blinked. "June, I'm no use to you anymore."

Vince felt a lump form in his throat. June stared at Taein, shook her head, and signed again.

But I need you.

Taein looked up at Vince, then back to the kid.

"I'm not going to make it," he said simply. He pointed to his leg. "I'm all shanked up."

June looked between Taein and his bloody leg. A splintering look of outright terror crossed her face. She shook her head violently.

You have to come with me. She said, *You have to help me fix things.*

"*Fix* things? Listen, kid," Taein began, but June had closed her eyes tight.

A moment passed, and then she reached out and rested a hand on the sticks Taein had just fashioned a crude brace out of. Her brow tightened, a pulse of light flared, and the sticks were suddenly run through by threads of pale, luminous green. They sprung new shoots which turned to flexible young branches that knit across Taein's leg, pulling tight where pressure was needed, forming strength where Taein had none.

June couldn't mend his leg. But she made him a cocoon to protect it, to see the journey done.

Vince's eyes had grown quite watery by the time June opened her eyes again and surveyed her work.

There, she signed. *No excuses now.*

Taein stared at the cast around his shredded leg, then looked at June. He struggled to say something before turning glassy eyes onto Vince.

"I'm not asking you to do this," he said.

Vince shook his head. "No, you didn't. But I'm gonna, all the same."

And to Vince's utter surprise, Taein stood up and hugged him.

Heat pricked behind Vince's eyes and he hugged Taein right back, and when he saw Taein was shaking, he held on a little tighter.

"Thank you," Taein said as he pulled away, his voice all choked up. "For everything."

Vince nodded. "Just get her there for me."

Taein hastily wiped his nose on his sleeve. "Don't get all sappy on me, old man, you'll be right behind us."

"Sure thing," Vince said.

Taein nodded, looking away as his eyes became suspiciously wet. Vince turned to June. He took the kid's hand and guided her over to Taein, then pressed her little palm into Taein's own gloved one.

Taein looked sharply at Vince and tried to rip his hand away, but Vince kept it closed tight over the kid's.

"Look at me, boss," Vince said.

Taein, his entire body gone stiff, looked begrudgingly up. His eyes had gone dark again, still glossy with tears he was too stubborn to let fall.

"You ain't gonna hurt her, because that's not who you are." Taein opened his mouth to argue and Vince didn't give him the chance. "That ain't who you are. Not anymore. You're a dirty rotten scoundrel, and you're always gonna be. But you're not a coward. Not even just a survivor. You're the guy who saves people."

At that moment, ten years slipped off of Taein's face, and he looked incredibly small in front of Vince. He was a little boy again, just for a moment, staring up at Vince as if he held all the answers.

"But Vince, I can't even save myself."

Vince faltered. No one had ever looked at him like that besides Kassie, and the truth was he never had the answers, not even for his own wasted life, and he never really had any idea what to say. But he drew in a deep breath and gave Taein a smile.

"You don't have to. You just have to save her."

Taein, tight lipped and wavering, gave a nod. A haze passed over his face as Vince watched him try to sort out just how the hell he could pull off this feat set before him, and in an instant, just as it had melted away, all the years came back and hardened his face.

"You're gonna be just fine, boss. Don't worry about it." Vince said, which felt right to say even though they both knew it was a lie. He then looked down at June, who stood slump-shouldered and gloomy next to Taein, looking between them with those big green misgiving eyes. Vince ruffled her hair and that little smile crept back onto her dirty cheeks.

"Be a good girl, will you? But not too good, or else life won't be any fun."

I will not be good, she signed. *Goodbye—*

"None of that now," Vince said, his throat gone suddenly tight. "Let's say 'see you later' instead."

June nodded and signed it back. *See you later, Giant.*

Then Vince gave Taein a nudge and the thief turned, still hand-in-hand with the kid, and slowly limped away into the woods.

Vince watched them go, his heart sinking, until Ka-el cleared his throat behind him and Vince remembered he existed.

The tracker was still hovering in his corner, looking at Vince with his brow tight. The question in his eyes was obvious.

Vince nodded after Taein. "Get going, Ka-el."

"You need back-up. This hunter is a real monster, isn't he?"

"I was always *your* backup, Ka-el. Since when do I ever need backup of my own?"

"Since you've gotten old."

"I ain't even that old," Vince grumbled. "Now get on with it."

Ka-el dragged himself onto his feet and followed after Taein, eyes on the dirt. He paused at the base of the little hill, his shoulders hunched tight, and looked back.

"Take care of yourself, Vincent," he said.

Vince nodded. "You too."

Ka-el turned and silently moved through the brush that Taein and June had disappeared into only minutes before, and Vince found himself alone in the forest.

He squared his shoulders, listening to the breeze moving through the trees and the distant sound of his group slipping away through the brush, and eased himself down against the cool dirt wall of the hollow to wait.

THE LAST STAND

In the end, Vince got to spend an hour strumming on his guitar before the hunter arrived.

Vince always thought he'd turn very regretful and reflective when facing down the end of his life, but nothing rested too heavy on his mind as he plucked a little tune. There was lots to feel sorry about, of course—he wished he would've left the Pearl with Jeaney, he wished he would've taken her to the sea and covered her with kisses in the salty warm air. He wished he'd submitted his journal of compositions to Callaga Hall for playing on the city orchestra instead of spending his life pounding people into the ground. He wished he would've found a way to get Kassie well, once and for all.

But really, who ever reached the end of the road without a list like that? Was there ever anyone who reached the end of their days without pining for one last kiss, one last walk about their favorite place, one last bite of their favorite food, one last *good day?* Who, really, ever got here and was *ready?* Vince didn't need to be ready, he didn't need to have done it all. He'd done his best, spent his time trying to do good in a world that scorned and swindled men like him, and that was enough. What good was fretting about it all now, when he had a perfectly amicable hour to spend in a perfectly amicable patch of forest with a guitar at hand?

A tremendous peace settled over him, all the way until the hunter himself dropped down into the clearing.

Vince had never met Vasily before, let alone any king, but he had met many murderers. When Vasily dropped down into the little clearing focused on Taein's blood-droop tracks, Vince knew his type.

He was a tall, broad-shouldered man, his frame obviously once muscular but now withered down to a battered husk, dressed in simple traveler's clothes and drenched in just as much blood as Taein, the only difference being Vasily was clutching at his shoulder and not gimping on a ruined leg, and his face was black, blue, and swollen almost beyond recognition as a human.

So focused was the hunter on Taein's tracks, he didn't even notice Vince sitting there until Vince announced himself.

"You lost, boss?"

Vasily didn't startle but instead looked up at him, his eyes a dark and dangerous black beneath all that swelling, his tangled hair cutting jagged across his gaze.

"Are you one of *his* companions?" The hunter asked in heavily accented Jinian.

Vince grinned, setting aside his guitar. "Sure am. Got any idea as to who?"

Vasily straightened, going to square his shoulders and trying to hide the way he flinched. "Should I?"

"Not unless you've stepped inside Pearl Jin. I'm Regor Snevets' best muscle."

"I'm sorry, but that means nothing to me, and I'm in a bit of a hurry."

Vince shook his head and stretched, a level calm settling over him like always when he sensed a fight brewing or saw a mark in a crowd. "Wouldn't rush off, if I were you."

"Do you intend to keep me here?"

"Oh, I very much do."

Vince watched a tension bleed into Vasily's frame. "Do you know who *I* am?" he asked, sizing Vince up.

Vince nodded.

"Then you understand my reputation."

Vince rose to his feet and cracked his neck, then his knuckles. "Sure do. But that's the thing about reputations. I find they're always overstated."

Vasily narrowed his eyes. "You may be surprised."

"Maybe. I'm not too old to find myself shocked now and then."

"And your companions never shocked you?"

"Nah. They're just people."

A hard glint leveled Vasily's gaze. "He's a monster. As is the child."

Vince shook his head, readying his stance. "'Naw. They're only human, after all."

Vasily looked at him for a long moment. "I don't suppose there's any use arguing. You seem like a man of principle."

"I do try to be."

"Rather remarkable, considering the place of your occupation."

Vince smiled. "Well, *I'm* full of surprises."

Vasily sighed and let his pack slid from his shoulder. "Let's get this over with, then."

Vince nodded. "Let's."

Vasily moved forward with the grace of a man carrying some twenty years of hard-won experience under his belt, drawing out a pair of slender knives. Vince watched their twin glinting lengths as he approached, and felt his opponent's resolve a tangible thing in the air. Vasily looked half beat to deaf, but he looked *determined*.

A whisper of fear tickled his spine, and Vince shivered. Something he hadn't felt for ages thrashed in his stomach.

Wait a minute—there were a *lot* of things he regretted: ratting out Taein, accidentally squishing that stupid diplomat with the door, not playing the piano more, not seeing Kassie every single day after work. Letting Jeaney ever walk away. There was *so much* he regretted, so much he had yet to fix, to make up for. Kassie still needed her treatments paid for. Regor was counting on him bringing Taein back. He hadn't taken Jeaney to the sea yet.

And he *promised*.

Vince's mind shifted to the thought of little June and he thought of

Taein, how those gentle dark eyes betrayed his smile. How the gentleness inside Taein was *winning*.

You always liked to take the easy way out, Vincent.

Jeaney had told him that, the day she left and he didn't go with her. And that had been true for a long, long time.

Not anymore.

Vince held his friends in the front of his mind as Vasily glided forward, light on his feet despite his many wounds, graceful like a man underwater, blades at the ready.

For June.

Vince squared himself, forcing his frame to stay loose, to stay ready.

For Taein.

It was getting harder, these days. His bones weren't as spry as they were when he first arrived in the Pearl, all those years ago.

For Kassie.

Vince's heart settled, and a calm washed over him like rain. Vasily was nearer, now. Near enough to strike.

The giant let him come, and braced.

❧ 69 ❧

ATONEMENT

There is a place where men go, where death cannot prevail. It is a walk on a knife's edge, a teetering on the spine of the world. One false move and you will fall. Death is waiting, eager to swallow you whole.

Cold is the water that shocks you back to life. Cold is the day that receives you again. Cold is the world you will remake at your feet.

But Taein Glass had never died and faced the Celestials, nor was he ever given a choice.

Taein Glass was the one who would live, despite it all, through everything. So was it fated in the grand making of it all, in the weaving of the night's fabric, in the spilling of the world, in the forging of the heart of every star. You were made to carry the weight. Made to see the work done, all the way to the end of days.

It is a strange place, this expanse where a soul resides. A door without a lock or key. A door you didn't open, a door that holds you all the same.

There is a place where men go, when death no longer holds them. Taein Glass had lived there all his life. Taein Glass would live there forever. To the end of days.

. . .

TAEIN FELT A SPURT OF BLOOD GUSH DOWN HIS LEG.

He felt the shattered bones protruding from his gnarled knee.

He felt his split lip and aching gut and cracked ribs and bruised back. He felt everything and yet nothing as his body faded in and out of numbness, so overwhelmed by pain it could barely function.

Taein was on the verge of collapse. Time was running out. He kept stumbling on anyway, dragging his bad leg behind him until he made the mistake of looking down. How dark and bright his own blood seemed, a deep ruby color against the pieces of bone jutting from his skin like little white splinters.

I'm not going to make it across the Fendall. It was the first time the thought had crossed his mind.

He swallowed hard and forced himself to keep going until the foot belonging to his bad leg caught a raised root and sent him pitching into the brush. He hit the ground hard and immediately tried to scramble back up on pure instinct, which just sent him falling back down in agony. He clapped a hand over his mouth to muffle a rising scream, but the pain fell away as he saw June.

She was staring at him, arms hugged tight around her torso.

Taein tried to turn his grimace into a smile. "Stop looking at me like that, brat—"

She cut him off with a few quick signs, her face going a little gray. If the kid was grossed out, Taein knew it must be bad.

What happened to your knee?

Taein accepted Ka-el's hand and winced as the tracker hauled him up. "I fell on a nail during my little tangle with the Raincloak Man. But at least I beat his ass."

June frowned. *Looks like he beat your ass.*

"No, if anything I beat my *own* ass."

Ka-el scoffed. "And you of all idiots would, too."

Taein glared. "Look, I'm sure Vasily is still after us, in which case I'm leaving a really obvious trail."

June's eyes glowed an eerie green in the receding light. *See, that's an idiot thing to do.* She signed.

Taein threw his hands up. "Well, my right leg is kind of in two halves right now, attached only by..." His eyes fell back on his knee and bile rose in his mouth. Shattered bone? Shredded flesh? What *was* holding his knee together?

Ka-el squinted. "Looks like meat to me."

June nodded in agreement. She seemed to have gotten over her prior revulsion and was peering at his knee with decidedly morbid interest.

"What are our options?" Taein asked Ka-el.

Ka-el shrugged. "I got you out of the Oldswood, what else do you want from me? The tourniquet is doing all that it can to keep your blood in you. The only thing that might help is rest."

Taein felt a wave of panic rise in his chest. "We cannot afford rest."

Ka-el narrowed his eyes. "But we left Vincent to—"

"I know what we did," Taein snapped.

June tugged on Taein's sleeve and signed rapidly. It took three tries before Taein understood.

You should've killed him when you had the chance.

Taein faltered.

"What's she saying?" Ka-el said.

We can just wait here for him, June continued, *and win the fight this time.*

Taein looked at Ka-el. "She wants to stay and wait for Vasily, so we can fight him."

Ka-el frowned. "But... that's why Vince stayed behind."

Taein ran a hand through his matted hair. "Well, here's to Vince. Let's get moving."

Ka-el's voice rose. "Are you saying there's a chance Vince was *bested?*"

Taein stared back at Ka-el. "Are you seeing what the Hunter did to me?"

"Half of that you did to yourself, Taein. You're a terrible fighter."

"But the hunter is Vasily Miinriel of House Slate, Ka-el. *Aal Salava?*"

Ka-el's face went slack. "Oh." He was quiet for a long while before his eyes fell to June. "Maybe she's got a good idea."

A little smile curled June's mouth, betraying the intensity inside. When she signed, her small hands were quick and careful.

If he comes, you'll have me.

Taein scoffed. "What're you going to do, bite him—"

I'll make things grow. That can hurt him.

Any words Taein had fell dead in his mouth.

I'll hurt him.

A cold sweat broke out on the back of Taein's neck. "No. We're not waiting here for him to find us like sheep in a slaughter pen."

June tried to argue, but Taein just stood up and got moving, clenching his jaw so hard he thought he might crack a tooth to keep from screaming.

They kept on toward the Fendall, dark shadows in a darkening world, and the landscape slowly began to change. The dense forest gave way to grassy, wide-open fields sloping incessantly downwards toward the distant Fendall, which was hidden by a distant crop of slender trees growing along the bank. Countless streams ran through the fields, connecting and crossing, consuming and feeding each other. Ka-el led them through as many of these little rivers as possible, trudging as a snail's pacing along some for what felt like hundreds of miles. Taein propelled himself after the tracker with tiny, ginger steps, feeling the way his body shuddered with each clumsy motion as if every single nerve ending was frying at once, intent on keeping himself from falling and royally screwing his knee over *again*.

They stopped when Taein could go no longer, taking refuge for a few sparse hours among a cluster of half-grown maples still working on unfolding their spring greenery. Taein laid down for the first time in what felt like a hundred years, struggling to ease his shattered knee out flat and realizing for the first time that he couldn't. Sleep soon stole June away and then Ka-el, too, and every tiny sound in the night became his sole responsibility to analyze.

Taein let his weary eyes wander to the stars above and tried to focus on breathing. It was getting harder by the hour.

I have to kill her, you know. The little girl.

Taein traced through the stars, trying to search out constellations, hating the way Vasily's voice was burned into his mind. The sky seemed so endless here, void of clouds, every silver speck bright and shining.

Taein peered over at the kid. She was curled into a tight ball a foot or so away, her back turned to him, mouse-brown hair brushing against the grass. He took a deep breath, let it go slowly.

This was his atonement. *She* was his atonement, he knew for certain. A chance not to run, but to do the right thing for once in his waste of a life.

Again, Taein heard Vasily's voice.

I have to kill her, you know.

Taein turned his gaze back up to the heavens. He wondered, just for a moment, if Vasily had noticed how clear the night was.

I know, he thought. *But I won't let you.*

———

THE RIVER

The next day arrived and didn't bring Vince with it. Taein's heart was filled with a gaping, cavernous ache that had nothing to do with the stinking blood oozing from his knee and everything with the giant's absence.

Taein trailed just behind Ka-el and June as they walked along the Fendall, separated from the river itself by a dense wall of trees and budding underbrush. His pain was a blanketing gray haze, growing thicker all the time. He hovered within that haze, the swollen river roaring in his ears, until Ka-el stopped short. Taein stumbled and stifled a curse, looking up to see why the hell they weren't moving.

He saw the ruins of the Fendall Crossing some thirty feet ahead, and his heart shuddered to a stop.

The river was twice as full as normal and had washed out a good portion of the crossing, splintering the bridge into some three broken-up parts. Each piece was barely connected by precarious skeletal stakes and broken-off beams that jutted from the water like the crude spears of some ancient, long-dead Celestial. The gray river below churned with a white-foam fury, overfed by the spring melt. The waters seemed to have risen up its banks some three times its normal level and was thickening the air with a heavy, rippling mist so dense Taein could not make out the other side.

Ersii was hidden from them. The path was broken.

Taein swallowed hard and searched for any possible way over. If they held any hope of crossing, they'd have to hop and climb along the high end of the wrecked structure, using the spearing beams and snapped ropes that once made up the railing as a guide to make it from chunk to chunk.

All this, to be done with one leg. Taein clenched his fists, fighting back the urge to sink down and just not get back up. He couldn't do this alone, and one glance at the heavy despair on Ka-el's face didn't lend much hope of a helping hand.

"Don't look so glum, Ka-el, we're still going to cross," he muttered.

Ka-el's glassy eyes slid over to Taein. "You intend to *cross* that thing?"

Taein slung off his pack and let it fall unceremoniously into the overgrown spring grass. "Do we have any other options?"

Ka-el looked back at the wrecked crossing, his perpetually sun-scorched cheeks draining white. "Not for another fifty miles."

"I don't have another fifty miles in me. We're going to cross that damn river and once we're in Ersii I'm going to find myself a horse before the lower half of my leg decides to sever its connection to the rest of me."

Ka-el took an unconscious step backward, his eyes still glued to the raging river. "I can't swim, Taein. The Faeish as a whole don't know how to swim. We're mountain-dwellers, we—"

Taein stripped off his coat, then his over-shirt. "You're Jinian today, then. Ditch whatever extra weight you've got on you and prepare to climb."

Ka-el fell silent, eyes trained on the river, brow knit tight. Taein stifled a sigh and glanced back, wishing for Vince's familiar form to come cresting the distant hills, and was instead greeted with the not-too-distant form of a rider on a dark horse, cantering down the rolling green slopes toward the river.

Toward *them*.

Taein stared as recognition drenched the world white.

Vasily.

"Oh, sweet hell." The words fell out of his mouth as he wrenched himself out of his stupor and whirled to June, snatching her by the wrist and forcing his mangled body toward the equally mangled bridge.

Ka-el glanced backward and, catching sight of the nearing rider, took three steps back. "I can't. Taein, I can't swim."

Taein continued to propel himself toward the river. "Move it, Ka-el!"

"I can't swim!"

"Risk the water or get shanked!" Taein faltered and looked back, holding onto June with a white-knuckle grip. "Ka-el! *Vince* stayed behind so *you* could come with us!"

Ka-el shook his head wildly and took another step back. Taein held his gaze, something beginning to snarl beneath his skin. "Are you really going to waste his sacrifice?"

Ka-el set his jaw, his eyes going flinty. "I sure as hell won't die like him."

Taein didn't wait any longer. He leaned down as much as his leg would allow and took ahold of June's shoulders.

"Look at me," he said, "*look at me.* To make it across I'm going to have to let go of you, yeah? But you stay right with me." He tilted her chin back toward him as her eyes snuck toward the rider. "You stay with *me.*"

June nodded once, and he let go.

Taein didn't give himself time to think about the cruel bite of the water or the stark emptiness of his gloved hand. He pushed the welling pain away and took a step into the river, then another.

Another. He heard June sloshing just behind, her steps barely audible above the river's dull thunder.

He was waist-deep before he finally found where the bridge once began. Taking hold of a strand of rope slick with algae, he hauled himself up onto the steeply angled platform, his head spinning as the shattered bones in his knee ground against each other. He leaned back and helped June as she struggled to climb, glancing up just in time to see Vasily cantering through the mists and onto the flooded bank.

Where Ka-el was *still* standing, ankle-deep in the rushing gray water, his eyes glued on the wrecked bridge.

"Ka-el!" Taein shouted, hauling June up with a burst of desperate energy.

Ka-el's gaze slowly loosened its grip on the water and rose to meet Taein's. He stared for the span of a breath, somehow unaware of the rider behind, and gave the barest shake of his head.

"No! Behind you! *Behind you!*" Taein bellowed, waving wildly.

But Ka-el didn't look behind. His eyes fell from Taein back to the river and stayed there. And in the end, he only managed to take three steps backward before Vasily shoved him in.

Taein felt his breath catch in his throat as Ka-el toppled face-first into the river, the water washing away his scream before it could reach Taein.

"Swim! Dammit, Ka-el, kick your legs!" Taein shouted, stopping himself from scrambling forward as the river dragged Ka-el sputtering downstream.

"Ka-el!" Taein bellowed.

The tracker surfaced for only a second before the crashing water came together over his head and pulled him under.

Taein waited, searching out the white water for any sign of Ka-el's dark form.

He didn't come up again. Taein's heart went tight. He forced his gaze up, surprised at the heat smarting behind his eyes, and looked at Vasily.

He met the hunter's eyes for only a millisecond before Vasily mounted his horse. Taein expected him to canter off down the river for the next crossing, but Vasily just stayed still, watching. Waiting.

Taein understood. Vasily would wait until they got to the other side, and *then* he would ride to the next river crossing. But he wouldn't have to do that at all, if they drowned first.

Well, watch me best the river, asshole.

Taein set his jaw, still clutching June lest she somehow topple off the skewed wooden ledge. He turned, swiped his water-logged curls out of his eyes, and started forward, pulling June after him until he was forced to let go again.

"Stay with me!" He called, unsure if she heard him over the river's raging.

He looked back and she nodded, eyes dark. Taein forced himself forward, the fractured bridge rocking with each step, and struggled from ledge to ledge as the river's thick mist drenched his clothes and hid Ersii's bank.

The bridge stretched before him in those three jagged parts, each sunk lower in the water than the last. The jump from the last portion to where it once connected to Ersii's riverbank would be a horrendous challenge.

Taein swore and kept going, hopping and stumbling and sliding from portion to portion, the wood slippery and rotting beneath his boots, so much tension coursing in his husk of a body he felt ready to burst.

They'd almost made it to the midpoint. Taein was just easing himself off the first platform down onto the lower half where it was bobbing among the white-water spray when something let out a *crack*. He froze, holding out his hand to stop June from following him down onto the second platform. She stared at him, wavering like a leaf in the face of a windstorm, as a low, guttural groan rose above the river's roar.

Taein heard that crack, and for a long while stood there waiting for the lower half of his mangled leg to finally drop from his body.

Then came the sound of wood scraping against wood, and Taein caught up. He swore as the lower platform shifted, the far end tilting deep into the water, and tried to brace.

Oh, sweet Geiin.

Everything was still but for his pounding heart.

"June. Don't move," he breathed.

Taein lunged for the first platform as the second broke away with the final snap of splintered wood and splitting ropes, his fingers just *barely* glancing the slick, mossy edge.

For a breath, he was falling, and above he saw June on her hands and knees, leaning over the edge, reaching for him.

Please.

It was the last thought to enter his mind before he hit the water and every other thought was shocked away. He forced his eyes open and jetted back up to the surface, just managing to snatch a spearing board still connected to June's platform.

"Stay there!" he screamed, scrabbling to keep his grip as he fought the current.

June was still looking over the side, gesturing wildly. Taein didn't have the time to read whatever she was signing. It was all he could do to hold onto the rotting board.

He groaned, thankful that the water had shocked all the feeling out of his body, and tried to haul himself up the length of the board.

But the wood was slick and his grip was weak, and before he even knew what was happening, he let go.

He glimpsed the terror on June's face as the river sucked him downstream, away from the rest of the bridge, away from *her*, still leaning over the edge of the Jinian portion of the bridge, flailing her arms wildly.

Taein fought the water, struggling to keep his mouth clear of the broiling, foaming surface. He could see June scrambling along the edge of the bridge, trying to get down. Trying to get to *him*.

Geiin, no.

A wild burst of alarm jolted him into action and he thrashed forward, fighting the current with every fiber of his being.'

Who are you to fight the water?

"No!" he shouted as she dropped down from the ledge onto a lower log, his voice stolen away by the river's raging. "June, no! Stop!"

She crept along the length of the log, shadowed by the fractured shadow of the bridge looming above, pulling a length of rope behind her. Taein struggled, his breaths coming in tight desperate gasps, trying to keep his frozen limbs moving.

June threw the rope out toward him, and the river brought it near. Taein dug for any last reserve and swam like bloody hell. The rope was bobbing just above the surface. Its frayed edges were so near.

Who are you to best the river?

Taein lunged against the current and took hold.

The rope went taught and hope flared to life inside of him. He hauled himself through the water toward the log June had tied the rope to, one hand after the other, his heart a drum inside his failing pain-shocked chest.

He'd almost made it when the log decided to give way for the rest of the platform, and with an explosive snap, the whole rest of the bridge shattered.

"Give me your hand!" Taein shouted, but his voice was lost to the explosion of splintering wood. The water roiled with hundreds of boards, beams, and logs, all of them cracking and falling into the water around June.

A scream tore from Taein's chest as a beam fell onto June's log and she toppled into the churning water below. The tension in the rope vanished and he was ripped downstream once again, water flooding his nose and stinging his eyes as he fought to keep from being swept under by the rushing debris.

But he was just a sun-starved sapling bent before the greedy eye of a hurricane, and he didn't have the time to draw a spare breath or scream her name before he was sucked under.

The world went impossibly cold. He forced his eyes open, squinting to see through the clouded water. There—some ten or twenty feet ahead. A glimpse of dull pink.

June's sinking form.

Taein swam, his bad leg trailing behind, his lungs searing. The river continued to drag her down and further away.

Who are you to scorn the depths?

Taein pressed his lips together, his chest spasming for want of air. His eyes burned. He kept swimming and yet June's dim shape only seemed to get farther away.

Please.

Even his good leg was failing him. His lungs were desperate, begging his mouth to open and search for air amongst the water like a drunkard searching for peace at the bottom of his cup.

Taein's lips were threatening to mutiny when he finally wrapped a hand around June's arm. He clutched her against his chest with one arm and fought back up to the surface with the other, kicking with everything he had.

We're going to make it.

He was just about to break the surface when he couldn't hold his mouth shut any longer, and water came flooding in. All of the sudden Taein was drowning.

He kept on helplessly gulping water, clutching the kid even as his arm began to give out, eyes trained on the dimming spot of light that was the sun above the surface. Some force kept him moving, and the spot of light grew bigger.

I will not die here.

At last, his fingers broke the surface.

Taein jetted up, gasping in only one panicked breath before he vomited water. He struggled to get June's head above the surface, thrashing and throwing up and trying so hard to just *breathe*. June's head lulled against his chest, eyes shut, her skin an eerie shade of gray. Taein held on tight and let the river push them further downstream until they reached a narrower bend. He flung every last fiber of his being into hauling them toward the shore until his numb feet knocked against rocks—the riverbed.

Still coughing up water, he dragged them just far enough up the bank that the river would not draw them back out before collapsing. His chest was heaving in huge breaths of that sweet, summery *Ersiin* air, his eyes dropping shut before he could fight them back open.

June. She wasn't moving. He needed to... he needed...

Taein's hearing faded out. He realized he could not open his eyes just before his body finally quit on him.

❦ 71 ❦

PROMISED LAND

"Hullo, friend. That's it, come on back."

A strange half-light glinted beyond Taein's eyelids. A voice cut through the silence of his mind.

"That's it, that's the way. Come on back now."

He heard himself groan. Someone was moving his head, his body. He felt himself be dragged from water onto grass. The softest bed he'd ever felt in all his life.

"Open your eyes, friend. That's it. Come on back."

Taein squinted as dull sunlight pierced his eyes. A hazy figure loomed over him, tapping his cheeks.

Vince?

A wild burst of hope shocked away the remaining darkness and Taein heaved himself up on his elbows, startling the figure back.

"Hey now laddie, take it easy."

Taein blinked, forcing his vision clear. The man who came into focus was dressed in forest green and cream-colored livery, a captain's hat sitting cock-eyed atop disheveled blond hair. An overgrown mustache hid his upper lip, not a beard.

All the hope inside Taein squashed itself in an instant. No tattoos,

479

no rings, no beard. No Vince. Instead, here was some twat in the dandy-boy livery of an Ersiin house guard.

A guard? Where was *June?* A cacophony of alarm chased the remaining fog from Taein's mind and he sat all the way up, ignoring his spinning vision.

"Where—" he cut himself off, peering around the guard and down to the riverbank, searching for a glimpse of pink. "I was with a kid. I—where's June?"

The guard's brow drew tight. There were dark circles beneath his eyes. He reached out with a muddied white glove and tried to force Taein back down.

"Just rest a while longer, sir, we've yet to check your health—"

Taein shoved the guard away as his gaze came to stop on two other guards in matching livery. One was standing, scratching notes into a thick red book. The other was crouched down ankle-deep in the water, peering at something. Something pink.

Taein was on his feet before he knew what was happening. He pitched face-first onto the grass the second he put an ounce of weight on his shredded leg and was back up stumbling on one leg and hurrying down to the rocky shore before the first guard could catch him.

"Sir, wait! Sir!"

"What the hell are you doing?" Taein shouted, trying to run. "Get her out of the water!"

The two guards rose and faced him, alarm breaking out over their features. Taein shoved past them and dropped onto his good knee, taking the kid up by the shoulders.

June was still, her face blue, eyes closed. She wasn't breathing.

Not breathing.

"Sir, the plague—" one of the guards said, reaching down to touch Taein's shoulder.

Taein whipped his knife from his boot in the span of a second and waved it in the guard's face. "If both of you bastards don't get the hell away from me I'm going to start freeing fingers from their hands," he snarled.

He dropped the knife even as he heard the rasp of a rapier sliding from its sheath and pressed his ear to June's still chest, searching for a heartbeat.

"Give him a minute," one guard whispered to the other.

Taein couldn't hear her heart. She was still. Too still. Not breathing.

"He's clearly mad," hissed the other guard.

"A minute," insisted the first. "She must be his child."

Panic came to life inside Taein like never before.

"June?" he said, voice cracking as he tapped her cheeks. "June, don't do this to me."

"We have orders, Hillipe. We can't just leave an infected body here—"

She was still, horribly still, and Taein forgot how to breathe.

"*No,*" he gritted out, forcing himself on his hands and good knee. He braced shaking hands over her slight chest and began to pump, pausing now and then to check if she was breathing, if any life had returned to her frozen cheeks.

It hadn't.

"C'mon, brat. Don't do this to me. Don't you do this to me," he whispered, forcing himself to keep pumping her chest. Her body was such a frail thing beneath his gloved hands.

A guard laid a hand on his shoulder again. Taein hardly felt the touch, hardly heard his baffled voice.

"Sir? Please, we're the Infection Squad, sixth unit of the Saeint Soldatt. We have... orders."

Tears streamed down Taein's cheeks. "Don't do this to me, June. Please don't do this."

He heard the third guard splashing through the water toward them. Two hands clamped down on his shoulders and tried to haul him away.

"No, stop! *Stop!* She's not breathing!" Taein shook them off with wild desperation and kept pumping his hands over her little heart like Ruein had taught him all those years ago. His vision blurred so badly he could hardly make out her features. Through his tears, her face and Reuin's were one and the same. He let out a strangled breath, choking on tears.

Not again.

"Take him—"

The guard stopped short as June jolted upright, her eyes flying open as she sucked in a huge, gasping breath. Taein toppled on his side and knotted his hands in his hair as she turned over and vomited and let out a hysterical laugh. As soon as June quit throwing up she started to cry, so Taein pulled her into his arms and held her tight, his laughter turning into hoarse sobs as an ocean's worth of fear oozed out of him and back into the cold river.

He could've stayed there for an age, holding her tight and sobbing, but the guards remained.

"Sir," said the first, clearing his throat, "that child is infected."

Taein didn't bother looking at him. "Her fever already broke. It broke last week, and she lived."

Another uncertain cough. "Do you have your passports? Proper documentation?"

Only then did Taein look at him. "Do I *look* like I have a passport? You just fished me out of the river yourself, dumbass."

The guard's eyebrows lifted. "Ersii is in a state of emergency, sir. Travel in or out of House Light's jurisdiction is currently forbidden."

Taein laughed deliriously. "Are you going to haul me back over the river yourself?"

There was an uneasy shifting between the three guards, and silence came to hang heavy over the river's edge. Before they could reach the end of their silent negotiation Taein forced his broken limbs to pull the two of them up. Without bothering to say a word he turned and started the long limping slog out of the water and up the rocky bank.

"Hey, you can't just leave!" said a guard, sloshing through the water to follow. "If you don't have the documentation we have to take you to Hautae Janxcome. Sir!"

"What the hell is Hautae Janxcome?" Taein asked.

"Just a jail, sir. We would only hold you until the child is proven clean of the plague and proper documentation can be found for you. It would only be a holding period."

Taein stopped short, faced the guard. "Are you offering to... help us?"

He nodded. "Of course, sir. We are sworn to protect and serve."

Taein narrowed his eyes. "You swear that no harm will come to the kid?"

"No, sir."

"And you won't separate us?"

"Not without just cause."

Taein well another bout of laughter rising in his chest as he looked deep into the overly-sincere eyes of the guard and smiled.

"Well, my good lad, you obviously have no idea who I am and I'm obviously not having the best day of my life, so I'm going to say something that I have only said once before in my life: please take me to jail."

A wash of confusion passed over the guard's face before he held out his arms. "I can carry her. We have a cart just above the hill, and horses."

"Not a chance," Taein said, and he started the long struggle up the hill.

THE CART IN QUESTION OF WAS FILLED WITH THE STILL, STINKING bodies the Grey Lady had claimed, and the horses were no more than a trio of beaten-down field nags, but one of the guards gave up theirs—a short, skinny, irritable chestnut mare with a lopsided blaze—for Taein. He helped Taein into the saddle and then handed June up to him, and off they went through the green fields of the promised land. A calmness was overtaking Taein with every stride taken toward jail. There, they could hide from Vasily, and they both could rest for just a while, and then they would finish it.

They were here, in *Ersii*. Taein smiled even as the pain returned, welling up everywhere, stabbing through his mind. He felt worse than he'd ever imagined possible to feel. But he looked down at the kid sitting in front of him, her head lulling against his chest as she slept, the fading sun drying the river water from her hair.

She was breathing. They were going to make it. There was no other way.

72

THE PATH ENDS

The sun was barely awake, streaking the sky with pastel pinks, blues, and purples. The colors were reflected by the endless array of flowers below, their scent so strong that Taein could hardly detect his own stench anymore.

Just a little farther.

He kept his hand twisted around a lock of the nag's chestnut mane and held on. Minutes had crept by like hours, like whole days. The landscape melted into something new as they left the tamed, open countryside and entered the Fields of Ten-Thousand Flowers. The Fields were just coming into bloom and with every step the colors grew more overwhelming, their perfume stronger. Along with them came a sense of salvation. After the Fields they were but a three day ride from House Light herself.

Of course, there was a little stop to be had at a jail soon, but that could be dealt with. The journey was almost at a close, what did Taein care if they spent a night or two in the clink?

Just a little farther.

They kept on, pulling their cart of dead alongside dense cliques of roses boasting blossoms twice the size of his fist and lilac bushes as big as grown trees. They were skirting the edge of the Fields, which were planted on a high, flat hilltop, either side sloping toward green valleys. The guards kept quiet—two on the cart's bench, the other atop a rangy bay gelding as he towed Taein and June's mare behind—and Taein followed suit. Each young man held a shadow in their gaze owed to the cart of dead bumping along behind them. But that was alright—they might be his saviors, but they certainly weren't his friends. The sooner they reached the prison, the sooner Taein could get a good night's sleep, sew his leg back together, and finish the job.

And... what after?

His gaze drifted to his swollen, shredded knee. The river had washed off much of the caked-on gore and laid bare what was left of his kneecap. Beyond the swelling and festering infection was nothing but masticated bone—the puncture had cracked and splintered with every fall he'd taken since. Whole pieces seemed to have chipped off. Taein wondered how many shards of his kneecap lay at the bottom of the Fendall and felt a smile tug at his lips.

What after? It didn't matter. All he had to worry about was a few more days.

A guard—the one with the wannabe mustache—looked over his shoulder and spoke. "How are you getting on, fellow?"

Taein's pain had long since fallen away—or maybe it had taken over his body so completely he had lost the ability to fathom it. Either way, he had entered a gray haze he was quite content to stay in.

"Just fine, thank you," he replied.

"And the child?" the guard asked, tugging Taein's horse after his own.

Taein looked down to June. She was still fast asleep against his chest, but her breaths came easy and even.

"Still chugging along," he said. "How far off are we from this little brig you spoke of? I want—" his words fell off as a figure cresting the hill on the other side of the valley came into view. The man was flying down the hillside like his pants were on fire, screaming at the top of his lungs for help.

Taein didn't bother wondering what the man was running from. He knew. The horses stopped short and threw up their heads as a howl dry as a desert wind and piercing as an arrow broke the quiet of the morning.

Dogs.

Sure enough, Taein watched as more than twenty dark shadows crested the hill after the screaming bloke and went tearing down after him.

"Gather arms!" the mounted guard shouted, tossing the chestnut nag's lead rope off his saddle horn and booting his gelding around to face the pack. The other two guards bailed down from the cart and set about tearing the harnesses from the horses before vaulting onto them bareback and chasing after the first guard. Before Taein could blink, he was left atop his frightened chestnut mare, clutching June to his chest as she startled awake and started crying, alone but for a cart of dead.

Taein watched as the guards' blue livery grew faint as they charged down the hillside into the valley, the speed of their small, worn horses so slow compared to the rate of the dogs as they raced to meet the fleeing man first. Taein squinted against the rising sun, fighting to keep the chestnut nag still. Could the running man possibly be Vince? Taein was too far to make out the man, but he could see his speed. The man was sprinting so fast his heels looked as though they were practically smacking the back of his head with every frantic step. Taein knew Vince couldn't run like that. The giant was far too bulky.

Taein's heart sank to his toes. The thunder of the horses' hooves faded—they were closing in on the pack, who'd almost caught up with the man now. Still they kept on, the guards extending their rapiers, the three of them shouting in unison. What sort of death-charge was this? What kind of courage did these fools have, to go galloping toward a pack like that to save a stranger? What strength was possessing those tired little horses, that they might run on so unwaveringly, so faithfully?

Pollen rained down as the wind stirred. Taein watched until the charging guards collided with the pack, the fleeing man swallowed by a collision of shadow, flesh, and steel. The screaming started.

Taein didn't bother watching the massacre. He booted his mare around and just got her cantering when dark shadows and snapping teeth cut them off. Taein cursed and held onto June as the chestnut reared, then reined her back around. She ran down the hill, letting the dogs herd her straight to the rest of the pack and the fighting men in the valley.

Taein spat curses and wrestled with the reins, unable to properly steer with his leg. June clung to him, crying her ever-loving eyes out, and it was all Taein could do to keep them both in the saddle. He looked behind and the dogs were snapping at the chestnut's heels, toying with her. Ahead were twenty more of the dark shapes, tearing at the only two figures left standing, their frenzied howls blurring together with the screaming of the men. Taein recognized one guard by his livery. The other man still standing was the stranger.

How the hell is he still alive?

Taein barely registered the thought before a dog dashed a little too close to the chestnut's flying hooves. She tripped as she trampled it and fell forward, and Taein found himself toppling from the saddle.

Rolling through the grass. Dirt in his mouth, the smell of earth. His shoulder took the impact and he felt something pop out of place, then pop right back in, his nerves so spent he barely felt a thing. He got back on his feet and sprinted to June, taking out his last knife and stabbing at the first dog that reached him.

Matches. Where were his matches? He slid onto the grass next to June and scaredy had time to check if she was conscious before the next dog was upon him. He jammed his knife into its snarling mouth and jerked it out. Ash smeared over his clothes, caked onto his face.

No time to think. Taein patted himself down, searching for anything of use. Anything that might've survived the Fendall. Out came his match box. Profanity of all sorts poured from his mouth like a veritable river as he struck match after match. They wouldn't take, not a single *damned* one—there! Fire! He threw down the match and kept at it. Another, then another—he dropped them in a circle around himself and June, slashing at dogs as they tried to dive after him, the whinnying of the chestnut mare as she fought off other dogs dim and terrible.

Soon, a wavering orange ring was eating away at the grass around them. Taein dimly registered that the dog's shrieking cacophony was fading. He looked up and spotted the Ersiin guard and the stranger still alive amid a spray of smeared ash and red gore. The guard was sunk down on his knees, holding one of his friends as he gasped out sputtering, dying breaths. The stranger was still up, his broad frame casting a small shadow in the strange smokey light as he slashed at the last dog.

His sword caught the dog on his side. One last demonic shriek, and the creature melted into a smear of ash like the rest. The stranger straightened, dirty, shoulder-length black hair cutting across his gaze, and Taein's exhausted mind comprehended the hollow face of the hunter himself.

No. They made it across the river. They were safe now. Free of him. For the love of Geiin—*how was he here?*

Taein crawled onto his feet and shook the kid as wind caught the ring of fire and riled the flames.

"June? June!" he pulled her upright and all she did was start crying again.

"Can you stand?"

She shook her head, scrabbling at his face. More tears. He realized she was trying to touch a cut on his face. Taein cursed, pulled her into his arms, and struggled toward the chestnut mare. She'd somehow remained standing, sweat-soaked and covered in bloody bites.

"Come here, old girl," Taein croaked out.

The mare took no notice. Taein crept closer, the sound of his voice almost drowned out by the crackling of flames. "Come on now, be a good girl. Please."

He glanced over his shoulder and caught sight of Vasily limping after him. The surviving Ersiin guard hurried to catch up, shouting. He reached Vasily just in time to support Vasily he buckled, and Vasily thanked the guard by putting that soot-stained length of steel right through his chest.

Taein felt tears pricking the backs of his eyes. He looked away and redoubled his pace, June's face buried in his chest, and kept coaxing the chestnut mare closer.

Her ears pricked, finally catching the sound of his voice. Taein prayed and pulled every trick he knew from his days learning the ways of horses in Efriel Shu. He stopped, turned his back, and waited.

Through the flickering orange veil of fire, Taein watched Vasily struggle to rip the sword from the guard's body. Watched him grow impatient and leave the sword lodged there in the guard as he unsheathed a shorter, curved blade. Watched him step through the fire like a demon crossing the threshold of hell into the world of the living.

Even through the smoke, Taein recognized the blade. He knew those green stones. Vasily had *June's dagger*.

So Vasily wasn't the only thing Taein shouldn't have trusted would stay in the silt back at the shack. But what in his life ever stayed dead, anyway? Nothing he left behind ever stayed gone these days.

Nothing except Ruein.

Taein could just make out the tears cutting white trails through the ash on Vasily's face when he felt the tickle of whiskers on his shoulder, felt a warm, blowing breath. He turned to the battered, bleeding chestnut mare, pried June's arms from around his neck, and heaved her into the saddle.

"Thank you," he murmured to the mare, laying a hand on her bitten neck before pressing the lead rope into June's hand.

"Here," he said, "Keep on north—"

The kid shook her head violently and leaned down to snatch Taein's hand.

There's no time. His first instinct was to shove her hand away and shoo off the mare, but instead Taein reached up to touch her face. Forced those pale green eyes to look at him.

"Please, June. Do this for me. You have to do this for me."

She kept shaking her head, tears gushing down her face. She wouldn't let go of his hand.

"Pinky promise me," he whispered.

No, she signed, shoving his extended hand away while gripping his other like the earth would swallow him if she let go.

Taein sensed Vasily closing in, heard the hunter's slow, unrelenting steps on the grass.

"I'll find you," he said, and he ripped his hand from June and slapped the mare's rump.

The chestnut turned and only shambled off a few steps. A few steps weren't *enough*. Taein hobbled after the mare, hollering and waving his hands as June cried and reached back for him. It took everything in him to ignore her and keep harassing the mare to get going. He slapped her rump a few more times before she finally picked up a staggering canter and started up the hill toward the flowers.

Taein stopped as soon as the mare outpaced him. He wanted to watch them make it up the hill, watched them disappear into the flowers. He needed to see her make it.

But Vasily had caught up.

Taein couldn't feel much anymore, but he could still feel Vasily's presence in his very bones. The old unbreakable tether between them. That unrelenting grudge.

The thief turned and faced the hunter, the path ended at last.

73

COYOTE

When she was eight, June watched a coyote kill a rabbit from her window.

She was supposed to be practicing handwriting, but the day outside was just so much more interesting; all thick fluffy white clouds and happy yellow sun beaming down onto the blue-green valley grass.

She saw the rabbit first. She didn't recognize him from the burrow beneath her reading log.

A visitor. Something interesting. Something new.

June saw the coyote next, creeping up on that oblivious little ball of fuzz, and watched with frozen horror when that particular *oblivious* ball of fuzz did finally take notice of his impending demise and did absolutely nothing. The stupid idiot hunkered down and just *waited for it.*

June never liked coyotes before then, and she certainly hated them afterward. But she hated that rabbit, too, for not even trying to save himself. For freezing, and letting death come so easily.

But June now understood something different. Sometimes, death came without a fight. It just happens.

Tears blinded June's eyes as the little red horse limped up the hill toward the flowers. She could hardly see a thing. The world was narrowed down to a gray haze, just as it had been when the Raincloak Man killed Mama.

It was happening again. He was taking everything away, and all June could do was hold onto the horse's mane and cry. Her limbs weren't working anymore, her entire body overcome with shakes. She wasn't even angry anymore. She was just a scared little girl again, just like when the coyote killed the rabbit, just like when the Raincloak Man killed Mama *in front of her*, just like she was right now.

The little horse carried on, her neck so dark with sweat her red fur looked black.

Do it for me.

June saw the Idiot again, saw the desperation in his sad, tired eyes as he held out his pinky—wait a minute. She didn't pinky promise. The last thing he asked of her, and she didn't even do it.

She held the chestnut mare's mane tight, too weak to fight the ropes securing her legs to the saddle, and cried.

Just for once, the kid wanted to be the coyote, and not the rabbit.

✥ 74 ✥

BREATHLESS

Smoke blacked the sky. Taein stared Vasily down, trying to find whatever strength remained in his ruined body. He just managed to shuck off his gloves and was blinking back the darkness behind his eyes when Vasily's boot collided with his good leg and toppled him.

Taein dragged himself back. The kid needed more time. She needed distance. She needed Vasily *dead*. Still, it was all Taein could do to get back to his feet. He faced Vasily, wavering like drunk, and raised his naked fists.

He'd always thought his praying days were long over. But here and now, fire all around, so far from the snow that he thought would hold him captive forever, Taein was praying again.

Let her live, Geiin. If you've any mercy at all you'll let her live.

It was the only thing he could think to say to the supposed maker of the world as he met the hunter's eyes. He heaved in breath after breath, looking at a man and finding only an abyss, and tried to find his voice.

You'll die at the hands of the Anathema just like your bastard father, is what he wanted to say. He wanted his bravado, his grandiosity, his flair. But all the idiot humor he'd once leaned on like a crutch was dead and

493

gone and there wasn't enough air in all the world to satisfy his lungs, so Vasily got to speak first.

He stood for a moment, the dagger waiting at his side.

"I just want it to be *over*, Glass," he said, eyes taking on a sheen. "That's all I need you to understand. And I don't know any other way... than this."

"I won't let you," Taein steeled himself for the last time, the wind on his bare hands a strange sensation. "Not again. Go burn the world for all I care, but the kid stays with *me*. It ends here, Vasily. *I won't let you*."

To Taein's shock, a single tear slid down Vasily's cheek. His hands shook.

"I know," Vasily said. And then he swept forward, the steel edge of his blade cutting through smoke. All the thief could do, standing there in his worn but beautiful boots as he looked death in the face, was pray.

———

RESTLESS

{TWENTY HOURS LATER}

Vasily sat beside a somber, slow-moving creek, lost somewhere in the openness of Ersii. He was looking at his hands again, at his filthy, disgusting, weak hands. He'd already washed up three times, and yet the bloodstains refused to leave.

He frowned. Whose blood even was this? Did it even matter?

Vasily shook his head and wiped his palms on his pants again, disgust roiling in his gut. So this truly was the price he had to pay for Babas' honor. The destruction of himself.

He looked down at his wavering reflection in the stream.

You carry him with you, Vasily.

He could not see his father's face in his own.

He lives in you now.

Vasily didn't think he'd ever felt further from Babas than now.

He sighed and picked up a mottled blue and gray stone, turned it over in his hand.

Let this be enough, Babas. Let me rest.

He'd done it to soothe his own weary heart, and to bring Babas the honor he'd been denied so many years ago. But the ache inside hadn't grown any smaller. It was a chasm that only wanted to grow, a dark maw that was always hungry and always would be. It'd taken to eating

Vasily alive years ago, little by little, and it certainly wasn't stopping now. But he wasn't the one to first open this wound in himself, was he? He should've known he wouldn't be the one to close it.

Vasily tossed the stone into the stream. Heat gathered behind his eyes and he blinked furiously.

Tell me I did the right thing, father. I need to know.

Silence was all he got in return.

Vasily pulled his cloak a little tighter despite the late-spring warmth. Surely, it was finished now. He'd done his best. Poured himself out on the altar of this quest. There was nothing left to give.

He lowered his head into his hands and sighed.

Mie durksil menwi tu son gaethoa, Babas.

The morning remained unchanged when he lifted his head. The hunter stood, wiped his bloodstained hands on his pants one more time.

The red stayed all the same, his father still so far away.

———

THE END

ACKNOWLEDGMENTS

Without my savior Jesus Christ, there would be no *Prince of Glass* nor Sarah herself. I owe both this book and my life to Jesus, who carries me through the valleys. From Him flows all good things—including forgiveness.

The most sincere thank-you's go out to all these great people who contributed to Prince of Glass Remastered:

Lauren, Jack, Mattie, & Amethyst. You guys are the real MVPs. Thank you to all my beta readers—for sticking with it, and for all your encouragements.

A huge thank-you to Miss Lisa. Your insistence that I start something new is what brought Taein Glass, fully formed with those stupid boots and all, to step into my imagination.

The biggest thank-you is owed to my sweet James, who didn't run off the minute I told him I was a writer—my love for you is fearless. Thank you for everything.

SNEAK PEEK FOR BOOK TWO:
FATHER OF RAIN

CHAPTER ONE: THE DEAD GIRL

The dead girl sat in a garden, surrounded by a thousand silent living things, and drew in a slow breath of incensed air.

Another. And another.

The Shade sat with eyes closed and legs crossed, listening to the wind as it feathered through the many fragrant blossoms in *Jarra* Havana's garden—heady crimson roses from Ersii, creeping velvet-blue starlings from Nown Jin, sturdy yellow foxgloves from Faeriel, bloody arrinvale native to the white sands of the Vandel Province. Every species of flora from every realm in Ieris, but for one.

Jarra Havana had nothing from Efriel Shu. To Jarra Havana, it was as if the realm had never existed in the first place. And these days, it almost didn't.

As will all Anathema, one day. The Shade reached out bone-white fingers and touched the rough, yellowed sandgrass making up the garden's pathways.

As will I.

She curled a finger around a blade of sand grass—too tight, and the rough fibers sliced her skin open. She opened her eyes and examined the split in her skin.

No blood, of course. She had no blood to bleed. One of the

innumerable little details that separated her from the race of living, breathing, red-bleeding men.

The sky above was bathed in a soft scarlet glow, the setting Vandel sun spreading tendrils of saffron and amber as it slunk low and heavy beyond the dark southern mists. She watched it creep away.

Oh, what she wouldn't give to feel the warmth of a sleepy sun on her skin one last time. To feel water caress her limbs, lean into the kiss of a papery summery breeze.

What she wouldn't give to be *alive* again, just for one day.

She'd never kissed anyone, after all. She was too shy for anything near a young romance to find her when she was small. And after it all had happened—the lie uncovered, the Sect come to steal her away, her soul pulled out from within and stuck back in this *thing* of a frame— there was no hope for any future loves, no chance for a tentative first kiss, no safe embrace.

Just quiet moments like this. A garden, a setting desert sun, and a darkness coming swift ahead.

"I never knew you were so sentimental, sister."

A voice like the scratch of flint broke the peace of the evening, and the Shade opened her eyes to spot the world's own reckoning come to stand before her.

Kovra loomed very different from the girl the Shade had once known—her eyes, made up of the greens and browns and golds of earth, were lined with coal. Those eyes looked out from a face changed from the softness of childhood and made gaunt by a hunger the greatest feast from the greatest hall could not fill, a hunger belonging not to men but of the beasts within them.

She was a lean, tan woman, tall and terrible, her hair a loose dark swath, her body a blade dressed in rather like a girl in shades of amber. She almost matched the look of the dying sun.

Needless to say, the Shade was a little at loss for words.

"Strange, to find you here in some tea-warden's yard pining over lost kisses like a wee girl." Another pause, and Kovra grew impatient. "Well, Aeyda? Aren't you going to greet me?"

The Shade was still sitting among those silly flowers, staring up at

Kovra and feeling especially small. She looked from the woman before her to the red sky beyond and sighed.

"That's not my name anymore."

"Sure it is. Still playing make believe, are we?"

The Shade eased herself up, hollow bones grown spectacularly weary, and looked Kovra in her terrible earthen eyes.

"I am called the Shade now."

Something like a smile curved the edges of Kovra's lips. She cocked her head and gave the Shade a thorough once-over. "Gods. Time really hasn't done you any favors. You're so much more... transparent than last we met. Your sickness is eating you now, isn't it?"

The Shade lifted one gnarled hand, looked over the webbing of dark scarring that wrapped each finger. Sure enough, in this fell light she could almost see the grass behind her palm.

"You could say that. It extracts a greater toll as I grow older."

Kovra hummed. "And we *are* older now, aren't we? Look at us. Grown women now. It's been so terribly long."

The Shade said nothing. There wasn't anything to say.

Sure enough, Kovra broke that silence before it could grow beyond a few scarce seconds. She'd never been patient when they were children, and what was growing up, if not a grand solidifying of all the things that once made childhood hard?

"See here, Aedya—"

"I know what you've come for. Don't bother asking, Kovra, my answer is still the same."

Kovra's face hardened in an instant, the glint in her eyes flashing a little brighter.

"They *exist*, Aedya. The Mothers. *We* exist."

Aeyda just shrugged. "You're really going to go through with it all?"

Kovra laughed a little, a sound like the crackling of fire.

That laugh once warmed the Shade inside and out. That laugh once meant *everything will be all right*. Now it heralded just what it sounded like: flames. Hungry, greedy fire.

"Of course I am. What else is there to do?" Kovra said. "Now listen. You have nothing I want, and I have not a single use for you. But you are my sister, Aedya, though you try very hard to forget. We suffered together in the crypts. We were *remade* together. The world is finally at my hands, just as I always said it'd be," she shrugged. "I'd hate to see you burn with it."

The Shade held Kovra's gaze. "I don't believe you'll do it."

"Please," Kovra drew near, reached out to cup the Shade's face. Didn't flinch from the chill.

For just a moment, the Shade went to lean into that familiar touch. She remained there, Kovra's hand unfelt on her cheek, those eyes that once held the world so near, yet gone so dark.

"We suffered so much, for so long," Kovra said. "But we never suffered alone."

"We always had each other," the Shade agreed.

"Are you really going to make me leave you behind? Are you—"

The Shade dared to cut her off. "You won't do *it*. I know *you*."

Kovra brushed along a scar stretching from the edge of the Shade's eye to her ear. The Shade wondered if the touch was tender, if it was cruel. If her sister's hand was still as warm as she remembered.

When Kovra's eyes flickered back to the Shade's, they'd gone dark as a starless light. "This world has been so cold to us, sister. Now I am set to burn it to the ground, to feel just for once its warmth. Aren't you curious to see what bones lie beneath?"

"You won't," the Shade whispered. "It's not your dream, Kovra. It's *his*."

Kovra scoffed. "So what if it is? I haven't a single reason not to. What has the world ever given you, besides pain?"

The Shade brushed Kovra's hand away, took a step back.

"Kovra. We are born of blood and remade in ashes. We are one and the same, you and I. Search the earth for my replacement, scour the world of its habits and make it new, and me along with it. It doesn't matter, because you left. I was all you ever really had."

Kovra stilled, and that terrible something twisted her features. "Perhaps you forget what I am, sister."

"Perhaps. But you're not even here."

Kovra opened her mouth, but the Shade waved a palm through her apparition and smiled.

"How are you doing this? The energy this projection would take... it must be killing you."

Kovra set her mouth in a hard line. "Come back. Come back, or I'll make you."

"I can't come back to something I never left in the first place."

Kovra snapped. "Have it your way! But let me remind you that you cannot be remade, sister. They'll *always* be afraid of you. You'll always be what they made you."

The Shade just smiled. "And you'll always be alone."

Before Kovra could open her mouth again—the Shade saw the way her mouth parted in that small, vicious *o*, that positively surprised look that always preceded the worst of her tempers—she snapped her palm close and severed the connection.

Her sister's projection faded to ash at once, and settled down among the rough desert grass.

The sun was all but gone now. The Shade stared at the ash among the grass and sank back down.

Gods. After all this time, after all these fell stirrings, the withering, this strange twisting of the land... everything made sense now. It was really coming.

She was coming.

ABOUT THE AUTHOR

Sarah Matey (née Martin) was raised among the unending green of the Pacific Northwest and spent her childhood riding horses, exploring the woods with her orange cat Dale, and writing stories. Today, she can be found fending off the soul-crushing drudgery of adult responsibilities with a pen in one hand, a guitar in the other, and Dale ever at her side; still resident of the PNW, married to the love of her life, and forever enchanted by storytelling.

Follow Sarah **@saarahwrites** on instagram or check out her website
https://sarahamartin21.wixsite.com/website
for special *Thorn and Ash* content + updates on forthcoming books, as well as information about her coaching and editing business, **High Sierra Creative Coaching.** For business inquires, please reach out to Sarah at
samartin975@gmail.com